GOWER STREET

Claire Rayner

SIMON AND SCHUSTER   NEW YORK

First printing

SBN 671-21550-7
Library of Congress Catalog Card Number: 73-3782
Designed by Jack Jaget
Manufactured in the United States of America

For my very good friend
MICHAEL LEGAT

DANIEL COOMBE m. CHARLOTTE STEELE m. JESSE CONSTAM   BRIDGET BURNELL
      1784   1790

b. 1754   b. 1765   b. 1750   b. 1770
d. 1789   d. 1810   d. 1811   d. 1798

DOROTHEA COOMBE   ABEL LACKLAND   LILITH (LILY) BURNELL
    b. 1786   b. circa 1789   b. 1789
                      adopted 1800   adopts name Lucas 1805

Part I

· ONE ·

SHE STOOD concealed behind the muslin curtains of the drawing room, watching him disappear into the darkness along Gower Street, his heavily caped shoulders swinging cheerfully behind the linkboy as the light glinted on the silver head of his stick and outlined the angle of his beaver hat against its smoky brilliance. And misery and frustration sank like a stone into her narrow chest, making her hunch her shoulders a little and pull pettishly and ineffectually at the gauze scarf about them.

How could he behave so? *Why* should he, indeed? Was not his home all a man could ask for, filled with every comfort and elegance she could contrive? She turned then to look at the room, at its white-paneled walls and curving light-mahogany furniture, the sea coal burning so comfortable and clean in the broad marble fireplace, the bright light of the many wax candles making the red Turkey carpet glow with richness. To leave this, to go *there*; how could he be so uncaring of his station in life? Had he been behaving as did other men, going to drink chocolate somewhere in St. James's, she could have borne it. Had he even behaved as did some other men and *told* her he was going to St. James's, while choosing to be elsewhere, it would have been less hurtful. But to go to the places he did, and to have the effrontery to tell her of it—she almost stamped her foot in her rage, almost wept in her distress.

Dorothea looked up from her book, her head on one side in its customary birdlike way, and said anxiously, "Mama? Are you well, Mama? Shall I fetch your hartshorn or—?" And Charlotte attempted a thin smile and shook her head.

"I am quite well, thank you. A little distracted by a momentary thought, no more—do not concern yourself. Perhaps you will read to me, my love, until the tea tray comes in and you retire. I should like that above all things."

And obediently Dorothea began to read as her mother settled herself in her chair beside the fire, holding the embroidered hand screen to her face with as much elegance as though there were ninety admiring guests in her drawing room to observe her, but feeling far from as happy as an elegant woman should feel.

Jesse, by now in Oxford Street and picking his way over the crossing so assiduously swept for him by the ragged urchin who leaped to his service, knew quite well how she felt. He knew precisely what thoughts were passing through her mind under the fashionable Grecian curls that so ill became her pinched and narrow face, and smiled a little maliciously into the high collar of his Garrick overcoat. That she should feel as she did about his jaunts was in some part the cause of the pleasure they gave him. Imagining her now, sitting there prim and icy in her insipid drawing room, gave an added piquancy to the sights that now were paraded before his eyes.

He had reached the far side of the street, and threw a coin to dismiss the linkboy before plunging into the muddle of the alleys that led to Seven Dials, hard by Covent Garden. He stood still for a brief moment, looking back over his shoulder.

There were the brilliantly oil-lit shop windows with their gleaming plate-glass panes behind which were heaped the delectables of the whole world—brightly colored spirits in crystal flasks, exotic pineapples, figs and oranges, the unbelievable riches of the jewelers and silversmiths, the luscious colors of the ribbon sellers; the well-fed shopkeepers obsequious even in their haggling as they stood waiting to serve the Quality till ten o'clock and gone.

But before him lay the ill-lit cobbled alleys, where the narrow houses lurched tight-packed against each other, spilling their half-starved ragged inhabitants into the ordure-slippery gutters, where the very air was heavy with the stench of poverty and misery and disease. And he raised his head and breathed deeply of it, feeling the familiar rise of pleasure in his belly, and pulled his coat more firmly about his shoulders before grasping his heavy stick stoutly by the middle to march, head high, into the squalor.

Sometimes, in his moments of self-examination, he had given consideration to the way he felt about the horrors of Seven Dials and the Bermudas, the filthy miseries of Porridge Island and the Holy Land rookery by St. Giles's, had wondered why in truth it should be that he found such interest in alleys and hovels where any other man of his stamp would find nothing but disgust. But he never allowed ponderings too much rein, preferring to assure himself—as he assured any inquirers among his acquaintance—that his visits to London's gutters were rooted in no more and no less than a deeply felt concern for the wretched lot of the inhabitants, a genuine philanthropy which demanded the satisfaction of personal involvement with those it wished to help.

"I'll not wash my hands of my duty with a few gold coins, my friend!" he would say to any of his coffeehouse cronies who jeered at him when he came blinking into their company after an evening spent in the alleys. "Not for me that easy salve to a Christian conscience! I go myself to see where my help is needed, and where it is, I give it!"

And though they would laugh and accuse him of having far more salacious purposes in his expeditions, and would make heavy jokes about the Muslins of the Gutter, the Pathians of Seven Dials, he would sip his drink and solemnly shake his head, clearly not caring in the least for their opinion.

And why should he? He knew, as an astute man always knows, that he held the good opinion of them all for his business sense, his market-place cleverness, his rare ability to continue to make profits—considerable profits—from a trade that depended on imports, all through these long-drawn-out years of the French Wars. While he continued prosperous and became ever richer, moving his home from behind his countinghouse in Eastcheap to the gentility and style of Gower Street, hard by the splendors of Bedford Square, he could be as eccentric as he chose in the matter of his evening jaunts. No man would care to turn his back on him for such a cause.

But he also knew perfectly well the real truth: why, in actual fact, he found such pleasure in the stinking alleys. Though the City streets in which he had grown up, hard-driven child of a poverty-stricken widow, had not been quite so foul as these, they had been foul enough. As he had dragged himself through his painful adolescence, scrounging, trading, bartering to give himself the handful of gold coins that was to be the basis of his eventual success as a merchant, he had suffered painfully the shame of his poverty. In his young eyes it had not been so much that the poor food he ate left him hungry, or that his patched and shabby clothes left him cold and shivering, but that his pride was injured. He would see the better-off sons of clerks and warehousemen go swaggering about his streets, and hate them for their affluence and himself for his poor showing. To saunter through the stench of Seven Dials in his middle age to be envied by all who saw him was his recompense to the dead child he had once been. To go there from his comfortable home to the Dials and back again underlined in a most satisfying way the heights to which he had climbed.

The thought of his home made his lips curl now with pleasure. There sat Charlotte, in the glory at which she had been aiming ever since the day she had married him ten years before—and too sick with rage to find it pleasurable. He could still remember how tenderly he had felt about her once, how he had been beguiled by her fair delicacy, her narrow bones and fine pallor, had been touched to gentleness by her widow's plight, alone in the world with four-year-old Dorothea. He had promised her the world and the sun and the moon then, and meant every word of it.

But that had been before he had known of the view she was to develop of him, before he knew how much she would come to despise what she was pleased to call his coarseness, his baseness, his essential "lack of gentlemanly sensibilities." Well, she had her gentility now, in the Gower Street house.

It pleased him to have given her that, while going on demonstrating in every way he could that in essence he remained as he had always been. Coarse? Base? Ungentlemanly? If that was what she said he was, if that was why she shrank from him, curling her pale bird-boned body away from his eagerness, then by God, she should be proved right. She should sit there in the midst of finery and know the man who gave it to her in all his lowborn reality.

But now, as he moved ever deeper into the maze, letting the lights and sounds of Oxford Street and then the Strand dwindle away behind him, thoughts of Charlotte shriveled away, as they always did, to be replaced by new satisfactions. They followed the same pattern, the reactions he observed, and he deeply relished it.

First, the few people aware of the presence in their alleys of one of the Quality; then the closing in a little, the moving round him carefully, the waiting for the moment to pounce on him and seize all they could—for any man dressed as he was who ventured into their world was too much of a gull, too stupid altogether, to be worthy of the least human consideration. And then that moment of recognition, when in the fitful light from a cookshop door his face would be clearly seen, and someone would say his name, and the murmur would spread, and some would cry a welcome. At which, beaming roundly, he would tip his hat to them, and wave his stick, and then, as from nowhere, the urchins would come to tumble round his feet to shout and tease and beg.

He enjoyed that moment of recognition, the fearful way some of the men fell back or slid away down the alleys. It had taken many years of venturings like this, some hearty fights and nasty injuries among these scrawny men, inflicted by his own skill with the blade that lay hidden inside his black silver-topped stick, to achieve this cautious respect. And he valued it. He was well known as a source of comfort and aid in hard cases, and though this whole area was populated by thieves and footpads, pickpockets and pimps, there were none who wished him ill, or who would take the risk of attempting to rob him before the eyes of their neighbors. Any man who set a finger on him knew well that he would be set upon in his turn the moment he had in his possession any object of worth. The very populousness of this hellhole was protection enough.

So, on this evening in late April in the seventh year of the French Wars, he moved through the alleyways toward the junction of the seven streets where the seven clockfaces stared down each one, with a crew of half-naked children at his heels, well pleased with himself and the world he lived in.

The boy was well pleased with himself too, on that same April evening. The day had started well, welcoming him with true spring warmth when he woke in the hayloft behind the cowkeeper's yard in Endell Street. He had lain there for a few moments blinking up through the broken roof at the scrap of blue sky, relishing the warmth of the sun on his face. Soon, if the summer was to prove a hot one, there would be fears of fever and the shortage of food that came when the muggy heat rotted almost every scrap there was to a stench and loathsomeness that even he, with his hardened young appetite, could not stomach. Behind him lay the harsh, cold winter, which again he had survived, during which he had even grown a little, for the tattered trousers that had closed well enough round his narrow flanks at the end of last summer now barely met across his belly.

But now it was spring, and the sun was thin and kind, and soon there would be new fruits in the market, new cheeses, even perhaps fresh meat to be had in Hungerford. At which thought he had tumbled from his hayloft to the street below, relieving himself cheerfully in the gutter before hopping away to the shrieks and hubbub and good pickings of Hungerford Market.

And the pickings had been very good. Before he had dodged beneath more than a couple of drays, had been shrieked at once by one of the straw-hatted fishwives or leaped out of the reach of a drayman's whip, he had stolen a handful of whelks, had pocketed two good hot pies and swallowed the almost half-full can of beer a coster had been fool enough to set down while he sold cabbages to a fat housewife from the Royal Mews across Union Square, where the Strand met Whitehall and Cockspur Street.

There had been time to enjoy the market in all its bustle,

to stroll cheekily, for all the world like a man of the town, eating his pies and staring at the crowds. Had he been asked if he liked the market, he would have stared in puzzlement, for who could not like it? The noise assaulted his ears with all the joys of music, as women and children shrieked their wares, as men bawled and hollered and jeered, and fought and swore at each other for every and any cause, real and imagined. The stalls, with their sheeps' carcasses and vegetables and flowers, rich and colorful now in the April sunshine, the beads and brooches and scarves and ribbons blowing in the breeze, the children leaping between them as they stole what they could, the lucky ones with mothers to catch them and cuff them and give them food, leaving the way free for those who, like the boy, had to steal to eat at all; how could anyone not like the market?

The best moment of the day had come very early, soon after he had stuffed down the last of his stolen mutton pies. A seller of old clothes, a small woman so wrapped in rags, so shawled and bonneted and beskirted that she seemed to have as much of her wares on her back as on her stall, started to fight with the woman standing next to her who was selling strings of gaudy beads. For a while he had stood and enjoyed the spectacle as the two harridans, their skirts blowing and tumbling, had fallen about the muddy ground, displaying their scrawny shanks and buttocks for all the world to see—much to the joy of several of the costers, who came to watch and cheer them on—until he realized what opportunities he was wasting.

They were so involved in their fighting, and the onlookers so entranced by the violence of it all, that he had time to examine the rags piled on the old woman's stall, to actually choose a pair of trousers that were almost in one piece, apart from a rent across one buttock, and that were patently much larger than those now straining over his growing body.

He had seen a shirt he liked, too—once good white lawn, though now a sour gray and with an ugly rip across the collar that made it clear the last wearer had been one of Jack Ketch's customers. But the boy was in no way squeamish about that.

He had tucked the shirt and trousers under one thin arm

and was reaching for a promising-looking coat before the fighting woman became aware of more pressing problems than the insults of her adversary, and pulled herself away from the clawing hands in an attempt to reach the thief so leisurely depriving her of so much choice stock; but he was away across the market, lost in the mob and shouting insults at her over his shoulder before she was fairly on her feet again.

He had dressed in his new finery, and sold his castoffs to a ragman for a few pence, before the sun reached the noon sky, and spent the afternoon basking in it, his belly filled with the jug of beer and pigs' trotters the sale had brought him, a very happy boy.

And the later afternoon had gone well too, for there had been a raree man to set up his show in Bedford Street, and the crowds had come, and with them a couple of drunken messengers wandering off course from the Strand on the way to their masters' shops in the City. He had spotted them very quickly after the raree man had started his patter, long before any of the other boys who shared the streets and its pickings with him had seen them, and was in behind them and had their pockets well and truly picked before the raree man had called so much as a one to peep and be amazed at the contents of his box; and was away into the fence's ken in Mercer Street and a good bargain struck over his pickings long before the messengers had been shocked into sobriety by fear of their masters' rage at the discovery of their loss.

A good day, in all—a splendid day, as good a day as he could remember in all his life. Now he lounged comfortably against the wall of the pie shop in Monmouth Street, debating with himself whether to swagger in and buy a supper or steal one in the usual way. An alderman, after all, is an alderman, and not to be lightly thrown away on what could be had for the taking. Why, with so much money to call his own, he might begin to be in a position to make more. Perhaps a little judicious buying of this and that, a little selling across Oxford Street, to the servant girls in the fancy houses there; why, in no time he could have a proper stall of his own. Be his own man, like the bully boys of Drury Lane, who drank and ate all they could hold just from selling their gear to the swells.

He had drifted into a complete daydream in which he was swaggering along Drury Lane dressed up all flash with a silver watch and a pocket full of good gold money, while the others slid away respectfully and boys like himself begged him for ha'pence, when he became aware of the man moving up the street in front of him.

A strange man, at first sight, because he was walking in the middle of the crowded cobbles—not sliding along the house fronts like a normal person, but swinging along like a Drury Lane ponce. But clearly not one, for there were no judys walking beside him, no girls in glittery clothes throwing bold stares at the men. And besides, his clothes! The boots, the coat, the angled curly-brimmed hat . . .

The boy stared, and thought, and stared again, and then remembered. The knowing cove, this one. He'd heard of him. The swell no one touched, for he was a downy bird, and ready with as fair a wallop as any man in the Dials. No use to any pickpocket, not even one as skilled as he, even though he was almost a top-class operator. And yet . . .

The boy watched the beaver hat move easily through the crowds, watched the people every other respectable citizen of the town feared fall back and let him go, and all the arrogance of the good day behind him came welling up to fill his throat with tension and his head with sudden dreams of wealth.

Hadn't he been standing there thinking of the need for a bit more money to add to his day's takings? Hadn't he been telling himself how just a little more would put him right in the top class, right above the local gentry, even into a house of his own? The fantasy trembled for a moment at that enormous and impossible idea, and then as the broadclothed back was about to disappear into the dimness at the end of the street, losing him his chance for good and all, it hardened, and rose up and whispered, Why not? into the boy's ear. And almost without knowing he was doing it he was lounging after the man, his hands in his new pockets, clutching his precious half-crown, its silver roundness comforting against the palm of his dirty hand.

Even as he went, fear was rising in him. He'd heard about Constam—about the sword he kept in that stick of his, the way he'd struck a man dead on the spot for no more than coming too close to him in a crowd. Had heard, too, of the way he was good for a touch, if he knew you, and that there were enough hard cases about the Dials to skewer the person who damaged that easy touch in any way, skewer him as thoroughly as Constam himself would do it, if he were harassed in any way. . . .

Yet still he went on, following that perky angled hat through the murk of the sour streets, weaving from side to side of the alleys with all the skill of the really professional pickpocket. No matter what, the boy was going to try to take Constam tonight. After such a day, it was meant that he should. After such a day, in which all had been right for him, he would have to be a very rum cove, queer in his attic, not to follow through. Constam was asking to be taken, one of these days, the way he came strolling down the Dials. The boy would be the one to take him.

And he watched and followed, and his heart lifted with fear and hope and the most exciting feeling of all: the hunter's feeling, with the prey, all unsuspecting, in his eye.

· TWO ·

IT WENT on so long, the following, the dodging, the losing of him and the finding again, that it was almost as though the purpose of his actions was only the chase, as though he had forgotten why he was doing it at all. There before him in the thickening murk, as the man plunged deeper and deeper into the alleys and courts and yards of the Dials, went the hat, and it became more difficult to keep it in sight, to be sure round which corner it had gone. The number of people in the streets had thinned out; this far into the reeking slum, even the inhabitants were afraid to be abroad once darkness was well established. But still the boy went on, slipping along in the shadows beneath the rickety house walls, his hand clenched in his pocket, waiting and watching for his moment.

Jesse would have been hard put to it to pinpoint the moment at which he became aware of the presence behind him; there had been the crowd of urchins, and then they had fallen away as they realized that there were no more ha'pence coming from him this night, and then the two or three painted women who had tried to invite him, until they had seen his face and recognized him, and laughed and gone away in search of less exalted custom; and then there was the follower.

Despite his many years of haunting the Dials and the Holy Land and the Bermudas and his pride in his special status there, Jesse had never lost a deep awareness of the dangers of the place. He feared it and its people with the same strength he had the first time he had ventured away from the safety of Oxford Street and the Strand; indeed, it was this fear and the sensations it gave him that was a large part of the attraction he found in his visits. And this fear kept alive in him an almost preternatural sensitivity; it was as though he could see without looking, hear without listening, feel without touching, while all the time dissimulating a casual, devil-may-care appearance.

So he marched on, never turning his head, keeping his shoulders as relaxed as before, but assessing constantly the information coming to him from the shadow slipping along behind him.

Not a big man; no great physical presence here. Small, light, and fast—a boy. One given to guile more than the use of brute strength, and as such to be treated with a little more respect; any fool could protect himself against a mere bully boy—any fool with a well-oiled blade in his stick, he amended, with a quirk of his mouth.

Deliberately, he changed his direction. He had been going steadily toward Covent Garden, meaning to walk through its more cheerful, amusing streets to reach his ultimate destination in the tangle of streets called the Bermudas, there in the corner defined by St. Martin's Lane and the Strand; but now he bore west, skirting the Garden, and twisting and turning with all the ease of long familiarity, led his shadow into the darkest and most dangerous of all the alleys.

Still moving with his deceptive ease, he allowed one hand to test the movement of the blade in the stick, and when it responded smoothly to his gentle pressure on the silver head, slackened his pace very slightly; and it was as though he were signaling the boy behind that the time was right.

They were in a tiny court, barely wide enough for two people to pass each other, but which led into a better-lit street where there were a few cookshops and a drinking booth; he knew that now was the time the boy must do whatever he intended if he was to do it at all.

And almost as though the man had in truth stopped and called him, the boy obeyed. He came out of the shadows with a sharp but silent rush, and Jesse braced his shoulders for the impact, knowing at once what the boy intended: no permanent damage, but an impact that would send him sprawling in the filth, a blow that would leave him breathless and helpless just long enough for the boy to dip his pockets and then go flying away over his recumbent self and into the safety of the streets beyond.

But the boy was surprised in his intentions, for moving with a delicacy that seemed absurd in a man of such solid if compact form, Jesse whirled, and arms outstretched and rigid, he held his stick before him in both hands so that it formed a fence that met the rush full on. And the boy, leaping to reach his shoulders as he thought, found himself winded as the stick caught him hard under his ribs, almost knocking the breath out of him.

But his own native cunning matched Jesse's, for winded though he was, he immediately realized what had happened, and using the stick as an ally instead of a barrier, he allowed his body to follow through its own movement and went over the stick like a monkey. As he tucked his head under and came round, he kicked hard with his heels and caught Jesse a sharp blow under the chin that forced his head back, small and bare though the feet were, and that was enough to make the heavier man lose his balance. His booted heels slid on the filth of the broken ground, and then they were both sprawling, the boy on top of the man.

For a brief moment both lay still, trying to adjust to the newness of the situation; and then, almost in concert, they moved: the boy to leap up and over and away, the man to stop him.

The man won, clamping one iron-strong hand over the boy's arm, holding it so tightly that for the first time the boy let a sound escape him, a sharp whimper of pain as he tried to pull himself away. But the man lay there and held him, making him half-crouch above him as he wriggled and whimpered and scrabbled impotently at the cruel grip that was making pain scream through his arm muscles.

Jesse peered upward in the darkness, just making out the white blur of the small face, never relaxing his hold one whit as he considered. And then he spoke easily, with no hint of breathlessness.

"Boy, stop your caterwauling. Do I caterwaul, though I lie

here in the filth where you threw me? I have you, and I mean to hold you, and none of your missish shrieking will make aught of difference. Stand up, boy!"

And without letting go, he stood up himself, using his stick to lever his bulk upward, and then tucked it neatly under his arm to release his hand to set his coat to rights.

"My hat, boy!" he said then, and half dragging, half pushing him, the man led him up the alley to the place where his hat lay just visible in a mud puddle. Sulkily, the boy kicked at it, but a sharper pressure still from those dreadful fingers made him wail in enraged pain, and duck and pick up the hat.

"Clean it!" Jesse said peremptorily, and after one swift glance upward at the square face glimmering palely in the darkness, the boy rubbed the hat ineffectually against his shirt before holding it out to his captor.

Jesse took it and clapped it back on his head, seeming quite unconcerned about the mud that still adorned it, and turning briskly he led the boy to the top of the alley and out into the street beyond. And now the boy felt a sudden surge of fear again, and once more tried to pull away, gritting his teeth against the pain as Jesse held on even more tightly.

"Afraid one of the bully boys will see, and know you were fool enough to try to take Constam?" Another cruel squeeze. "Eh, boy? So you should be, so you should be. The boy who can take Constam isn't born yet, nor ever likely to be, d'you hear me?"

"I'll kill you—yes I will, I'll kill you!" the boy cried, his voice thin with the pain and fear that filled him, still struggling. "I will, you see if I don't, you stinking son of a . . ."

Jesse stood still, peering more closely at him here in the light where he could see him, listening almost admiringly to the string of curses the boy produced, and after a while he threw his head back and laughed aloud.

"You're a game 'un, and no mistake about it! There's not a boy or man in all these parts wouldn't be begging me for mercy, and you curse! A rare plucked 'un! Who taught you such matters, boy, a bird-brained nothing such as you?"

"Bird-brained? *Bird-brained?*" The boy stopped his swearing and stared furiously at him. "I ain't no fool, and don't you go believin' it. I'm a fly one, I am, best dip in all these parts, and never been rumbled; not never, and don't you go thinkin' it, you—"

"Aha!" Jesse laughed again. "So it's got its pride, has it? So! Never been rumbled, hey? Till today! Picked a fly one this time, didn't you? And now I've got you, I could turn informer and get you topped, d'you know that? Hey? D'you know it?" And he shook the boy hard, so that his head snapped to and fro on his shoulders.

The boy looked at him for a moment, at the face now very close to his own, for Jesse was leaning down and staring hard at him, his expression almost ferocious in its severity. For a moment he felt new fear rise in him like a lake of cold water, but he held his own face rigid, merely staring back, and then after a moment, he pulled his lips back in the travesty of a grin and said, "Gammon!"

"Hey? What's that? Gammon, is it? And why should it be? I could take you to the beak right now, and you'd be up in court before nightfall tomorrow, in Newgate and meeting Jack Ketch before you were a week older! How should *that* be gammon?"

"You comes down the Dials too much! Flash cove like you! What does the likes of you want in the Dials? But you likes it, or you wouldn't come. And if you get me topped, you won't come down so friendly ever again, because they won't let you out again, that's what. Not even the bully boys could stop 'em takin' you if you gets me 'anged. You wouldn't be so safe 'ere no more, and you likes comin' here, so it's all gammon."

Very slowly, Jesse smiled, and then slapped the boy on the shoulder with his other hand and beamed at him, and the boy stared back at him, doubtfully at first, and then, as sureness filled him with relief, nodded almost cheerfully back.

"Boy, I was wrong! Bird-brained you never will be. A very downy bird you are, for one so young! The man isn't living that Jesse Constam would ever send to the hangman, nor boy neither. And you know it. So what do we do to the boy who tried to take Constam, hey? I tell you what we do. We buy him a daffy of gin. And a bite o' supper, too. What say you to that, hey, boy?"

The boy put his head on one side and stared up at Jesse, his face filled with suspicion.

"You wants to give me—what for?"

"What for? What for? Why, to reward you, boy, reward you! You tried to take me, and that is very remarkable. And though you wailed and caterwauled to a degree when I hurt you, you showed you was a well-plucked 'un. And then you rumbled me, knew what I was about when I threatened you with the magistrate. And I'm hungry and thirsty and in sad want of company. So, boy, are you coming with me or no?"

"Let go my arm," the boy said, still wary, and immediately Jesse laughed again.

"Damme if I hadn't forgotten. There, boy—did you think I was still going to take you to the beak? Well, it's not surprising if you did. But I will not, I promise you!"

The boy stood there, rubbing his arm and flexing his fingers as the sensation painfully began to return to them, and then nodded with a sudden wisdom.

"Is it boys you comes down the Dials for? Because I don't do that lay, I'll tell yer now. I told you, I'm a dip."

"Boys? *Boys?*" For a moment Jesse looked genuinely puzzled, and then comprehension dawned on him. "No! And don't you ever let me hear you say that Constam does! I come here for my own purposes, which are none of your interest, boy. Now, I ask you again. A daffy of gin and some victuals? Say your yea or nay, and stay or be off. I care not either way. But I like a boy of spirit and sense, and you have a rare deal of both. I offer you a good supper for no other reason. So, is it to be?"

"What d'you take me for? A gull? If it's not boys you wants, then a daffy and grub it is, and glad of it." The boy grinned widely, and capered briefly in a sudden access of glee.

"Come then, boy! To supper!" And with another convivial slap on the boy's narrow shoulders that made him reel, he turned and marched away along the street.

Pattering along beside him, full of satisfaction, the boy peered upward and asked, "Where was you goin' when you came down the Dials? Was you goin' to your supper then? Why do you come here to get victuals when you could go to any of the fancy kens where the swells are?"

"Where was I going, boy? Ah, now, that is an interesting

question. A very interesting question, to be sure!" Jesse laughed fatly, and beamed at the boy. "What other questions do you have to ask? Observe, boy, that I do not intend to answer any that I choose not to. But ask away, ask away! I like a boy of spirit!"

After a moment, the boy asked, "Where we goin'?"

"Now, that I will answer. To Maiden Lane, m'boy, as ill named a thoroughfare as any in all London, but no matter! To the cookshop of my old friend Thomas, that is where we are going. Next question!"

"To Maiden Lane?" The boy stood stock still. "You're gammoning me again! There's not a chance they'll let me in there! That's for the swells, that is, not for the likes of me! They'll take one look at me and be away to Bow Street for the Runners! Not me, not to Maiden Lane—not for anythin'!"

"Stuff, boy! You're with Constam now! No one says nay to Constam, not even the swells of Maiden Lane." He laughed his fat laugh again. "Thomas Rule a swell? Bless me! They'll be making a belted earl of me yet, if Thomas Rule's a swell!"

And the boy didn't argue. This strange man was too authoritative altogether, too sure of himself in every way, to be gainsaid. And besides, the boy told himself, anyone who could rumble him as he'd been rumbled, after all his years in the game and never once caught, was a most remarkable man. If he said the boy could march into Rule's cookshop in Maiden Lane without being thrown out amid great noise and fuss, why then, it must be so. The day was indeed proving to be the best he'd ever had, one way or another!

· THREE ·

HE STOOD there in the doorway blinking at the brightness of the lights and feeling exceedingly small beside the bulk of Jesse Constam, who, four-square and arms akimbo, stood looming above him, his black stick held in one fist so that it thrust out fore and aft of him in a very insolent fashion. And almost without realizing he had done it, he shrank a little closer to the man, to peer at the scene before him round the skirts of Jesse's mud-spattered coat.

And such a scene! Such a profusion of light from masses of heavy wax candles and the excessively luxurious coal-oil lamps that sat on shelves and tables and on the great wooden dresser that almost filled one wall; such a spread of scrubbed wooden tables and benches, on which sat men in thick clothes, with silken handkerchiefs about their necks and great hats on the floor beside them; such a belching of steam from vast tureens of soup and huge pies and platters of meat and bowls of fish; such a sawdust-covered floor, such noise, such smells, such overwhelming magnificence! His belly contracted into a tight knot of exquisite pain at the glory and wonder of it all.

"Hey, Thomas! Where's Thomas, God damn his eyes to hell and his heart to the devil's own plate! Thomas!" Jesse roared, and many of the diners turned and stared at him and shouted a welcome, and Jesse beamed round at them all, and then upended his stick to rap it against the floor.

And this time out of the glitter of hazy light a man came running, a fat man with a great white apron tied about a vast belly and an old-fashioned wig slipping sideways on his head, with a face so lined and red and sweaty that it reflected light from its every facet, for all the world like a vast crimson diamond.

"Jesse Constam, to be sure!" this splendid man cried, and the boy stared in great interest, for even he knew that this was the owner and a man of substance, eating his own beef every day of his life and still with his pockets well lined with cash. "How long do we wait to see you again, my good friend? Not an oyster have I opened this past se'ennight but I've asked myself when next Jesse Constam will be here to partake!"

"Thomas, you lie in your teeth, but I thank you for it. Never a thought of me has passed your mind since the moment I set a foot beyond your door at New Year! But e I am, and with me a companion—who fears you'll turn out of doors to eat his supper in the gutter! But I told hat in your eyes any companion of mine was as welas I myself, and was I not right to so assure him, my old friend?" And he stepped aside, leaving the ling there where he could easily be seen.

ite-aproned man stared at him, and the boy stared nly very conscious of the difference between his and sagging breeches and filthy bare feet and the well-shod appearance of the people all around

vled furiously and slid his eyes sideways at

Constam, this is the outside of enough! ttersnipe of such filth and such evil to eat 'riven the little prig a dunnamany times ith all the other villains and thieves, and

boy said loudly, swallowing his fear has you seen me and chased me, on afore you knows it!"

25 ·

Jesse roared his approval, and slapped Thomas hard across the back, and laughed until his eyes ran.

"You hear that, Thomas? Such a villain, such a prig, such a sin and blot on the face of the good God's earth and such a pride in itself that won't be gainsaid! You'll grant me, Thomas, in all the Dials you never met such a one as this!"

"No, nor shall I ever!" the other man growled. "For I'll not hang about with such scum, no, not if you were to pay me hard gold for it! If that's to your taste, Mr. Constam, it's your taste, but I'm not one to . . ." He stopped, for Jesse's hand had tightened on his shoulder, and then he grimaced. "Oh, to be sure, what is't to me? Feed the brute, if you so choose. But I tell you, boy, set foot here once alone, without the protection of your good friend here, and you'll see the moon and the stars as you meet the ground beyond these doors! Now, hear me!"

"I hear you!" the boy said perkily, for he was beginning to feel safe under the elbow of the redoubtable Jesse Constam. This was indeed a remarkable man to so cow so many people with little more than a word or a grip of the hand! And knowing little of the power of real money, of the many pounds that Constam had spent here in the past, and would undoubtedly spend in the future if he were well enough contented with his landlord's care of him, he saw only the power of a personality and, without knowing it, began to fall into a state of admiration.

They settled themselves at a scrubbed wooden table, nea the vast sea-coal fire, and the boy stretched his toes toward under the table and marveled at the sensation of it, the w the heat licked his toes and traveled up his scrawny legs warm his buttocks and belly.

Constam sat and looked at him, then shrugged off his g overcoat and put his hat upon the floor beside it, and the could now see him far more clearly, and stared unabashed

The most noticeable thing about him was his head, shone bald as an apple in the candlelight, flanked by a c reddish fringe that sat upon the small points of the collar which framed his neck. Beneath the collar we cravats, a white one peeping out behind a shining bla one, on which were a bow and a discreet jeweled glittered in the light as he moved. His waistcoat w pea green and pearl-buttoned, his frock coat a rich and lustrous black, and his trousers, though much mud-bespattered above the now dirty Hessian boots, had clearly been a gleaming white at the start of his evening.

The man stretched his legs beneath the table and, tucking his chin into his collar, opened his rather small hazel eyes wide at the boy and said, "So, boy? Did I tell you aright or not? Are you here in the warmth with me, or out in the gutter of Maiden Lane? Hey, boy?"

The boy shrugged and turned his head away, to stare about the room and watch hungrily as food was carried by. The man sat and studied him in his own turn.

A thin boy, pitifully thin, with his bones sharp-etched under his throat beneath the appalling rag he wore as a shirt. Thin, birdlike bones, reminiscent of the younger Charlotte's, Jesse thought, and pushed that idea away to look harder at the boy. Thin, yes, but with a toughness that could be seen in the set of his shoulders, the line of his back as he sat there. With half-decent feeding and a decent shirt to his back, he'd be a respectable-looking lad indeed, one that would go through the world with head high, for he was a handsome boy.

It was his eyes that were most striking, being long and narrow and heavily lashed, and a most peculiar shade of green. Cat's eyes, Jesse thought with a rare departure into poeticism. A head of hair which, though clearly solid with the dirt of years, and undoubtedly supporting a large number of extremely active lice, was thick and springing, with a tendency to curl about the small ears and the high forehead. Just such a boy as he would himself be happy to call his own, had he fathered him. But that was an idea not to be borne, and almost viciously Jesse thrust it away from him. There were thoughts that must not be thought, wishes that must not be wished, hopes that were hopeless.

"What's your name, boy?" Jesse asked abruptly, and the boy turned and looked at him again, his green eyes wary and slightly narrowed. But he did not need to answer, for a waiter, also wrapped in an apron but one much less white and capacious than that which encompassed the important Mr. Rule, arrived to slap down on the table before them the food that Jesse had called for with a gesture of his thumb as they sat down.

A platter of oysters, with barnacles still clinging to their rough black shells; a pasty in a deep dish, with the pastry glowing golden-brown and fragrant; a tureen of thick green pea soup; a slab of best wheaten bread. The boy stared, and then looked up at Jesse, and then back at the food, and the man put out his hand and patted the boy's shoulder with a sudden rough kindness.

"Eat, boy. Eat all you can stuff inside you! There's time and to spare for all else."

The boy needed no further invitation, and Jesse watched him, amused, despite his regrettable eating manners, for he snuffled and gulped and gobbled exceedingly noisily. Then, while the boy mopped up the last of the soup with chunks of bread, Jesse, using a large knife with a wicked flat blade, attacked the oysters, twisting each one open with a sharp turn of his powerful wrist, and pushed them toward the boy, who greedily swallowed several.

And then, with more leisure, he set about the pie, doing more than his fair share toward its destruction, and not until the last piece of mutton, the last sliver of onion and clove-scented gravy, had been wiped up with a piece of bread did the boy stop, and straighten his back to look at his companion with his face damp with sweat and a faint flush across the pale cheeks, his eyes half glazed with the satisfaction of it all.

"A daffy o' gin?" the man suggested invitingly, but the boy shook his head.

"Makes yer slow on the dip. Don't know your time right, like. So I drinks only beer, if I can get it."

"Wise in your generation," Jesse murmured, and the boy looked uncomprehendingly at him.

"Thomas! Beer for m'young friend. And for myself! Hurry along, now!" he roared, still not taking his eyes from the boy, and then he leaned forward and said, "I asked you your name, before the victuals came and took your attention."

The boy looked at him, then stared down at the table and sulkily drew up his shoulders.

"Still afraid? Goddamme, boy, what more must I do before you believe me one of the family—when I choose? I live among the swells, but come to the Dials to be with my own kind of people. No fear I'm aught but what I seem—a man of my word, to be trusted. You can tell me who you are. There'll be no handle against you made of it! You have my word!"

He leaned back, to let the waiter slap foaming tankards of beer before them.

The boy looked at him then, his green eyes opaque and half closed, and after a moment he grimaced slightly.

"Call me aught you care to," he muttered.

"By God, I'll not be so mistrusted by a foul and evil young prig such as you!" Jesse began to raise his voice. "To sit there and deny me the mere—"

"Call me aught you care to on account there's no name to be told you," the boy said, and though his voice was quiet, it could be clearly heard.

Jesse stopped, and stared at him, and had the grace to look a little ashamed.

"Like so, boy? No people of your own? No father, mother, brother?"

The boy shrugged.

"Where do you live?"

"Where I can," the boy said, "I'm a skipper, and allus has been."

"A skipper? Sleeping rough? You live the winter thus? Where can you sleep on such nights?"

"There's the haylofts about, the cowkeepers' yards. And while I come late and wake early, I sleep safe enough, and warm enough. And sometimes, if I'm flush, and things is running good, I buys a night, when the frost is about, in the lodgin' house in Drury Lane. When it's very cold and I can't get no boots nohow. Only wears boots of the wintertime, when I can get 'em."

"Always lived thus, you say? But surely, once, you had some people of your own? No child, not even so bright a one as you, can live quite alone in these parts, as well I know."

The boy sat hunched on his bench, his head down so that Jesse could see only the top of his head and the dullness of the dirt that caked his hair, and after a while he looked up at Jesse, his eyes again narrowed and opaque.

"What's it to you?" he asked flatly.

"I know not!" Jesse said, and spoke as much to himself as to the boy, for he was in truth a little puzzled by his own interest. That the boy was a fly boy, a downy boy, a capable boy, was clear. But was that the only cause? Or was it the memory of himself growing up in the alleys behind Smithfield, long years ago, and of the poverty and misery of the childhood from which he had dragged himself by the exercise of his own sharp wits? He shook his head a little at his foolish maunderings and looked again at the boy, and smiled one of his broad smiles.

"I'll tell ye, boy. I have it in my mind that I'm ripe for some philanthropy. The care of my brother man! I'm known well in these parts for it, as you'll have heard, or could find out if you'd a mind to ask some of your villainous friends. When I take a care to a person, why then, I take a care! Perhaps I'm about to take a care to you? Tell me of yourself, so that I may decide. Now, does that not seem to you to be a worthwhile consideration?"

The boy looked at him carefully, running his eyes over the round red face, the jowls resting on the points of the collar, and tentatively let his mind stretch itself. He had an alderman, a single alderman (and his hand slid into his pocket to curl about his half-crown still miraculously there, in spite of the topsy-turvy tumble he'd taken). This very afternoon, had he not been considering ways and means of setting up a real straight selling lay for himself? Enough to buy a little gear, to sell again, and buy again? He looked at the man, who looked back at him silently. And then decided.

"I wants to be a Manchester man, or a peddler, or have a shop of me own," he said flatly.

"So, a proud boy *and* an ambitious boy! A rare collection of wishes from a Seven Dials pickpocket! Hmph! Pickpocket. Who taught you your trade?"

The boy grinned at that, and shook his head. "I taught meself. Had to. There was none to show me the way to take their lay, now, was there? I've been taking what I needed this—oh a dunnamany years. Always."

"Not always, boy. Come, you must remember something other than this? A time when you had a place you called a home?"

The boy put his head on one side and after a moment said simply, "Weean."

"What's that you say?"

"She called me Weean. Like that—Wee-an. In a soft way. I disremember—"

"She? A woman who looked after you?"

The boy nodded. "There was a time—I disremember—I know she died. I—have a view of that." He wrinkled his face a little, his eyes almost disappearing into narrow slits, and it was as though he were looking at a picture somewhere just beyond Jesse's line of vision, and he spoke almost dreamily, hugging himself in the firelight, curling his arms about his knees, which he had pulled up against his full belly.

"I sat on the floor, and there was dirt, and she did not call at me for playing in the dirt, as she always did—for she was always lifting me away of it, for fear of the rats, she would say. And I played in the dirt and she lay in the corner as she always did, but she lay and lay—and then others came. I saw their legs and they took her out, and she let them. Picked her up as she picked me up, and she said nothing, but lay there on the man's back, and he took her out and banged her head at the door, and she did not cry out, nor tell me to leave off the playing with the dirt for fear of the rats—and the men took her out into the alley, and I went after, for she told me. Always. Always she said I must stay with her, and never to go off on my own. 'Wee-an, stay by me,' she'd say. And she was letting the man take her, so I followed. I didn't know she was dead. Not then."

His voice dwindled away, and after a moment Jesse asked gently, "And then what?"

The boy looked at him and shrugged. "I disremember. I've always been a skipper, since then. I disremember exactly."

"How long ago? How old are you?"

The boy frowned at that. "How long? How shall I tell that?"

"How many summers have you slept in the cowkeepers' haylofts?"

"How many . . ." The boy blinked and closed his eyes, and it was as though he watched the years of his childhood marching away before the lids, for suddenly he smiled.

"The year of the French Wars," he said triumphantly. "The first summer, the year of the French Wars!"

Jesse shook his head at that. "What can you know of the French Wars, here in the stews? What cares have the people here for politics? How could you know of such matters?"

But the boy nodded his head vigorously. "I know! Of course I know! Over there . . ." And he jerked his head in the direction of Union Square and the Royal Mews. "Soldiers, and marching, and music. That was the first summer. I would watch them, and the soldiers gave me food. I slept in the stables there then, till I got too big. 'Twas a good summer, the first year of the French Wars."

"And have you no notion what age you were when your—when she died—the one who called you Wee-an?"

The boy frowned and creased his face and shook his head, and then, suddenly, stopped.

"I disremember . . ." he said again, uncertainly, but Jesse leaned forward and said with a curious urgency, "But you have recalled some matter, some matter you had not recalled before?"

The boy smiled a little, then. "Don't think much about it, not on the dipping lay—too much to do and watch. But she told me once—a foolish thing to remember—'I'll teach you how to cipher,' she said, 'to make a merchant man of you, and you shall keep me warm and rich when I am old. I'll teach you how to cipher. Now, I,' she said, 'I . . .'"

He faltered and stopped, frowning as he tried to remember, and Jesse put out a hand toward him and then almost instinctively pulled it back, for the boy was again staring glazed and remote beyond him, as he struggled to extract from his clouded memory the remainder of the little colloquy.

"'Now, I,' she said, 'I am five times your age, my Wee-an, five times. And I am old, I'm twenty years, twenty years since—since . . .'" he shook his head. "I disremember. I don't *want* to remember. Is it not enough? Enough to—for you to make me a Manchester man or a peddler or . . ."

But now it was Jesse who was staring with glazed eyes and remote air, and the boy looked at him, puzzled.

"Is't enough?" he asked again after a moment, and more

loudly, and this time Jesse started, and looked at him.

"Boy," he said after a moment. "D'you wish to know for how many years you have been on God's green earth? For I can tell you."

The boy blinked.

"Indeed I can. 'Tis simple arithmetic, no more. You were four when your—whoever it was started to teach you to cipher. If this was shortly before you took to the gutter life—which it must be, for you could not learn to cipher earlier and would remember more were it later—and this, you say, was the first year of the French Wars—why, you are eleven! Eleven years old, which looks about as it should, for one so half starved and ill served by the good things of the world."

He looked again at the boy, and then suddenly swept their beer tankards aside and set his hands upon the child's narrow shoulders.

"You are an ambitious boy, a willing boy, a boy of hopes, and—a boy, beyond any doubt, marked out by Providence for a future that is better than you will ever find here in your present life. Hey, boy? What future for you here on the dipping lay? How long before your fingers slip in some man's pocket, a man less good at heart than Jesse Constam, and you find yourself in lumber, hey?" And he turned his head to one side and crossed his eyes, and thrust his tongue between his teeth and produced the thick gurgle of the newly hanged man. "Is this not so?"

"I want to be a peddler," said the boy after a moment. "With a little more than I have—I've an alderman, a half-a-crown, good money—with a little more, a little stock, I could—"

"My boy, you shall have better! I have decided. I have found in my heart the wish to—well, let be, let be. You shall discover! Thomas!"

He turned his head, roaring, and Thomas Rule came hurrying across the floor, spurts of sawdust marking his way, and Jesse threw a gold coin at him and lifted his coat to his shoulders, scurrying the boy before him toward the door.

"Thomas, next time this boy comes here, you'll welcome him, I promise you, as you have always welcomed me. And you'll not know you do it!" And laughing hugely, he swept the boy ahead of him, out into the dark and chill of Maiden Lane.

"No, you don't, my boy!" Jesse cried, and his voice was jocular; but his hand was heavy as it came down on the boy's shoulder, for he had turned and was about to dart away through the crowds, taken aback at the change of mood in Jesse. He seemed suddenly to be so eager, bursting with energy, and the boy was even more alarmed than he had been at the commencement of his adventure, if that was possible. But he could not get away, no matter how hard he wriggled, for Jesse's grip was as firm as ever as he hurried the boy through the streets.

"Where are—where do we go?" the boy managed to gasp, for indeed the impact of the chill air following the heaviest meal he had ever eaten, combined with the headlong speed to which he was being subjected, had made him breathless.

"Where? My boy, you are no fit sight for man nor beast. To Lucy's in Panton Street, that is where! And when she and her ladies have done with you, you'll not know yourself, nor your future, that I promise you!"

· FOUR ·

CHARLOTTE had let her maid undress her long since, but still she sat there on her elegant silk brocaded sofa beside the glowing fire in her dressing room, her silk peignoir pulled about her and her nightcap tied firmly beneath her chin, staring at the flames.

Would he be back at all tonight? The Watch had long since called midnight, and generally when he went on these jaunts of his he had returned well before this hour, for however irregular his private behavior on occasion, he was a careful man of affairs who was in his countinghouse each morning by eight. Tonight, she brooded, he was behaving in a more than commonly ill manner, to stay among his evil companions so long.

It did not for one moment occur to her that he might come to any harm, for inevitably she shared Jesse's own sublime confidence in his ability to look after himself.

His particular lateness tonight was undoubtedly due, she told herself somberly, to the way she had remonstrated with him after dinner. Had she bitten her tongue and let him go with no word from her, he would surely have returned by now, to stand in the door of her dressing room smelling of the cold night air, his hands in his pockets, his hat under one arm and his stick under the other, staring at her insolently over the points of his collar and asking her how she did and saying perkily that he trusted that she had passed an agreeable evening. . . .

Tonight, for some foolish reason, she had chosen to linger in the dining room after dinner, when the cloth was drawn and the wine was set before him, instead of accompanying meek Dorothea to the drawing room and leaving him in his solitary masculine splendor. She had asked him not to go; had reminded him of his new station in life, of the style of his home; had been unwise enough to point out to him that any pretensions he might have toward making acquaintance among the *ton* could not fail to be damaged by such expeditions as these.

And he had raised his sandy eyebrows at her over his wineglass and said in his sneering way, "Indeed, ma'am, it is not I who have ambitions towards making acquaintances among those milk-and-water people! Such desires are all yours, and I have no part in them, nor ever shall, upon my word! No man yet has called *me* tuft hunter, nor had cause to regard *me* as having encroaching ways, and so I tell you! As for such people shunning me for my interest in matters philanthropical—I tell you straight, ma'am, I would rather lose the regard of twenty such than the gratitude of one of my poor friends!"

And she, in her stupidity (she now thought bitterly), had flashed back at him her old accusation of seeking other satisfactions than those he claimed, and even as she had said it had known her error.

"I do not, ma'am, have to apply to you for permission to do aught, and so I tell you!" he had said, his voice rough with anger. "If I chose to seek in the Dials the pleasures and rights *you* deny me, there would be no man in all the world who would despise me for it! In truth I do *not* behave so, and had you the style and elegance to which you so constantly aspire, I believe you would not be so shocking vulgar and ill bred as to speak of such matters!"

And she, stung in her turn, had snapped, "Aye, sir, I believe you, for none know better than I of your capabilities—or lack of them—in that sphere! Nor of your desires, which in all truth are—"

"Madam, you have the tongue and soul of a fishwife! There's no Billingsgate slattern that would not be ashamed— aye, madam, *ashamed*—to speak so to any man! There are husbands in this town would turn you out of doors for half such a cause, and well you know it, ma'am! I tell you again, as I have told you these many years, that I seek only to discharge my Christian duty tu my fellow man. And if you choose to sit here in the richness and comfort which *I* provide for you and your daughter and think evil thoughts of me, then it is your soul that is in jeopardy, not mine. And so I bid you goodnight, Mrs. Constam!" And he had swept out of the dining room to call loudly for his coat and hat, leaving her to join Dorothea in the drawing room with such composure as she could muster.

Beyond the curtains that shrouded the window, she heard again the distant wail of the Watch and moved her shoulders irritably inside their silken covering. She should go to bed; she would look haggard beyond recognition in the morning unless she had her rest; but where was the sense in going to her bed? She would not sleep until she heard his footsteps on the stairs. Surely he must return soon!

She sat on for a long time, brooding, letting the core of misery and resentment in her grow and flourish, seeking all through her mind for a way to punish him for his abuse of her.

At what point it was that she first saw her way to both please herself and punish Jesse, while yet behaving as a good wife should in furthering his interests, she could not be quite sure, but there it was. The idea came to her mind, and as she sat and thought about it for a while, her anger melted away, to be replaced by a creamy self-satisfaction.

The fire dwindled and the candles guttered a little, low in their sconces, but Charlotte did not notice. She felt much better than she would have believed possible a few hours earlier.

On the floor above, Dorothea too had been wakeful. She had gone to bed when her mama had bidden her, as she always did, with a dutiful curtsy and a kiss for Mama's proffered cheek, though she had not been in the least tired.

She had submitted to the resentful attentions of Kate, the housemaid who acted as her abigail (for Charlotte could see no sense in employing a maid to do nothing but wait upon a mere child like Dorothea), and had said only a meek "Good night" when Kate had blown out the candles and closed the bed curtains before stamping away to her own bed.

Then she had listened carefully, sticking her head out between the bed curtains to be sure there was no sound from outside, and, satisfied, slipped quickly out of bed to run softly across the floor to the far corner beside the fireplace. Now her real life could begin.

She had found the loose floor board almost as soon as they had moved to the house and she had been given the room, and had immediately hidden her silver thimble in the gap below it and left it there for a whole week, undisturbed. And when at the end of that time it had not been discovered, despite much urgent searching on the part of Kate (and during which Dorothea suffered much from Mama's tongue and listened, head bowed, to her animadversions on the subject of harum-scarum hoydens who could not keep aught about them for five minutes together), she knew her hiding place was safe.

She had taken out the thimble and replaced it with her journal and gone to Mama and told her with limpid innocence that she had found her thimble tangled in the fringe of one of her shawls, and stood by while Kate was roundly scolded for failing to find it there, feeling happy. And from then on had kept her journal safe hidden in the corner.

Now she lifted out the journal, together with the inkhorn and quill, and crept to the fireside to gently stir the embers to flames before squatting beside it, the precious journal open at a new page, to start writing.

It was a curious hotchpotch, the journal, which would have puzzled any reader, but since none but Dorothea herself ever saw it, that didn't matter. She wrote in it each night, sometimes covering as much as three whole pages with her spidery writing, stopping only when she had to mend her pen. She always tried to keep it purely truthful, and indeed often succeeded in her attempts at first. It was only later that the pen seemed to move of its own accord and carry her recollections of her day onward from their humdrum reality to more interesting matter.

And so it was tonight. She wrote carefully of all that had taken place between Mama and Papa Constam (she could never bring herself to abandon the use of his name in her journal, even though Jesse had succeeded in making her do so in conversing with him), faithfully recording every word, for she had heard it all; but then she always did, for she was a small and light-footed child who had had many years of practice at listening to her elders, of being sure she was near enough to hear them, yet far enough away to appear unaware of their conversation. She understood very little of what had been said today, familiar though it was from many drearily similar conversations, realizing only that her mama was angered by Papa Constam's absences from home and that she was in some way disappointed in him; yet still she punctiliously set it all down. . . .

It was at this point that her pen took over, starting to write its account of the secret life she led inside her head, and she let it speed over the page, dropping occasional blots in its anxiety to get it all down, her small, narrow-lipped mouth curving with pleasure. Her pen wrote of her experiences with her dear Lysander, her perfect, her beautiful, her adoring, her rich and totally beguiling Lysander.

Never under any circumstances, her pen told her Lysander had said that afternoon, would he behave to his dear Dorothea as Papa Constam had behaved to Mama. He could not *bear* to leave his Beloved Angel for so long as five minutes together. He agreed with Dorothea, the recorded conversation went on, that in True Love there could be No Parting and reiterated his Constant and Undying Devotion to her, his assurances that he held her always in Perfect Esteem and would Never, as long as either lived, Forget his Love and Duty toward her. Dorothea should Nestle Always, her pen wrote fervently, in the Security of her Lysander's Bosom, a bosom filled only with thoughts of her Well-being and Happiness and . . .

She wrote until her wrist ached and the fire had dwindled down too far for her to read the pages at all clearly, and then, regretfully, she dried the ink in front of the embers before hiding all away again under the floor board in the corner. And then she crept into bed, to plan the day she would spend tomorrow with dear Lysander, of the dresses she would wear to accompany him to Cremorne and to a picnic and to the Opera House and to the Palace for a Rout . . .

Somewhere alongside her visions of her bright tomorrow scuttled the real Dorothea who would undoubtedly spend the day as she always did, wearing plain white muslin with the minimum of ribbons, spending the morning hours in the schoolroom with Mama and her indifferent attempts to teach French and Drawing and Music; eating her bread-and-butter luncheon with Mama in her boudoir; paying morning visits with Mama before hurrying home to receive such callers as might feel constrained to visit them that afternoon; the dismals of dinner with Mama—and perhaps Papa Constam—and the long evening—and then Lysander again. Without Lysander, Dorothea thought as she drifted into sleep, her life would be quite impossible to support at all. . . .

· FIVE ·

CAUTIOUSLY, the boy stretched himself, letting the water move luxuriously across his body, and took a deep breath, filling his lungs with the scented steam. Across the room somebody laughed, and immediately he drew himself back into the tight knot in which he had been holding himself ever since the big woman had so unceremoniously dumped him into the bath, and turned his head to look over his shoulder.

There was a girl standing there beside the curtain that covered the door, her head on one side, her face split into a huge smile that showed her rather blackened teeth very clearly. Not that the teeth mattered much, for the rest of her was very glorious, being adorned with a yellow muslin half-dress cut so low in the bosom that part of her nipples showed above the edge of the bodice, and so transparent that the rest of them could be almost as easily seen through the fabric. The muslin clung damply to the rest of her body too, clearly defining the round belly and the slightly protuberant navel and the smudge of darkness above her heavy thighs. Her hair was almost as yellow as her dress, and piled in elaborate curls on top of her head, and her face gleamed incredibly white and red with paint.

She leaned against the curtained door in such a way that every line of her body was displayed, yet with a curious lack of interest; it was as though she stood thus because she knew no other way to stand rather than because she wanted the boy to take notice of her exhibition.

"I'll lay any odds that's the first time those legs o' yours 'as touched soap and water as long as you've 'ad 'em! Not to talk of the rest of you! You'm a grand-lookin' lad, ain't you? I should have guessed as lads might be Jesse's fancy. Still, it takes all sorts and all, don't it?"

"You lay hold o' yer tongue or I'll lay hold o' you!" the boy said furiously. "I ain't one of those, and nor is *he*. And if you—"

"If I what?" the girl jeered. "You'll lay hold of me, will you? You haven't the meat on your bones to do aught with me, lad, nor will have for a year or two yet, let alone the dibs. Expensive I am! One of the real fancy, that's me. Got all the swell mob askin' for me, I 'ave. Mind you, come back in a year or two and there'll be a chance I'll be interested." She came a little closer, and the boy shrank back even more and shouted in real fear, "Get away!"

Behind her the curtain billowed and lifted as the door was opened, and the big woman came back into the room bearing a pile of clothing in her arms, and at the sight of the girl now standing beside the bath she let out a great roar of anger, which made the girl jump and turn and run. The big woman let fly a kick with a leg as heavy as a young tree trunk, catching the girl cruelly across the shins, and gave a great yell of laughter as the girl went sprawling, her skirts flying to reveal her bare backside.

"Much good it'll do yer, showing your stock in trade to this one!" she shouted, and her voice made the boy shrink again, for it was as huge and overwhelming as the rest of her, even louder now than when he had first heard it. "Go on, you heap of rotten meat—get about your business! I'll take care of this one! There's work to be done belowstairs, so go earn your victuals, or out on the street you'll be before dawn!"

"You'll stop pissin' before you'll throw me out, you stinkin' old carcass," the girl said sulkily as she picked herself up, but there was no real rancor in her tone. "You lousy heap of—"

"Ah, get away with you, yer stupid tail. I got work to do."
She moved threateningly toward the door, and the girl made
a face at her and winked cheerfully at the boy before she
disappeared.

"Right, my young sprig!" The big woman dropped her
pile of clothes on the bed at the far side of the room and
came toward the bath, bending to pull at her dress, taking the
back part of the hem through her great legs and hauling it up
to tuck it between her huge breasts in front. "Now we'll set
about you." And she flopped down on her knees beside the
bath, and indeed did set about him.

At first he resisted, panting and shoving at her as she
reached for his head and dunked it before starting to scrub it
with heavy great hands, but ever practical and economical of
his efforts, he soon realized that she would not be denied, and
let her have her way. He sat there in the bath, his eyes
screwed shut and his mouth clamped hard against his teeth,
and waited out with what stoicism he could her energetic and
thorough ministrations.

And in a curious way, he even enjoyed it as the hot water
sluiced through his hair, tickling his scalp with unfamiliar
sensations as her hard fingers scoured away at the thick mass
of soap and dirt and poured jug after jug of water over it
before again scrubbing him, and finally wrapping his head in
a towel before turning her attention to the rest of him.

Now he yelled in real earnest, for the rough handling that
his hard skull and thickly carpeted scalp had found tolerable
was cruelly painful on his arms and legs and back, but she
merely laughed her great roar of laughter and scoured on.

And then at last she hauled him out of the water by one
arm, and his feet scrabbled against the wet floor, and then he
hopped up and down in anguish as she set about drying him
with the same ferocity with which she had washed him.

But then at last it was finished, and she took a bone comb
from her pocket and dragged it through his hair, ignoring his
shrieks of pain, before, after looking at him for a while with
her head on one side, she seized a pair of scissors from another pocket and, to his horror, began to chop at the ends of
his wet hair.

"Be quiet, yer young limb o' Satin," she growled, "an' keep

still, or as the good God is my witness, I'll stick you through yer gullet and think nothin' of it." And she jabbed at him with the scissors, so that obediently he stood still.

She combed and clipped and combed again, clearly enjoying herself, and then dragged him with the same roughness over to the bed to seek clothes for him. He went willingly enough, for the air was cold on his bare damp skin now that he was out of the bath, and he was shivering more than a little. She noticed this, and threw an arm across his shoulders and hauled him up to sit upon her great lap, enveloping him in her body as she reached across him for the clothes.

"There, lad, let Lucy take care of you! A likely lad as you are—a sin it is you've no mother to care for you! Let Lucy warm your bird bones for you." And she gave him a hug that almost suffocated him. But he didn't mind her heavy-handedness now, for it was clear to him that it had naught of malice in it, but was just her way of handling anyone, and he said cheekily—and in a voice muffled by the billowing breasts against which he was thrust—"I'll lay odds the bully boys as come to you don't go chilled away." And she hooted her laughter and gave him another rib-creaking hug.

"A likely lad! Here. We'll put these upon you first."

Under her direction, and not without some waggish assistance (for she was much given to tweaking his bare buttocks and making a pretend grab for his private parts, just for the pleasure of seeing him hop and hearing him yelp), he dressed, putting velvet smallclothes on over the drawers—a garment that amazed him, for he had never worn such—and a fine cambric shirt with real bone buttons, and a silk cravat to tie at its neck, and black hose and good leather shoes, with rags stuffed in the toes to keep them on his feet, for they were mighty large for him. The shoes felt very strange indeed, for although he had sometimes worn boots in winter months, when he could steal a pair, never had he worn on his feet such light and supple objects, and he moved his toes inside them with delight.

"Come, my fine friend!" she said at last, standing back to admire him. "We'll see what our friend Jesse says of you now. Away with you!" And pulling her dress down to cover her legs again, she pushed him to the door and out of the room, to chivvy him down the stairs that faced them.

Turkey-carpeted, they stretched away to the black-and-white-tiled floor of the hallway beneath, and everywhere there was gleaming white paint, and heavy candles and draperies, and much gilt and glitter from mirrors. The place was alive with candles and oil lamps: altogether, a scene of total dazzlement.

When they reached the bottom, Lucy pushed past him to open a door, then pulled him in behind her, and he could see people, a great many of them girls. There were gentlemen too, some of them very swell indeed, and all were talking and laughing and drinking.

He came in behind Lucy, and she roared in her great voice, "Jesse! Here's your young varmint—and if you know him as the lad you brought to me, then I'm the Great Chinee!" And she shoved the boy before her, and he stood there in the middle of the room, aware of every inch of the clothing on his back, deeply conscious of the leather shoes upon his feet, and blinking a little in the brightness at first, but then lifted his chin, giving back stare for stare with them all, as good as they gave him.

And stare they did. What they saw was a small figure, looking slightly absurd in clothes patently too large for him, but with a curious dignity in him as he stood with his hands clenched lightly at his sides, his head held high and his chin thrust forward. They saw a head of thick springing hair which shone a rich red-brown in the lamplight, curling a little damply against his high white forehead, framing a face of considerable beauty, with its milky skin and vividly green eyes.

"By God, the boy's a real human creature, now he's washed and barbered! Damme, I wrought better than I knew when I found this one!" Jesse came across the room to stand in all his solid bulk beside the boy, his hand on his head.

"Well, Lucy, did he fight you much when you pulled the lice from him? He's a hard-bred one, this, with pride and ambition, and not one to truckle to any lady—not even you, I believe."

" 'Twould take more than me to fight such a one!" the boy said suddenly, feeling his confidence in himself building as he saw the approval in Constam's face and became aware of the smiles and winks thrown at him by many of the girls in the room. "She's meat for you, maybe, but not for such a one as me."

A great laugh went up, which Lucy led as much as joined, and she patted his shoulder with all the impact of a ton weight, which almost made him reel, and he looked about him at the roomful of people, at the richness of its gilt, its mirrors, its hangings and its sofas and huge pictures of naked women on the walls, and produced a wide and impish smile.

He would remember that evening the whole of his life. One of the girls, a great tall creature who was merely voluptuous now but would one day clearly be as vast as Lucy herself, came and swung him up into her heavily scented arms and nuzzled his cheek and bore him away to one of the sofas, to sit there with him upon her lap and feed him sweetmeats and sugarplums from a silver dish, while the other girls crowded about him and cooed and laughed at all he said, greeting every one of his saucy comments (and he made many of them) with shrieks of laughter and kisses and hugs.

He enjoyed it all hugely, and could have gone on talking and giggling with these new friends forever. But then the group about him rustled and moved as Lucy came plowing toward him, Jesse by her side, to scold the girls and send them back to the men, who had been talking to each other in the background but were now beginning to look sulky at the way the girls had turned their backs on them.

"Well, now, boy. To business!" Jesse cried, and sat down on the sofa beside him, planting his muddy-booted legs foursquare and uncompromisingly on either side of his stick, on which he folded his hands and rested his chin so that he held his head at a level with the boy's and could stare him direct in the eyes.

"Hey? To business. What next, d'you imagine, have I in hand for you?"

"I want to be a peddler," the boy said at once. "I gave thought to it, there in all that water, and I thought, A peddler'd do best for me."

Jesse laughed and winked at Lucy. "Indeed, to help you do as much was all I had thought to do when last I talked to you! But suppose I was to tell you now I can do you better than that? Suppose I was to tell you I have a new plan, one that'll make a better job of you than just a peddler, a costermonger? What would you say to *that?*"

"A better job?" the boy said uncertainly. "There ain't no better lay than the peddlin' lay, not if you wants to keep away from the beaks. And I don't aim to do anythin' that—"

Jesse shook his head, almost impatiently. "Boy, lift your eyes from the gutter you was born in, as I did! Look above and beyond it! You see me? A merchant, as respectable and as warm a citizen as ever drew breath. Fit company for the *ton* whenever I fancy it. Whenever *I* fancy it." His face darkened for a moment, but then he was himself again, and he put his hands out to lay them on the boy's shoulders. "I'll put you in the way to being one day as I am. You'll have to work hard, and struggle and push as I did, if you're to make it, but I'll give you what no one gave to me. If I'd had the start I'm willing to give you, why, boy, there's no saying where I'd be today!"

"Sitting next to Mr. Pitt! An' I don't think!" Lucy cried, and laughed hugely, and Jesse turned his head and swore at her till she scowled and subsided; but she didn't go away.

"What do you want me to do?" the boy said, and the suspicion in him showed so nakedly on his face that Jesse laughed again.

"No need to look like that, boy! There's naught in my budget to throw you into a quake! Listen, lad. It's in my mind to make a use of you. In my making a use of you, you'll learn, and you'll grow and one day—well, we shall see. I'll take you to my business, boy, make a spice man of you. If you shape up, then there's the whole future ahead of you. Money, the esteem of your fellow men, position in the polite world, whatever you want. If you're as good as I was at your age, as I think you might be! What say you, hey, boy? You'll come to work in my warehouse at the docks, and learn the trade at my own hands. And until we can take you there, in a day or two, we'll lodge you here with Lucy and her bonny *filles de joie*. What say you to that, hey, boy? Doesn't that beat the peddling lay you had a fancy for?"

· SIX ·

SINCE it was Sunday, the family dined at two o'clock, for Charlotte kept fashionable hours. She had ordered a more than usually elaborate meal, even taking the unusual step of coming to the dining room herself to check the table.

"She's about some villainy," the footman told the cook. "For's there's only themselves, and she's going about it as though the Lord Mayor and half the Corporation were to dine!" At which the cook sniffed and so viciously beat the cream for her cheesecake that it curdled.

Jesse too was suspicious when he returned home to find his wife sitting busily at her writing table, for it was unusual for her to spend Sunday in any but religious pursuits, and he said as much as he stood at her door shrugging out of his coat.

"Indeed, Mr. Constam, I have been to church," she said calmly, "and my present activity, while it may seem at surface frivolous, is in actuality a most religious pursuit, as I will explain to you in course of time. We shall dine first, I believe, before I open my budget to you." And she left the room with a serenity that made him frown sharply.

"Damn her, damn her!" he thought viciously as he let his valet complete the alterations considered necessary before he could eat his dinner. "Were she wholly the shrew, I'd know where I was with her, but she follows one suit with another so fast, she turns me on my ears."

His suspicion deepened as they ate, for she had ordered

a purée-of-artichoke soup, a cod's head in oyster sauce, Provençal cutlets and sweetbreads in white sauce for the first course, the whole removed with a saddle of mutton, and proffered as a second course a roast partridge and a duck, jelly of fruit and cheesecakes, all removed with an ice pudding and beignets soufflés.

"Hmmph! We dine as well as though we were offering hospitality to the world!" he grunted, waving away the footman's offer of dessert. "I thought, ma'am, that you regarded the eating of so vast a meal as excessively vulgar on a Sunday!"

"Indeed, so it may be in generality, but I observed that you dined sparingly yesterevening and considered it a matter of some importance to your health that you be well protected against the dangers of contagion by eating well today. I am persuaded that such ills and diseases that a man may contract from mixed company are best held off by a stout constitution," she said sweetly.

"Come, ma'am, you press too hard on this matter! I'll not be made to change my ways by such guiles, and so I promise you."

She raised her eyebrows at him, bending her head very slightly toward the footman, and he grunted and drank the remainder of his wine.

"Dorothea, you may leave us," Charlotte said. "Instruct Kate to accompany you to walk about Bedford Square, for it is a pleasant afternoon and the air will be of value to you. I myself shall not be venturing out this afternoon."

Dorothea murmured politely and slipped away, silent and wraithlike as ever, leaving her elders sitting in an atmosphere of guarded silence and staring at each other down the length of the table. The footman moved about his tasks for a while, and then at a sign from Charlotte departed to the kitchen regions, to tell the cook with great relish that there was a rare storm brewing abovestairs.

"So, madam, and now let's about it!" Jesse said at length. "For I'm a plain man and have no patience with these womanish tricks of yours! Set about your tongue-lashing and let's be done with it—but remember, well as I know what is due to a wife, so well do I know a husband's rights, and I'll not tolerate any more such talk as yesterday's."

"Indeed, Mr. Constam, I have no intention, I assure you, of saying more upon that score. We shall, if you please, adjourn to the drawing room, for our greater comfort." And she rose majestically and led the way out and up the stairs to ensconce herself before her fireplace, leaving him to stand with his back to it, his hands caught together behind him beneath his coattails.

"I have been considering, Mr. Constam," Charlotte said, looking at him with her face smooth of any expression and her eyes shadowed by her half-closed lids, "that your concern for matters philanthropical is one that as your wife I should not merely comprehend and applaud, but share."

"Eh?" He stared at her, his forehead creased a little, and then laughed his fat laugh. "Come, ma'am, are you planning to accompany me upon my visits?"

"Indeed, if that is necessary, I shall do so," she said, and now a faint expression of distaste moved her pale mouth. "Although I believe I know the station in life to which it has pleased God to call me, and would not wish to set myself against Providence, I know also where my Christian duty lies. The talents which it has pleased Divine Providence to bestow upon me it is my place to use. I can best use them to pursue the same aims as yourself. I cannot give in your fashion directly to the welfare of the—ah—unfortunate, but I can perhaps endeavor to provide them with matter more valuable to them than even the generous amounts of money and your time that you bestow."

He moved restlessly and said irritably, "Come, ma'am, I've no patience with these circumlocutions! What scheme is it you have afoot? For clearly there is one."

"I have decided I must set about relieving the lot of the ignorant and vicious poor. Mr. Spenser preached a sermon not a month ago on the need for education and salvation for the children of the gutters, who are in grave danger of sinking into a life of total degradation from being the object of—of lewd practices by people who should know better than to use them thus, since they themselves have had the benefit of scriptural education."

He was frowning now, but she went smoothly on.

"So I have decided to form, together with several ladies of like mind, a new Charity. Our object will be to save the children of fallen women from following their mothers into the vileness by which they live."

His face reddened now as he stared at her, his thoughts twisting and turning in his head. That she was about more than the simple charitableness she professed was clear to him, but what that more was he could not at first determine.

And then he seemed to see it. She would go into the Dials, with conspicuous charity, to preach to the prostitutes and thereby shame him. That he, as a man, should enjoy the company of such women could be accounted normal, but that his wife should so behave would be to make him not merely an object of derision, but to be despised for his weakness in allowing her to do it.

He could not speak, so conflicting were the emotions within him, for added to his anger there was a curious sick shame. That he should have need of easy women, when married to a wife who refused to give him what he wanted—indeed, had to have—might seem obvious enough, and had his wishes in bed been those of ordinary men, he would have been able to shrug away any sense of impropriety. But they were not so, and it was bad enough, God knew, that he was as he was without having his wife show the world that she cared not who knew it as well as herself.

She was not looking at him, sitting erect and rigid and keeping her eyes fixed on the wall above his head. Her voice went on as smoothly as ever.

"I have no doubt whatever that the many people to whom I have already sent cards of invitation to the supper at which I shall launch this Charity will support me in every way. I shall read to you, with your permission, a list of the names of people I have asked to be Patronesses."

She opened her reticule and took from it a folded sheet of paper, and began to read in a steady low voice. And as name followed name, his anger rose until he looked almost apoplectically engorged.

"I have in my letters, most of which were sent out this very morning, and to the remainder of which I shall apply myself this afternoon, said that I know that you, with your well-known interest in matters philanthropical, will be happy to be of aid to us and suggested that they should likewise apply to their own husbands for similar support and—dare I say it?—pecuniary aid. I trust you will agree that I have chosen my lady colleagues well?"

His color began to drop a little as he stood and stared at her, and she stared back, her eyes steel-hard and her chin held rigid below her set lips. After a while, he nodded heavily.

"Aye, ma'am, exceeding well. Oh, exceeding well! Is there one City alderman of any worth whose wife is not upon that list? So, you'll hold me up to ridicule in this fashion before all my friends and business acquaintances, will you? Do you hate me so much, madam, that you . . ."

She shook her head suddenly, and her mouth moved awkwardly before she could easily speak. "No, Jesse, indeed, no. I care deeply for you even if I cannot—even though you are the man you are. But it is not fitting, it is truly so *improper*, for you to do as you do, and you cannot go on so, for your own sake! For an Eastcheap man to visit the stews—none think unduly ill of that. But you do not fully comprehend the world as it is for you now, the society in which you live today! Believe me when I assure you, my dear husband, that it is for love of you, and deep and true concern for your welfare, that I plead with you to cease such activity! I give you with this plan of mine the opportunity to satisfy your Christian generosity without any longer exposing yourself to the—to the ills of the gutter!"

"Enough, madam, enough! I've heard this budget of delight before, I assure you! You will never cease to recall to my mind the affliction that I suffer. And affliction it is, not a matter of my free choice as you profess to believe. So! You shall have a Charity, shall you, and set out to save the souls and children of the women you believe me to be debauching so that you may . . ."

He stopped quite suddenly, and stood staring at her with so strange an expression upon his face that she became alarmed, and stood up to move nearer to him and look into his face.

"Mr. Constam? Jesse? Are you well? What ails you?"

He blinked, and his eyes lost the glassy stare that had so alarmed her, and then he smiled—a long, slow, and strange smile that almost frightened her more.

"So, you shall have your Charity, shall you? For children in danger? And when, pray, is the supper to be held at which this shall be launched upon the unsuspecting world?"

She put her head on one side, puzzled by the joviality in his voice. "Yesterday se'ennight."

"Then you shall indeed be busy, shall you not, between now and then! Such a list as you have there—why, the kitchens will be in a pucker from night to noon with such preparations! Here, give me the list—yes, the list, madam, the list! There are perhaps some names you have forgot and I shall put your errors right for you."

He took the sheet of paper from her startled hand, hurried across the drawing room to the small writing table in the corner, and seated himself heavily on the small gilded chair beside it before starting to read carefully. After a few moments he nodded and seized the quill pen from the stand and began to scribble furiously.

"Indeed, ma'am, you have left from the list a number of persons of consideration!" He completed the list to his satisfaction, and then reread it before standing up and coming across the room to give it to her. She took it from him with a cold hand, her startled eyes never leaving his face.

"You—you are content with this plan, then, Mr. Constam?"

"Content? Aye, madam, more than content!" He threw back his head in his characteristic fashion and laughed a long, hard laugh which was full of true mirth, for the tears sprang to his eyes so that he had to mop at them with a large silk handkerchief. "So content, madam, that I shall take myself tomorrow, before I go to my countinghouse, to Mr. Jackson's shop in Piccadilly and arrange for him to send you a range of victuals for your supper party, so that it need not be too great a burden upon the household books! Some York hams, I think, and the like, and a good large Stilton—what say you? They will bring their husbands, these good and charitable ladies of yours, and all are men of my stamp who will seek more at table than mere flummeries and ratafia biscuits! And my good claret you shall have, to boot—William shall see to it! Away with you, my dear! You have much work to do if you are to be sure your supper is all set ready in good time!"

Then he put an arm about her and kissed her cheek roundly and went stamping out of the room, leaving her in a stunned silence.

· SEVEN ·

THE BOY sat perched on a high stool in the middle of Jesse's countinghouse chewing happily at an apple pie so vast that it had to be held in both hands, his eyes flicking about busily to take in all the information they could.

He looked a rather different boy from the one who had tried to take Jesse Constam in the alley on Saturday night, for the three days he had spent living with Lucy and her girls had had an excellent effect upon him. He had eaten steadily of Gargantuan meals at mealtimes and quantities of pies and sweetmeats and the like in between, for all the girls were generous to a fault and gained great pleasure from watching him eat, calling on one another to "only see how he fills his face!" He had in consequence lost the rather transparent look that denotes a person living on the edge of starvation, although he was still pitifully thin; it would take a year or more of such eating to put any true flesh on those bones. But his eyes were clear and bright, his hair clean and bouncy, and his cheeks gently tinged with the hint of health.

Beyond him, standing at a tall desk over which he could barely see, was a stout little man whose gray hair stood up in a quiff, and whose face was so lined and twisted from years of peering shortsightedly at ledgers that his eyes could hardly be seen for the pouches of flesh that enclosed them. He was scribbling away at the great ledger before him with a quill so tall that it was higher than his shoulder. From time to time he shot a suspicious glance at the boy, then sniffed lugubriously and bent his head to his columns of figures again.

The boy liked the room very much. It was so snug, so warm, so crowded, so heaped with so much to look at. There were piles of leather-bound ledgers in all directions, and a great globe sitting on a table; there were shelves laden with black boxes which he shrewdly suspected contained cash in some form or other, and hempen bags which also had a moneyed look about them, and pens and inkhorns and more ledgers.

On the other side of the room were two more clerks, obviously much less exalted than the fat little man, for they stood either side of the same desk and had to jostle for space in which to work; and anyway, in contrast to his middle-aged seriousness, they were young and lively, flicking ink at each other from time to time, or dealing each other shrewd pinches when the senior clerk wasn't looking, only to bend limpidly innocent gazes upon him when he raised his eyes sharply at the sound of a muffled yelp.

The boy enjoyed watching them, a fact of which they were well aware, for they performed assiduously for his benefit while all the time loftily ignoring his presence. The boy knew this and was somehow comforted, for this was just how the bully boys of the alleys behaved when they knew the younger boys were about and watching them. It was good to discover that even swells who could read and write and wore white linen and broadcloth every day of their lives were swaggerers, flash coves, just like any others of their age.

In the special spot before the window was Jesse, and he had a desk with a high stool so that he could be clearly seen to be the master, the only one with the right to rest his backside. His desk's being twice the size of any other also indicated his status, had he needed any such proof of it. But he didn't, for here in his own domain he was a very different person from the one he was at home or in the alleys. Gone was the swagger of the Dials walker; gone the bluster of Charlotte's husband. In its place a man of true authority, who knew what he knew, and had no doubts of his abilities and neither need of approbation nor fear of disapproval. Facing the facts of his success, as he did every time he checked one of old Hunnisett's ledgers, he had no need to prove anything, for the proof lay there beneath his hands as money mounted and thickened, always on the credit side of every transaction.

He closed the ledger before him and turned his head to look at the boy, now stuffing the last mouthful of pie into himself and carefully brushing the crumbs from the velvet jacket Lucy had put upon him this morning. He gazed at him consideringly, trying to see him as he would appear to others, to people less accustomed than he to the sight of true poverty. Would they see the beauty that was in that pinched little face, the potential in those scrawny limbs? Would they see in the boy's quick glances and sharp movements the intelligence and native wit that Jesse knew to be there? By people he meant people like Charlotte, not the girls of Lucy's establishment or the men who frequented it, for the comfortable protected women of Charlotte's world had little chance or, indeed, desire to see how the poor who so outnumbered them in this city of London lived.

He thought of Charlotte and her new Charity and smiled sourly to himself; by God, but they should know of the waters in which they had chosen to paddle—should truly *know* and not merely stand beside them with eyes closed in pious prayer. He'd bring the object of their milk-and-water charitableness right under their eyes and noses; he'd show them. . . .

"Boy!" he said peremptorily. "Be ready to take your leave. Hunnisett, I shall not return today. Bring the keys to me at Gower Street before you go home, you hear me? And you two"—turning and glowering at the young clerks—"do not deceive yourselves that you have not been closely observed this morning with your chaw-bacon addlepated tricks! What are you, a pair of giggling yokels, to behave so when you should be about your business? Apprentices to a merchant of standing do not perform such apish antics, and such as do are turned out of their indentures faster than you can reckon! If I hear from Hunnisett that there has been any further such, your fathers shall hear from me, and so I tell ye! Hunnisett, my hat and coat and stick! Parker, call me a hackney—and be spry about it!"

He shrugged on the coat, Hunnisett standing absurdly on tiptoe to help him, and sweeping the boy up in his wake, surged out to the rush and bustle of Eastcheap, leaving Hunnisett bowing and hand-rubbing on the doorstep.

The boy took a deep breath of pleasure, for he was now on known territory again. Although his manor had been the Dials and the Bermudas and Covent Garden, he had, in good weather, often ventured as far as the City, skipping through Holborn and picking up what he could on the way. It was a long journey that would take him half a day, but well worth it, for City men were good prey for as experienced a pickpocket as he. His only problem had been to watch out for other boys on the same lay as himself who would bitterly resent any attempt by a "foreigner" to cut in on their territory, and would show their resentment with considerable personal violence. But now, standing perkily beside the important Jesse Constam, he could hold his head high, enjoying the luxury of letting laden pockets, good gulls, go by unmolested by him.

"Hey, jarvey!" Jesse shouted above the din of the streets, and the driver leaned down, touching his whip to his forehead as his horse stood dejected and weary between the shafts. "Take me to Wapping Walk, next the 'Bull and Mouth,' d'ye hear me? And if that poor screw of yours can't do better than walk it, then say so now and we'll seek another, for I've no patience to be ambling on my way!"

"Aye, she'll move you and fast. 'Bull and Mouth,' you say? Get up, you!" The mare laid her ears back and tossed her head, and satisfied, Jesse climbed in, and the boy scuttled after.

He sat there entranced, his cheek pressed against the musty old squabs of the carriage, staring out the small window as the streets went jolting by. Past the Monument, lifting itself with a dizzy, effortless elegance high against the blue April sky; past the Tower of London on their right, its great pale gray stones gleaming in the sunshine above the press of horses and carriages and pushing, sweating, shouting people; curving left past St. Katherine's Docks to join the notorious

Ratcliffe Highway, almost jammed as it was with traffic, but safe from the attentions of footpads and robbers in these broad daylight hours (though nightfall would make the whole area a wilderness of danger); eventually to turn sharp right into New Gravel Lane. Here warehouse walls loomed high above the narrow cobbled street, and great drays and overladen carts had to make way for the cursing jarvey, pushing his way through the mob. Until at last, the man leaned down and shouted, "No farther, not for half the Royal Mint—they'll crush me flat, and you with me!"

Grunting a little irritably, Jesse climbed out and threw the man his money, before leading the way down toward the end of the street, never looking back to see whether or not the boy was following. But follow he did, dodging the draymen and warehousemen, keeping close to the skirts of Jesse's coat.

On their right, the masts of the shipping in London Dock cut sharp edges against the sky, soaring above the crumpled, close-packed roof tops, and then the roadway curved left, leaving the masts behind them, and they found themselves in another, even narrower cobbled street with high walls cutting off their view of the river; but still it made its presence felt, for the boy could hear the sound of water and smell the heavy stench of rottenness that hung over the whole area like a miasma.

But there was another smell underlying it, and he wrinkled his nose a little, finding it interesting, as he followed Jesse past the entrance to the yard of the "Bull and Mouth"—a dirty, messy tavern of the common sort—down a narrow alley that plunged away from Wapping Walk toward the riverside.

The smell grew stronger—a curious, hungry, almost edible smell—and then Jesse twisted again and pushed against a narrow doorway in the wall, and with a jerk of his head indicated that the boy should follow him inside.

He stood there for a moment, trying to adapt to the dimness and above all to the scent, for the air here was thick with it—a splendid smell, full of excitement and pleasure, that made his eyes and his mouth water together.

"Well, boy, does it please you?" Jesse's voice came from the dimness, and the boy blinked and squinted round, and now he could see that he was in a vast warehouse which had for light only two immense open doors at the far end. The place was so large that here, at the greatest distance from the doorway, they could hardly see at all, for there were great tubs and barrels, bales and boxes piled up all around, forming barricades, between which narrow walkways had been left. At the far side the boy could see the river framed in the doorway, sparkling and winking in the sunshine, with barges moving steadily on its gray-blue surface, passing the slab-fronted warehouses on the far bank in stately slowness.

"It smells," the boy said. "Strange smells, but some I think I know."

"Come, boy, we'll try your nose and see how much of the makings of a spice man you have in you!" Jesse cried jovially, and began to pull off his coat. "Nidd! Hey, Nidd, damn you, where are ye hiding your ugly face?"

There was a scuffling sound, and out of the dimness a man came—a tall, drooping man, as thin as Hunnisett was fat, as bald as he had been well thatched, but with the same anxious wrinkled look about his face.

"Good day to you, yer honor," he muttered. "Good day to yer. I'll give your coat to the lad." He turned his head and shouted in his own turn, "Jem!" and a boy of about fifteen came bobbing round a corner made by a pile of boxes and, touching his forelock at sight of Jesse, took his heavy coat and bore it away into the shadows.

"Now, Nidd, we're trying the boy's nose for size!" Jesse said. "We'll see if he's the understanding and the sense a spice man needs. Bring me the boxes, my special boxes—d'you hear me?"

The man nodded and went away, and Jesse led the boy farther into the warehouse, eventually stopping in what appeared to be the center, where there was the broad slab of a pocked and shabby wooden table on which an oil lamp sat producing a thin yellow light. There were a few piles of sacks beside the table, and Jesse plumped himself down onto one of these and clicked his fingers in irritation as Nidd came panting out of one of the aisles with a large wooden box clutched in his arms.

"Come, man, you get slower by the hour! Put it here—aye,

here, that's it. Now about your work, and leave me with the lad. The Indiaman is shed of its load, I believe?"

"Almost complete, yer honor, almost," Nidd said. "I'll get the men to—"

"Aye, that you will, and they'll put their power into it if they want paid a penny piece this week! That ship should have turned round an hour since! About it, now!" And Nidd scurried away, and after a moment could be heard shouting and urging the invisible unloaders of the Indian merchant ship to "Double up, double up!"

"She's time to sit a half day yet," Jesse said complacently. "There's not a warehouseman on any part of this river can spur a team of stevedores faster than can Nidd, for all his namby-pamby looks. He'll have the gear in here and checked and the right cargo laden on the coasters before the tide is half turned tonight. Now, boy! To our business. Here."

He opened the box with a large gilt key taken from his pocket. "Here is my testing box. Observe, and use your nose, and use it sparingly. Don't damage your senses by abusin' 'em, for there's no virtue in a vast great sniff which only serves to stun the delicacy of your apprehensions. Just let the scent drift into you, and hear the names as I tell you 'em. Now, pay heed!"

The next few hours were curious for the boy. He sat there while Jesse put into his hand small box after small box—some containing powders, brown and gray and yellow and green-ish white; others with seeds and strips of bark or pods—and lifted them to his nose and let the scent of them enter, just as Jesse had bidden him, and the names of them all as Jesse said them in rote made a song in his ears. Coriander and cin-namon, nutmeg and mace, vanilla and turmeric, allspice and cardamom, cassia and dill, peppers and cloves and anise and ginger and myrrh and caraway . . .

And then Jesse locked the box away again, and gave the boy a draft of small beer taken from a barrel beneath the table, and seized a small lantern to lead the way between the piles of boxes and sacks, stopping from time to time to open one and take out a handful and thrust it at the boy.

He acquitted himself fairly well, correctly identifying at least half the spices, particularly those of which he had some knowledge, like pepper and cloves and mace, which some of the cookshops he regularly robbed used to disguise the badness of the meat in their pies. Jesse said little, whether he was right or wrong, except to correct his errors, making no sign of either approval or displeasure, and the boy became more confident, and made fewer mistakes as time went on.

Until the moment came when his nose was stunned with all it had sampled, and his eyes began to run with tears and his nose to leak in watery sympathy, and Jesse laughed, and said, "Let be, let be! You've had enough for one day," and led him back to the central table.

Nidd was there waiting for them, and at a nod from Jesse took away the box and came hurrying back with Jesse's many-caped coat held respectfully across his arms, and Jesse put it on and said, "Well, Nidd, the boy has the makings in him! There's much to be thought on in this case, but I may be sending him to you one day, to learn the trade. But not yet, not yet. I shall return tomorrow, Nidd, to oversee for myself the shipping of the Edinburgh order, so tell the men to look sharp about it. For today, I leave you again in charge. 'Ware fire, now, and douse those glims with water when you lock away! Good day to you, Nidd!" And again he went sweeping away, with the boy chasing after him.

It was not until they had made their way back to the Ratcliffe Highway and found a hackney to take them back to the City that the boy ventured to speak.

"You said as how you was going to put me to the warehouse to work, but you told that Nidd you'd send me there one day. When? Ain't yer doin' it the way you said, now?"

Jesse had been leaning back against the squabs of the cab, his face shadowed, but now he leaned forward and looked very seriously at the boy. "No, boy. I am not now dealing with you the way I first considered would be best. I have even greater plans for you. Not for you the bed beneath the table in the warehouse, snug and good though it be for any apprentice lad. Not for you only the chance to learn Nidd's tasks, but better—the chance to learn Hunnisett's, perhaps!"

"Hunnisett's?" The boy almost squeaked the name in his surprise. "But I'm no—I never learned to cipher, nor to write nor read. How could such as I—"

"Nay, boy, listen before flying up into alt! I'll unfold all—well, not quite all; as much as is good for you. Next Saturday there is to be at my house in Gower Street a supper party. A great gallery of old cats there'll be there—but a few good men besides. Their purpose there does not concern you, but you will concern them—oh, yes, you will concern them! On Saturday at about nine of the clock, Lucy will see to it you're dressed in your rags again—nay, don't look like that! It's barely for one more evening!—and shall set you in a hackney coach and bring you to Gower Street. And there I'll be waiting for you."

He laughed suddenly and leaned back again in his seat. "Yes, there I'll be and waiting for you, and all of them waiting for you too, though they'll not know it! Do exactly as I bid you, boy, and not only will you eat a supper next Saturday the like of which you've never seen in all your life, set aside tasted; not only that, but—well, let be. Much can befall from this little junketing I'm planning. I'll not say now what will happen after, for I can only see my way in part. But 'twill be good for you, you have my word." Again he laughed. "Not that anything that I plan for you could ever be anything but good, for the life you've had hitherto has been naught but evil—"

"No!" the boy cried, indignant even in his bewilderment. "I wrought well, I did, the best dip in all the Dials—aye, and the Bermudas and the Holy Land too—and don't you let others tell you different!"

"Keep that, boy—never lose it, no matter what befalls! Such pride! Such proper pride! Oh, the old cats next Saturday, the old cats next Saturday!" And he crowed his great laugh again, and refused to say any more.

· EIGHT ·

LUCY paid off the hackney and then turned to look up at the house, and the boy could see she would as lief turn and get in the cab again as go on, for her face had none of its customary heavy cheerfulness about it, but seemed pinched and tight, for all the weight of flesh on her bones. But the hackney had gone away with a rattle of hoofs and the jingle of harness, and after one anguished backward look she moved resolutely forward, holding the boy firmly with one great hand.

She looked remarkably fine, wearing a dress of cloth of gold beneath a silver-gauze shawl trimmed with gold fringe and bearing on her head three nodding plumes of yellow ostrich. Around her neck were hung many strings of amber beads, and her reticule too bore amber embroidery on its silver and gold sides. The boy thought she looked a complete lady with her white face and scarlet mouth, and looked down at himself with a spurt of shame that almost surprised him.

He was once more wearing the clothes he had stolen from the ragpicker's stall in Hungerford Market, and he marveled that he had ever thought them fine. For a whole week he had been one of the swell mob, he thought mournfully, with velvet to wrap his backside in, and drawers and shoes besides. And now to be again in rags and barefoot, and dirty too—for Lucy had taken a delight in rolling him in the gutter of

Panton Street that afternoon, in preparation for the visit—was a matter of some chagrin to him.

"I don't know, no more than you," she had grunted, gasping a little with her exertions, when he had shouted and shrieked and asked her why he had to be smothered in mud and ordure and rags again when she had been at such pains to get it all off when first they met. "I don't know, and I knows better nor to ask. He's payin' me well for this, for I'd not venture on such a matter otherwise, and so I tell you—and I've give my word. So do it I shall, the way he bade me. So come about, and do as I bid or you'll feel the other side of my hand!" Which threat had made him hop and jump to her directions immediately, for he knew he had met his match in Lucy, fast as he was.

In the week he had known her, he had developed a curious respect for her. She was rough of tongue and rougher of hand and treated her girls with a casualness that often came close to cruelty, and yet there was no evil in her; indeed, she had shown the boy more physical affection than he had ever remembered having and for which he was fast developing a liking, for she gave him her great hugs interspersed with cuffs and kicks, but in a way that showed she cared for him. He was her "likely lad," as she often said, and he much preferred her to any of her girls, generous as they were with their sugarplums and comfits. They treated him as a toy, but Lucy as if he were a person like herself.

She surged forward with him now, and he looked up at the house and blinked. A tall house, with rows of shining windows all gleaming in the dusk with the light of many candles, and with a front door stood half open to show the richness of carpets and furnishings within. On either side of the door, in a metal ring attached to the stucco, a link was burning smokily, and all about stood boys leaning on the railings that fronted the house and perched upon the steps that led down to the area below, while sedan chairs and carriages were ranged on the other side of the street, and coachmen walked the horses up and down.

When Lucy took the boy up the steps that led to the front door, several of the linkboys jeered and shouted, but he took his cue from Lucy and behaved as though they were not there. He was feeling strangely frightened now, catching some of Lucy's uneasiness in his contact with her hand still clamped hard about his wrist, and fully expected that when Lucy had knocked upon the door as she did, a man would come to chase them away with a club at the very least.

But although the footman who, dressed in stunning finery, came to the door in answer to her knock showed in every line of his body and every lineament of his face his disgust at their presence, he clearly expected them, for he held the door open even wider and stood back to admit them, curling his nose in condescension as great as any shown by a lord.

"Stand there," he commanded, closing the door firmly behind them. "I'll inform my master of your presence." But he got no farther, for at the back of the hallway a door opened, and Jesse came out. There was a rush of sound emitted from the room with him, and he closed the door behind him with a snap, grimacing at Lucy and the boy as he came toward them.

"Such a din and a clatter as a roomful of stupid old hens can make! So, Lucy, let me see you both! Hmm. Aye, you've done well, very well, and timed it to a T! Now, Lucy, you're not to be surprised at aught that happens here this evening, you hear me? Whatever I say is my affair. As for you, boy—just listen, and do as you're bid, and you will see what you will see! Now, William!"

The footman stepped forward, and Jesse looked at him and snapped, "Take that damned sneering look off your face, man, or I'll show you the street so fast you'll not make contact with the door! *And* I'll rip the fancy livery from your backside as you go, so you'll land in the mud as mother-naked as when you arrived in this world! These people are worth ten of you, and you've no call to look down your damned dirty nose at 'em!"

William stood impassive, storing up every detail for later recounting to Cook, and let Jesse rant on.

"Now, go and open those doors, do you hear? They're all in there, chawing up the victuals as though they'd not seen a bite nor sup these twenty years, so none will miss a word! You are to announce us, you hear me? Call—um—call, 'Mr. Constam and protégé!' Can you say that? Aye—that's it—protégé. Go on, now! Lucy, and you, boy, follow me!"

It was all curiously dreamlike for the boy. The footman

pacing solemnly and opening the door upon a shrilling of female voices and the clatter of dishes, and then his stentorian roar, and then the silence that fell so sharply as he followed Lucy and Jesse into a room he thought quite good, but not in the same class as Lucy's parlor for glitter and light and style (an opinion clearly shared by Lucy, he realized when he looked swiftly up at her).

The silence grew heavier and people were looking at him, just as they had looked on the night he had arrived in Panton Street, but it was different now, very different, for in Panton Street the people had looked at him approvingly with winks and smiles and nods. But these people stared at him in horror, clearly regarding him as quite the most evil thing upon which they had ever clapped eyes, and one or two even put handkerchiefs and vinaigrettes to their noses and cast up their eyes in horror.

"My dear!" Jesse's voice came booming above his head into the stupefied throng before him. "My dear Mrs. Constam, here he is! The lad I see as the first beneficiary of the Charity! I have given you your first moneys, so let me have, I beg, the honor of providing the first poor child of a Fallen Woman who shall benefit from it!"

The boy whirled and looked up at him, his face twisted with anger. "What's that you say? What's that? A fallen— who's a fallen woman, eh? What's that you're sayin' of me?"

Jesse's hand came down firmly on his head with apparent benevolence, but the boy could feel the steel in his grip.

"You see, ladies, why I chose for you this child? Despite the horror of his life, despite the many evils and degradations to which he has been exposed, he remains a boy of spirit, not yet quite cowed by the misery of the gutter! Indeed a worthy recipient of all our benevolence!"

He turned and looked at Lucy then, and said in carefully modulated tones, "Now, madam—ah—this boy. He is in your charge, I believe?"

Lucy gaped, and frowned, and then nodded. "Well, aye, an you say so, though why you should be asking me is more than I—"

"To be sure, to be sure," Jesse said, speaking more loudly. "And tell me, madam, you would be content, for an—ah—

consideration, to allow me to keep the boy here and feed and clean and dress and educate and house him? In short, to adopt him and treat him as my own?"

There was a sharp hiss from somewhere near the boy, and he turned his head to look, and saw at the front of the group of women a new figure, a small, pallid woman with a pinched face, so white now that it looked to be the same color as the dress of the child who was standing beside her, and upon whose shoulder she was leaning. The child, who looked to be a little older than the boy himself, he decided, was staring at him with her mouth half open, and her blue eyes very round and staring.

"To adopt him and treat him as my own?" Jesse said again, even more loudly, and with a curious emphasis, and Lucy shook her head in puzzlement, and said, " 'Tis as you please, indeed, Mr. Constam, and none of my concern. Do as you say you will and—"

"Ah! You see, my dear?" Jesse turned and, taking the boy by the arm, led him across the room to the woman with the white face. "You see? We have all the necessary consent to our plan. Here he is—your gutter child, your helpless, ignorant scrap of infancy, saved from the depredations of those who would prey upon him and his like, brought to you in all your charitableness to rear! I've no doubt you will find him no easy task to rear as he should go, but equally no doubt that you will accomplish much!"

The fuss and noise was over. There had been that long stunned silence, and then a sudden uplifting of voices as women crowded round the pallid lady, chattering and cooing and telling her in solemn tones how Good she was, how Christian and how Splendid an Example of True Charity, while Jesse stood sardonically by, his arms folded, and watched and listened.

Lucy had gone, with a final hug and breath-stopping kiss, whispering, "You knows where I am, boy," before taking firm hold of the money Jesse put into her hand and marching out past William to the street.

The pallid woman had subsided onto a sofa and sat there with her hands rigidly folded on her lap, and looked the boy over from the top of his head to the muddy, manure-stained feet that were so firmly planted on her Turkey carpet, and gone paler than ever, if that was possible. And as the smell of the boy became heavier in the oppressive warmth of the candle-lit room, people murmured and departed at first one by one, and then in a rush, promising much and talking vaguely of calling soon to discuss the further progress of Charlotte's Charity.

And now they sat alone in the dining room amid the wreck of the elegant supper, Jesse with a piece of ham in one hand on which he chewed with bright-eyed relish, watching Charlotte over the top of it, the girl in the white dress sitting at her mother's feet on a footstool, and the boy standing in the middle of the room.

"How could you do such a thing—how *could* you?" Charlotte burst out. "Can any man be so wanting of concern and care for his own station in life, let alone for the welfare of his wife and child, as to do so cruel a thing?"

"Cruel, ma'am? How so, cruel? Did you not tell me with your own lips that you were to start a Charity for children such as this? That I demeaned my station in taking myself to the stews to distribute my philanthropy? I listened to you, ma'am, I listened to you—and brought my philanthropy to the respectability of Gower Street! Is't not that you wanted? Come, ma'am!" He looked at her with his head cocked, his face alight with the pleasure he was finding in her discomfiture, and after a moment she took a deep breath, her nostrils narrowing as she looked at him, and then nodded sharply.

"Very well, Mr. Constam. Very well. So be it. This is the child you wish to adopt and rear as your own. As your wife, even though you exposed me to the possibility of much calumny and indeed public shame, it is my duty to do as you wish. So be it! The boy *shall* be reared as you say; I *shall* make it my personal concern to see that he is cleaned, and clothed, and fed, and then educated. I *shall* teach him, and—"

Jesse laughed comfortably. "Come, ma'am, no need for there to be too much effort on your part! The servants shall clean and feed him, and as for his education—why, I shall see to that at the warehouse! He knows that—eh, boy?" He looked at the boy with a wide smile upon his face, but the boy looked woodenly back at him. "So there is no need to discommode yourself one whit. Admit, ma'am, you've been choicely hoist by your own petard, and cry Pax!"

"As to that, Mr. Constam, we shall see. First"—she looked back at the boy, raking him with a dispassionate look—"first, clean him, then feed him and bed him. For the rest, we can consider tomorrow. What is his name?"

"Ask him," Jesse said succinctly.

"Well, boy?" she said, addressing him directly for the first time.

"Ain't got a name. As well 'e knows," the boy said sulkily.

She shot a sharp look at her husband, frowning slightly, and then looked back at the boy again.

"I see. Well, a name must be given you. And mark me, Mr. Constam, whatever the strange humor it is that is making you behave thus, I'll not tolerate it if you attempt to give him your own name!"

He looked genuinely startled at that.

"Good God, ma'am, no such thought had crossed my mind! To play the philanthropist is one thing; to give the benefit of my name as well as my purse, quite another. Indeed, ma'am, it is against my desires not least because one day, perhaps, we shall see a boy more justified in . . ."

She turned her head sharply and looked at him hard and he stopped, and there was a long silence in the room for a while, and the boy looked from one to the other in some puzzlement.

"So, a name!" Jesse said at length, with a curious bravado in his tone. "We must find you a name! What shall it be?"

The girl on the footstool spoke suddenly, her voice a little breathy and high. "King John," she said unexpectedly, "King John was called John Lackland since he had no place to call his own. The boy should be called Lackland, should he not, for he has no place, has he?"

Jesse cocked his head to one side, and then laughed aloud, sounding his old relaxed self again. "Indeed, Miss Dorothea, a capital notion! Lackland it shall be! And what further?"

"Er—Adam?" she ventured, pinkly. "The first man?"

"Nay, child, too much of a—but why not—ah—um—Abel? Aye, I like that. Abel. It means, as I recall, breath. And since the boy is the first of his house to draw breath, why, Abel it shall be. Have you any objection, boy?"

The boy shook his head, sulkily. " 'Tis little of my concern, for if I said I misliked it, you'd still call me by it," he muttered, and Jesse laughed and said almost gaily, "Aye, Abel Lackland. A solid name, a good name, and the name you shall have. And into the Church shall you be baptized by it when you're fit! And now, Master Abel Lackland, to the lower quarters with you! You begin to stink too much even for my nose!"

・ NINE ・

ABEL sat curled up on the floor beside the schoolroom window, his nose pressed against the lowest panes, staring out into the street below—a sight quite bereft of any interest, since rain was sluicing heavily from a gray sky, emptying the pavements of any foot passengers and discouraging all but the most intrepid of coachmen from venturing into the muddiness. He was feeling thoroughly uncomfortable and could not quite understand why.

After all, he was well dressed. He looked down at himself dispassionately, at the dark blue nankeen trousers and jacket over a sober white linen shirt, the dark woolen hose, and the shoes upon his feet, and felt no pleasure in any of it. He remembered the day Lucy had put him into those clothes that were so much too large for him and those splendid rag-stuffed shoes and how he had felt about them, trying hard to recapture the sense of satisfaction that had filled him then. But he could not, even though he now wore shoes that had no need of rags, and drawers that really fitted him beneath the snug trousers.

And well fed he was, too. Not as excitingly as in the days of Lucy's girls, with their cornucopias of pies and comfits and sweetmeats, but well enough for any boy who had grown up on the edge of starvation. Mutton broth and bread and butter and boiled meats and fowl at dinner time were not to be sneered at by such as he, and well he knew it.

And in addition to all this, in addition to the room with a real bed in it and a washstand and a cupboard of clothes that was all his own (a most sumptuous apartment in his eyes, despite the fact that it was high up under the roof slates in among the servants' rooms), he had been Learning. He had discovered the simpler secrets of ciphering (to which he had taken very well, earning even Charlotte's grudging approval), had so far mastered more than half his alphabet, and had learned by rote much of the catechism and the Ten Commandments—the latter material striking him as totally irrelevant and ridiculous, but a burden to be carried in exchange for the benefits he was enjoying.

For there was no doubt that the boy—who by dint of much effort was coming to think of himself as Abel, strange as the name sounded in his ears—was well aware of his good fortune. To live, as he had lived for these three months and more, in such a swell ken with regular food and the surety of a bed each night must bring nothing but pleasure to one who had lived his life hitherto as he had done. Yet now he felt uncomfortable and could not comprehend why. And he pressed his nose again to the windowpane and scowled out at the rain.

Behind him the door swished, and he turned to look, but with lackluster eyes, expecting to find little satisfaction in anything that he saw, for already he knew the pattern of the household, and lack of daily incident was very much a part of it. He was justified in his lack of expectation, for it was only Dorothea, carrying a workbasket, who met his eyes. He turned back to his window-gazing, saying nothing, having been well trained by Charlotte.

"You shall not, Abel," she had said firmly on the very first day of their shared lessons, "speak to Miss Dorothea except as part of lessons, and in my hearing. I make this rule not solely because she is, of course, above your touch, but because there is a very real danger that she will take from you some turn of speech or method of speaking that would not be suitable to a young lady of her station. The time will come, of course, when you will speak more as the adopted son of a gentleman should speak, and will have forgotten the dreadful cant that lards your every utterance at present. Then, perhaps, it will be suitable for you to converse with Miss Dorothea on a more natural basis. But until then, you shall not, I insist, speak to her on any but the simplest of matters, as part of the inevitable intercourse of daily life. You understand me?"

He had nodded mutely, and had been hard put to it to speak at all for some time, nodding and shaking his head at all Charlotte said to him, until she lost patience with him and adjured him sharply to speak his lessons and do as he was bidden if he did not wish to have his rags put back upon him and find the street his home again. This threat—which she constantly used to control his every action, keeping his rags (well washed) set upon a table in a corner of the schoolroom so that they would be always before his eyes as an Awful Warning—had the desired effect. He spoke, but as little as he could, and always with care, imitating her speech sounds and trying to use only ordinary words. It was difficult for him, since he did not fully know the difference between cant and normal speech, but he had a good ear and was a fast learner. He was making progress more swiftly than he knew—but never yet had he spoken to Dorothea unless her mother was present to correct his errors.

So he started in considerable surprise when she spoke to him.

"What do you look at out there, Abel? There's naught of interest in Gower Street on such a day!" she said in her breathy little voice, standing just inside the closed door, her head on one side.

He looked at her over his shoulder, and she giggled at the look of alarm that filled his face.

"Nay, don't look so! She's not about, you know!"

He turned his body round now to look at her more directly, his head to one side in unconscious imitation of her own pose as he stared at her, his expression very guarded.

"It's quite true!" Dorothea said airily, and went tripping across the room. "She went to a special meeting of her Charity Board, and since I am still not quite shook free of my putrid throat, she said, I must stay quietly beside the drawing-room fire and do my sewing. I was not to speak to you, of course, and to mind my stitches. So I said, 'Yes, Mama' and 'No, Mama' and 'Yes, Mama,' and as soon as she was gone I came to see you!"

"If she finds out, there'll be the devil to pay," he said, swallowing a little over the unaccustomed experience of talking to her.

"She will only if I learn any cant or vulgarity of speech from you," Dorothea said; "but I shan't, shall I? Oh, Abel, I've been wanting to talk to you ever since you came into the house, and what chance have I had? But I knew if I waited long enough, until Mama was more accustomed to your presence here, that she would be away from home one day and leave me behind, and I would have my chance. To be sure, I was quite recovered enough to go with her this afternoon, but I told her my throat hurt still, which it does not in the very least, and here I am!"

"Why do you want to talk to me?"

"Why? *Why?* Oh, Abel, such a question! Here I am, with no sight of any person but Mama and Papa Constam and the servants, of course, and sometimes such people as we visit or may visit us, and so *dull*. I am half dead with ennui most of my life, you know, and here you are, in my own home, the most *romantic* situation imaginable, and you ask me why I wish to talk to you! There is so *much* I wish to ask of you, and—"

"Ennui?" Abel interrupted, staring at her with his forehead creased. "What is that?"

"Oh, blue devils—finding life insupportably dull—being bored, you know! That is ennui, and I have it all the time." She stood very still beside the table upon which she had set her workbasket, for the first time not holding any special pose of toe set forward to reveal her ankle, or shoulder turned to show the line of her sparsely developed little breasts—just a mournful child. "All the time, I promise you!"

"What does it feel like?" His questions were abrupt and his voice husky, and she made a little *moue* of pleasure at the sound of it, and sat herself down in the chair beside the table and took her work from the basket to bend her head to it.

"I must do my sewing still, of course, for she will inspect it

upon her return and be most put about if I have not completed my set task. But I can still speak as I work. What does
it feel like? Ennui? Oh, horrid. Like—oh, I am not sure I can
explain. As if there is a great piece of something disagreeable
deep inside you and the whole world is a black and silly place
and nothing good will ever come again. That is what it feels
like."

"Ennui," Abel said slowly. "I did not know of it." And he
turned and looked out the window again, and marveled at the
way she had managed to explain in so simple a way the cause
of his discomfort. Ennui. A splendid word for a most disagreeable sensation. A strange sensation, too—one totally
new to him. Whatever else his former life had held, boredom
had been no part of it.

"Oh, do not sit there so silent, Abel, when I am risking so
much to speak to you!" she said after a moment. "Indeed,
have you not wished to speak to me? I do not, allow me to
assure you, ask you this in any spirit of—of—er—coquetry,
but because you too are situated as I am, with no congenial
company to make your existence more agreeable!"

He looked at her again, at her flustered pink face and wide
blue eyes, and considered her question with the same seriousness with which he was wont to consider everything that was
said to him. "Wished to speak with you? I do not know. I
have never thought about you."

She seemed to shrink a little at that, and looked at him with
her eyes wider than ever and her mouth screwed up into a
trembling pout.

"Oh! You wish me to go away."

"No," he said after a moment. "I do not think so. I have
not thought about it."

"Oh, must you speak so—so stiffly? She is not here, you
must understand! She cannot hear aught you say, and she will
not send you away! Indeed, Abel, you know, she cannot! For
all her threats to you, and those horrid clothes she keeps
forever on display, Papa Constam will not permit it. And
anyway, she gains much from your presence here, you
know! Her Charity Board—oh, they all say such things of
her, because of you! She will not send you away, I am persuaded of it!"

"I am not so persuaded," he said somberly, returning his gaze to the window. "One day she may do as she says, and find some other Dials boy to fill my place."

"Oh, the Dials!" breathed Dorothea, casting her hands together in ecstasy, to the marked detriment of her handwork. "Do, I beg you, Abel, tell me of the Dials! Is it indeed as wicked and dreadful and *sinful* a place as they all say?"

"I know nothing of sin and wickedness, for all your mama's speeches to me of the matter. I have still to learn of it. But I tell you this: the Dials is a cold and hungry place for some."

"Is that why you are so afraid of Mama? Because you were cold and hungry there?" Her eyes shone with a liquid sympathy, ready tears trembling on her lashes. "You poor boy!"

"Indeed I was not!" Abel flashed. "I said 'twas so for *some*. But for my part, I led as good a life as any swell—according to the ways of the Dials, that is. I ate my fill many a day— though not always, of course. And there was many as I helped with a little of my blunt when they was doing worse nor me."

"You sound quite like your old self!" she said warningly. "Beware of slipping into your old cant ways, Abel, for she will hear it in my voice, perhaps, and then we shall be in disgrace."

"Then do not speak to me," he growled after a moment, carefully altering his voice. "I did not ask it of you, but you of me."

"Ah, forgive me, Abel," she said wheedlingly, "please! I cannot tell you how much I have yearned to hear of your life before Papa Constam brought you here, and how he found you, and of the woman in the gold and silver gauze who brought you here—Kate says she was a woman of the streets! Is that so? And was she your mama? And did she not object to—"

"You ask too many of your silly questions!" Abel snapped. "I'll tell you none of that—except perhaps of the Dials."

He turned his head to look out the window again at the gray, teeming rain. "I'll speak of that, if you must know of some things, but not of—of anything else."

"Oh, whatever you wish to speak of, *dear* Abel," Dorothea

said eagerly, and came to sit beside him on the floor and put her hand a little shyly upon his sleeve, looking hopefully up into his face. "*Please* to tell me, dear Abel, for you must know I know so little of the world outside these walls! Mama will keep me so close, you know, that I may not even have a governess—only Mama to teach me—and as for being permitted to attend a school, which is my dearest wish—well, all I have to tell me of the world is the novels I may sometimes obtain from the circulating library, when Mama does not forbid me to read such matters, as she does from time to time. And to talk to you will be *so* much better, for it is all real, is it not?"

He looked down at her—at the pleading pink face looking up so hopefully into his own, at the wide and pale blue eyes under the carefully arranged fair curls on her forehead—and felt a strange stirring in him. It was a little like the way he had used to feel when some of the very small boys of the Dials, those who survived the horrors of trying to pit their meager wits against their world, had come to him for food. In part protective, in part irritated, but in part something else, something quite new which he could not recognize in himself, for he had not felt it in quite this way before.

A little shy himself, he leaned back against the wall, so that her hand perforce fell away from his sleeve, and began to plait at the fringe of the curtain that shielded the window.

"Well, as long as you do not tell your mama that I have told you, for she will be— Whatever you say about her keeping me here, I cannot be sure you are right. And I mean to make my way in the world, and I can do that better when I can read and write and cipher, as I shall learn to do here, so I would not— Well, what is it you wish for me to tell you?"

"Whatever you choose to tell me, Abel!" she said at once. "For it will all be quite remarkable to me, you know! Whatever you choose."

Haltingly at first, but gradually with greater fluency, he began to speak. He told her of the streets of the Dials and the Bermudas and Covent Garden. Of Hungerford Market and its costers, painting a word picture of the place and its people that brought it vividly before her eyes in all its color and stench and awfulness and excitingness and humanity. He told her of escapades that left her breathless, of pocket picking on dark nights, of pie-shop robbing on high noons, fruit stealing from the early-morning drays, shed burglings on dark midnights. She felt with him what it was like to sleep in a corner of a doorway on a rainy summer's night, and on a freezing winter's one to curl up warm and snug and dry—albeit itching with all the fires of hell—in the straw-filled racks of a cowkeeper's byre, warmed by the breath of the cows beneath. She discovered in his words what it was like to have hunger tie your inside into knots, and truly felt it, for all she had been so well fed all her life. She entered into his story with him—sitting rapt at his feet, never once taking her eyes from his face, watching the expressions move across its curves, watching his eyes darken with memory of things uncomfortable, but lighten to a sparkling wickedness when he recalled his more successful exploits—and was part of him.

In later years she was to know that this was the moment that altered her life, that patterned her future for good or ill. Fascinated as she had been by this strange and hauntingly good-looking boy the moment she had first seen him standing filthy and bedraggled in Lucy's formidable shadow on that evening in her mother's supper room, it was on that cold July day, sitting on the floor beside him in the dull and severely furnished schoolroom in Gower Street, that she learned to see him as a person who was of importance to her.

As the rain drummed on through all that English summer afternoon, chilling the drafts that came whistling through the windows' cracks, his physical presence warmed her, completing her in some way that she did not understand but recognized. It was as though the daydreams of romantic heroes, culled from the reading of novels, that had for so many years filled her imagination had been transmogrified and come to reality before her. True, her heroes were always tall and fair and excessively noble, whereas this boy was slight and dark and a veritable guttersnipe. They adored and worshiped her, while this boy patently gave her no more than a passing thought. True, Lysander was strong and masterful, while this boy was as frightened of her mama as she was herself, and as incapable as she of standing up to her chill controls. But he was a hero all the same, in all the essentials. She knew it with every part of her body, and shivered with delight at the knowledge.

She was so startled at the interruption when it came that she found herself shaking, her very head trembling upon her neck as she turned and stared in wide-eyed shock at the door.

"Well, Miss Dorothea, and it's here you are, is it? Oh, a nice tale I'll have to tell your poor mama, and won't I just! There you was, sitting like all the angels there is as your mama bid you, by a fire lit expressly for you and your putrid throat as you made so much of, and where do I find you but 'obnobbin' with this piece of rubbish! Oh, I tell you, miss, but your mama'll have plenty to say to *this*, as well you know!"

She stood there, arms akimbo, staring sourly at them both, and Abel looked at Dorothea, sitting there huddled in fear at his feet, her face white as she stared at the other female's insolent, sneering face, and then back at Kate, and he felt anger rising in him. But he said nothing for the moment, just putting his hand forward to rest it on Dorothea's arm. She threw one agonized look at him and convulsively grasped the hand with her other one.

"So, is that what it is!" Kate cried jeeringly, with a high note of triumph in her voice. "Oh, but she shall know of this, for it's no more than my bounden duty to tell her of it—asittin' here all alone with this creature. Why, if it was to get about, you'd be ruined, miss, that you'd be! For who would care for soiled goods such as all will think you after such an escapade? Oh, yes, and all! My bounden duty! Not if you was to offer me a mint-new crown could I hold my tongue! . . ."

She stopped and looked at them suggestively, and then grinned. "Mind you, for more than one—a lot more—I might be able to forget *some* of what I sees here this afternoon. I'm not sayin' I would, mind, but I *might*."

Eagerly Dorothea moved, and began to scrabble in the reticule hanging from her waist for the few coins she had in it, knowing it to be pitifully little, and knowing that Kate would take it and all she could get for months to come besides and knowing she would have to pay it. But Abel pulled her hand away and stood up to walk across the room toward the woman beside the door.

He spoke to her very softly, standing there in front of her and looking up into her face, and Dorothea, still sitting on the floor beneath the window, could not hear what he said, just the low murmur of his voice; but she could see Kate's face, and marveled at it, for she went a sickly gray color as she listened, and then opened her mouth, and closed it again, and shook her head. But Abel said something more, and this time Kate turned and opened the door, and bobbing awkwardly in Dorothea's general direction, said flatly, "I never say aught, miss. Not aught. Your ma says I was to give you a cordial in the drawin' room, and it's there now, please, miss." And then she was gone.

"What did you say to her?" Dorothea breathed, staring at Abel across the room, at his nonchalant pose as he leaned against the door, his face for the first time that afternoon adorned with something approaching a smile.

"Nothing I should say to a lady like you," he answered, almost gaily. "But I keeps my eyes open and my wits about me, even within walls. I always has been a knowing cove, and one as notices things, and I jest kept on when I got here. And there's things I've noticed about them as works here—her and that William, and the cook—and kep' quiet about, for all their nasty ways to me. But I was waiting my time, and today it come. I told 'er of things I've seen and things I know of—some of 'em matters for the beak, if all was known. She'll say naught to your mama—not now nor ever—I'll take my oath!"

"Oh, *beloved* Abel," she said softly, and then flushed hotly, for fear he'd noticed. But he hadn't, and was opening the door for her.

"You'd best be gone," he said a little roughly, for shyness and his new stiff speech had suddenly returned to him. "Your mama must surely return soon, and there is that cordial you're to take waiting in the drawing room."

"Dear, *dear* Abel," she murmured, as she got to her feet and hurried across the room toward him. "I— You cannot know how— I cannot tell you—"

"You'll forget your workbox," he said, and slipped past her

outstretched hands to get it for her. She took it from him, and grasped his wrist before he could get away.

"We'll talk again, Abel? Please say we shall! I'll teach you many things, I promise—things my mama will not teach you, for she cares only for reading and writing and counting for you. I know French and music, and I shall teach you those if you wish to learn, and more besides, for I am quite bookish! Only speak to me sometimes, secretly, so that—so that— Oh, please, Abel!"

"Oh, I cannot say," he muttered, suddenly brick red. "If chance allows, perhaps—"

"Oh, it shall, it *shall*," she said fervently, "for I shall make it allow, somehow. I shall make it allow—especially now, with Kate— Oh, I *shall*! Dear Abel!" And in an excess of emotion, she leaned forward and kissed his cheek rather inexpertly and, with her workbasket beneath her arm and her skirts held clutched in one hand, fled to the drawing room with her hot cheeks, to clutch to her heart her dreams of masculine perfection as exemplified in the thin boy left standing alone in the ugly schoolroom.

· TEN ·

LONG after he had gone to his bedroom that night, to sit on his hard bed wrapped in his nightshirt and staring up at the stars above him through the narrow skylight which was all that lit and aired his sleeping quarters, he thought about the afternoon's experiences. Not because of Dorothea or Kate, but because of the discovery that he was suffering from boredom.

The sense of stifling misery, the achingness that had filled him these many weeks, had alarmed and puzzled him in equal measure. He had not been able to understand why he should feel so, when he was so well fallen on his feet. But now he did understand and bent his mind toward seeking a remedy for his situation.

There was help in this search to be found, yet again, in the afternoon's events. In speaking as he had to Dorothea of his childhood years in the Dials, he had discovered something which, now he thought about it in his solitude, was most surprising. He was homesick for the Dials. He longed for the life and companionship and excitement and reality of the Dials in a way he could never have imagined possible in the early days after his escape from it.

But yearn though he might for some aspects of Dials life, he knew well that he had neither the desire nor the intention of leaving behind the satisfactions he found in his present situation, tedious and dull as it so often seemed. He had begun to soak up the meager teaching Charlotte had to offer with an eagerness that made all he was told stick to his mind like a bur. While Charlotte was laboriously teaching him his alphabet, his mind was far ahead of her, part of it worrying out the actual words of the book she used, while his lips obediently repeated the letters as she told him to. He did not himself realize how close he was to being an able and fluent reader. He knew he could read a little, of course, but had had no opportunity as yet to exercise his newfound skills on any more complex words than those to be found in *Dame Joan's Book for Infants,* on which Charlotte based most of her educational practice. But that he wanted to know, to be an educated man, was as sure as that he breathed.

So any remedy for his boredom and this sneaking aching need for the familiar sights and smells and sounds of the Dials that threatened in any way his position in the Gower Street household could not for one moment be countenanced. He needed to enjoy both, and somehow, he told himself, this should be possible.

It was the episode with Kate and her tricksy ways that gave him his answer. Until that afternoon he had been as frightened of the servants as of Charlotte—more so in fact, for he had more to do with them than with Charlotte. She taught him his lessons, filling the schoolroom with her grim determination to Do Her Duty, but he ate with the lower servants (for neither William nor the cook would tolerate his presence in their snug little room) and suffered much in consequence. They made his life misery in many ways, treating him as though he were the lowliest scum of all the earth, as indeed in their eyes he was—Kate's in particular. Her resentment was the most intense, for it was she who waited upon the schoolroom, and had perforce to wait upon Abel during those hours in which he was in the company of the family.

But his defense of Dorothea had redounded to his own benefit. When he had gone downstairs to his own dinner after Jesse and Charlotte and Dorothea had gone into their dining room, the servants had treated him with an exaggerated respect, piling his plate higher than usual and offering him all manner of good things. William and Cook had bidden him come and take a daffy of gin with them beside her fire in the Pug's Parlor (as the others called this upper servants' fastness), but he had refused, almost instinctively knowing that if he was to keep his strength and his position against them, he must remain aloof. He had eaten his dinner in silence, and departed as usual to his room in the attic to think.

And now, his ideas crystallized into a full-blown plan. He had clearly no need to fear the servants any more. Even if one of them should notice what he was about, there was not one would risk splitting on him for fear he would retaliate with his own much more dangerous information against them.

He slid to the floor, his feet curling against the chill of the bare boards, and rumpled his sheets and blankets and pillows to make the bed look occupied. He did not for one moment suppose that anyone would ever look at his bed, but he wanted to be sure.

Below him the house lay still, some lights gleaming from the half-open drawing-room door and along the stairs and passages, but that was all. He had but to get past the drawing-room door, past Jesse and Charlotte's chamber door, and to the schoolroom. The rest would be simplicity itself.

Abel slipped noiselessly down the stairs and crept with infinite care past the drawing-room door. He could see Jesse sitting inside, sprawled in an armchair that was patently far too delicate in design for his bulk, staring morosely at the fire and drinking steadily from his glass of rum and water.

For one fleeting moment, Abel wanted to go in, to stand beside the man and talk to him: of nothing in particular, just to talk to him. But he easily conquered that strange notion, and went on, wraithlike.

In the schoolroom, he left his nightshirt neatly folded on the table in the corner in place of the ragged shirt and trousers. He had some trouble getting into them, for they were as much too tight for him now as they had been too loose on him those long weeks before. But he managed, and was away to the window on silent bare feet within a few moments of coming into the room.

He had seen that afternoon, without any conscious reason for noticing it, how easy it would be to get out of the house by means of the little balcony outside, and how easy to return. The schoolroom was one of the rooms that flanked the drawing room, and whereas the drawing-room windows had only the steps that led up to the front door beneath them, the schoolroom looked over the area, and the railing that edged it from the street. He had seen how an agile person could make the transition from the first-floor balcony to the railing beneath without too much difficulty.

Outside, the street was almost dark, only the distant light of a pair of links set outside a house some distance up Gower Street breaking the heaviness of the moonless night. He stepped out upon the balcony and pulled the window down behind him—not fully down, but with enough of a crack for him to reopen it on his return.

And then, with a twist of his rubbery young body, he was hanging over the sill, clinging carefully to the edge with tight-gripped fingers while his feet swung, seeking the toehold below. After one sick moment of doubt he found it, curled his almost prehensile toes about it—and let go, forcing his body to curve backward as he went. He uncurled his toes as he launched himself into space, and with a mighty muscular effort twisted himself into a ball. The resulting backward somersault took him over the railing and landed him tidily and silently in the middle of the street.

He went padding away into the darkness, his throat tight with the old mixture of excitement and doubt. How he had needed this exploit! He felt new blood moving in him, a new strength filling his muscles, and almost danced his jogging steps as he made his way with the unerring certainty of a homing pigeon toward the raw streets in which he had been born and lived.

It was the first of many such jaunts. That night, in a gently experimental way, he picked a pocket in the Strand and found his haul was hard cash, which made him jubilant. No need to go hunting out a fence! He spent the money on such of his old friends as he could find, slapping them on the back and offering to sport his blunt and give them a supper if they wished it. And wish it they did, accepting his easy generosity without question.

He sat that night watching them eat wolfishly at the pies his stolen money had bought them, and knew again how fortunate he had been, for their faces, he could now see, were pinched and gray as his must once have been. He knew now he was rounder and sturdier, that his clean skin shone with the developing glow of good health. He knew his well-fed muscles were stronger than any of theirs—though they were still in better training than he—and above all, he knew that their wits were being dulled by the life they led.

They listened in a lackluster way to his story of what had befallen him, having neither the interest nor the mental energy to either disbelieve or marvel at his tale. They just sat there in the gutter, four or five half-starved adolescent boys, watching him dully as he talked, only half listening as he told them of all the good fortune he now enjoyed, and then went slouching away with not a backward glance at him.

He returned dispirited to Gower Street that night, almost sure he would never again venture so. But his intent did not hold for very long. Not a week later he again slipped out of the schoolroom window, to make his silent way back to Short's Gardens and Monmouth Street and the alleys round about. Again he wandered in familiar streets and among the familiar people, and once more filled the bellies of his erstwhile cronies with the gains he made from a little judicious operation of his old trade. And as this second escapade ended in success, it was inevitably followed shortly after by another and then another, and yet another. . . .

He could have gone on so for a long time, living this curious double life with no change in either his Gower Street existence or his Seven Dials one, with the two partaking of a sameness, each giving small spice to the other by the contrast between them. He could have gone on so, had it not been for the night in late September when he met the girl.

· ELEVEN ·

IT WAS a warm night, with a heavy yellow moon lying low above the chimneys, seeming to press the heat of the day down into the streets and gutters, filling the air with the faint, distant stench of rotting food, and worse. He used the roof to leave the house, having long since decided that there was little point any more in going out through the school-room. He could no longer easily get into his old ragged clothes, and anyway there was a growing risk that Charlotte would one day notice the increase in their tattered state due to his wearing of them, for there was not a time went by when he did not tear or stretch the ancient seams a little more. So he had rearranged them on their display table for the last time and gone prowling silently about the house to find a better way out, and something different to wear upon his outings.

He had found a route that took him from his skylight over the roof slates and down the back of the house from window sill to stucco ledge to window sill and on to the narrow yard at the back, thence through a slit of a window that led to the kitchens, and through the house to the area door at the front. It took him at least fifteen minutes to make the journey however accustomed he became to it, but it was easy and safe for his agile limbs, and he enjoyed it.

As for clothes, he had solved that with the easy insouciance of his past. He had waited until the laundry woman who visited the house each week had left her great basket beside the area door while chaffering with Charlotte about her payment, and removed from it one of William's shirts and a pair of his own trousers. The washerwoman had been soundly berated for the loss of the garments, and turned away from the house for good and all (a scene that gave Abel considerable, if callous, amusement, for the sound and fury of the washerwoman's denials contrasted with the icy outrage evinced by Charlotte was as good as a raree show), and he had hidden the apparel in his mattress, to bring it out and put it on whenever the weight of boredom in his life overcame him and he needed the restorative drug of a visit to his streets.

Tonight he had lain abed for a long time debating with himself whether or not he would go. It was curious how he felt about his jaunts, for often, while he was there in the alleys wandering about looking for old familiar faces and places, he was as uncomfortable within himself as when he sat alone in the schoolroom on those long and dreary mornings while Charlotte and Dorothea paid their visits. Sometimes, to be sure, when he picked up a little blunt and could treat people to food and drink, he recaptured the heady pleasure of that first secret visit, but mostly it was not like that. Often he would return tired and aching in the small hours of the morning, sick at himself and filled with a sort of anger (though he did not recognize it as such, only as an uncomfortable sensation), to sleep but fitfully until morning and his solitary breakfast in the kitchen before lessons.

Curiously enough, such nights were succeeded by mornings in which he did even better than usual at his books, when he felt supernaturally aware and alive and able to understand and absorb. He would sit there, pale and tight-lipped, racing through his set tasks in a way that made Charlotte uneasy—for she was becoming more and more anxious about her own ability to keep up with this strange gutter boy's mind—but filled him with a curious triumphant satisfaction.

On this September night, it was as much the desire to feel

this special alertness and strange, edgy weariness the next morning as any true adventurousness that made him get up and go out. It was past eleven o'clock, for he had heard the call of the Watch while he was scrambling over the roof, and the street was empty of people, though he could hear ahead of him the sounds of traffic along Oxford Street. There the swells and the thieves and the women of the town would be abroad for hours yet, but here in the respectable gentility of Bedford Square and Gower Street, well-conducted citizens were long since abed, snoring virtuously under their snug nightcaps.

As Abel slid himself into the bustle of Oxford Street—not so well lit now that the shops were closed, but still with light enough to see from links and carriage lamps as well as from the full moon—he thought, as he always did when he saw the women of the town with their red-and-white painted faces and extravagant clothes, of Lucy and her girls. It would be so good to visit them, to go and boast to them of his good fortune and to show off his prowess as a reader of words and counter-up of figures; he had come very close indeed to doing so many times, reminding himself of Lucy's hugs and whispered "You knows where I am, boy" when she had left him that first night in Gower Street; but he controlled this childish desire with some sternness. He could not be sure that Lucy or one of her girls would not tell Jesse of such a visit, thus exposing him to the danger of banishment from Gower Street.

He hesitated uncharacteristically there in the muddy gutter beside the broad thoroughfare of Oxford Street, and then on an impulse turned his back on his usual haunts and went on up Oxford Street, moving west. He would go somewhere different tonight.

For once he decided not to even try to pick up any cash. He was in no mood for the quick jostle and dip and headlong flight that were the trade of the pickpocket. He had noticed this lack of interest in himself more and more this past month or so, and had wondered briefly whether his distaste for his old livelihood was due to Charlotte's interminable preaching on the subject of Sin and the Wickedness of his Past Ways, but had decided, with a shrewdness that he was coming to recognize as very much a part of himself, that it was because he was well fed. Hunger drove pickpockets to the skills of their trade, just as a full belly robbed them of their speed and delicacy of touch.

He crossed Soho Square, his hands deep in his pockets and slouching a little as he moved, his head down and his eyes on the roadway beneath his feet as he pondered this thought, considering the changes that his new life had wrought in him. Of late he had become ever more interested in this business of thinking, this use of time to explore his own mind. It had been a strange activity at first, one almost forced upon him by the need to do something in those long dull hours in the schoolroom when he had exhausted the resources of the book Charlotte had left him to study. But this was the first time that his new habit of consideration had spilled over into his nighttime activities.

He had been walking so for some few minutes before he became aware of her. When he did, he stopped immediately, standing quite still but with every muscle bunched in readiness for atttack. He slid his eyes sideways at the figure that he had suddenly realized had been capering along beside him, peering a little in the dim light, and then relaxed very slightly.

She was small, even shorter than himself, which made him feel a little strange for a moment, for Dorothea was taller than he, and he had become unaccustomed to having people of his own generation physically near enough for such comparisons.

She was as shabby and dirty and ragged as he himself had once been, but she did not appear to be as hungry and thin as he knew he had looked then. She stood there beside him in the thin light of the moon quite relaxed and unafraid and staring up at him, her arms folded inside the ragged skirt which she had hoisted so that it showed long, slender legs and dirty feet.

"'Ullo," she said after a moment, and smiled at him, a wide smile that split her face into creases of good humor.

"What d'you want?" he growled, still standing with his bunched fists in his pockets and his shoulders squared.

"Gi's a fadge," she said invitingly, "Eh? Go on, gi's a fadge."

"Scarper," he said shortly, "I ain't got no farthin's for the likes o' you."

"Yes, you 'ave. I seen yer. Go on—gi's a fadge. You gives to lots o' people—I seen yer. Only a farthin', that's all—just enough to buy me a bit o' bread to me supper. Go on."

He stood there staring at her, swept by an extraordinary sensation. It was as though he had somehow changed places with her, that it was he standing there pleading for money, while he himself had become a shadowy version of Jesse, the fount of good things. He blinked and looked down at himself, at his voluminous shirt tucked into the waistband of the cloth trousers, and tried to see himself through her eyes. Did he look a swell, as Jesse had looked a swell on his visits to the Dials? Surely not! How could he, a scrap of a boy in a stolen shirt and trousers, look anything like as good a touch as the richly dressed, fleshy Jesse? The very idea made him laugh aloud.

Immediately she moved closer to him, dropping her dress and tucking one hand confidentially into the crook of his arm and peering beguilingly up into his face. "Eh, Guv? Gi's a penny, eh? You wouldn't let a poor little kid like me starve, would yer?"

"Where'd you get the notion I've got blunt to give to the likes o' you?" He made no attempt to move away from her clutch on his arm. "I ain't got a penny to bless m'self with."

"Yes, you 'as," she said wheedlingly. "I seen yer, di'n't I? Not more'n a se'ennight since down Endell Street with six of the bully boys, di'n't I? And they was eatin' your mutton pies like they was sittin' in a toff ken! Go on, gi's a fadge."

"How long you been on the cadge? Or d'you have another lay?"

She pulled back from him, to stand for the first time with an air of caution about her. "What's to do with you?"

He shrugged slightingly. "Nothing. Do as you please, and the devil take yer. You asked me for money and I asked you a question. Do as yer please about it." And he began to move again, walking toward the other end of the square.

Immediately she came pattering along beside him. "I ain't no cadger—only when I can get good out of it, or reckons I can. I got a regular life, I 'ave, but sometimes I picks up a bit where I can. So go on, Guv, gi's a bit."

He stopped. "I ain't got nothing to give you. Not tonight. Sometimes I has and sometimes I hasn't, and tonight I hasn't."

She stopped too and stared at him, pouting suspiciously, and then drooped her head forward so that she had to peer up at him under her lashes, and he saw for the first time how very pretty she was. Her face was small, but broad across the forehead under a mass of dark curly hair, and her eyes were widely set, the whole making a finely etched line which curved down to a very small pointed chin below a straight and delicate nose and a wide pink mouth. He looked at her and felt her coaxing coming at him in great waves and wanted, quite urgently, to put his hand into his pocket and bring out a fistful of coins to spill into her eager grasp. The knowledge that there were no coins there enraged him, and he said roughly, "Regular life, you say? I should just think so! You looks like a Covent Garden tail, you does, standin' there mopping and mowin' like that."

She jerked her head up and stared at him, her eyes narrowed with rage, and then suddenly lashed out at him, and he had to duck fast to dodge the blow aimed at his head. Immediately his irritation was dispelled, and he reached out and grabbed her wrists and held her with cheerful unconcern as she began to kick and tried to claw at his face with her nails.

"I ain't no tail!" she gasped, almost weeping in her rage. "I got more class than that, you, you—muck snipe, you!"

He laughed at that. "Do you always go beggin' from muck snipes, then? You'd not get much of a supper from such as they! Stop your screeching, you stupid blower! D'you want the Runners comin' to see what's afoot?"

Immediately she stopped, and sniffed, and pulled one hand away from his grasp so that she could wipe the back of it across her nose, and stood there staring at him, her face sour and sulky.

"So if you ain't givin' me nothin', get away out of it! Let go o' me, and scarper!"

"Why'd you come beggin' from me, if you got a regular life and beggin's not your lay?" he asked with real curiosity. "And I believes it ain't, because no one as knows anythin' at all about it would spare a look at such as I, no matter what I might have been seen doing with my blunt in Endell Street!

What's this regular life that you have to go on the cadge besides?"

She sniffed unappetizingly and pulled ineffectually against his grasp. "Why should I tell you aught?"

"Because like I said, sometimes I has blunt and sometimes I hasn't. If I hasn't now, it don't mean I won't have later on. If it's worth my trouble to get it."

He really wanted to know about this girl, and why she had chosen so obviously useless a touch as himself to cadge from, feeling a curious unwillingness to let her slip away back into the shadows from which she had so suddenly appeared. Standing there in the deserted square with shuttered silent buildings all about and only the distant sound of traffic, thinning now as the night wore on, to show there were any others in the world besides themselves, he needed to keep her there, and all unknowingly his hand tightened on her wrist so that she whimpered slightly.

" 'Ere, Guv, I done nothin' to you. Don't set about me, now, will yer, Guv? I'll not come next nor nigh you ever again if you'll just let me go. Please, Guv."

"There's naught to cry havoc about!" he said, and though he spoke gruffly, there was a note of friendliness in his voice which seemed to reassure her. "But I've talked to no one of any mark this se'ennight, and I'd as lief talk to you as myself."

And then, as he realized that this was exactly why he was so unwilling to let this ragged piece of human rubbish go, he dropped her wrist and shoved his hands back into his pockets.

She didn't run, although she turned her body and stood poised for a moment as though she were about to, but stood there rubbing her bird-thin wrist against her scrawny chest and staring at him.

"You're a rum cove," she said after a moment. "Saw you in Endell Street and thought you was a toff on the run from school or suchlike, lookin' at the cut o' your jib and the way you was flashin' your blunt, but you talks like one of the family."

"I used to live round the Dials," he said after a moment's pause, "only I've been took up by the Quality and lives in Gower Street now."

"Gower Street?" She turned back and came to stand close

beside him, peering interestedly into his face. "That's a real swell drum, 'n' it? You're on to a good lay, ain't you? What does you do all day? Just eat and sleep, and that? And what are you doing down here if you've been took up by the Quality?"

He laughed. "Now who's asking the questions?"

"I am. You are too, though, ain't you?" She stopped and took a sharp little breath and then nodded with a sort of sudden resolution. "I mean, Quality livin'. Comes in the way you talk sometimes, like it did then."

"I told you. Wouldn't say it if it wasn't so, would I? Where'd be the benefit?"

"I'll stand you a daffy of gin," she offered after a moment's silence.

"Don't want it," he said, and then frowned sharply. "Didn't you say you wanted a fadge for bread?"

She laughed a fat gurgle of laughter. "La, sir, what a maid says and what a maid means! Have you never heard *that* said? I've no need of your farthin's, and don't you think it! But I was never one to see an opportunity pass m'door without comin' out to say 'Good day' to it, and I saw you and remembered seein' you in Endell Street, and came to pass the time of day and see what was about! Will yer come and take a touch of ale, then? M' ken's not so far from 'ere."

And she turned and slid away into the darkness, and without stopping to think he followed her, hurrying along behind her rushing steps, feeling more life in his bones than he could remember feeling there since the first time he had left Gower Street for a private journey on his own.

· TWELVE ·

IT WAS a small room, little more than a tiny hole in the wall leading off a basement. She had pushed her way past the heaped garbage and reeking gutters beyond the square into the comparative respectability of Frith Street, and then into a tiny narrow passage that ran parallel with Old Compton Street, and finally into this ramshackle house.

It was dark and silent and smelled indescribably ill, and Abel wrinkled his nose as he followed her in through the low doorway, ducking his head and holding on to the back of her skirt so as not to lose her in the pitch blackness as she pushed forward and down the stairs to the cellar. His months of easy living in the cleanliness of Gower Street had clearly partially destroyed a lifelong ability to ignore such unpleasantnesses as greeted his senses here.

Once they had reached her own domain the smell diminished somewhat, only to be replaced by the reek of a tallow dip, which, disagreeable though it was, was far less offensive than the other.

"The air smells foul out there," he said, as he looked about at the room revealed by the smoky leaping flame of her light in its shallow saucer. "Is't a slaughterhouse, or something of that nature?"

She looked at him sharply, putting the light down on a

rickety wooden table in the center of the small room. "Aye, something of the sort," she said. "Will you have aught to eat with me? I've a rasher or two to spare, and an egg besides, mayhap, not to speak of a heel of bread and some good beer."

He stared at her, his forehead creasing. "For one that was begging, you're very generous with your victuals," he said, his voice thick with suspicion. "I've come this far with you, but look you, not a thing else before you tell me what it is that keeps you so proud! I thought you to be as I was before—as I used to be. One alone and living as best you could. But to have a place like this, of your own . . ." He shook his head.

And indeed his surprise was justified, for the basement, though small, was far from being the desperately poor place he had expected, the like of which he had seen many times in the past. Instead of the walls running with foul water, the heap of filthy rags that made up a bed on the damp and dirty floor, the clear evidence of the presence of rats that would have seemed normal to him, this basement was snug and dry, the walls painted with whitewash, for all the world as though it were the back kitchen in Charlotte and Jesse's splendid house. There was a real bed in one corner, narrow and low but a bed nonetheless, with a thick brown witney blanket neatly spread upon it, and beside it a chair with a red calico cover thrown over. There was a tiny fireplace, at which the girl was even now kneeling to put a light to the kindling that lay in it, and in the center was a scrubbed wooden board table upon which the tallow dip stood. On the stone-slab floor was a scrap of almost threadbare carpet, but carpet all the same, and a heavy plush curtain, once blue but now very faded, hung on a string over the arched entrance to the small room.

"What is it that's your lay, then? If you aren't a tail, then I'm a . . ."

Still crouched before the fire, she turned her head to glare at him, and fixed on him a steady regard that made the words dry in his mouth.

"I'm no penny whore, and don't you never say such a thing again, you hear me?" And her voice was low but crackling with controlled anger, sharp as a whip. "I've got class—*class*—and no one can ever say as Lil Burnell is anythin' but class! I got better ways to make my days go round than walkin' the streets, as you'll discover if you keep your tongue betwixt your teeth! Now, do you believe what I say, or will you start again on this tack? For if you do, then you can be about your business right now, and leave me to mine!"

He looked at her, puzzled, and then nodded. "If it has so great an importance, then so be it! You're no tail! But I'm hard put to it to know what you do to get your bread—for you're small use on the begging lay, that much is certain!"

She stood up and smiled at him, the same wide smile she had produced before and which had so beguiled him with its prettiness.

"I've my friends," she said simply. "There's three as lives in this house, and runs their business from here, and they lets me have this room for no more than my company and my eyes and ears! Aye, and gives me good victuals, too. Only sometimes when I've a mind to it I dirties meself up and walks about a bit to cadge. Not that I need to, mind you, but because I've a mind to." She laughed suddenly, and twisted herself on her toes and threw herself toward the bed, to sit there curled up and impishly clutching her knees in her arms. "Because I've a mind to!" she crowed again, and laughed with huge satisfaction.

He watched her, a little bedazzled by the way the light of the fire, now leaping with high and crackling flames, etched her face, outlining the curves of her cheeks and enriching the color of her large eyes to a sparkling green gaiety that cheered him in a most remarkable fashion. She sat and hugged herself in huge self-approval, and beamed upon him with that bewitching slit of a smile, and he blinked and swallowed, and almost tentatively smiled back.

"Indeed, if you live here for no more than your company to pay for all, then you've a right to laugh so mightily," he said. "But, still, you say you cadge when you've a mind to— for the sport of it, as I imagine you mean, and that I don't comprehend." He shook his head in genuine puzzlement. "Why should you try to beg from one such as I, clearly without a groat to scratch himself? You must either take me for a flat, to tell me such a tale, or be a Bartholomew baby on your own account!"

She shook her head, still grinning at him, and then, scrambling to her feet, "I'll speak of that when the fancy takes me!" she said airily. "Now, will you take aught to eat?"

He nodded, and she laughed again and reached across the table to take his hand and tugged, making him move until he was standing beside the bed, and then with a thrust at his body that doubled him up, made him sit down upon it.

She disappeared beyond the curtain for a while, and he could hear her rattling about, heard water running from one vessel to another and then splashed about a little while she sang in a high, shrill voice which yet had a certain sweetness about it and which was undeniably true and clear. Then she came in again, bearing a broad tray with dishes upon it, and he gawped, for she had washed herself and put on a different dress, a blue one, faded and patched but very clean. She laughed at the sight of his face, at the way he stared at her hair tied back prettily with a frayed blue ribbon, and then she crouched before the fire to cook the bacon and eggs on a rattly old pan, and to toast the bread before the flames.

They ate in companionable near-silence (for neither was exactly genteel in the way in which they smacked their lips and chobbled at their food), and then, when every last scrap of bacon grease had been mopped out of the pan with the bread and they sat with mugs of beer in their hands, she looked at him and nodded cheerfully.

"So, friend! We've done a tightener and now we can be comfortable! What's your monarch? You heard mine."

"Aye, you're Lil, did you say? Lil Burnell? What sort of name is Lil?"

" 'Twas one my mother chose for me," the girl said shortly. "She came from Ireland and had a fancy for the names of flowers. But none say Lily to me these days. Only Lil. What's your name, then?"

He blushed hugely. "Abel Lackland," he muttered, and waited, cringing, for the hoot of laughter he was sure would come. But she put her head to one side and repeated it thoughtfully.

" 'Twas they gave it me," he said defensively. "I never had

another as I know of, and so it made no nevermind to me. I let him have his way with it. But for my part—"

"Abel Lackland." She ran the syllables gently over her tongue. "Abel Lackland. Aye"—she nodded that decisive nod of hers that he was beginning to realize was characteristic of her—" 'tis a good name. It has a good sound about it. You shall call me Lil, and I shall call you Abel. And we shall be friends."

"We shall?" he said, and she looked up at him quickly and smiled and said softly, "Aye, we shall."

He looked at her for a while, and then said bluntly, "Why?"

"What sort of a question is that? Should I not choose my friends where I will?"

He shrugged. "So you may, but why should you choose me to be your friend? You never saw me before this night, yet now you give me your grub and talk of friendship as though you were some fancy lady! It's strange."

"I choose my own ways, with none to tell me otherwise!" she said with a sudden gaiety, and he looked at her with an upsurge of his earlier curiosity about her.

"Have you no people of your own? The people in the house—are they not yours? Mother or brother or—"

She slid her eyes sideways at him. "No, they're naught to me but what they are—friends with business of their own and lives of their own the which I don't meddle in. As for the rest—what's it to you? Have you mother or brother or . . ." and she imitated the tone of his voice as well as his actual words with such accuracy that he was startled and stared at her till she laughed again with a huge self-complimenting glee.

"I've as good an ear as any on the chanting lay!" she cried. "Have I not? So, tell me! Have you?"

"Have I what?"

"People of your own?"

He shook his head. "And you?"

"My mother died of a bloody flux when I was nobbut nine years old. There was never more than the two of us."

"When was that?"

"Two years come Christmas."

"Then according to the reckoning of— Well, we're about

of an age." He said it almost shyly, and she flashed a quick and companionable smile at him.

"Are we so? Then all the more cause we should be friends."

There was a pause, and then he asked abruptly, "Did you live here with your mother before she died?"

"Aye. And Barliman said as I could stay and he'd not put me to Coram's Hospital."

"It's no bad place, as I've heard."

She grimaced. "I was never one for doing as others bid me, be it good or bad. I must be my own woman. So Barliman said I could stay and—"

"Who's Barliman?"

She jerked her head upward. " 'Tis his house. I works for him sometimes. And watches the house for him when he needs, and when he and Fitch and French John are all about their business. French John is abovestairs now. That's why I was out tonight."

"What business is it that they need you to—"

She shook her head in sudden irritation. "You ask so many things! It's none of my concern, nor yet of yours. I know what I know, and I keep my tongue between my teeth when I should, and don't concern myself with what is naught of mine. And you should do as well. Now you tell me of your history. How is it you're with the Quality and lives in that swell ken? I've told you all of me."

"Jesse Constam," he said shortly. "Did you ever hear tell of him?"

She frowned and narrowed her eyes. "Constam—Constam— I've heard such a name somewhere about."

"He's a very downy cove, very downy, and well breeched besides. Comes down the Dials and Bermudas and flashes his blunt—and cuts the throat of any as interferes with him as soon as look at 'em. Oh, he's known all about, is Jesse Constam!"

Her face cleared. "Aye, I know the one! A fat man, with red hair, such as there is of it, and a fair choice spirit, from all accounts! Is that the place you live?"

He nodded. "Aye. And if you ask me why he should have took me up and be keeping of me in his house and making his

fancy madam teach me my books, I cannot tell you, for I
don't know! There's some air of trouble between them and
he's making some use of me to settle it—so much is clear
from what I see and hear. But for the rest"—he shrugged—"I
take my luck where it falls, and don't spit in its eye."

She nodded in full comprehension and turned her head to
stare at the flames of the fire, her chin propped on her fists
and her elbows on her knees. He watched her as her face
seemed to move and shimmer in the uneven light, watched
her forehead crease and then smooth, her eyes narrow and
then widen as she thought—for she was clearly cogitating
very hard upon something—and was totally fascinated by
her. He could never remember meeting such a person, so
adult and so capable and so sparkling for all her youth and
the hardness of her life. And he felt suddenly very young and
humble comparing himself with her, for she seemed so much
more knowing in every way than he could ever be.

They sat on in silence for a while, as the flames dropped a
little, and then he stirred unwillingly.

"I must be on my road to Gower Street," he said, and was
surprised at how sad the thought of going made him feel. "It
must be past two of the clock, and if I'm not careful I'll not
be back before dawn. And I've no doubt they'll not like it
above half."

"They doesn't know you goes out of doors?" she said
quickly. "I'm a flat! Of course they doesn't. And you're not
to let them know if you're not to lose your place there!"

He smiled at her lazily. "What is't to you if I do?"

"What is't to me? I'll tell you, Abel Lackland. It's a lot to
me. A great lot!"

"Why? You know naught of me but what I told you, nor
who I'm there with, nor anything of what happens there. So
what is't to you?"

"Will you tell me of all that? Will you, Abel? For I've a
great desire to know! Will you tell me of all the things that
you see there, and do there, and what they speak of, and
what you eat and how, and—"

"Hold hard!" he cried, and laughed again. "You sound for
all the world like Dorothea with all her questions about the
Dials—only you wish to know of the house!"

"Dorothea?" She frowned ferociously, and he felt a moment of chill.

"Aye. The daughter of the house. She—she's kind to me, speaks often with me, and—"

"How old is she?"

"How old?"

"Don't repeat all I say, fool!" She stamped her foot in sudden rage. "Answer me! How old is this Dorothea?"

He shrugged. "I never thought of it. Some years more than I, I daresay."

"*How much* more years?" She almost howled it in her impatience.

"Some two or three," he said sulkily, much put out by her sudden change of mood, "so she would be about fourteen. Though why it should matter, I cannot for the life of me—"

"Will you come and see me again, Abel?" She was kneeling before him, her hands on his knees, and peering up into his face through her lashes just as she had done before, and every sign of her temper completely gone. "Will you? For I like you, indeed I do, and would so wish to see you again!"

He blinked down at her, bewildered, and she looked up at him with her eyes wide and appealing.

"You're talking differently," he said uncertainly, and she produced a crow of laughter.

"Am I, Abel? Am I truly? Oh, Abel, you will come and see me again, please will you? Don't you see how it is with me? When I'm with one that speaks Quality, why, then, so do I! But when I'm with these"—she jerked her head scornfully in the general direction of the rest of the building—"why, I talk like Billingsgate! And I want to be like the Quality, Abel, so much! That's why I spoke to you, why I chose to play the cadger with you, for I thought you had a touch of Quality. Will you teach me, Abel? Will you? Come and see again, and tell me of your Dorothea and all she says and does and all the clothes she wears, and more besides? And we shall eat and drink here and be such friends! Will you come again to me, Abel?"

He grinned and nodded, feeling for all the world like a donkey in a stall nodding and becking over a manger. "Aye," he said simply, "I'll come again."

· THIRTEEN ·

THE DRAWING room rustled with sound, a susurration of silk skirts and a hiss of fans moving in the heavy, overheated air. Charlotte, sitting with her hands folded on her lap and her ankles neatly side by side, looked about the room and felt a wave of satisfaction pass through her so strong that she almost feared for a moment that someone would observe it; and she raised her own fan, opening it with a click to smooth its painted chicken-skin folds before her face.

Across the room, Lady Hawkins bowed slightly, her turban of satin trimmed with pearls moving majestically over her tiers of chins. Ever behind the fashions for all her aristocratic *ton*, Charlotte thought with satisfaction, smiling sweetly back.

"I think, dear Mrs. Constam, that we might commence our Discussions," Lady Hawkins said with immense graciousness, and pinkly pleased, Charlotte rose to her feet and coughed very gently. The remaining half dozen ladies turned toward her, moving with elegant languorousness, and with gently raised eyebrows and calmly composed expressions prepared themselves to attend to matters of greater moment than the talk of servants' depredations and the fashions currently available at Exeter 'Change and Grafton House, which subjects had hitherto occupied them.

The Sixth Meeting of the London Ladies' Society for the Rescue of the Children of the Profligate Poor settled to an agreeable afternoon discussion about money and its uses—agreeable because it was permitted; talk of money was excessively vulgar, except when the matter was charitable.

Charlotte had been a little surprised at the success of her venture. Already endowment funds amounting to the value of seventy pounds per annum had been bestowed upon them (largely by husbands anxious to provide their wives with activity and interests that would occupy them sufficiently to ensure that they would leave their spouses in more than usual connubial peace), and they had not in fact been prepared for the handling of so much actual finance.

The past five meetings had gone by in attempts by the self-appointed Board of Ladies to decide on the best activities for them, and so far they had agreed to the provision of Bibles to be distributed in the slums (although they had not yet decided precisely how this was to be done, for it was unthinkable that any of the Board should themselves penetrate the horrors of those streets and alleys, yet who else could be trusted to do so and not to run away with the Bibles to sell them?) and the arrangement of an annual service at Mr. Spenser's fashionable church.

Today they bent their minds to a plan for seeking out respectable houses in the country to which Rescued children could be sent to work and live and be protected from the sins of the great metropolis.

"It will have a double benefit, dear Mrs. Askerley!" Lady Hawkins said in reply to that lady's comment on the excellence of the idea since it would cost so little to arrange. "For not only will these houses accommodate the children, and apprentice them at half premiums either to the household's trade or to domesticity, whichever is most suitable to their sex, but a portion of the child's earnings should surely be required payment to the Society at such time as the child reaches a useful age. This will be a very small recompense for the Saving of a Soul, as I have no doubt the children in their adult gratitude will understand, and will provide further funds for the rescue of more children. It will also make up in some small measure for the inevitable loss of revenue to the

Society that will occur from the deaths of those children which do not survive to earn. They are, by and large, sickly creatures, and we must accept with what equanimity we can the sad truth that much of our money will enter the grave-yard with them."

"True, true," murmured Mrs. Askerley, much gratified by Lady Hawkins's condescension in so carefully explaining the matter to her. "I fully concur with the suggestion, and would wish to see it arranged without delay. Will you arrange that, dear Mrs. Constam? Or if you cannot, then upon whom shall this responsibility fall?"

"Much as I should wish to be fully responsible for the selection and appointment of rural persons for the purpose of caring for our rescued children," Charlotte said, "I feel I cannot at this time accept this further demand upon my time. In due course, undoubtedly, but not at present. It is not, I do assure you, that I lack in any way the desire to do my duty in full. Indeed, no, ma'am, for it is my most earnest desire that this work should proceed apace. It is, rather, that my respon-sibility and duty toward the—the first child brought to our care by my own dear husband—who, as you all know, is deeply concerned with the progress of our work—precludes my spending too much time in—"

"Ah, indeed, indeed, Mrs. Constam, I do comprehend, none better, the personal burden that you bear." Mrs. Lar-rett, a pallid and very plump lady in yellow muslin that ill became her sallow complexion, sounded a shade nettled, for she regretted considerably that her own husband had not had foresight enough to provide her with so splendid an illustra-tion of her Charitable and Sensitive Soul as an orphan of her own to rear. "And I shall take it upon myself to offer my own services in this matter, for I have many connections, you must know, of excellent respectability and irreproachable worth through my work for the Children of the Clergy. My experience in such affairs—"

"Indeed, Mrs. Larrett, we thank you for your offer, and I, for my part, am disposed to accept it." Lady Hawkins rose majestically. "And that settled, you will I trust, permit me to make my farewells. You will recall I spoke to you, dear Mrs. Constam, of the matter of the Rout at St. James's to which we are bid. 'Twill be a shocking squeeze, and a dead bore, no doubt, but . . ."

Smiling, she took her leave, thus permitting the remnant of the London Ladies ample time in which to discuss her nasty, overbearing ways and shocking high instep as well as settling such Society matters as remained undiscussed. And when they in their turn departed in a clatter of carriages and a froufrou of lacy shawls (for the October afternoons were drawing colder now), Charlotte could sit in her boudoir feeling exceedingly satisfied with herself.

So much of what had happened since she had commenced her Charity had fallen precisely as she had wished it—the respect of those ladies to whose society she most aspired (to include among her acquaintances a Lady, albeit only the wife of a first-creation knight, was deeply gratifying); the sense of charitable worth that came from her efforts to teach Abel—these pleased her so well that she had almost buried the prime reason that lay behind the foundation of the London Ladies. In many ways she had forgotten the ire that Jesse had used to arouse in her, rarely concerning herself with his comings and goings as she had in the days before Abel's arrival and the foundation of the Charity. There was so much to do now that the summer had whisked by in a flutter of collating registers of the names of charitably disposed persons, the preparation of lessons for the voracious mind of Abel as well as for the less demanding Dorothea, and the inevitable discussions and plannings with the clerical Mr. Spenser that had been required in order to satisfy the religious side of her new tasks.

Sitting now with her feet outstretched upon her elegant chaise longue, a fine Paisley shawl thrown across her legs, she relaxed, and even dozed lightly for a little while, as the darkness of early evening filled her boudoir window. In the schoolroom along the passage Abel was, she knew, sitting with the Bible before him and a long passage marked to be committed to his memory, while Dorothea was in her own room, ostensibly resting until it should be time for dinner, but in fact sitting on the window sill staring at the sky and dreaming a long, complicated dream about Abel. All was well in Charlotte's world this evening, and she relaxed even more, drifting ever more deeply into sleep.

She woke with a start when light from the fire suddenly leaped to throw great shadows upon the plaster cupids that gamboled all around the ceiling, and she lay still for a moment, bewildered and blinking upward at their round plaster behinds. Then she turned her head and saw him standing there beside the fireplace, one foot upon the hearth and with ashes on the toe of the highly polished leather boot to show that it had been a hearty kick at the coals that had started the leap of the flames.

"Well, Mr. Constam!" she said, and her voice was a little thick and drowsy. "You return early to your dinner today!"

He merely grunted a reply and shrugged out of his coat and waistcoat, dropping them upon the floor before stumping across the room to seat himself heavily upon her chaise longue, making her drop her own feet to the floor so that she was sitting upright beside him.

"M' boots," he muttered, and thrust his legs forward, and she blinked again and stifled a yawn and said, "Shall I ring for your man?"

"Nay—you weren't too proud to remove my boots for me when first we were wed! Are you now?"

She frowned sharply, turning her head to look at him in the firelight. "You are in your cups, sir! That is no condition in which to come to a lady's boudoir! And at such an hour of the day!"

He laughed rather loudly. "In my cups, ma'am? If I were, I'd not need you to tell me so! You have not nor ever shall see Jesse Constam the worse for wear. A trifle disguised I may be, not to say a little bosky, but in my cups? Never!"

In fact he was a good deal more incapacitated by drink than he cared to admit, for he had been drinking smuggled brandy with the captain of his biggest India merchantman since noon and eaten little, and his head was swimming with the fumes. His humor was good, however, for the captain had reported some excellent sharp dealing in Bombay that had improved the value of the cargo by almost fifty per cent, and he had, in addition, the assurance of a further good business deal to come in loading the merchantman with a cargo of spirits to take to Spain on the journey back to the East. He had stopped at the schoolroom door on his way to Charlotte's room and greeted Abel with a noisy bonhomie that had made the boy respond with a smile, and had had him say over his catechism to him, and been most agreeably impressed by the boy's ability to read with such fluency; he had wrought well the day he had selected this boy to bring him to his house and make a citizen of him. One day—quite soon, going by the boy's progress so far—he would have a new man at the office to replace the plodding Hunnisett. He would have twice the work for half the cost, a thought that pleased him mightily as he went stumping on his way. Altogether an excellent day, and he was as content with himself as was Charlotte with herself.

"I take leave, sir, to regard you as rather more than 'disguised' or 'bosky.' I dislike it above all things when you come to me in such a state!" she said sharply.

"You speak as if I had come to you so on every other day of the week!" he snapped, some of his self-satisfaction dissipating. "Be so good as to remove my boots, ma'am—a wifely duty I believe may be asked of even so great a lady as yourself!"

She primmed her mouth, and looked enraged for a moment, but obediently slid to her knees to tug at the heavy boots that fitted his calves so snugly, and he sat there, half leaning back to give her leverage and looking down at her with half-closed eyes. She seemed to his brandied gaze to be shimmering with light against the dark background of her room, for her robe was a silvery pink one that seemed to melt into her skin, and her fair head above her pale face looked to be made of the same finespun silken material as the dress. As she leaned even farther forward to gain a purchase on the boot, he could see above the neck of the robe the swell of her breasts, small and rather pendulous now as she moved further and further away from her young years, but recognizably female breasts all the same.

The surge of need for her that rose in him was so sudden and so unexpected that he could not, even had he wished to do so, control it enough to coax her as he had attempted to do in the past. He simply leaned forward and with one sharp and almost vicious gesture pulled her dress from her shoulders to reveal the whole of her breasts in all their inadequacy, and grasping her shoulders in a grip tight enough to control an ox, he pulled her toward him and kissed her, thrusting his tongue into her mouth so violently that her teeth were forced apart, and dragging her body against him so that her skin was abraded against the buttons on his shirt.

She writhed and pulled back, but he ignored that, feeling his desire increasing with every effort she made to repel him, and he opened his knees wide—in part for his own comfort—and then clamped them on each side of her narrow body to hold her firm, and, his hands thus released, reached for her breasts, to clutch at them with iron-hard fingers while he tried to kiss her again.

And then she retched, heaving under his hands horribly, her throat contracting and the muscles of her belly tightening so convulsively that he could not help feeling it, and he let her go at once, almost terrified at so intense a response, and leaned back again. She remained crouched on the floor at his feet, her face livid and her eyes watering as she made feeble gestures toward her ripped robe, trying to cover her hunched shoulders.

"You—you . . ." She tried to say more, but retched again, turning her head away from him and wiping one shaking hand across her mouth, and shook her head, and he jumped up to move about the room, throwing his arms about with the same violence he had directed toward her, flailing with impotent rage at the air about him.

"What sort of woman are you?—what sort of hell-born bitch that behaves so? What have ever I done to you that you should treat me so? Why, *why* should I so—so sicken you that the merest of kisses should—"

"Kisses! You call that kissing?—that attack, that— You are evil, evil, *evil*, you hear me? If I had come to you an untaught girl who knew no better, you could have made me do the things you want—aye, even the most hateful of them!" She was still crouching on the floor, holding her torn robe about her shoulders, upon which the bruises were already beginning to appear. "You could have used me thus and told me it was the sort of kiss an honorable man bestows upon his wife, and I, poor wretch, would have known no better! But I was not so—no, I was *not*! I was wed to a man who knew how to behave like a man, and not an animal of the filthiest of farmyards—a man who used me as every man must perforce use his wife, but with a—with decency and due gratitude for my forbearance. But you—you treat me like some drab of the streets, and then expect me to— Faugh, man, you sicken me, you hear? You sicken me to death!"

"I could have today. I know I could have." He was standing still now, his hands hanging limp at his sides as he stared at her with a maudlin lugubriousness that sat ill upon his stocky frame. "I could have been as others today. I knew it. I was—I felt it in me; I would have needed no more than your willing wifely duty, no more, to have got a child upon you. And you have—you— It was no more than a kiss, I tell you, a kiss! What is in a kiss to make you heave in my face in such a fashion?" He sounded almost pitiful, his voice shaking a little, but she shook her head, moving awkwardly until she was on her feet again, and holding her robe clutched at her breast with one hand, rested the other upon the head of the chaise longue for support.

"So you say—so you say!" She jeered it, her eyes very bright in her pale face, though now there was on one cheek a patchy red flush where his roughness had scraped her skin. "You get a child upon me, as other men do upon their wives? Not you, not you! Not as long as there is a God in Heaven will you do so! Because I will not, I cannot, nor ever could do the unspeakable things you need before you can behave as a man and not an ape! And so it is, sir! You can never have a son—you hear me? You are not fit nor able to become a father! The best you can do is pull a wretched beggar's brat from the gutters you sprang from yourself and call him your son! Well, make the best of him, for I tell you, no other son shall *you* ever have!"

His face was now as white as hers as he stood and stared at her, and his voice when it came was shaking with controlled rage.

"Shall I not, ma'am? Shall I not? Oh, but you take too much upon yourself to make so wild a promise, and so I tell you! Think you I have never yet gotten a child? Suppose I tell you, you bloodless, gutless, useless bitch, I have got children beyond counting upon any number of Seven Dials whores, every one of them a woman worth ten of you with your dried-out bones and ungiving soul! Got children— I have got children that would turn the knife in any who saw them, children with hearts and heads and limbs that shame those useless sticks of creatures you and your precious friends are so proud of!"

"Your ranting jealousy will gain you nothing," she sneered with a fine, disdainful ice. "Oh, I know how it galls you when we are in company and people comment on Dorothea and her well-turned manners and her charm and beauty and her accomplishments! I know how you ache that she should be yours! But she is not yours—she is mine, mine and my dear dead Daniel's child! He could be a husband and father— he was a *real* man! But you? All you can give me as a son is a dirty gutter brat who—"

"Well, guard him good, ma'am, guard him good, for though he may be no child of yours, he may well be mine! Had you thought of that, in all your fine posturings, ma'am? You use the boy, and happy enough you are to do it, to show your fine ladies what a charitable, angelic creature you are— mighty glad to have him for such a purpose! Oh, I have heard you and watched you, sitting with your fan before your simpering face while all those old biddies tell you how good and virtuous and God-loving you are! Well, consider, ma'am, that this child might be the child *you* could have had, were you what a woman should be, and meekly desirous of her husband's pleasure! But he is not, is he? He is the child of a whore, and you in your virtue have the rearing of him! Oh, it's a ripe joke, is it not?"

He lifted his chin and produced a heavy, raucous laugh with not an atom of true humor in it. "Oh, a ripe joke! My gutter boy, and you with no way to know whether he's my blood or not—and can't send him away, for fear of what your fine old biddies will say of you behind your back! A fine joke!" He moved then, thrusting across the room to the door to stand with one hand upon the knob as he stared at her with a huge malevolence.

"Aye, ma'am, think on it! There's the boy, and you shall never know, shall you? He is as bright and knowing as I am, is he not? As strong and healthy, is he not? As your precious Dorothea with her drooping ways and scrawny limbs is clearly yours, so well may the boy be as clearly mine! You shall never know, shall you, ma'am? You shall sit there beside him in the schoolroom and try to teach him—and he is so much quicker at his books than you or your Dorothea that he must scorn your teaching!—but you shall sit there and teach him, and seek for the truth about him, and you cannot know! Oh, a ripe joke!"

And he opened the door and went out, slamming it viciously behind him, and she stood there in the firelight, leaning on her delicate chaise longue, staring at the door and trying to absorb what it was he had actually said.

· FOURTEEN ·

"LIKE this, Abel? Is that the way? Do observe, you silly boy; don't just sit there grinning like a great ape, but observe! Now, I shall try again, and you shall tell me if I have it right!"

To Abel, sitting cross-legged on her bed with his back resting against the whitewashed wall, she was sheer enchantment as she paraded about her tiny room. His eyes followed her faithfully as she moved, watching the way her limbs flowed beneath the folds of the silk gown, the nodding of the plumes of the bonnet that was tied beneath her chin, delighting in the flick of her wrists as she tossed the shawl across her shoulders and turned again to stand with one small foot thrust forward to peep saucily from beneath her gown, her thin chest pushed forward in pigeon fashion in a perfect imitation of the posture of the ladies of fashion who thronged Oxford Street each morning and paraded in the politer purlieus of Hyde Park each afternoon.

"Exactly so!" he cried, and she stood there flushed with self-satisfaction and beaming upon him. "Exactly so! You're the outside of enough, Lil, in truth you are! How can you do it so exact? I shall never understand it!"

"I told you, I've as good an ear as any on the chanting lay—and as good an eye as any screever! Only I don't try to write down such matters, but choose to do them! Is it truly so? Is that how your Dorothea does it?"

"She's not my Dorothea!" Abel said almost wearily. "How often must I say that to you? No, it is not as she does it—"

Her face immediately darkened to a scowl. "But you said—"

"—because she moves very ill. Like a drunken hen." And he slid to the ground to go mincing about the table with a very crude imitation of Dorothea's awkward attempts to walk in a modish manner. Even as he did it, he felt a twinge of shame. He knew he was being cruelly unjust in his imitation of Dorothea, but he would do much to please Lil. Dorothea could be awkward, even gawky sometimes, but she was not so foolish as he made her out to be, nor yet so plain. But he felt instinctively that to please Lil he must make it clear that Dorothea was no rival, could never be as pretty, as enchanting, as clever as Lil herself. And since this was to his eyes quite true, he was able to swallow his shame at his dis-loyalty to the affectionate if sometimes tedious Dorothea, especially when Lil crowed her approval, and slid round the room to hug him warmly, and smack a great wet kiss upon his cheek. At this he blushed furiously and muttered, "Stow your nonsense, you stupid great gull!"—which protestation deceived neither of them as they sat down again on the bed side by side and inevitably as close as a pair of puppies in a basket, for the bed was a very small one.

Sitting here with her weight heavy upon his arm, and able to smell the faint hint of apples on her breath (for they had gorged themselves on several pounds of fruit he had stolen for her that evening), Abel did not feel as comfortable as a puppy. This girl disturbed him, very deeply, and he was curiously angered at the effect she had on him, for he could do nothing about it. In the few short weeks he had known her he had become her unwilling slave, and knowing that she was aware of the control she had over him and took it as no more than her due did not help his self-esteem one whit.

He would come to see her as much as three nights in the week, if she would let him, and was much put about when she said in her insouciant, uncaring fashion, as she sometimes did, "You shall not find me to home if you come before next

Friday se'ennight, Abel, so save your breath to cool your porridge!" and then refused to tell him why, adjuring him sharply to "hold your tongue and mind your own affairs, if you please!" And he would stay within doors for the next week, fuming and glowering with damped-down temper, counting the days till he could see her again.

He had, just once, gone out on such a night, knowing he would not find her if he wanted her, to wander his streets as he had used to do, hoping to find some of his old satisfactions in such a jaunt, but it had been a miserable experience. He had done a little desultory stealing, but that had given him no pleasure, for without Lil to produce her crow of approval at the booty he brought to her there could be no satisfaction in the exploit.

It had been Dorothea who had suffered most because of his ill temper. She had taken to creeping away to the schoolroom whenever she could in the afternoon, to sit with him behind the door ("In case Mama comes in, Abel. If she does, then you shall run across the room to draw her attention, so that I can escape to the drawing room again, and she none the wiser!") and to coax him to talk of his past, while she warmed her loneliness with the comfort of his presence.

She suffered because he became so very strange in his ways. The careful politeness of their first meeting had soon given way to bouts of ill-disguised scorn of her "silly missish ways" which were sometimes reinforced by loud and frank statements of his disapproval of her. She had tried very hard to be as he wished her to be—which was impossible, for how could she show the dazzle of Lil, so totally unknown to her? But still she tried, wanting only to please Abel, to coax him out of his sulks and miseries, aching to make him begin to love her as much as she knew she now adored him.

She had been almost in despair, so surly had he become, when he seemed to her bedazzled eyes to undergo a complete change. From being sour and unapproachable, he suddenly showed a vast interest in her ways, asking of her how she did at the dull morning visits she made with her mama, and how she comported herself at the few other social engagements upon which she accompanied her elders, and displaying a remarkable taste for discussion of her clothes, all with a desire for a wealth of detail that quite turned her head with delight.

Dorothea, welcoming with pathetic gratitude Abel's new attentions, was happy in her ignorance of Lil's existence. Lil herself had at last explained to Abel, a little unwillingly but yielding to his demands for information (especially since he strengthened them with a flat refusal to do aught she asked until he was told why), that she had no notion of ending her days where she had started them.

"I've got class, Abel!" she said to him, sitting crouched beside her minuscule fire and staring hypnotized at its flames. "So my mam told me before she died, and so I believe. And I have such ideas and wishes, Abel, you'll never know of! I shall be a lady, Abel, a true Quality lady, and then everyone shall know of me, and talk of me, and . . ."

He had been ill advised enough to laugh at that, and she had turned on him, blazing. "You think I shall not? Then you are a gull, a muck snipe, a stupid great flat! For I shall do it, and if you would be my friend in the days that I shall be the desire of Lords and Ladies as a friend, then you will help me now, and not laugh! Do you hear me, you great lummox? Do you dare to laugh at me?"

"No, I was not laughing at your wishes for a great life, Lil," he said, sobered by her tirade. "Indeed I was not, for I have such wishes too, sometimes, and I know how strong they are when they come upon me. I was laughing only because you said it so—oh, I don't know precisely. So romantic and foolish, you know."

"Romantic is not foolish!"

"It may be sometimes," he said shrewdly, "and if you don't want to be taken for a Bartholomew baby, then you'll tell none but me of your desires, for there are those that would scorn you and make much mockery of you for it."

She nodded slowly at that, keeping her eyes fixed on his face. "Have you learned that from Charlotte, together with your books? Did she teach you this about romantic ideas and foolish desires?"

He grinned sourly at that. "Nay, she tells me naught of that! I am there to have my head stuffed with the Bible and to be taught reading and ciphering that I might one day work in Jesse's countinghouse! She tells me none of the ways of polite society! But she tells Dorothea, who suffers much at her mother's hands, and I hear, you know, and understand. Charlotte says that swooning missish ways are not genteel, and to be romantic and read three-volume novels is to make a mockery of oneself in the Polite World, and that such matters are not for the true *Haut Monde*."

"What is that?" She spoke with great eagerness, putting a hand on his arm.

"I don't really know. The Polite World, I believe. She is always speaking of the *ton* and the Polite World, is Charlotte, and making Dorothea speak well, and me also, for she says a well-spoken clerk is always a better reflection on his master, and I am to remember the gratitude that is due to my benefactors, and their great condescension in caring about me, and to mind my manners and mend my ways as they bid." And his nostrils curled into a sneer.

"What else does she tell Dorothea about her behavior and her speech? And am I talking right, Abel? As you do? For I listen with great care, you know, and use as many of the words as I may that you do."

He had looked at her curiously, his forehead creased a little. "Do I talk so strange, then? I had not noticed it."

"Had not noticed it!" she echoed, with another of her uncannily accurate imitations, and he smiled shamefacedly at the clear, round vowels and uncluttered consonants she produced.

"I don' always talk the swell lingo," he growled, "and can talk the family's way any time as I chooses, and there's all about it!"

"I know," she cried impatiently, "but it is better that you do! Better for you and best for me, since I must learn of you if I am to be as a lady born! So will you tell me all that Dorothea does, and of her clothes and her ways, and all of it? And perhaps bring me her unwanted clothes and bonnets? You can get such for me without her knowledge, of that I'm sure! Will you, Abel? To help me? And I shall help you all I can, in my own ways, *dear* Abel, however they shall be!"

And of course he had agreed, bewitched by her as he was, and Dorothea had reaped the benefit (if lost some garments, to Kate's puzzlement) in his renewed interest in conversation with her, and gone happily to her bed on many a night to plan a golden future with dear Abel at her side, while he shinned over the roof and away down the house to speed through the streets with his budget of new information and new finery for his Lil.

Tonight, as they sat in companionable silence upon her bed and stared into the fire, he tentatively explored the feelings within him. His new habit of introspection had had little play since his first meeting with this girl, who had come to take so important a part in his life, but it was still there, and he let his thoughts dip down into his mind to see what they should find.

What they found startled him not a little, for he discovered that, for the first time in all his life that he could remember, the idea of love came to him. He could not put a name to it, but when he looked down at the dark, curly head that was resting on his chest just below his chin, he felt it again, that wave of protectiveness and need and amused pleasure and sharingness. Sitting here, in this narrow little basement by a fire of a few scraps of sticks, he felt complete, a whole person at ease with the world; when he was away from her, it was as though there were a gap in his covering, a sort of blank area all down one side of his body into which the wind would whistle and the cold air could stretch cruel fingers. All he heard and saw and thought when they were apart was for the times when they could be together, when he could pour out into her receptive ear all that he had gleaned for her since their last meeting.

He did not consciously know it, and indeed might never know it fully, but it was at this time, on a bitter-cold November night, sitting beside a half-dead fire in a London slum basement, that he knew himself to be in love. He did not in truth know of love at all; how could he, this eleven-year-old piece of human wastage, who had been spawned and born in a gutter to grow up in the obscenity of total poverty?—how could he know what love was, let alone know that he felt it? But there it was; that night he was aware at some point deep within himself that he loved his Lil with an enormous, if closely controlled, fierceness. And his arm tightened across her shoulders, making her move her head to peer up at him questioningly, and he looked down at her and was about to speak. But was prevented.

The curtain had moved in the darkness with such slowness and stealth that not until he was standing looming over them did they realize he was there: a tall and heavy man with a huge head that was covered in startlingly incongruous wiry yellow curls, and a face that looked as though it bore a perpetual smile, but that was in fact very sour, since it was twisted by an ugly scar that ran from the corner of one eye to the lobe of his ear, giving him what passed at first glance for a quirk of amusement, but was belied by the chilly regard in his eyes.

"Well, there's a pretty sight, and no error!" he said, and his voice was incongruous too, for instead of the deep and resonant sound that should surely have come from so deep a barrel chest, he produced a shrill and mocking piping note that sounded quite remarkably frightening in the startled Abel's ears. "And 'oo might our pretty Lil be achattin' to in so friendly a fashion, if I may make so bold as to ask?"

She had at first shrunk closer to Abel, and he had reacted by holding her even more tightly, but now she pulled away from him and said cooly, "'Tis none o' yer affair; git aht of it"—and Abel looked at her sharply, noticing how swiftly her voice had returned to its old nasal Cockney note, but he could hear the underlying fear in her voice and looked up at the big man with his eyes narrowed, assessing his weak points and strong points in case it should come to an argument.

But the big man with the shrill little voice moved away, to set his great haunches upon the wooden table and to stare at Abel with a considering and decidedly chilly look in his eyes that made the boy feel really alarmed for the first time.

"None o' my affair, ain't it? 'Ow can you say that to yer old friend, Lil, now, I asks yer?" the big man said reproachfully, still staring at Abel, and he pulled from his pocket a piece of twisted blackened rope—or so it looked to Abel—and bit a piece from it with a twist of his strong jaws that almost made the boy wince.

"Don' stare so, boy! Ain't yer never seen a chaw o' 'bacca afore? No, I daresays as you 'aven't, not bein', as you might say, one of the travelin' fraternity, nor yet ever served yer time at sea, like what I did. No." He chewed reflectively for a moment, and then turned his head and spat copiously at the floor. "No, the likes o' you wouldn't know o' such things. Not Quality like what you is, eh?"

Lil sat up sharply, and said in a very breathy voice, "You lay orf 'im, Fitch, you 'ear me? 'E ain't nothin' to do wi' you, not no'ow! 'E's my pal, that's what, and you got no call to—"

"You shut yer face, girlie. No, little sparrer, don't you curl your bunch o' fives at me! There ain't the fist of a boy alive as could tap my claret, so don't think it!" Abel saw the man's hand slide to his pocket, and knowing almost as surely as though he could see it that there was a knife there, he let his fists uncurl and relaxed his shoulders, but still remained totally alert, every muscle ready to make a leap off the bed and throw himself at the man's throat at whatever risk to himself should he make any attempt to touch Lil. But she at his side, though tense, seemed unafraid now and said again, "Lay orf, Fitch! You don't need the likes of 'im, any more'n you needs anyone. Just you leave 'im be."

"I ain't 'ere to spoil your lay, my little pigeon!" the man said, and Abel knew somehow that the man genuinely meant no harm to Lil and was interested only in himself, and relaxed even more. "No, my little love, o' course I won't queer your pitch! Only I bin watchin' and listenin' and waitin', not knowin' as when it might come in 'andy to know one o' the Quality like your friend 'ere, and now, well there you are, my dear! I didn't waste my time, on account the time is 'ere and now, and I 'as need of your friend's services, like! Barliman got took up on a larceny charge—the which I promises you they'll not get to stick on 'im—and French John is out of these parts on a game of 'is own, and me, well I got an order to carry out, see? I needs some 'elp, and this lad'll do nicely—nicely! And I'm sure 'e'll be only too 'appy to give me this little bit of assistance like, in exchange for which I don't tell no one of anythin' I knows—not 'ere, not in the Dials, nor yet the Bermudas, nor even Gower Street!"

"What sort of 'elp?" Lil said sharply, and the man turned his head in the firelight and grinned at her—a wide and yet

sinister smile, for half his teeth were missing, leaving yawn-
ing black gaps in his mouth.

"What sort? There's a daft question from a smart little
pigeon! Di'n't I tell you? I got an order to carry out, for
Great Windmill Street, see? And I needs some 'elp. Now.
Tonight."

He turned his head back to stare at Abel with a smile on
his face, but an underlying threat there all the same.

"Well, my fancy Quality lad? Does you 'elp me as a friend
should be 'elped, or does I go visitin' in Gower Street come
mornin'?"

· FIFTEEN ·

THEY moved in a silent procession along the narrow alleys that flanked Old Compton Street, Lil leading the way, her shoulders and head hunched under a dark woolen shawl, with Abel close behind her and Fitch a couple of yards behind them, his great shadow seeming to lie on Abel's shoulders with all the weight of a physical hand.

As they moved deeper into the darkness, bearing steadily east, Abel whispered forcefully into Lil's ear, "Where we going? What is't we're to do? How can I help with whatever it is if I don't know what to—"

"Will you be quiet!" she whispered back at him, drooping her head even farther forward and hurrying a little faster. "You'll find out soon enough."

"Hist, there!" Fitch whispered too, and even his whisper had the same shrill quality as his voice. "I've no mind to be taken up for the sake of a pair o' squallin' brats! Hist, now, you hear me?" And he came closer to them with a couple of long strides, and poked a hard forefinger into Abel's back with a sharp cruelty that made him wince. But he bit his tongue and held his peace. Never one to waste his efforts where they could do no good, Abel had no intention of attempting to take on Fitch. Not yet, anyway. Not till he knew what it was he was about, and what his part in the man's activities was to be.

They reached the end of the alley, and ahead of them lay the broader thoroughfare that was Crown Street. Ill lit by a few cookshop and roast-pork sellers' windows though it was, still it was a good deal brighter than the narrow ways through which they had come, and also a good deal more populous, and Lil stopped at the end of the alley and looked questioningly back over her shoulder at Fitch. He immediately moved forward, brushing Abel roughly aside and shoving into his hands the heavy sack he had been carrying in one of his great meaty fists, though Abel needed both hands just to take it from him.

"Carry that!" Fitch muttered. "Like it was nothin' much. Under yer arm, if so be you're too feeble to 'old it in yer 'and like a man! An' follow close, or it'll be the worse for you when I gets to Gower Street in the mornin' and tells what I 'as to tell."

Even as he was speaking, he picked up Lil as though she were no more than a rag doll, and immediately Abel moved forward, his free hand curling into a fist, his face tightening with rage and fear.

"What are you doin', you great—"

"Abel, will you be quiet!" Lil raised her head from Fitch's shoulder. "He does me no harm, you fool! I'd not be here if it were to be any harm to me, so do as you're bid and be silent! You'll see soon enough!"

She dropped her head back on the young tree trunk that was Fitch's shoulder and gave herself a sort of wriggle, reaching up to pull the shawl across her face. And then sagged, letting her head fall helplessly into the dark and musty folds, and her legs droop heavily against Fitch's chest.

Abel blinked and stared and felt a sudden sick surge of fear rise in him. It was as though time had slipped sideways somehow; he was small, very small, and playing in the dirt on the floor, and a man had come and picked her up from her place in the corner, and she had lain there on his back, and as he took her out he banged her head at the doorpost, but she had said nothing, just lay there on the man's back. . . .

"Right, Lil?" Fitch's whisper came out of the air above him, bringing him back hard to the present moment, and even as he was about to reach up to pull his Lil to safety he heard her replying hiss of assent, and stopped, half bewildered, half resentful.

"Right, you. Follow close, walk sorrowful, and do all as I does or you'll be the sorrier, and don' you forget it. Come on."

And Fitch moved into the traffic of Crown Street, and Abel followed, the sacking-wrapped whatever-it-was lumpy beneath his arm. For a few moments no one seemed to notice their heavy progress, until they had almost reached the far side, and then a man who had been hurrying along with his head down and moving so fast that he nearly bumped into Fitch stopped, saw the load on his back, and stepped hurriedly backward, pulling his battered old hat from his head and muttering something.

Fitch nodded lugubriously at the man and plodded heavily on, and Abel, still following, saw the man mutter again and make a sketchy sign of the cross against his dirty old coat before hurrying on his way.

They reached the shadows of the alleys on the far side, and immediately Lil slid to the ground and moved back into her original position leading the way, and again Abel followed her, with Fitch close behind him, though he made no attempt to take back the heavy package, content to leave that in Abel's care.

For a while Abel padded on in silence, moving as stealthily as ever he had in his old pickpocketing days; but then he could contain himself no longer.

"Why, Lil?" He whispered it so softly, his head so close to hers, that it could not have reached Fitch's ears behind him. "We've done nothing yet! Why that fancy business in Crown Street? Why've we got to be so silent now?"

She turned her head in the darkness, so that he could see the glint of her eyes as she looked back at Fitch, but he still didn't appear to hear them, and after a moment she whispered back, so softly that Abel had to strain to hear her. "Be careful there an' back, Fitch says; no one sees you goin', they can't say you was there. Carry me over Crown Street goin', and there's always the chance as you can confuse 'em when you comes back. So Fitch says. He likes to do all properly. So do as he bids."

"But where are we *going*?" Abel whispered, almost despairingly.

"St. Giles's." Lil moved a little faster then, pulling away from him, and shook her head furiously when he tried to whisper again, and he gave up, recognizing defeat when he saw it.

And then, quite suddenly, they stopped. Ahead of them was darkness, and openness—he could feel that in the air on his face, knew that there were no looming buildings thrusting their weight into the space above and before him, and then he almost jumped as Fitch reached forward and pulled the heavy parcel from under his arm.

"Right, we're goin' in. Not a sound, boy, you hear me? Or I tears your gizzard out of you and makes *you* into a job. Now, over you goes."

Hard hands about him, a sick lurching sensation as he was heaved into the air and thrust forward, and then he was falling, to land heavily on hands and knees on damp earth. He stayed there for a moment, winded by the suddenness of it, and then there was a soft thump and Lil was on the ground beside him; he could smell the wool of that shawl and the heavy scent of her hair. A faint creaking sound and another thump, and he knew Fitch was beside him too. He reached forward with one tentative hand and felt the rough coldness of iron railings, and knew they were inside St. Giles's churchyard. And shivered suddenly, for stoic though he was, he had the normal superstitious fear of the dead and their environs, and had more sense than to go meddling in churchyards in the middle of the night.

"Lil!" he whispered urgently, and then caught his breath as Fitch's hard hand caught him a sharp blow on the side of his head.

"Be silent!" Fitch muttered. "I'll not tell you again!"

Roughly he pulled the boy to his feet and half pulled and half led him forward into the darkness, Lil trotting silently beside them, round lurching gravestones against which Abel's legs scraped cruelly once or twice, forcing him to be more alert, so that he peered forward trying to accustom his eyes to the blackness, straining to see.

They moved closer to the building, and Abel put up one

hand to feel the comfort of the rough stone, knowing it to be the church. The words of the Lord's Prayer, so carefully instilled into him by Charlotte, rose bubbling into his mind, and he heard himself repeating it inside his head, over and over. "Our Father which art in heaven, our Father which art in heaven, our Father which art . . ."

Then they were round the corner of the building, and ahead of him there was a faint glimmer of light that outlined the gravestones with a soft mistiness, and he stopped short, shrinking closer to the comfort of the church wall. Lil moved in to the wall too and came closer beside him, and the warmth of her filled him and made him feel suddenly better, and he put out his free hand and touched her and she came even nearer, patting him comfortingly.

Fitch put a heavy hand on Abel's shoulder and squeezed warningly, and then put the parcel delicately and silently on the ground at his feet before starting to move forward very slowly. The two children stood there in the shadow of the wall and watched in total silence.

It seemed a long time before they heard it: a soft thump, so soft it was almost like a sigh; and Lil tensed for a moment or two, and then relaxed and put her chin on Abel's shoulder and giggled softly.

"There! That's *that* over and done with!" she said, no longer whispering quite so softly.

"*What* is?" Abel begged. "Will no one tell me what this is about? I'm as lost as—"

"Have you not heard of the resurrection men, you great gull?" She sounded truly amused. "I thought sure you'd have known by now what it is we're about."

"Resurrection men? I don't think— No, I've heard naught." But somewhere at the back of his mind there was knowledge, a memory of mysterious nods and becks made by some people he had known in the Dials in the old days who had made a good living, but not on any of the lays he understood.

"You'd best tell me," he said roughly.

"There's some as will pay good money for new corpses. They gets all those as is topped, of course—you knows that much . . ."

He nodded, feeling a sick cold surge rise in him again. Yes, he knew what happened to the bodies of those the gallows spoke for. Taken away in carts and delivered to the surgeons to do unspeakable things with . . . He shivered involuntarily and rather painfully.

"Well, that ain't enough for 'em, so they pays for others, all they can get and no questions asked. Fitch and French John and Barliman 've been resurrection men these ten years and more—diggin' up newly buried corpses and takin' 'em to the surgeons."

"And you *help* them?" He peered at her in the darkness. "Is that why you gets your keep for—"

"Oh, why not, Abel? Don't be so missish! What's it to me? 'Tis all dead meat, after all, and if there are those that'll pay for it, why, then, I see no harm in it." But she turned her head away from him as she spoke, so that he could no longer see the glint of her eyes in the dimness.

After a moment he whispered, "Where is he now?" and stood peering forward into the misty dimness.

"There's some pay the sexton a mite to keep watch over the place until such time as a gravestone can be set to hold 'em in. He's gone to deal with that. He'll be back presently, and then we must set about the real work."

He swallowed, feeling his mouth drying suddenly. "Real work? What . . . ?"

And then Fitch was back, incredibly silent for all his great bulk, and Abel looked up at the looming figure above him, trying to see his face, and shrank fearfully inside himself as one part of his mind told him what was to come next and another tried to deny it.

"Right, now, me young limb!" Fitch sounded almost jovial. "No need to be so silent as the grave as we was, on account of this place is a' full of graves and none to come near nor nigh, not now I've tucked up that little one back there!" And he jerked his head back over his shoulder and produced a shrill, breathy little giggle in the back of his throat that made the fear that already filled Abel's chest thicken so that it almost stopped his breathing.

"Did you do for 'im?" Lil asked interestedly.

"You knows better nor that!" Fitch said, kneeling on the

ground now and untying the rough string that held his sacking parcel together. "I don't go for any toppin' jobs, not Fitch! Got my wits about me, I 'as! Leaves it to 'Eaven to do the toppin' for me, and then sets about making a honest livin' out of the leavin's." And again he produced that curdling high giggle. " 'Twas no more'n an oldish man—I'll 'ave 'im in Windmill Street before the year's out, natural-like, from the cut of his jib! 'E'll sleep the night cold on a gravestone there, and wake a sorrier man in the morning—and we'll 'ave been long gone. Right, young Quality lad! Now's the time for some work from you! Take 'old o' that."

A heavy iron shovel was thrust into Abel's hand, and then Fitch was leading the way across the wet grass to the glimmer of light at the far side, and Lil came alongside him, carrying under her shawl some of the things Fitch had taken from his parcel.

"Don't go gettin' any notions as this'll be easy, now," Fitch muttered, "on account it won't be. The grave was filled this very afternoon, but it's been a wet time this past week or so, and the earth'll be as 'eavy as a first mate's rope end. So set to with all the might you got, boy, for I don't want to be 'ere above an hour or two, and so I tells yer!"

They reached the glimmer of light: a dark lantern with only one slide open, set on the ground beside a heap of newly turned earth. Abel looked at the piled mound, at the few flowers set upon it, and swallowed hard, turning his head away. Which brought more of the churchyard into his line of vision. He saw lying huddled on a heavy moss-grown slab a few yards away the figure of a man in a sober black suit of clothes, breathing stertorously, with his eyes rolled back in his head to show a rim of white beneath. On his head, an ugly gash was oozing redly onto his sparse graying hair, and for a moment Abel wanted to go to him, to move him so that he looked less uncomfortable.

But Fitch again gave him one of those cruel thrusts with a forefinger as sharp and hard as an iron poker, and obediently he turned his attention back to the matter in hand.

The next hour was misery. At first the work hadn't been too hard; he had thrust in the shovel, hauled out a load of earth, dumped it to one side, with mechanical ease. It had been his mind that had felt the strain as he imagined with all too much realism what they would find when the earth had all been moved. He had imagined his shovel hitting against something solid, or worse still, something yielding, and wanted to drop it and run yelling away into the mist. But Fitch was there facing him, digging with a controlled ferocity that made it clear he was full of strength and speed and that no attempt to get away from him would be likely to succeed. And even if he could run away successfully, where would be the point? The man knew where Jesse's house was, and would, Abel had not the least doubt, keep his word about visiting there with his tale if he were crossed in any way.

And then the shovel grew heavier, and his hands shrieked pain as more and more skin was rubbed off them with each lift of the great clods of wet earth, and his shoulders, his back, his legs, every muscle in him cried their protest at the effort demanded of them. The sweat poured off his forehead, getting in his eyes and dripping off the end of his nose, to mingle the smell of salt and his own skin with the heavy reek of wet earth and rotting vegetation.

Lil sat perched on a gravestone to one side, watching them, and after a while she slid to her feet and came across to wipe Abel's face with a corner of her shawl.

"You'll do well to let him rest, Fitch," she said calmly, "for if you don't, he'll be in no shape to complete the job, and that's all about it."

Fitch looked up and peered at him, grunted unwillingly, and then returned to work himself, and gratefully, Abel dropped the shovel and stretched his back, grimacing at the pain of it. Lil grinned at him and patted his hand, and then reached into the fastness of the pocket in her skirt to bring out a small bottle. He took it from her gladly enough and took a great gulp from it, which made him cough and splutter, but it warmed him through and through, for it was a raw brandy that seared his gullet comfortingly. Fitch too took some, and then with a jerk of his head at Abel, both returned to work.

Abel went on with a dogged determination, mindless now, for he could think no farther ahead than the next shovelful and then the next. It was as though he had spent his entire life digging, and would not stop until he dropped dead.

And then, it happened, bringing him back to the reality of

what they were doing with a sick jerk. It was Fitch's shovel that grated on the coffin lid, and Abel, terrified, dropped his own and clambered up the sides of the hole in which they were now standing as though the very devil were about to creep out and catch him. Fitch laughed thickly, and reached out to pull him back.

"Scared of the ghosties, little gentleman, are you, then? Think they'll catch you by your tail and wave you over their heads? Come back 'ere, you lazy 'ound—there's more to be done yet."

They scraped away at the earth, each thrust of the shovels making its hateful sound against the wood of the coffin, until the whole of it was uncovered, and Abel was standing on the bare wood while Fitch was straddling it, his huge feet set in small holes he had deliberately made to accommodate them.

"Right, now," Fitch muttered, and raised his head. Lil was standing at the edge of the grave peering down at them, and at a nod from Fitch reached out to take their shovels from them and then handed down a jemmy and an iron bar.

Fitch tossed the iron bar to Abel and took the jemmy himself, and grunting a little with the effort, worked its thin edge under the lid of the coffin at his end. It creaked a little as it moved, and again Abel began to shiver with his barely controlled fear and scrabbled backward to stand behind the coffin rather than on it. But Fitch did not notice, and shoved the jemmy into his hand, taking the heavier iron bar, and indicated with a lift of his chin that Abel should do the same at his end of the coffin while he levered away with the bar.

It took them the best part of ten minutes to finally free the lid, for it had been nailed down with great care, but at last Fitch straightened his back and wiped his face on his sleeve and nodded up at Lil, still staring down at them from the grave edge.

She disappeared for a moment, then came back to drop down a large sack, which Fitch caught and draped across one shoulder. And then he bent and seized the lid at his end.

"Come on, boy—take yer share o' the weight! Lift it, you 'ear me? Lift it, and slide it to one side, like—see? *That's* it—we needs all the space we can get."

Together they raised the lid, Abel trying to keep his eyes

averted, and slid it down beside the coffin. And after a moment Abel made himself look down, and felt a great lift of relief. All that could be seen was a white shroud, glimmering softly in the faint light, and he breathed again. It wasn't going to be so bad after all. . . .

"Right. We'll start down this end," Fitch said, and leaning down, he began to pull at the cotton shroud, and Abel heard the faint sound of rustling, and could not for a moment see what Fitch was doing. But then, after a moment, he could, and cried out, almost yelping it, "What are you *doing*? Why are you—"

"You've got to strip 'em." Lil's voice came calmly from above, and he looked up wildly. "Don't look like that, Abel! I told you, it makes no difference to anyone! It's all dead meat, and not important to them!"

"Why? Can't you just take 'em out, all covered up decent, and put 'em in the sack and bear 'em away?" He knew his voice was rising and could not prevent it.

"Shut yer face, you young varmint!" Fitch said sharply, and leaned over and slapped him ringingly. "You want to call the Watch out, damn you? Bite your tongue, you hear me? We strips 'em and takes 'em mother-naked, on account it's a toppin' matter if you takes coffin or shroud, but only a few days in the nick if they gets you with a deader. So get on with it."

Shrinkingly, Abel obeyed, helping Fitch manhandle the weight of the corpse from side to side as they stripped the cheap shroud from it. And then they'd finished, to stand looking down at the white naked body lying awkwardly in the narrow box.

"Well, there's a bit of beautiful luck, and no error!" Fitch crowed softly. " 'Ere, young Lil, get a butcher's at this! You'll get a basinful of best butter out o' this one, and there's Fitch's word on it! If she wasn't right at 'er time and died of it, then I'm as dead as what she is! Worth twice as much, she is, twice as much!"

Abel stood there looking down at the body before him. He could see it more clearly now, for Lil had brought the dark lantern nearer and was holding it over the edge of the grave. She was lying with her head at his end, and he saw her face upside down. A young face, very white, with some bluish markings on it, looking like faint bruises. The mouth lax, showing small yellowish teeth. And below that the sweep of small globular breasts before the great curving swell of the belly. Even in this light it looked tensely taut, the skin glistening whitely with silvery streaks of stretch marks running away down the sides, and surmounted by the small bump which was the navel, turned inside out by the weight of the burden behind it.

It was extraordinary, the effect this unknown young woman had on him. He stood and stared at her, at the way her narrow white hands flopped helplessly against the wood of the coffin, and felt tears prick his eyelids and fill his nostrils. In all his memory he had cried only for pain inflicted upon himself, and to feel this surge of grief for a totally unknown person who should be frightening him rather than filling him with such unfamiliar sensations was extraordinarily strange.

He blinked and stared at her and blinked again, and said gruffly, "I thought it would be worse than this."

"You see? I told you!" Lil said in a triumphant whisper. " 'Tis only so much dead meat, no worse'n a piece of mutton!"

"Not mutton," he said, still staring at the swollen belly, trying to see the infant curled up inside it, trying to see it as dead as its dead girl of a mother. "Not mutton. People."

"Well, 'tis dead, anyway, and not to be feared, that much is sure."

"Come on and about your business now! And handle it carefully! Wilson pays less for damaged goods than perfect, and this'n's worth a mint. Come on—away, now."

Abel helped Fitch put the girl's body into the sack, and then helped lift it to the edge of the grave in quite a different mood from the one that had gripped him the whole night hitherto. His fear was quite gone. The sick feeling of trembling that had filled his belly from the moment he had realized what the night's business was to be was no longer there.

He wondered briefly whether it was sheer tiredness that made him so stoical now, but he knew this was not all of it. There was something new in his feelings now: an intense curiosity. He very much wanted to know what was to happen to this sacking-covered helpless corpse he had helped to resurrect. It was very important to him to know *why* someone would pay for her, would pay more because she had so obviously died in childbed.

And above all, what they would do with her once they had bought her.

· SIXTEEN ·

THE WORST part of the return journey was navigating the iron railings that enclosed the churchyard. They had scrubbed the mud from themselves as best they could, cleaning up with the wet rags Fitch had packed in his holdall of a sacking parcel. They had repacked the tools and loaded the lot onto Lil's back, for there was no one else to carry them, and then with great effort had together manhandled the sagging sackful of corpse to the edge of the railings.

Abel thought his back would break as he lifted it unaided toward Fitch's reaching grasp from the other side of the barrier, over which he had shinned first, but somehow he managed it, and then helped Lil over before pulling himself across onto the cobbles of the road beyond.

They stood there panting with their efforts for a moment while Fitch listened for distant sounds, and then, satisfied, he nodded and with Abel's help took the corpse on his back, just as he had carried Lil earlier, and Lil draped her shawl across it carefully. Apart from its greater size, and the problems Fitch found in accommodating the swollen belly, he looked much as he had when he had crossed Crown Street with Lil four hours before.

It was a lot quieter now, with few people abroad in the streets and only the occasional cry of the distant Watch to be heard, and as the little procession started off, moving as silently as it had before, Abel let his thoughts take hold of him.

He tried very hard to imagine what sort of person it would be who would want a dead body. He knew it was surgeons that bought them, but what did he know of surgeons? It was no more than a word to him. Never in all his life had he come across anyone who gave help to the sick. In his experience, all that happened to the sick was that they got better of their own accord or died of their illness if they were of a mind to. There was naught else to be expected. Surgeons. Strange creatures, from all accounts, who took dead bodies and . . .

And what? He pondered, and explored that sense of pity that had filled him at the sight of the dead girl in the coffin, and marveled a little, and yawned and thought again. He was very tired, and the night was getting ever shorter.

He became aware suddenly that behind him Lil was arguing in a bitter whisper with Fitch instead of walking just ahead, and then that she had lost the argument, for Fitch swore softly, and Lil dodged a blow he aimed at her with his free hand and skipped forward to come and walk again beside Abel.

"What's afoot?" he whispered.

"Ah, he says, the great dolt, that we must deliver tonight. I'm tired! I don't see why we cannot take it back to the house in the usual way, and set about carrying it to Windmill Street tomorrow night. You'd come again to help, would you not, if I asked you?"

"I'd come if you didn't," he said unthinkingly, and she peered up at him in the darkness, frowning her puzzlement.

"Well, it makes no matter, either way," she said irritably, "since he's bound and determined we shall take it now. So you'll not get much sleep this night, and that's all about it, Master Abel." She finished in a spiteful whisper, and pinched him sharply, and slid ahead of him to walk alone in the dim light.

But he didn't mind her display of temper, for he was used to such exhibitions, and they rarely lasted long with her. She would tell him in her own good time, no doubt, what was to be.

They crossed Crown Street, once more play-acting the sorrowing funeral procession, and stopped in the darkness to breathe a little when they reached the other side, glad that no one among the few hurrying late travelers had seemed to heed them. It wasn't until they started to move forward again that Abel realized that Lil was no longer with them.

"Where is she?" he hissed at Fitch, who shook his head, as best he could with the burden he was carrying on his huge bent back, and scowled. But Abel was not to be gainsaid and stood still.

"I'll not go a step further until you tell me," he muttered, "and for all your threats about what you'll do, I'll call the Watch, and then what chance to tell your tales in Gower Street? Where is she?"

"Gone ahead, is all," Fitch grunted. "And move on, boy, move on! Good and big a man as I may be, this one's breaking my back. We've a long way to go yet, and I can't stand still, not for aught. Here, take the weight of the legs before me, now we're where we can't be seen. I'll tell you what's afoot then."

Obediently Abel stepped in front of him and took the weight of the woman's legs across his back, and as they started moving forward, more swiftly now the load was shared, he turned his head and whispered doggedly, "Well? Gone ahead where?"

"To tell them at Great Windmill Street to be ready for us. I don't wish to be standing crying my wares at the door like some fool of a muffin man! They must be there and ready as we arrive. You'll see. Now, hist, for the love of God."

Satisfied, Abel did hist, and they plodded on and he felt weariness fill him more and more. He knew Great Windmill Street to be as far on the other side of Fitch and Lil's house as St. Giles's was on this, and that there was a long walk ahead of him. And though he missed Lil's company near him, he was satisfied she was in no way to come to harm, and that was good enough.

They reached their destination just at the point when Abel felt he could go no farther with the weight he was bearing, and Fitch with one mighty heave swung the sacking load from his back and put it down on the step beside the door with a sickening thump. Then he scratched on the panels, and after a very few moments the door slid open a few inches, to reveal Lil's face peering whitely through the gap.

"Aye, it's them," she said in a matter-of-fact tone over her shoulder. "Are any about, Fitch? No? Right then, Mr. Wilson, you can light your glim."

There was a small rattle of sound, and a glow, faint and guttering at first and then stronger, appeared in the doorway, and the patch of light grew as Lil held the door invitingly open.

Behind her Abel could see a thin, spare man, wearing black broadcloth trousers and a white linen shirt open at the neck, the sleeves rolled up about his scrawny arms. He was holding a towel in one hand as well as the candle in the other, and almost bobbing about in his anxiety as he looked out into the darkness of the road.

"In, in, in—fast as you can! Come on, man—do you want to tell the world what we're about? Move faster, man, d'you hear me?"

Fitch carried in the body in his arms and grunted, "No need for such a pother! We've come this far with no trouble, and we'll not have any now. Make way, man, this one's heavy! A rare treasure, I promise you!" And he pushed familiarly past the thin man and went plodding along the passageway beyond.

Lil slid the door closed behind Abel, and then moved closer to him in the darkness, for the thin man had gone fussing away after Fitch, taking the candle with him and leaving strange shadows dancing on the paneled walls of the passageway.

"He'll not be long, Abel, and when he comes back, you make him give me some of his cash, will you? He's not like Barliman—he always gives me money on the spot, and even French John will, but Fitch tries to get off with some miserable victuals, and I want both. So will you—"

"Where have they gone?" Abel asked, peering ahead into the darkness to the cellar doorway that he could see outlined at the end of the passageway. He could hear the stumping footsteps as the men went downward, and he pulled away from Lil almost roughly in his eagerness to see what was to be seen, and she immediately dropped her hand and stamped her foot.

"What's to do with you where they've gone? Did you hear what I said, Abel? Will you—"

"In a while I shall, Lil. Just let me see." He spoke over his shoulder almost absently, for he was away from her now and peeping round the cellar doorway.

Below him he could see light and hear the sound of deep voices and then the chink of coins, and after a moment's hesitation he went forward, slipping away down the steps as softly as he had ever moved.

Neither man noticed him when he reached the bottom and made the half turn that brought him right into the room. He found himself in a commodious cellar, very cool—so much so that it made him hunch his shoulders against the cold bite that seemed to seep into his bones—and very well lit. He stared about him with his mouth half open, fascinated.

There were brackets set against the walls, each bearing a large oil-burning lamp with a glittering naked flame, but no glass globe to hold it. It was these that filled the whole wide cellar with the light that made him blink a little with its brilliant clarity. The floor was stone-flagged, and set against one side was a long bench on which was an array of implements the like of which he had not seen before. Saws and knives and chisels, they were familiar enough, but there were others that looked most strange. He moved his eyes onward, and now saw that in the center of the room there were three long wooden tables. On one of them was a sheet-covered mound. On another was the newly delivered corpse still tied in its sack, and beside it stood the two men, their heads together as Wilson counted coins into Fitch's outstretched palm. And on the third . . . Abel's eyes widened.

It had clearly been the body of a young man. He could see the curve of the cheek on one side, the springing dark hair, the clean line of the jaw. But on one side only, for the other side of the head had been flayed, with a flap of skin lying to one side of it, and the exposed eye glaring bluely upward with a sort of surprised rage.

Almost hypnotized, Abel moved forward, crept nearer until he was standing right beside the table. He was aware of a smell now, the sweetish, sickly smell that he had become accustomed to when visiting Lil. It did not perturb him unduly, seeming almost agreeable in its familiarity.

It was the rest of the body that so fascinated him. The chest too had been flayed, the skin flaps lying neatly on each side across the upper arms, and he could see rows of bones lying open to the air. For all the world, he marveled inside his head, like the butcher's meat on the stalls in Hungerford Market. And the belly . . .

"And what is't you find so fascinating there, boy?"

He jumped sharply, and turned round to see the thin man looking down at him, his hands clenched on his hips as he stood arms akimbo, and for a moment he was frightened. But the man did not seem angry, or even anxious now. Clearly his edginess abovestairs had been due entirely to his fear of Fitch's being seen from the street. Now he was relaxed and half smiling as he stared down at Abel.

"Is this what you do with them?" Abel asked, swallowing his sudden nervousness. "All of them? Really make meat of 'em, as Lil said?"

"Whatever your Lil may have said, m'boy, I'm no cat's-meat man, though this indeed is what I do with 'em. I and my students, that is."

"Students?" Abel could see Fitch glaring at him from behind the thin man's shoulders, but did not care. This was altogether too interesting for him to give a snap of the fingers for Fitch's displeasure.

"Aye, lad, students. Those that will be surgeons if ever their natural indolence and stupidity can be overcome. But there are hopes that their cupidity will ensure that. They spend enough of their fathers' money to get their teaching here, so ultimately most of them learn their business."

"What is their business?"

The thin man laughed, and looked over his shoulder at Fitch. "A strange boy, this one, Fitch! Asks me more questions than do those with a right to my answers! No—don't admonish the lad—I've a taste for honest curiosity."

He turned back to Abel. "What is their business? Why, surgery, to be sure. Or will be if I can cram sufficient facts into their doltish heads. There's not above one in fifty of 'em's worth bothering about, but there—it's worth it for that one, or so my teachers always told me."

He smiled then—a wide smile that stretched his lips thinly but made his eyes half close with friendly wrinkles. "My teachers. Great anatomists they were, believe me, lad! The younger Hunter, you know, was one of them! Couldn't lecture, not to save his poor soul, but a great man with the knife—oh, a great man! Yet to hear him talk— Why, shall I tell you what he said once, lad? 'Twas a lecture on gunshot wounds—I'll never forget it, not if I live to be ninety." He chuckled richly, his eyes, misty with nostalgia, staring at Abel but not seeing him. "There we were; must have been— let me see—back in 'seventy—or was it 'seventy-one? Aye, that would be it. In the winter of 'seventy-one. Well, there we were, all young and eager, and accustomed to the words of great scholars upon our ears. And he said—let me see, now—he said of this man on whom he was lecturing us that 'the bullet, having gone into the man's belly, hit his guts such a damned thump that they mortified.' And there were some that laughed, and one young blood that walked out, saying the man wasn't fit to teach the sons of gentlemen to speak so inelegantly. But bad a lecturer though he might have been, he taught me well enough, and many others—and here I am now, in his very own anatomy school. Well, well. Time goes."

He looked down at Abel then, and shook his head ruefully and patted the boy's shoulder.

"How I do prose on, to be sure! But you asked me, lad, and I'm not overly accustomed to people who ask me anything of much interest. Not even my students."

"Why do they have to do this to do surgery?" Abel flicked his eyes sideways to stare in fascination at the naked cage of ribs gleaming redly in the lamplight. "I know naught of surgery."

"I doubt you do, lad, I doubt you do! There's few enough of your stamp, God help us, get any care for their ailments. Surgery, my boy, is the use of the knife to cure men's ills. There's pains and troubles that come to a man that the fast use of a sharp knife, the careful tying of bleeding vessels, the removal of some wen or tumor can cure, and make a man's life fit to live again. Surgeons are those that do these things. And to do it, they must learn their trade. No man can go using a knife upon his fellows without knowing what lies beneath the skin, hey? So I teach 'em, as I was once taught, the art of the surgeon by teaching anatomy."

"Why do you buy corpses? And what is anatomy?"

"Too many questions!" Fitch growled suddenly, moving toward Abel, but again the other man shook his head.

"Don't punish the lad, Fitch. It's good when a lad takes an interest in the trade he's apprenticed to. He'll make a better resurrectionist knowing why he does it! Anatomy is the study of the structure of the human body. And we buy corpses to give the students practice in the understanding of it. To rehearse on living flesh would be a sin against God and nature. But on dead flesh it's no harm, no harm at all. But to find enough dead flesh! That's the difficulty. You and your master, here, are the people we seek to solve it. You see?"

"And why—"

"Enough!" Fitch cried. " 'Tis enough, in all conscience, yer honor! I want to be about my business, and I daresay you do too. It's enough."

"One more question, lad!" the thin man said jovially. "You can ask me more again next time Fitch, here, brings me a consignment. What is't, then?"

"Why is today's—that one—worth more to you? Because she was so—because of being young and sad?"

There was a short silence and the thin man looked at him, his head on one side.

"What's your name, lad? You're a cut above the usual Dials meat, and—dare I say it? . . . " He shot a sharp glance at Fitch. "Well, let be. No, lad, not because she was young and sad. But because she was with child. To help a surgeon accoucheur learn how to bring a child safe into this painful world, it's mighty useful to have a dead woman with her infant still within her. Then we can see why it stuck in the passageway, why she could not be delivered of the fruit of her womb. You see?"

Abel opened his mouth to speak again and then, seeing Fitch's scowl, closed it, but unwillingly.

"Next time you come I'll answer more such questions, if

you have them. So, Fitch? You may bring him again to aid
you when your usual cronies are away on other matters."

"That's as may be," Fitch said, his shrill little voice sharp.
"I'll be here on Monday as ever I am, Mr. Wilson, for the
usual, as you'll recall. And we can talk then of other matters.
Good night to you, sir. Come on, you."

They reached the street in silence, and Mr. Wilson closed
the door behind them with a return of his original nervousness, leaving them standing out on the cobbles. There was no
sign of Lil, and for once Abel just did not care. He was
bemused and puzzled and thick with fatigue, and stood
almost swaying with it all beside the burly figure of Fitch.

"You'd best be away to your fancy Gower Street ken,"
Fitch said after a moment, "and I'll say no more about—
Well. We'll see."

He stood for a moment chewing at his lower lip and looking down at Abel, who stood staring vacantly into space, his
mind filled with a mass of conflicting thoughts. "Tell me,
boy, you'd come again on such an expedition? Willing, like,
without fear of me splittin' on you?"

Abel was at once full of attention, and stared up at him.

"Would you bring me back here to talk to that Wilson
again?"

"Aye."

"Then I shall. I'd know more of what he talks about if I
could. It's strange the way he— Well, I'd know more if I
could."

"I'll get a message to you if I need you and you're not
about the Dials. And I'll pay you a little, too. Not a great
sum, and never think it. But Fitch is a fair man and none can
say otherwise, so I'll pay you."

"Give it to Lil tonight," Abel said, remembering, "and tell
her I shall come to her again as soon as may be."

"I'll tell her," Fitch said, and melted away into the darkness, leaving Abel to plod his exhausted way back to Gower
Street, his head buzzing with all he had seen and felt and
done. He could not remember ever feeling quite as confused
as he did this night.

· SEVENTEEN ·

CHARLOTTE was puzzled. Had the boy really changed in some way, or was it merely that she had become more aware of him, and that it was this that made him seem different? She would watch him covertly during lessons, looking at the line of his cheek and the shape of his forehead as he sat with his head bent over his books, seeking constantly for some evidence that Jesse's wild statements had some grain of truth in them. She would watch him as he moved, looking for similarities of gait as well as of build, but for every fleeting resemblance she thought she noted there would be some other aspect so very dissimilar that it quite destroyed the effect of her first observation.

She argued much with herself during these months. She knew, none better, how cruelly Jesse could react to the sting of rejection of his husbandly demands with some wild and vicious bite of his tongue. It was, she often thought, as though he spent his masculinity in words since he could not do so in any more normal way. She was by no means a foolish woman, she told herself, and had some understanding of the ways of a man's mind. Had she not been married twice? Who should know better than she how urgent a man's needs could be, and of the pains of male continence? Daniel had suffered much during the enforced abstinence of her pregnancy—for of course he had understood that no man of sensitivity could force himself upon his wife while she was in an Interesting Situation—and although she had of course felt no sense of guilt about his distress, she had indeed felt pity for him. She felt a curious pity for Jesse, too, but what could she do about it? His demands were so dreadful, so far outside what could be regarded as a normal wifely duty, that . . .

She found herself remembering much at this time. Over and over again it would rise unbidden in her mind, that memory of the first night on which they had shared a bed; her sick shock, her fastidious withdrawal from him. That scene had been repeated many times in these ten years, and on each occasion she suffered almost as much as he, for although she could not possibly expect to gain any pleasure from the rigors of the marriage bed, she had hoped to gain a son from it.

That she would have liked another child was well known to Jesse, for she had told him often enough, had taunted him—for how could she not taunt him?—with his failure to father one on her. But so it had gone on, over and over again, each hurting the other viciously with words, each punishing the other, and neither finding any satisfaction in it; for she knew he cared much for her, just as she did for him. That was the most miserable part of the situation: the abiding affection that existed between them, twisted and poisoned though it was by their ten years of marriage. They had married for genuine love, however convenient a marriage it might have seemed to be for Charlotte in the eyes of her friends (and indeed it was, for Jesse had been a warm man then, and was even richer now), and it was because that feeling persisted that each was able to punish the other so cruelly.

And was this new seed of doubt he had planted in her mind just another example of his attempts to hurt her? Was he punishing her through her desire for a child, a desire he could not satisfy, nor she help him to satisfy? She would look at the boy, and ponder and look again, and emerge no wiser.

Abel, for his part, was quite unaware of her scrutiny, as unaware as he was of Dorothea's dumb adoration. The two females would sit and stare at him, but he would sit and stare at his books, seeking always for more information about this strange new world into which he had stumbled: the world of the surgeon.

There had been further exploits with Fitch, for whom he was beginning to develop a curious affection. For all his size, his quick response of blows and cuffs when he was put out in any way, there was no malice in the man. Once he realized that Abel was glad enough to help him with his "orders" and needed no threats to spur him on, Fitch had become quite at ease with him, and indeed, a sort of friendship had sprung up between them at which Lil would sometimes rail in her rage; hitherto she had been able to manipulate both Fitch and Abel at her will. Now, sometimes, they would present to her a united front, laughing at her temper. But she soon learned how to detach them from each other. She had only to turn brimming eyes and trembling lower lip upon Abel for him at once to ally himself with her, and turn on Fitch and rant at him. Such arguments were always about payment for work done, for Fitch had a streak of parsimony in him that made him try to pay off Lil and Abel in food, while she demanded hard coin, and the food besides. Her urge to take was as great as Fitch's to hold.

Many times, during these long winter months, Abel had settled the fight between them by good-naturedly giving Lil his share of their earnings, a proceeding that annoyed while it obviously gratified her (she wanted the money, but why should Abel give it her?) and puzzled Fitch mightily. He could not comprehend why Abel, a sensible enough sort of a boy in other ways, should be soft about a bit of muslin. But that was something Abel would not talk of, telling him shortly to mind his business. At which Fitch would laugh coarsely and turn his attention to other matters.

Another relationship that was developing was between the boy and the thin, acidulous anatomist, Wilson. At first Abel could ask his questions only when a corpse was delivered, and ask he would, with great eagerness. Sometimes Wilson would answer as freely and easily as he had on that very first occasion, while on others he was distrait and sharp of tongue and would send Abel packing in his fussy, complaining way. But sometimes he would allow the boy to come to talk to him on the night following a delivery of goods. At such times

Wilson would be preparing the body for his students, and was glad enough of company. He used the boy to fetch and carry instruments for him, and in his dry and chattering way taught him more than he knew.

It was now well into the New Year, and during these long months Abel had discovered the names of many of the principal muscles, bones, and organs of the body, information that he stored carefully in his mind, saying it over to himself by rote as he lay in bed at night.

He had, tentatively, spread his net a little wider in his search for more knowledge of his new interest. If the bodies of his fellow men could be of such fascination, why not the bodies of other creatures? So he initiated a friendship with the cook, allowing her to think he sought her favor in exchange for tidbits and an implied promise he would not tell her mistress of the way she was busily lining her own pockets by sharp practice with the tradesmen from whom she bought on Charlotte's behalf. In actuality, it was meat that interested him. He would watch her skin hares, paunch and joint rabbits, dress a chicken, or butcher half a mutton carcass, making mental notes of similarities and differences between the brute creation and man, and marveling at how much there was that was the same. He would look from rabbit carcass to the fat cook and back again and try to imagine her without her skin, and would laugh aloud at the vision thus conjured up. And she, all unknowing, would laugh back at him, and each would be content with the other.

He had wished to question Charlotte about other matters that puzzled him. Another of Dorothea's putrid sore throats had afflicted her shortly before Christmas, and Abel had been fascinated to discover that the apothecary had been sent for. He had watched from the schoolroom window as the well-dressed, bustling little man had alighted from his carriage and then crept out to listen as best he could from the head of the stairs to what went on in Dorothea's bedchamber. Charlotte had seen him there and sent him sharply about his business before he could discover aught, but once Dorothea was well again, Abel had been free to ask her to explain.

"Apothecaries, Abel? Oh, no, of course they are not surgeons!" Dorothea had laughed merrily at the very thought. "The surgeons are a very rascally lot, you know, or so says

Mama. They do dreadful things to people, though to be sure it is sometimes necessary. I remember Mr. Cantler, who lived in the house across the street from us when we lived in the City before we came here, he had the surgeon to him to cut for the stone. He shrieked and wailed so you could hear him clear to Temple Bar. It truly was a dreadful time, so Mrs. Cantler told Mama, but he has been much better since. He was afflicted with dreadful pains, or so I believe, but they will not tell me much of it, for it is improper for young ladies."

"But apothecaries?" Abel said impatiently. "What of them?"

"Well, they make the medicines and pills, you know, that the physicians order them to do, and cataplasms and the like, for putrid throats, and congestion of the lungs, and irritation of the nerves," said Dorothea, listing all the illnesses she could think of, "and—and such things. Papa Constam has many among his acquaintance, I believe, for"—she giggled softly—"Mama likes to use their complexion washes and salves, but she will not buy them from any who may know Papa Constam for fear they would tell him, you know, and he would laugh coarsely at her. So she has to buy such from the apothecary who is patronized by Mrs. Lister, who lives near to Southampton Row. . . ." Dorothea chattered busily on, reproducing with ear-numbing faithfulness the inconsequential chatter of her mother's friends' drawing rooms.

Abel interrupted ruthlessly. "Physicians—what of them?"

"Physicians? I don't know," Dorothea said blankly. "Well, not to really know, you understand, for Mama always calls Mr. Hancock, the apothecary who came to me. Physicians cost a great deal, I believe. Perhaps Mama will start to call the physician to me when Papa Constam becomes richer again— as he often does, does he not?—and she wishes to cut more of a dash than ever. Shall I ask her to do so, Abel? Would it please you? I will, if you wish, although she may perhaps tell me to mind my affairs—but I will ask her if you wish it."

Dorothea sounded both hopeful and brave, and Abel again found rising in him that wave of irritation that she could so easily tap and shook his head brusquely. "Such a stupid idea! As if she would pay any heed to aught you told her to do! I only asked to see what you knew, but you are very stupid after all."

And, crestfallen, Dorothea had sat silent for a while, cogitating on how to win his interest again, and wondering where she had gone wrong this time. And found no answer, any more than she ever did.

And so the weeks of February merged into March, with Charlotte still wondering whether or not there had been any truth in Jesse's words, with Jesse appearing little in his own house, for he was much concerned with an expansion of his business at this time, and Dorothea and Abel working steadily through Charlotte's carefully prepared and excessively dull lessons.

In early February, Dorothea had celebrated her fifteenth birthday, and it was decided, for want of any better information, to settle on Ash Wednesday, which this year fell on the eighteenth day of February, as Abel's birthday. "For you must age as do all others, and have some record of it. Mr. Constam told me you were about eleven years when you came to us, so now you shall consider yourself to be twelve. Ash Wednesday, although it is of course a movable feast, is a highly suitable day for you to celebrate. You may occupy some part of your time in considering the evils of your past life and contemplating the good fortune that attends you now and which you enjoy as a result of Mr. Constam's generosity of spirit," Charlotte had told Abel in her most depressing tones.

Still, he had found a curious pleasure in the idea. To be able to count his years would be very comfortable, he had thought confusedly, for there were times he was not quite sure who he was, when memories of his past collided with experiences of his present, or particularly exhausting nights spent resurrecting from stinking graves with Fitch were succeeded by days spent sitting primly in Charlotte's soap-scented schoolroom.

They could have gone on so for always, with Charlotte no nearer knowing more about Abel's parentage, or Abel in any way disturbed by her watchfulness, when the weather changed and brought in its train events that were to alter much. In later years Abel was to marvel at the ways of Nature, and how unknowingly she could interfere with men's lives, such ponderings bringing him as near as ever he came to a belief in the existence of an Almighty Providence.

But at the time it occurred, he gave it no more thought than that the weather had changed.

It became suddenly much milder. The winter had been a sharp one, with much frost, if little snow, in the middle of London. It had sorely hampered the work of the resurrectionists, in that the ground was devilish hard to move, and sometimes needed the use of pick as well as shovel to disturb the earth on even a new grave; but that difficulty was offset by the fact that in such conditions the bodies putrefied less rapidly. They lost little good stock to noisome decomposition, demanding hasty reburial on a darker-than-usual night. They were able to charge higher rates for those bodies they did manage to snatch from the iron-hard earth, and could rest assured that they would not receive new orders sooner than they could fill them, for the bodies remained suitable for dissection far longer than they usually did.

But as March crept in, lamblike, bringing crocuses and snowdrops to Gower Street back gardens, it brought with it a heavy warm rain. There was a sharp increase in the number of deaths from congestion of the lungs and tertiary fevers and suchlike disorders. Since hand in hand with this larger number of burials came a more rapid rate of body decay, inevitably Fitch received more and more demands for new material. He served more than one anatomy school, being a sharp man in his way, and for the first week or so he managed to keep pace.

But then, on one unfortunate night, Barliman, the wizened little bowlegged man Abel had met only once (since on the nights when Barliman was available for work, Abel's efforts were not required), was taken up by the Watch and clapped fast in Coldbath Fields—much to his rage, for he did not consider that his misdemeanor warranted so cruel a sentence as the treadmill.

"And nor does it," Fitch said somberly to Abel, who fortunately enough had come that night to visit Lil and bring her (much to her delight) a lace cap he had filched from Charlotte's own boudoir. " 'Tis a cruel thing indeed to set a man to the cockchafer for so small a matter as the disposal of a dead body as no one's got no further use for 'ceptin' us and our customers—though, to be sure, it ain't so bad for Barliman as it might be on account of those bow legs o' 'is." And he had laughed coarsely and nudged Abel to make sure the boy fully understood the significance of the nickname of the treadmill to which old lags so often found themselves apprenticed. Since Abel had known of this for as long as he could remember, he found no special humor in the joke, and merely asked, "So what shall you do now, Fitch? Will French John return soon, do you think?"

Fitch shook his head. "Don't know where he went, nor what he was about, and that's the truth o' the matter. And since 'e's been gone this dunnamany months, it's no nevermind to me if 'e never comes back. Not that 'e's like to, for after all this time it stands to reason 'e's done for. Transported, most like, if 'e 'asn't been 'anged for summat. And 'ere I am, with an order to find every blessed night this week, if I'm not to lose me good name as a man to be relied upon, an' three weeks to go before the students is sent about their business and every surgeon in the town goin' on somethin' cruel. You'll 'ave to come out every night, me lad, until such time as I'm abreast o' meself again. What do you say, boy? It's a bit o' luck, the way the weather's gone, as well as it meanin' a lot o' extra effort. You'll not waste the chances, now, will yer?"

Abel had agreed gladly enough to sneak out of the Gower Street house every night until Fitch had satisfied the demands being made on him. The work was no longer as exhausting as it had been at first, as his muscles hardened and grew, and he had learned the tricks of his trade: how to turn his wrists so that they took the strain from his back, and how to get the best results for the least physical effort. And coming to Old Compton Street every night would mean he would see Lil every night too, for whether she accompanied them on their expeditions or not (it depended on which churchyard they were using, for on some routes through the town she was not required), she was always there when they returned, with a pan of hot punch brewing on her little fire and a plate of good mutton pies awaiting their work-sharpened appetites.

For the first three nights, all went well. The churchyards were unattended, for the rain continued to pour down, and only the most conscientious (or best paid) of sextons would stay out to watch a new grave in such weather; the earth moved easily, if very wetly and heavily, yielding up the coffins with small argument; and carrying the burden through the streets was safer than usual, for in such weather there were few concerned to watch the comings and goings of others, however heavy-laden they might be.

By the fourth and fifth consecutive nights, however, Abel was beginning to wilt. Young and well fed as he now was in Charlotte's household, he could manage well enough if he slept no more than a couple of hours on one night in the week. But after so many backbreaking work-filled nights, his body shrieked out for want of sleep, and once or twice he even fell to snoring over his books and pothooks and ciphering, which startled Charlotte considerably.

She chided him for his inattention, and dosed him with Gregory's powder, which stung his tongue with its ginger, afflicted his bowels with its rhubarb, and made him grimace at the taste of its magnesia. But to no avail, for he became more and more pallid each day and more and more weary as the week went on.

On Saturday night, the eighth of the marathon of body collecting, Abel made for the first time a great mistake. Hitherto he had gone to his bed at nine of the clock and lain there on his pallet waiting until the household was abed before making any move to quit the house. But on Friday night he had been within an ace of breaking the promise he had made to Fitch, since he had fallen fast asleep as soon as his head had touched the bed. Only the fortunate yowling of a neighboring tomcat, aroused by the imminence of spring, had brought him muggily to his feet to set out yet again.

So tonight, he dared not risk lying down. Nor could he even risk standing up against the wall to rest himself as he waited, for he was sure he would fall asleep even there. Instead, he would set out now, he decided. It was but half an hour past nine, but he would wait no longer. And wearily he began to change his clothes, ready to start the familiar but still dangerous journey across the roof tops and down to Gower Street.

Charlotte was sitting in the drawing room, with Jesse sprawled in a chair on the other side of the fireplace. Dorothea too had gone to her bed, and Charlotte sat over her embroidery work, even more than usually silent as she pondered, not for the first time that day, the state of Abel's health. If he was afflicted with an outbreak of some disease of the slums, was there not a dreadful chance that he would not merely sicken himself (and she was a little surprised at the slight pang that thought gave her), but pass it on to Dorothea or herself?

She almost paled at that thought, and raised her head from her embroidery to say impulsively to Jesse, "Tomorrow, Mr. Constam, I believe I shall have Mr. Hancock to see the boy. He appears sickly, and I would not have disease rampant in the house. You will, I believe, be content to pay his fees and for such medicines as he advises? He is a costly man, as you know."

"If the boy is ill, then of course you shall." Jesse frowned sharply. "Have you been feeding him well, ma'am? Has he been beaten or otherwise chastised? Slum boy he may be, but that does not mean you may—"

She reddened furiously. "Indeed, sir, you have no right to suggest such things! The boy receives nothing but a mother's care at my hands! You have seen for yourself how well he has grown in the time since he has been here! Indeed, you do me a great injustice to—"

"Well, let be. I daresay you deal well enough with the boy." Jesse had the grace to look ashamed. "'Tis no more than a disorder of the spring, I daresay. Dose him yourself or call in your precious apothecary if you wish. I'd not have him anywhere about me, the popinjay that he is, with his finicky ways! 'What is it that afflicts you, sir?'" Jesse produced a rough copy of the apothecary's conciliatory whine. "What does he know of such matters? I could do more good for the boy with some of my own ginger and cinnamon and a little honey and brandy than any of *his* fancy mixtures! It was a bad day when honest shopkeepers set themselves up as physicians and went about to people's houses, seeking to add to their business by tellin' honest men they was sick and dying!"

"So you will pay for it," Charlotte said, and suddenly stood up, setting down her embroidery upon the console table beside her. "I shall see to him now, I think. He seemed at the end of the afternoon to be in some sort of decline, I must say, for he was very pale and much given to gaping and blinking when I spoke to him. If he has some contagion, then the sooner Mr. Hancock comes to him . . ."

She reached the top floor of her house, unfamiliar territory to her, just as Abel was thrusting up the skylight. He was so tired he had not even remembered to set a chair beneath his doorknob to prevent unwanted entrants, and also was not nearly so silent as when he was in full command of himself.

Outside the door Charlotte heard him, and with a considerable degree of courage blew out her candle, which she had been holding with one hand curled round to shade it, and listened again. Once more she heard the sound that had alerted her: the creaking of a hinge. And although she felt alarm, she also felt intense anger; was this a cracksman daring to enter her house? And through the room of a sick boy at that, who would not be able to repel him? In her frightened anger she did not think very clearly, but simply swept forward and set her hand to the knob and pushed the door open.

It was a moment or two before her eyes accustomed themselves to the darkness, but then she saw the empty bed, its crude copy of a sleeping body on it (for Abel had botched that task too in his weariness) and the open skylight with the chair beneath it.

She blinked and shook her head to clear it, so puzzled was she, and then stood as still as a startled animal, for she heard another sound: the crash of a falling slate. Indeed, Abel was showing no vestige of his usual skill on this wet and muggy March evening.

Charlotte, whatever else she lacked, was not completely deficient in imagination. She stood there, her head up and listening hard, and knew what was happening. The boy was leaving the house for some reason; she did not know why, nor where he was going (though she could make a shrewd guess, she thought), but she could trace his noisy route as he went clambering, clumsy with fatigue, across the roof slates and down the drainpipes to the yard below.

She ran then, speeding silently down the stairs with inelegant haste to call peremptorily to the footman, who was spending the evening cozily in Pug's Parlor with the cook. William came hurrying out to her in the hall just in time to prevent her from coming in to them, tying his neckerchief as he went and then smoothing his hand nervously over his head. What the devil was afoot? Had the master dropped dead or something of the sort, or set about her with a vengeance?

"William—come at once! And be quiet, you hear me? Take your coat, man—you may need to go out. Come, and *hurry*."

He gaped at her, at her face uncharacteristically flushed with urgency, and then obediently ran to take his coat from the pantry, shrugging it on over his livery as he reached the front hall.

He could just see her in the dimness, and gaped even more, for she was standing beside the partly open door, peering out for all the world like an eavesdropping housemaid.

"Hush, man!" she hissed as he came up to her. "Now, wait—yes, there he goes! Do you see? The boy—Abel—he's sneaked out of the house, and is away somewhere. I thought as much. I *thought* as— Now, you are to follow him, do you hear? I want to know where he goes, and whom he meets. And when you know and can pinpoint the place for me, then you may come back and bring him with you. But be careful, you hear me? I would not wish him to know you were following him until you are ready to fetch him back."

William grinned—a long, slow, and satisfied grin. "Young Abel, madam? Indeed, madam, it will be a pleasure. Sneaking back to his cronies, is he? Going to arrange for us all to be robbed and murdered in our beds, is he? Why, madam, I'll catch him fast enough, I promise you. And then won't he be sorry!"

And he slid out onto the street, pulling his coat up about his ears and slouching along behind the boy to the manner born; not that it was difficult, for Abel was lurching along the street in an almost somnambulistic state and could have been followed by a herd of elephants and not known it.

Charlotte stood at her front door, watching them disappear into the darkness, and gnawed at her lower lip, not sure what report she wanted William to bring back with him. If the boy did turn out to be arranging a theft . . . She shook her head sharply and went in to sit and wait in the chilly breakfast parlor for the man's return. For some reason she did not herself fully comprehend, she chose not to tell Jesse, still sitting in the drawing room abovestairs, what was going on. Not until she knew herself.

· EIGHTEEN ·

WILLIAM stood in the center of the hall, flushed with pride and seemingly quite unaware of the mud upon his coat or the sharp scratch marks that bloodily decorated one side of his face. He was holding Lil by her hair, his fingers twisted in the curls so firmly that she had to stand with her head held painfully to one side. She too was flushed, and her eyes sparkled with a glitter of rage, but she made no attempt to free herself. Clearly she had already tried hard enough—witness the scratches on William—and failed. On William's other side stood Abel, one ear firmly pinched between the man's hard fingers. He stood sullenly, not looking at Charlotte but holding himself lumpishly still, his eyes hooded as he stared at the floor.

Charlotte stood looking at them, biting her lower lip as she tried to assess the situation. That William should succeed in bringing back the boy she had never doubted; had she not given him her orders? But that he should bring back another slum child . . .

"What is this? Are you clean out of your wits, man, to bring such as *that* to me? I told you to bring him back, but—"

"Ah, but madam, I knew as you'd want to talk to this one!" William said eagerly, and twisted his hand a little more as Lil tried to pull away from him. "And I had to think of myself, madam! This young limb o' Satan, this wicked boy"—he pinched Abel's ear even harder, making the boy wince—"this 'orrible creature's been making such accusations and tellin' me of as wicked a pack of lies that 'e'll tell you about me as'd put the very Devil hisself to the blush! So I 'ad—had to bring the girl with me for evidence to show you why he was tellin' such lies."

"It's not lies!" Abel roused himself with an obvious physical effort. "It's true, every word of it! You've been robbin' 'em blind all the time I've been in this house, and well you knows it! He has, ma'am, and you should know of it! He and the cook and the whole boiling of 'em! Fiddling the bills and selling your food at the back door and—"

"It's lies, all wicked lies!" William cried shrilly. "Don't you heed him, madam, trying to get me turned off just to get out of what trouble'll come to him now I knows what he's been about! I brung the girl with me to prove it, and prove it I shall! Been sneakin' off these dunnamany nights to meet 'is bit o' skirt 'ere, and behave like—well, like it isn't fitting to say before a lady like yourself, madam."

"What in the name of God and all His angels is this din? William, what the— Mrs. Constam! What are you about? Will someone tell me why my house is turned into Hungerford Market in the middle of the night? What's afoot here?"

Jesse was standing at the top of the stairs gazing blearily down at them, obviously just awakened from the deep sleep into which he had drifted, alone in the drawing room, and they all turned and looked up at him with a jerky unity of movement that made him produce a sudden spurt of laughter.

"Well, whatever it is, you all look fit to bust with it! Standing there for all the world like marionettes in a Punchinello show! So will someone tell me what all the noise and hubbub is about?" And he came down the stairs in a leisurely way, raising his eyebrows a little as he took in the state of William's face. And his expression changed as he caught a clearer view of Lil.

"Well, well, well! And what is this? A young lady, as I live and breathe! A friend of yours, William? Believe me, man, you'll make no progress with the fair sex if you treat 'em as rough as you're treating this one! Let go the girl, man! What do you suppose she can do if you hold her so? I never thought you had so much spirit in you as to bring your lights o' love into your master's house! Nor such excellent taste, by God!"

He had reached William's side by now, and put out a hand to turn Lil's chin upward so that he could see her more clearly, and William immediately let go of her. She stood there for a moment looking mulish, and then, as she saw the look of approval on Jesse's face, suddenly produced one of her most bewitching smiles, dimpling up at him, and dropped a little curtsy.

"Good evening, sir! I would have wished we'd met in better circumstances."

Jesse roared with laughter. "Well said, my dear! You are indeed a—"

"Mr. Constam, enough!" Charlotte came sweeping forward to interpose herself between Jesse and the girl. "There's matter here you must know of—and indeed that I must understand, for I do not yet know what's afoot for myself! In short, sir, when I went to see after the health of the boy—for you will recall I was concerned for his well-being, since he had been behaving so odd this past few days, and not having so evil a mind as to think his condition was due to aught but sickness—I found him gone from his room through the skylight and away over the roof! What think you of *that,* sir? Is that the action of a grateful boy, who has been given a home such as this, to go sneaking out of the house in so harum-scarum a fashion? I knew at once what it was he was about, of course, and sent William after him to see what he did and where he went and to see who were the cracksmen he was to bring here and—"

"I was not about to bring cracksmen here, ma'am!" Abel cried furiously. "He said that was what it was all the way back, and I told him it wasn't so! Had I wanted to do that, I'd have done it long since! I've been here nigh on a year! Why should I wait till now to start on any robbin' lay? Only a fool'd think it!"

"Be silent!" Charlotte said icily. "We shall hear from you in due time. William shall tell us first what is the truth of the matter."

"He's a liar and a thief himself!" Abel shouted desperately. "You shall not believe him, ma'am, indeed you shall not! He's been robbin' you all blind for—"

"That is a matter that is no concern of yours," Charlotte snapped. "If I choose to concern myself later with such tales— Well, let be. Now it is William I shall hear."

"Aye, William! Tell us all you know!" Jesse said, still in a high good humor. He was leaning against the newel post at the foot of the stairs, staring at Lil with the same grin on his face, and Charlotte's jaw tightened as she saw it. "It should make a merry tale for a dull evening!"

"I follered 'im all the way to Oxford Street and along it," William said importantly, "and 'im walking like a person in a dream. 'Twas a wonder 'e wasn't run down by a carriage half a dozen times! But 'e went like one who's gone the same way many times—familiar-like, you know, sir? Well, sir, he got to this house in some dirty alley off Old Compton Street"— William produced a grimace that clearly indicated how far above such places he was—"and I took the great risk of following of him right into the house. In the service of my mistress, sir, I am as faithful as a man may be, and Madam had said as I was to—"

"Well, well, man, we know what a paragon you are! Get on, get on!"

"Well, sir, there she was, this piece of rubbish here." He jerked his head at Lil, and immediately she flew at him, her hands outstretched and her fingers clawed, aiming for his face, at the same time as Abel, with one sharp tug of his head, released his ear from William's slackening hold.

"Don't you call me out o' my name!" Lil shrieked, and at the same time Abel swung a wide blow at the man's belly. Charlotte screamed, and Jesse roared his crack of laughter again, and came across the black and white tiles of the hall with deceptive ease, but to some purpose, for he caught Lil by the waist before she could reach William's eyes, and held Abel back with one hand, clamping it hard onto his upper arm.

"We'll have none o' that!" he said jovially. "Not in a gentleman's house! Be glad I'm in a good humor, or I'd tan the hides off both of you as soon as speak to you! Now, William, continue."

William gulped, and moving with some difficulty, straightened himself and went on in a rather choked voice that made Lil throw a triumphant sneer at him.

"Well, sir, she kissed him—begging your presence, madam—throwing her arms about him very unrestrained, and then—"

"And then he fell over his own feet, so eager as 'e was to spy on what doesn't concern 'im, and I set about 'im fast, for I've no mind to 'ave stinkin' spies creepin' into *my* house!" Lil said shrilly. "As if Abel was doin' anything wrong! Why, sir"—and she turned and ran to Jesse to stand looking up at him appealingly—"why, sir, you understands, don't you? You're a man o' the world, and your adopted boy here—why, he's truly worthy of you! Fallen into good fortune as he has, there's many as'd expect him to forget old friends and turn his nose up at those who've not had the great good fortune to catch Mr. Constam's eye! But not Abel! My friend Abel, why, he went on coming to visit me, down there in my little house—and I'm the first to know it's not as rich a house as it might be, but what can such as I do but my best?—and didn't say to you or your good lady as he was visiting me for fear you'd think he was begging on his friend's account! For he's a good boy, is Abel, and cares for his friends, and though there's been many a time I've said to him, 'Dear boy,' I've said, 'would not kind Mr. Constam do for me all he's done for you?' and he's said, 'Why, dear Lil, no doubt he would, were he asked, but I can't ask him, for he's the most generous soul alive, and would weep to know of your hardship and would suffer so, and how could I do so cruel a thing to my kind benefactor? He cannot care for all the poor people of the town, dearly as I know he would wish to, and . . .'"

Jesse had been staring at her, eyes wide at first with surprise and then with a great grin of appreciation spreading across his face; and now he laughed aloud.

"Why, child, you've the tongue of an angel! Where did you learn to talk as sweet as that? To hear such lies told with such style! Abel never said anything of the sort, and well you know it! But it's a credit to you to defend him so well in pleading for yourself! I like you, young—Lil, did you say? Indeed, I like you! A girl of spirit and one of my stamp!"

Charlotte was standing very still at the edge of the little group, and Abel, looking away from Lil and Jesse in considerable embarrassment—for to hear Lil turning her wheedling ways upon him seemed to him to be almost as though she had taken off her clothes—saw her face and was puzzled. He was almost comatose by now with fatigue and alarm and confusion, yet even through the mists of his own preoccupations he could see she looked strange—white and drawn somehow, and suddenly older than she had ever seemed.

Charlotte was indeed feeling as she looked. It was as though she had been struck a blow in her belly as physical as the one that had made William gasp and double up. Although she had been looking so carefully all these months for some evidence that would prove to her that Abel was Jesse's son, to have it thrust at her so sharply and in so shocking a way was almost more than she could bear.

For she was now in no doubt. This boy, this child she had sat beside and taught his letters and his pothooks, was precisely as Jesse was. They might not look alike, not show any physical similarities at all, but there it was. In the blood. Just as the man crept out of his house, leaving behind the comfort and cleanliness and peace of a good establishment to paddle in the muds and filths of the slums in search of the most degraded of female company, so did the boy.

She closed her eyes, sick at the thought. Bad as it was that Jesse should have so evil a strand in his character, how much worse was this child! For child he was, yet one that sought females of so low a type, so debauched a nature, that any normal mind must shrink from contemplation of it.

For a moment, a memory of the day she had first seen the boy came vividly into her mind, limning itself clearly against her closed eyelids: the child standing reeking and filthy beside the woman in the yellow dress with her painted face and brassy hair . . .

She snapped her eyes open to look about her almost desperately: at Jesse, still gazing with that warm and leering regard at the girl; at Abel, standing white-faced and swaying beside William; at William's face, half triumphant and half afraid as he looked slyly at her.

"Well, Mr. Constam? And what shall we do about this situation?" she asked harshly. "For all this boy's actions so parallel . . ."

She stopped sharply, aware of William again. "William,

you may go. Go to your bed at once—no, we'll lock the house ourselves. You go. I'll speak with you again." Even in the middle of her distress and confusion, she remembered the boy's accusations against the man, and noted the need to investigate the facts. It could indeed be true, and if it was . . . "Go on, William! Do you hear me? I have private matters to discuss!"

Sulkily William departed, casting one look of loathing at the boy before disappearing through the green baize door at the back of the hall on his way to the back stairs, leaving a thick silence behind him.

Then Charlotte spoke again in the same strained, harsh voice. "Well, sir?" she repeated. "What's to be done?"

"What's to be done?" Jesse looked at her, his eyebrows raised. "What can there be to be done, ma'am? Send the boy to his bed, let this child go about her business, and forget the whole matter! What else?"

"Forget it? Forget— Indeed, sir, you go too far! How shall I forget so—so wicked a course of action as has been followed by this—this creature you have foisted on me? In all these long months while I have done all in my power to bring him to a knowledge of all that is good and virtuous, to expunge from his mind the memories of his evil past, he has been sneaking out and meeting— Faugh!" And the sound of disgust she produced was so filled with emotion, so expressive of her revulsion, that even Jesse looked away in embarrassment.

"Well, ma'am, if you feel so strong about it, then—what should you wish done? I'll tell you now, I'll not willingly suffer your complaints about it should I try to force you to continue as we are."

"Don't send me away! Don't send me away!" Abel's voice came shrill and thick, and Jesse turned and stared at him, his eyebrows raised a little. "It matters so much to you, boy? You have an affection for us, perhaps?" And he looked at Abel with narrowed eyes, his chin up a little.

Abel stood for a moment, trying to think what he should say, but he was too tired for deviousness, too exhausted to say anything but the truth. He shook his head jerkily.

"I want to learn," he said simply. "I want to keep to my books."

There was a silence, and then Jesse said softly, "Good boy. You're a good boy, Abel. Had you lied to me, I think perhaps I should have sent you out of the house now, back to your slums—but you're a good boy, straight with me. I'll be as straight with you, on every chance there is."

"Well, sir?" Charlotte said it again, her voice cracked and icy. "What decision shall you make? For I'll not have him in my house a moment longer than need be, and that you should keep well in your mind when making your plans!"

"Turn him out of doors, ma'am, and then what happens to your precious Charity? Hey, Mrs. Constam? Come, you know as well as I that cannot be!"

"If I told the truth of this evening's revelations, then none would think the worse of me, and well you know it!" Charlotte said, her chin up. "I have no fears on that score."

Abel lifted his head again to stare at her, his eyes dilating. "You're sending me back, ma'am? You . . ."

She looked at him—at the eyes seeming so huge as to be almost black in the pinched face, the white, luminous skin and the springing hair—and felt her throat constrict. Send him back? How could she? Jesse's son, who had inherited only the bad that was in him and, it seemed, none of the good; who was as evil in his desires as—as . . . She swallowed hard and shook her head.

"No, I'll not send you back whence you came. I have a conscience after all, a Christian conscience that bids me see no person suffer. But I'll not have you in my house while you remain so bad a boy, for I could not bear to look at you."

"I'll do as first I planned, I believe, but do it sooner," Jesse said suddenly. "You shall come to the warehouse, Abel. I'll see to it you have the books you want to study in your own hours, but for the rest you shall work with me, and sleep below the counter as have many apprentices before you. It's a good life and offers great beginnings."

"No!" Charlotte said it almost without thinking, and Jesse looked at her in surprise, for she had sounded very vehement.

"Why not, ma'am? Is it not the best solution?"

She shook her head. How could she explain to him the rush of feeling that had come up in her narrow chest as Jesse had spoken, the vision of the two of them, Jesse and the boy, side by side for the long daytime hours, out of her eyes, growing closer together as father and son, caring for each other and leaving her outside, unneeded and unwanted . . .

"He will debauch the other apprentices. To introduce to the company of your apprentices one that is known to be of evil ways is not to be thought of. You do so and I must inform such as are interested in the welfare of apprentices of your actions. Their parents who paid their indentures, the Guild . . ."

"So what would you have me do, ma'am?" Jesse was growing impatient. "You speak no sense! To inform against your husband and make business troubles for such a reason? You must be half out of your wits!"

"And why should I not be, with such a night behind me? Such shocks, such fears, such matters as no well-bred woman should ever have to consider! But I am not out of my wits, sir, nor likely to be. I tell you only that I'll not have the boy in this house, nor about your business either, if I can prevent it. And you know full well I can: if not prevent it fully, make it all so much a pother for you that you'll wish you'd not crossed me in this matter!"

He nodded, heavily. "Oh, yes! I know. You can make more distress for a man than any other woman ever born, as I have found to my full cost! But you have not yet said what you would have me do—only what you would not!"

She bit her lip, and looked at the boy, and then said slowly, "You could apprentice him to some—"

Jesse gave a crack of sour laughter. "What, ma'am? Is it fitting to debauch another man's apprentices with his company but not my own? Fine sentiments for a Christian lady!"

"—but that will not serve," she went on as though he had not spoken. "He needs much correction and training and controlling if ever he is to overcome this fatal flaw in his character. And I am woman enough and soft enough, despite the ill way I have been used, to wish the boy only well, and would see him cared for. He should be sent away to some— some establishment where he will be taught and trained and made into a good and useful man. Mr. Spenser has an interest in a school at Islington, a Christian establishment where boys are taken by the term to learn their books and be brought to a knowledge of their own sinfulness. Mr. Spenser will, I have no doubt, obtain a place for him there. And the costs shall be borne by the Committee of the London Ladies."

Jesse shook his head vigorously. "Indeed, ma'am, I shall pay any costs involved. If the boy wishes to learn, then a time at a school will be of use to him, and I have no objections. There is ample opportunity yet for him to come to the business. But none shall say I shirk my responsibilities, ma'am! I took him on as my adopted child, and so he shall remain! I pay his fees."

She nodded after a moment, her head heavy with weariness and the weight of the discovery she had made.

"As you wish it, Mr. Constam," she said, and turned to go toward the stairs—and stopped as she saw Lil.

She was leaning against the wall, her arms folded beneath her shawl, watching with bright-eyed alertness all that was going on. She seemed to show no signs of fatigue, or even to be particularly alarmed about her situation, and Charlotte's lips tightened.

"Abel," she said, without turning her head to look at him, "go to your room at once. We shall discuss further our plans for you, and you shall try, if you can, to express some contrition for your behavior. But now, to bed."

He raised his head, for he had been standing with his hands hanging limply by his side and his chin resting on his chest, almost asleep on his feet. He looked blearily at her, and then, after a long moment in which he seemed to be gathering every scrap of energy that was in him, he nodded heavily and moved toward the baize door.

"You may use this staircase tonight," Charlotte said, and he paused and blinked and obediently changed his course.

As he put his foot on the bottom step, Lil said softly, "Good night, dear Abel!"

He turned his head and looked at her and essayed a smile, but it was no more than a grimace, and then, with immense effort, began to climb the stairs. He looked back once at the top and saw her standing there, her halo of dark, curly hair outlined against the white paneling of the wall, her head on one side in that perky way of hers, and muttered, "I'll come to you again soon." But they only saw his lips move, and heard nothing, for there was no power in his voice at all.

The three of them stood there for a long moment after Abel had gone climbing heavily up the further flights and they could all hear his clumping footsteps. They heard the door of his distant attic room open and then close, so silent was the house now, and then Charlotte turned to look at Lil again.

"And, now, you," she said harshly. "Decisions must be made about *you*."

· NINETEEN ·

THEY stood and looked at each other for a long time, the two females: the one with her back erect, her face pinched and white above her fashionable dress and looking every moment of her thirty-six years; the other dirty and disheveled and dressed in the shabbiest of clothes, but so full of controlled energy and life and the strength of her twelve years that she seemed to fill the narrow hallway with her presence.

"Well, Mrs. Constam?" Lil said perkily when the silence seemed almost to crackle about their ears. "What decision shall you make about me?"

Jesse, once again leaning on the newel post, gave a sudden thick gurgle of laughter, and Charlotte turned furiously on him.

"I do not see what there is to laugh at in this situation, Mr. Constam! Your levity throughout this dreadful evening has been no credit to your sensibilities!"

"Oh, I'm sensible enough to what is afoot," Jesse said, still grinning in that infuriating fashion. "Here's matters that shock you, on which, as always, you put the most evil of interpretations."

"I put no evil interpretations on aught, sir! I see what is to be seen, and no more."

He raised his eyebrows at that, and his face hardened a little. "Indeed, ma'am? Then you behave out of your usual character! You have always thought the worst of any person's behavior, and tonight indeed you have excelled yourself! Oh, I know what you think! You think this little miss is young Abel's light o' love—that he has been searching out her company for lustful causes. Did you never think it possible the boy was lonely for his old haunts and old friends? That perhaps he went to the Dials as I do—in search of friendly company and an absence of censorious gentility and criticism of the sort that fills this house to overflowing? That—"

"Mr. Constam, I will not discuss such matters in company—even in such degraded company as this."

"I—am—no—whore!" Lil's voice was low, but came at them with a controlled ferocity that made them both turn and stare at her. She had straightened herself, no longer lounging against the wall, and her eyes were narrowed to black slits of rage. "I am no whore!" She said it again, a little louder this time, and moved threateningly forward. "And not you nor any other shall ever say it! Abel visited me, as you said, yer honor"—she turned her head and looked at Jesse, and her face softened, taking on again the look of innocent charm that had previously filled it when she spoke to him— "for the sake of friendship and kindness, and to help me."

"To help you? How could he help you—as ignorant and dirt-born as yourself?" Charlotte said, her voice thick with scorn.

"He taught me a lot. How to walk and talk and be a lady . . ." Lil flashed, and then reddened and looked at her feet, discomposed for the first time. She had not meant to say as much.

"To be a lady!" Jesse said. "Well, well! There's a new breath abroad in the Dials these days! To meet two such ambitious creatures in the space of one year! To be a lady! Well, well, well!" And he laughed again, but not unkindly, and Lil smiled up at him, all dimples and sparkle.

" 'Tis late, and I for one am too weary for all this nonsense," Charlotte said sharply. "I care not what you are, nor what you wish to be. My only concern is that you should no longer concern yourself with Abel. We have agreed to rear him as a boy should be reared, with full regard for religion and the respect due to his betters. You have been, clearly, an evil influence on him, for why else should he sneak out of his comfortable place here to go to your foul slum?"

She did not look at Jesse, standing so close behind her, and went on, with her color a little heightened and speaking more rapidly. "If we are to rear this boy to any semblance of respectable manhood, it is essential he shall have no more contact with such as you! If you will agree to go away and not to see him again, not even if he comes seeking you—which I think he will not, when I have done with him, but there is always the possibility—if you will so agree, then you may go now and no more said, although it would be a matter of moments to call the Watch to you, and have you sent to some House of Correction. What sort of girl you are, at your young age, to be in a house alone and visited so is not my affair, though what your parents can be thinking of—"

"I have no parents. None but myself," Lil said sulkily.

Charlotte raised her eyebrows. "And live alone?"

"Aye."

"Then indeed you shall give me your promise, for if you do not, the Watch shall be called forthwith so that you may be set to Coram's Hospital or the like! No child of your age should be living so free."

Lil shook her head vigorously. "If you do that, I shall make so great a trouble of myself that they'll throw me out—or at any rate, I'll run away from them. There's no place can hold Lil Burnell against her will, and so I tell you! You'll need better than a threat like that to keep me away from Abel"—she dropped her eyes and then swept the lashes up to look devastatingly at Jesse over Charlotte's shoulder—"who teaches me so much of the matters I want to know of."

"She's bargaining with you, ma'am!" Jesse said, hugely amused. "The little wretch is trying her hand at browbeating you! What is it you want, child, to try such tricks? You've some plan to mind, I've no doubt of that! You've been as saucy as a bird since you walked in here, when any other would be frightened half to death!"

Lil grinned up at him again, and then shifted her gaze to

Charlotte's face. "I want to learn to be a lady," she said with great simplicity; "to talk right, and move right and dress right. I practice a little with Abel to guide me, but it isn't enough. Will you arrange for me to be taught such matters as you arranged for him?"

Charlotte moved away to walk along the hallway, suddenly much disquieted by the girl's steady gaze, and needing to think clearly. That the girl was the prime mover in the friendship between herself and the boy was becoming more and more clear, although that did not alter the fact that Abel was cut out of the same piece of cloth as Jesse, with his slum jaunts. She had no doubt that the girl would indeed make sure of seeing Abel again, unless she had what she wanted. But what an absurd thing to want! To be a lady! What chance had a creature of her stamp of ever learning of such matters? The most she could ever hope for would be to be apprenticed to some useful trade, or get into service in a good household. . . .

She turned back to the girl then, an idea coming to her that would solve the problem very simply, marveling at herself that she hadn't thought of it sooner, and opened her mouth to speak. And stopped, for though Jesse was still standing as he had been when she had moved away from him, although the girl too had not moved, still there was something between them, a sort of movement as of invisible air, for he was looking at her with that same foolish leer, and she staring up at him with the same dimpled knowing sparkle—yet there was more to it than that, and Charlotte knew it.

Suddenly she felt lost and bleak—so far away from Jesse, and so lonely, that to her own amazement and almost horror she felt a prickling behind her eyelids. She swallowed hard and sniffed sharply, banishing the feeling, and swept forward again.

"Well, I shall think on this," she said crisply. "You shall go now, and return tomorrow at eleven. To the area door, mark you, not this one. No—tomorrow is Sunday. On Tuesday, if you please. I require time to consider—well, on Tuesday I shall tell you what is to be done. You need not hope you shall see the boy, for he will be constrained to keep his room until such time as he goes away to school, which will be very soon—as soon as I can arrange it. So away with you, and return as I bid. And come with a clean dress on you and clean hands and face. You're not fit for a decent house the way you are."

Lil looked at her narrowly, and then, satisfied, nodded. "At eleven. I shan't fail. And if you can make a way for me, well"—she pulled her shawl up over her head, arranging the ends deftly about her shoulders—"Abel will soon forget me, I daresay."

She came promptly at eleven on Tuesday, wearing a clean print stuff dress and with her hair tied back beneath a plain white cap, announcing herself demurely to the cook as one expected by the mistress of the house. It said much for her self-assurance that the cook took herself upstairs without argument to tell Charlotte of her arrival, for generally Cook would have sent such as she packing, fearing she had come about a place as a maid and preferring to find a crony of her own to fill any place in the house.

The girl walked easily into the breakfast parlor, to which Cook was told to bring her, with a lightness of step that, while it did not in any way show obvious insolence, still had more of spirit about it than Cook liked to see in one so young—and certainly in one who might join the household. She went glumly back to her kitchen, much put about, for with William turned out of his place without a character, and fair warning given to the rest of them (herself most particularly) about the watch that would be kept on the kitchen traffic in future by Madam herself, the servants' quarters in the Constam household were not a comfortable place to be. Charlotte had gone like a whirlwind through her establishment, and all of them were feeling the sting of her tongue.

Now, in the breakfast parlor, she sat and looked at the girl standing so calmly before her and frowned. She should look at the very least nervous or eager or something of the sort! But there she stood, as calm and comfortable as though she were in such situations every day of her life.

Irritably, Charlotte said, "I have given much thought to you—not because I regard you as so important, or in any way an irritation to me, but because of my concern for such as you. I am, you must know, the prime mover of an excellent body of ladies dedicated to the rescue and care of—of such as you. Since you have asked me to give you help, then I shall, through the efforts of our Committee, do so."

"And I shall promise not to see Abel again, if that is how you wish it," Lil said cheerfully, and smiled widely at her.

"I am not interested in your promises or implied threats!" Charlotte said icily. "Indeed you shall not see the boy again, simply because the opportunity shall not be given you. I have considered the list of placings available to such children of the profligate poor as I should select to benefit from our Committee's work, and have decided on a place at Edenbridge, in Kent. It is some considerable distance from London, and you will be hard put to it to maintain a contact with any of your—old friends of any sort. Which is in many ways our object, for only by separating such as you from the evils of your background is there any hope of ever bringing you to any semblance of decent living."

"What sort of place?" Lil spoke more sharply now. "For if I don't like what you choose I shall say so, and that's all about it."

Her lips tightening at the insolence of the girl's manner, Charlotte went on as though she had not spoken. "The owner of the farm, known as Carter's End, is one Mr. Samuel Lucas, and he is in need of an extra person for his household. There is a housekeeper, a lady of strong will and excellent morals, who will be in charge of the training and care of the girl who is sent to the house, and—"

"And what of Mrs. Lucas? Will she teach me too? For it is from ladies that I most wish to learn."

Charlotte looked up sharply. "There is no Mrs. Lucas, although that is of no interest to you. In the normal course of events, such girls as work in the house of a widower do not attend on the master. His needs are served by the housekeeper and his valet, both of whom, I am informed, are excellent persons of exemplary character. This house has been recommended to our Committee by the vicar of the parish in which Carter's End is situated, and as such is totally suitable for our purposes. You shall go tomorrow morning, bearing a card of introduction from me, and will make your way from

Edenbridge, where you will leave the stage, to the farm. I am informed it is no more than a mile or two to walk, and you should reach the place before nightfall. And you are not to return to London for the full five years of your apprenticeship, for this is the light in which this arrangement shall be considered. You understand me?"

Lil stood and stared at the thin-lipped woman at the desk and tried to think as rapidly as she could, while keeping her face as calmly inscrutable as she was able.

If she refused this place, what would occur? To return to Fitch's house and the old life was clearly not to be thought of. Now that this woman knew of her and where she lived, she would surely watch and spy upon her—and the lucrative resurrection business would soon be discontinued in such circumstances.

To seek a new home here in London, a new lay? But what new lay could there be that did not approach the life of the night-houses and divans? And that life was not for Lil! Life in a gentleman's household, on the other hand, even as an apprentice dairymaid, had much to offer. Perhaps more than this woman could ever imagine. Lil smiled her long slow smile.

"I shall go. It will serve me well enough, as long as I can learn the matters that I wish there. I shall go."

"As for that," Charlotte said, rising dismissively to her feet, "you will learn what is necessary for you to learn, which is the running of a gentleman's household, the ordering of his kitchen and dairy, and like matters. It is an excellent opportunity for you."

"Oh, yes, ma'am," Lil said softly now, smiling up at her. "An excellent opportunity."

Charlotte stared down at her, at the lovely little face with its delicate vivid coloring and the lashes that so thickly fringed the wickedly sparkling green eyes, and felt a little stab of doubt; it seemed the best place to send her, inasmuch as it was the farthest away, but yet . . .

"You shall learn, too, not to look at your betters in so insolent and vulgar a fashion!" she said with sudden spitefulness. "With such a brazen look upon your face you should as soon be called Lilith, like the serpent in the Garden of Eden, as by your own ridiculous name."

"Lilith?" The girl tilted her head to one side and looked up at her, her eyes wide. "Lilith? A serpent?"

"Indeed a serpent, a most wicked and designing creature, who caused the Fall of our mother Eve."

"Lilith." She said it slowly, savoring the sound of it on her tongue. "Lilith. I like that."

She sighed softly then, and looked up at Charlotte fleetingly. "I shall be sad not to see Abel again to say goodbye! Ah, well, that is the way of it! Will you tell him that I have gone, and wish him well, and tell him of your goodness to me, yours and kind Mr. Constam's?"

"This is none of Mr. Constam's doing, but that of my Committee," Charlotte snapped, "and so you must remember. The time will come when you will pay back into the funds spent in your behalf—for we must find the price of your premium for your apprenticeship to Mr. Lucas's household—as you will discover. But you need not fear about that, for we shall keep track of you and receive reports on you, and if your behavior is not as it should be, you shall reap the consequences! Now be off with you. The stagecoach leaves from Charing Cross at seven o'clock tomorrow morning, and your ticket will await you at the booking office there. And remember! We shall be keeping our eyes on you!"

The girl produced another of her winning smiles and went cheerfully away, leaving Charlotte feeling baffled and sore and thoroughly put about. The interview had been all wrong. The girl should have been humble or afraid or at least clearly grateful for her good fortune, but she had been none of these things. There had been a mocking note in her voice, a sharpness in her glance and a self-awareness in her that had made Charlotte feel uncomfortable and uneasy, almost as though she had been weighed in the girl's balance and found wanting.

At which absurd notion, she swept out of the room to set about the remainder of her planning for the future. With Abel's school to be arranged, and the boy to be equipped and transported there, there was much to be done before she could rest comfortably.

And much she did do that day and the next, for when Jesse returned on Thursday evening from his countinghouse to take his dinner with her, she could report to him that the school had been sent a message by Mr. Spenser's hand asking them to be ready to receive a new pupil in a few days, and the boy himself had been apprised of the fact.

"He is well enough now, then, I understand?" Jesse said, grunting a little as he settled himself to table.

"Well enough," she said shortly. "His only ailment, I believe, was lack of sleep, and who can wonder at it if he had been spending his nights out of his bed and—"

"—in hers, would you say, ma'am?" asked Jesse, grinning hugely. "Nay, don't look like that! Without Miss Dorothea here to note it, surely we can talk as grown men and women! Where is she?"

"Dorothea is to keep her room for a few days yet," Charlotte said. "I have told her she should rest a little and dosed her carefully, for in this treacherous spring weather care is needed. And I would not have her in any contact at all with Abel at the present time, if you would have the truth of the matter. Better she should remain within her own chamber until he is gone. This is why I have made all arrangements for the school as soon as may be."

"And the girl?" Jesse asked, his mouth full of crimped cod. "What of her?"

"The girl?" Charlotte raised limpid eyes to his. "I cannot say. She did not return Tuesday morning, and when I sent William to seek her, before I told him he should leave our employ—and I have much to tell you on *that* score, Mr. Constam—he found she had gone no one knew where, taking all her belongings with her." She looked down at her plate, appearing to be giving her full attention to the removal of a bone from her own fish. "I do not think we shall be perturbed by that one again."

"No?" Jesse grinned a little. "A pity, that. I thought her a charming child."

But Charlotte did not pick up the challenge in his voice, and he lost interest in the matter, for amusing though he had found the occurrences of Saturday evening, they had not mattered much to him; he had other concerns on his mind, and fell to talking of them. For all their disagreements with each other in most other spheres of their shared life, Charlotte did at least understand many of the complexities of his business, and took a lively and intelligent interest in them. In talking business matters to her, he found himself as close to her as ever could be. And she for her part was glad indeed to lead him away from talk of the girl. It would be a long time before she would forget the expression on his face when he had looked at her, or the jealous despairing anger that had risen in her. But the episode was over now, and she felt the better for that.

And when a week later she watched Mr. Spenser escorting a pale and silent Abel in his own carriage, the small tin trunk filled with essential clothes tied on behind, to his new school in Islington, she felt even better. The truth about the boy could not be gainsaid, but life would be a great deal easier without him under her roof, reminding her of Jesse's perfidy and dreadful ways at every turn.

Perhaps, she thought optimistically, as the carriage disappeared in the distance and she dropped the drawing-room curtain into place, perhaps now the boy is gone we shall return to some semblance of normal living. Without his presence in the house, perhaps Jesse will no longer be reminded of the slums, and will stop making his still all-too-frequent visits there. . . .

Perhaps.

Part II

· TWENTY ·

ABEL stood before the drawing-room window staring out at the dusty sunlit stretches of Gower Street and making a conscious effort to be comfortable in his mind. But it was exceedingly difficult now that he was in this house again for good after so long a time. Of course, there had been occasions during the four years of his school days when he had returned to Gower Street; he had gloomily celebrated Christmas here (thinking all the time of how much less disagreeable it would have been even to be with some of the other boys at school), and had spent long, boring weeks in the summer holidays in the schoolroom. But those visits had not touched him in any way: they had been so patently temporary, mere breathing spaces in the school year.

But now it was different. School was over. He had mixed feelings about that. There had been good people at school whom he had liked and whose company he had enjoyed after they had got over the early days of jeering at him for his slum origins; once he had begun to achieve some status by showing himself to be better at his books, for all his lack of early learning, and had shown he could fight harder and run faster than any one of them, they had accepted him and indeed, in the last year or so, quite admired him. But they had been hard years, for the school was run on harshly ascetic lines, with strong concern for spiritual welfare, a grudging respect for intellectual achievement, and no interest whatsoever in physical comfort. There had been many times when he had suffered from the cold as sorely as in his gutter days, had yearned to fill his belly with good food as eagerly as when he had had to steal his victuals. But all in all they had been tolerable years, and now that they were over it would all be different.

He smiled a little wryly as he thought that. He had been sent there as a punishment, to be kept away from the evils of his visits to Lil, yet had emerged an educated person with his head stuffed with Latin and Mathematics, Natural Philosophy, and Theology. A strange bargain.

Lil. He let the thought of her slip into his mind, knowing it would hurt as much as ever. Not once, in all this long time, had he been able to think of her without pain. That she could have disappeared from his life so totally, with no word, no message even of farewell, had at first alarmed him (she must be dead! or ill! or in danger!) and then deeply depressed him. That had come after he had managed to go to the house in Old Compton Street.

It had been in the autumn of his first year at school. They had made him stay there for the first summer holiday, keeping him at his books under the disdainful icy gaze of Headmaster Loudoun himself, while other pupils disported themselves at home. But just before the term was due to recommence, Mr. Loudoun had departed for a hard-earned and refreshing visit to the cathedral at Canterbury, and Abel had been able to escape from the school for a whole night.

He had gone, of course, to Fitch's house, trudging his way heavily through the muddy lanes to the City and thence to the middle of London. The house he had found deserted and silent, and daringly he had knocked to awaken the people who lived on each side. There had been some swearing and complaining at that, for even slum dwellers take to their beds at night like more sober and respectable citizens, but there had been one boy willing enough to tell Abel what he wanted to know.

"Them in that 'ouse?" he'd said, leaning against the door of his own filthy home and staring curiously at Abel. "I knows about 'em. What's it to you? And what'll yer give us for tellin' of it?"

Since Abel had no money at all—the school disapproving totally of pocket money for boys—he could offer only the jacket from his own back, knowing full well that he would have to think of some very plausible lie to explain the loss. But it would be worth it to know what had happened to Lil, and so he parted with it cheerfully enough, though doing so left him shivering in the cold; it had been a warm September, but in these chill small hours there was a marked smell of October in the air.

" 'E lorst 'is partners, ol' Fitch," the boy said, tucking the coat under his verminous shirt, "an' took up wiv others. But it weren't never the same, and 'e got took by the Watch wiv a corpse on 'is back, and that were the last I ever 'eard of 'im. There's none in these parts cares much for resurrection men, so there was none to come to 'is 'elp, and for all I knows 'e's been transported or topped. 'E ain't 'ere no more, an' that's for certain."

"And the girl—the one that lived in the basement below. What of her?" Abel asked eagerly. "Where did she go?"

The boy shrugged. "No way of knowin', 'ave I? Comes out of the 'ouse one morning—saw 'er wiv me own eyes—all 'er gear tied up in a yeller straw basket, 'air tied up in a cap and wearin' of a blue dress as sassy an' as fancy as yer please, sees me 'ere aloadin' of me barrer—I bin sellin' fish this summer, though I've a fancy for a new lay nah it's gettin' 'arder to get the stock—well, I says to 'er, 'And where's you off to, all done up like a dollymop?' And she spits in me face, on account she was never one to let a body talk sideways to 'er, and says as 'ow she's fallen in good fortune and orf she's goin' to live in a gentleman's 'ouse. An' I tells her what I thinks of such lies, and away she goes, but I never sees 'er again, so maybe— Gawd knows she was saucy enough for anythin', she was . . ."

Abel had gone trudging miserably back to Islington, to be whipped eventually for the loss of his coat and to mourn even more unhappily the loss of his Lil. That first winter had been a painful time. Numb with his distress, more embittered than he himself fully realized by Charlotte and Jesse's rejection of him, he had only his books to comfort him and had worked so relentlessly that even the sour Mr. Loudoun was moved to unwilling approval.

But when spring came, he stirred himself to seek her yet again. In March the chance came, for the news of the Peace of Amiens drove everyone wild. Abel had never been one to think much about political matters, concerning himself with talk of the wars and the doings of Old Boney only when they seemed to have some bearing on his own affairs, which was rarely enough; but the excitement that came with the Peace had given him just the opportunity he needed.

The school allowed the boys a half-holiday in which to celebrate, and in the excitement (by which even Mr. Loudoun was affected, to the extent that the tip of his nose became quite pink and stayed so for almost a week) Abel contrived to slip away from the school for the afternoon and obtain a cart ride into London.

He spent the long afternoon hours prowling about the town, from Piccadilly, with its crowds of drunken, squealing merrymakers, to Hyde Park, where thousands of the poorest congregated, deliriously shrieking their delight not so much at the end of the threat of Boney as because of the free beer being distributed. Back to Haymarket and Regent Street, Leicester Square and the Strand, pushing and thrusting, seeking through the milling mob for a glimpse of her, but to no avail. He could not imagine she would miss any of the pleasure to be found in such a day, and was so convinced that he would find her that time and again his throat thickened with excitement and his hands shook as he got a glimpse of a curly head, or a delicately curved pair of hips beneath a narrow waist. And time and again disappointment left him drained of feeling, or sometimes so full of it that there were tears hurting his eyelids.

He had returned to school in so lugubrious a mood that Mrs. Loudoun had dosed him with one of her most disagreeable concoctions and sent him to his bed; and it was almost a month before he had quite conquered this new misery and disappointment.

And so it had gone on, as he had grown up at the school, mastering his Latin—enough to read books of zoology (which quite entranced him)—and becoming deeply enamored of Natural Philosophy, with its emphasis on the structure of matter and the workings of the world, both animate and inanimate. And whenever the chance presented, he slid away to London to haunt the streets and alleys, always looking. Hoping and looking.

On one such occasion he had seen Jesse, surrounded by a group of street Arabs for whom he was buying hot eel pies and peas. Abel had shrunk back against the alley wall, his head tucked into his coat collar, to stand and watch the way Jesse's expansive movements and great laugh seemed to fill the whole street with his personality, to watch him swallow the gratitude and fawning of the ragamuffins as eagerly as they swallowed the food he gave them.

It's that he comes for, Abel thought wonderingly; just that. Not for girls, nor any such matters. Just for that. And he thought confusedly of the way he himself felt when he was cheered by his schoolfellows for coming first home from a chase, and half sympathized with while half despising the man he was watching. He *was* a man, after all, and should have no need of such; if Abel thought at all about the benefits of growing to manhood, one of its greatest virtues in his eyes was that it conferred freedom from the desire to excel in such paltry ways.

And now, he thought, somberly staring from the window, it was over. School was over. He was a man now, for good or ill—or near enough—and here he stood waiting to hear what had been decided for his future occupation. His jaw hardened. He knew what would be said by Jesse, what Charlotte's views would be, but he had made up his mind on the matter. They should not make a spice man of him, no matter what. The time had gone for that. Had they set him to sleep beneath the counter four years ago, he would have gone quiet enough and glad to do it. But that was four years ago. Now he knew what he wanted and would not be gainsaid. No, he would not.

But all the same, his heart lurched fearfully in his chest when the door opened behind him, and he turned to look as straight as he could and with all the obstinacy he could muster in his bearing at the person who had come in.

But he did not look obstinate to Charlotte. She stood there just inside the door and stared at him with a faint sense of shock. He had grown alarmingly this past half year; he had been in Gower Street at Christmas but not at Easter, when she had asked Mr. Loudoun to keep him at school, for Dorothea had the chicken pox and Charlotte could not be kept from her sickroom duties by the presence of a boy in the house. And now, looking at him, she saw not the boy she remembered, but a most elegant and well-grown youth, who wore his hair cut fashionably short at sides and back but with loose curls upon his forehead, and had the faint shadow of an icipient moustache on his upper lip as well as shadows of masculinity on his shaven cheeks. The long eyes with the absurd lashes that had been so much a feature of his childish face seemed longer and narrower than ever now above the well-developed contours of his bony face, although his mouth had the same drooping curve that had made him look so vulnerable as a child.

"Good afternoon, ma'am," he said, and she was startled again, for his voice had completed its change now, and the husky uncertainties of last Christmas had given way to a clear, deep tone that was well matched to his long body and neat squared shoulders. She bowed an almost embarrassed response before moving with some majesty across the room to her favorite sofa.

He saw, in his turn, a figure heavier in build than it had seemed when last he saw her, although that could be due to her adoption of the new fashionable line; the fuller skirts and heavier draping of the bodice that were now *de rigueur* would make even the slightest of women look agreeably plump. She was wearing her hair in a chignon now, too, which gave her an even greater severity of mien, and his courage failed him a little as he looked at the clearly defined notches running from her nose to her mouth, the determined line of her lips. But he would not be bullied; no, he would not.

"Well, sir, so you have completed your education," she said in a flat, colorless voice.

"My school days, perhaps, ma'am. But not, I think, my education. There is much I must yet study before I can consider myself ready to enter the world as a man should."

She raised her eyebrows a little. "As to that, I cannot say. That shall be a matter for Mr. Constam to discuss. I, of course, am naturally concerned that there shall be a suitable decision about where you shall live now. You appear, at first sight, to be much benefited from your years with the Reverend Mr. Loudoun. Mr. Spenser assured me he would make a dutiful and God-fearing man of you, and indeed he spoke the truth. To *superficial* appearance. I cannot, of course, be sure that all the evil of your birth and early experience has left you sufficiently to allow you still to live here with us. After all, I still recall—"

"Come, ma'am, that was long ago!" Abel said, and his voice was a little louder. "I believe it to be a matter of Christian kindness to forget past misdeeds when all efforts have been made to overcome them!"

"Your education has certainly sharpened your tongue!" she said after a moment. "As to forgiveness—indeed, sir, I am the first to forgive. But I am not so much a fool as to engage upon a situation that might . . ."

The door opened noisily and Abel turned to see Jesse standing there, his hands clasped behind his back under his coattails, staring at him with his head cocked to one side.

"Well, lad! You've grown as fast as a weed since I saw you last! I'd not have thought those pinchpenny Loudouns would overfeed you, but seemingly you've found enough victuals to grow sufficient for two! How do you, hey, boy? As perky as you look?"

"I am well enough, sir, thank you. I believe I have grown considerable this year. It is not unusual in persons of my age."

"Hark at him!" Jesse said, and grinned hugely. "As smart a tongue as ever he had, but with a little school polish set upon it to make it really shine! Well, well!" And he came across the room to sit down at the other end of the sofa, and leaned back with his booted legs outstretched to stare consideringly at the tall figure before him.

"Well, now. To matters of business! We are to decide, are we not, the plan for your future activities. Not that there is so much matter to discuss, of course. I gave my word, and Jesse Constam doesn't go back on it. There's still a place for you in—"

"No, sir!" Abel did not mean to make it sound quite so crisp, and stopped sharply, as startled by the firmness of his refusal as they were.

"Eh? What's 'at?" Jesse frowned and peered up at him. "Damme, boy, come away from that window! Standing there like that I can't see your face, and I want to! Come and sit down like a Christian and tell me what the devil you mean by such a 'No'! No what?"

Obediently Abel seated himself opposite the two of them, folding his long legs awkwardly beneath the gilded stretchers of the chair.

"No, thank you, sir," he said after a moment. "I know indeed that the offer you make to teach me your business is a good and generous one, and I am sensible of your kindness to me. Indeed"—and there was a hint of a smile in his voice—"even if I wanted to be unaware of it, I could not. Mr. Loudoun has been at great pains to cry your praises to me these four years."

"And well he might, the money he's had of me," Jesse grunted. "But what d'you mean, 'No, thank you'? You sit there and tell me you have no wish to learn my business? Why not, pray? What better can you be offered?"

Charlotte was sitting very straight, looking at the boy with her eyes fixed and her mouth firmly closed. She could not have said for all the world what it was that so disturbed her about him. As a boy he had worried her enough, God knew, for tainted as was his inheritance, he needed great care if he were to be brought to any degree of respectability. But now, staring at him, she was moved by the look of him in a most curious way. He was sixteen; not much older than would have been the boy she would have had herself if Jesse had— had she borne a child of this marriage. And so good-looking a sixteen-year-old: too much so, indeed. She looked then at Jesse, at the expression on his face as he too stared at the boy, and she knew in some strange way that the same thoughts had come to him. There was a curious avidity in his expression, as though he were pleading with the boy to like him rather than feeling anger at what he was saying.

For Abel had taken a deep breath and launched himself upon what was so patently a prepared speech that it was almost amusing.

"Sir, ma'am, I am deeply sensible of the goodness you have displayed to me these past five years. That you removed me from the gutter in which I was born to bring me to your home was generosity enough. To have arranged so good an education for me was beyond the call of any Christian charitableness. I would not wish you to—to think I am not fully grateful for all the benefits you have heaped upon me, nor that I display unduly headstrong—er—willfulness in seeking now to persuade you that much as I value the offer to teach me the affairs of the spice trade, I have been seized of an ambition that, while it may seem strange to you, yet means a great deal to me. In short, sir, ma'am, I wish—er—that is to say, it has long been a matter of great interest to me to—er . . ."

He stopped and stared at them for a long moment and then shook his head slightly. "I think you will not understand," he said miserably, "and there is no reason why you should."

"I shall not while you mutter and mumble so," Jesse said roundly. "You might as well out with it, boy! What is it that means so much to you that you cannot talk of it? It must indeed be a strange ambition! Unless, God help me, you've been infected by that milky idiot Loudoun, and want to enter the Church! Now, that *would* be a waste of a likely—"

"Than to enter the Church there can be no higher goal," Charlotte said sharply. She looked again at Abel and let her mouth relax a little. She was not as angered by his words as she would have expected herself to be, and in a confused way she knew why. Just as she had not wanted Abel to join Jesse in the business four years ago, had balked at any plan that would throw the two of them together into any degree of intimacy, now she was strangely relieved that the boy was unwilling to become Jesse's creature at countinghouse and warehouse. So she looked at Abel with a less forbidding expression on her face and said pleasantly enough, "You had best say clearly what it is that you wish to do, now you are educated. We are, I trust, rational persons and can talk sensibly of all possibilities without displaying ugly prejudice."

There was a moment's pause, and then Abel said baldly, "I wish to be a surgeon."

They sat as though stunned, their faces blank with astonishment, and then Jesse cried, in a voice so startled that it came out as a squeak, "A surgeon? A *surgeon?* Good God, boy, where got you such a notion?"

"Long ago. I misremember," Abel said evasively. "But I have always been very interested in such things. And at school I have studied Natural Philosophy, you know, and learned much of the animal world. Now I would like to learn of—of human needs and human ills, and help to deal with them as a surgeon. It is not so strange a career, after all. I have heard of many men who are well thought of by society, and indeed, who have names that are— There is Mr. Astley Cooper, you know, who is at Guy's Hospital, and—"

"But a surgeon!" said Charlotte. "Such ruffianly creatures! All blood and swearing and nastiness—why, I have heard such tales as— Well! This man Astley Cooper: indeed I have heard of him! There was a report but a month or two back of a most dreadful affair. A man sold him the body of a pauper he had taken from its grave in shocking circumstances, not fit for decent people to talk of, and this man Cooper stood up in the court and defended him, and paid money to a lawyer for him, and when the man was sent deservedly to prison, said he would pay for the upkeep of his wife and child until such time as he came out! Ah, no, Abel, you cannot wish to be such a one!"

"They cannot learn to be surgeons on living flesh," Abel said. "A student must learn, and some must find the bodies for them to learn on."

Charlotte shuddered and shook her head. "For my part, Abel, I see no reason why you should not learn another business if the spice trade does not suit you. I am sure Mr. Constam will not stand in your way. But not surgery. I could not bear to be in the same house as one that spent his time with corpses!" And again she shuddered with great delicacy.

"Oh, I am to stay in the house, then, ma'am?" Abel looked at her sideways, a glint of humor in his eyes. "I thought perhaps—"

"Not if you are apprenticed to a surgeon. To any other, perhaps. But we have not educated you so far and brought you to such a state to see you throw yourself away on a way of life that is little better than being keeper of an abbatoir!"

"Such a waste!" Jesse said suddenly, and they looked at

him almost startled, for the sound of his voice made them realize how silent he had been. He looked at Abel now and shook his head. "Do you remember, boy? I took you to the warehouse and taught you the spices, and you learned fast—very fast. Such a nose as you have—it seems a sorry waste not to make use of it."

"But it would be of use to me in the work of a surgeon too, sir," Abel said eagerly—but with little hope. Charlotte's rejection of his desire had been so violent that he could not see how he could change either of their minds. Other plans would have to be made, undoubtedly. . . .

"How so? A surgeon uses knife and bowl and surrounds himself with blood—has no more need of a delicate nose than any other butcher."

"Had you said you wished to be a physician or apothecary I would not have been so set against it," Charlotte said unexpectedly. "For these are men of some gentlemanly ways. No physician would behave so bad as to take the part of the evil men that rob graveyards"—again the shudder—"and an apothecary, of course, is a man of business as well as science, is he not, and needs to be as sensitive in the matter of scents and the properties of herbs and spices as does yourself, Mr. Constam."

Abel felt hope rising tentatively in him. If they would apprentice him to an apothecary, he would at least be part of the way to being a surgeon. He could do as had others before him, and go to lectures on surgery. Perhaps to Mr. Wilson at Great Windmill Street. . . .

"I should be happy enough to be an apothecary indeed, ma'am, if you would think that more fitting. The art of the surgeon will always be of—of great interest to me, but if I may learn the craft of the apothecary I will be content enough. I have a great wish to—to seek out the illnesses that afflict people and—and that perhaps can be cured."

Prudently he said no more, for every instinct told him that any mention of a desire to help women give safe birth to their infants would shock Charlotte immoderately and quite ruin any chance he had of gaining his way; as it was, he was amazed he had found both of them as amenable as they were appearing to be. He had been quite sure he would have to leave the Gower Street house and find some way of his own to fulfill his ambition. But he had time and to spare, for however long it took, surgery was to be his way of life: that much he was determined upon. If they would agree to pay his premium to an apothecary, there would be no harm done, and once started upon that path, why, the road to the hospitals and the true human art for which he longed lay open.

Even after they had agreed, and Jesse had grumblingly said he would speak for Abel to one of his apothecary friends, he could not believe his good fortune. He would never know of the mixture of motives that led them to agree: Charlotte's jealousy; Jesse's respect for ambition, however bizarre it might seem to his taste; Charlotte's dawning realization that it could be agreeable indeed to have an apothecary of her very own available to her; Jesse's tendency to find pleasure in gratifying others' desires. And for both of them, an emotional response to the boy's sheer good looks. Neither of them fully understood that they had been so beguiled by those green eyes and that pale skin and sensuous mouth, but so they were.

And so it was arranged that at the end of December of 1805 Abel Lackland was apprenticed to Josiah Witney, apothecary, of Piccadilly, for a period of five years.

· TWENTY-ONE ·

DOROTHEA had managed to spend the entire morning with the flowers. She had arranged them first in large vases and then, dispirited by the thought of the morning hours stretching endlessly before her, taken them all out to make tasteful arrangements in much smaller bowls, which now were sitting on little tables in the drawing room and the schoolroom. They looked rather dilapidated, it was true, since her handling of the blooms had been somewhat excessive, but at least it was now gone noon and she had not looked at the clock above four or five times since breakfast.

Now she sat in the schoolroom, her hands folded in her lap, staring out at the street below and considering how she might fill in the long hours of the rest of the day. She would never have thought, in the days when she spent those tedious hours with Mama over those tiresome lessons, that she would ever regret the ending of her education, but she could not deny that the days had not seemed so interminable when most of the morning and part of the afternoon had been occupied with study.

She could, perhaps, read a novel. When she was eighteen Mama had stopped fussing quite so much about what was suitable reading for her, but though she had in her younger years heartily wished for the freedom to read what she chose, even that no longer mattered much. Now she could read novels whenever she wanted, she had to admit she found most of them insupportably dull. But then, almost everything was insupportably dull. She shopped a little, sewed a little, helped Mama arrange the household a little (never progressing much beyond flowers, to be sure, since Mama preferred to keep affairs in her own capable hands as far as possible), but none of it was really very amusing.

She ached for something to do, something to be. In all her life she had never amounted to anything much in anyone's eyes, she would tell herself mournfully. If only, now she was grown up, they would let her be more busy, life would be much more bearable. But as it was, she moved through the days and weeks and months, a slight and prettily delicate girl with her fair hair and her wide blue eyes, shadowed always by the mists of boredom. All she had to support her was her private thoughts and dreams and imaginings, and all these curved themselves about one person: Abel.

These days her mind was more than ever full of Abel and his doings, real and imagined. All through his school years she had thought about him, using the fleeting contacts of the holidays as fuel to feed her imagination during the eternity of months that separated their meetings. But now he had come back for good, it was all very different.

Not, to be sure, that she saw a great deal more of him now than she ever had. He had by special dispensation been allowed to live in Gower Street rather than in his new master's house, as was the usual lot of the apprentice. Jesse had intervened here, really wanting to see more of the boy, but maintaining that such an arrangement would be cheaper for him, and since Charlotte too was curiously loath to let him leave her house completely now he had returned, Jesse had been able to prevail upon her to permit it.

So each morning Abel left the house at six o'clock, after a most hasty breakfast, to make the long walk to Mr. Witney's establishment, which lay just east of St. James's Street. He still had the long, rapid strides of the London slum child, the ability to move swiftly and easily through streets and alleys, whatever the weather and however dense the traffic, and would arrive at seven in good time to take down the shutters of the shop and set about the preparation of the day's work before the first customers arrived.

Dorothea had managed to persuade Abel to tell her something of his day's work, which did not end until nine o'clock in the evening, when the shutters were put up and he was free to take the long walk back to Gower Street. He had told her some of what she wanted to know, since it gave him some pleasure to sit in the schoolroom for an hour or so on Sunday afternoon, the only free day he had, and bask in her undisguised admiration. Whatever he told her that he did, she would gasp and widen her eyes and say breathlessly, "And what then, Abel?" in a way that would endow with extra excitement and interest the most meager of his daily tasks.

And some of them were very meager. He quite enjoyed the mixing of Mr. Witney's brews, although there was little skill to the work. Mr. Witney kept a great book of recipes, in which detailed instructions were laid out, and each morning Abel would check the great bottles and jars and then mix enough to bring them up to full. He would measure squills and camphor, rhubarb and ginger, laudanum and nux vomica according to the rules; would roll pills of senna and quassia chips and licorice and alum, skillfully twisting his thumb and forefinger until each soapy little globule could be dropped into its box indistinguishable from its fellows.

He made cachets, too, filling with powder the little rice-paper shapes, sticking them together lightly moistened with spit (it was one of the driest of jobs, that. He did not know which was worse, the taste of the paper or the flying fine powder which filled his nose and made him sneeze) and made cataplasms by rubbing great slabs of heavy doughy masses into linen with a plaster iron until his wrists ached.

But he did not tell Dorothea that, any more than he told her of the dismal hours spent casting up accounts for Mr. Witney, and stocktaking for Mr. Witney, and sweeping the floor and polishing the mahogany counters for Mr. Witney. These were the most boring hours of all, for at least when he was working with the drugs and mixtures he was doing something toward his chosen vocation—though little enough, since he did not know for which ills the drugs were to be used, or how it was decided which a sufferer should take. Mr.

Witney would promise, whenever Abel asked, to tell him in due course if he minded his manners and his tasks and did as he was bidden for the first year or so. A year or so! Abel would think miserably, and then bite his tongue and get on with whatever was to be done.

He was able to tell Dorothea with all truth, however, that Mr. Witney liked him and that he liked Mr. Witney. He was a jovial man, a widower, fat and bouncy, and with a voice still heavy with the Norfolk accent of his country childhood. He would shake his round bald head at Abel, his chins wobbling cheerfully above his starched shirt-collar points for all the world like one of his own herb jellies (For the Delectation of Invalids, and All Those of a Delicate and Refined Nature in Need of Digestible Sustenance, Consisting Entirely of the Purest Natural Substances), and launch into an account of his own apprenticeship fifty years before, when he had had to clean his mistress's house as well as the shop, and had been "'prenticed full two years before he was allowed near the customers."

Abel would say perkily, "Times have changed! I'm an educated man, Mr. Witney, and one that will benefit from early learning of his trade, and will give back good value for his indentures!" But Mr. Witney would merely nod and laugh and say, "Well, we shall see, we shall see!" and hurry off to see one of his many patients at home, leaving an envious Abel behind to mind the counter and sell rubbishy potions to silly girls.

But Dorothea knew nothing of these irritations of the apprentice's lot. She knew only that Abel—tall and beautiful, remote and exciting Abel—was a man of great importance, taking his rightful place in the world, and yet her friend, the one in whom he confided his concern about his manifold affairs.

That he was three years her junior somehow never seemed to matter. Other youths of her own age whom she might know, the sons of her mother's friends, were tedious and childish and ugly in the extreme compared with splendid Abel. If she had thought of the matter of his age at all, she would have imagined a mistake had been made and that he was twenty at the very least.

She sat this Thursday afternoon in early March, not long

after Abel's seventeenth "birthday," and thought about him and all he had told her the last time they had sat here in this dull room. He had been unusually pleased with himself, bright-eyed and cheerful, and had sat before the fire with one leg casually flung out to the fender, the other with the heel set on the edge of his chair so that he could hug his leg and rest his chin upon his knee as he stared into the flames, and told her he was now to start visiting patients with Mr. Witney.

"I think, you know, that it is in his own health that I must seek for the reason. I have no doubt he would have made me wait a full year, till gone next December, before allowing such, as he had first said. But I have got on well enough these past months, and he has had some illness. . . ."

"Illness, Abel? Do you know what sort of illness?"

"Well, he has said nothing to me, you understand, but I have watched him, and he stops on occasion, and holds himself so"—Abel grasped his right arm near the shoulder, holding the elbow close to the chest, and grimacing—"when he is working busily, sometimes, or has hurried from his carriage, and I have seen him look sometimes quite a blue color about the lips. It's hard to see clearly, of course, for he's a red man—has a very ruddy countenance. But he looks *too* red sometimes, and then has this strange look about his mouth. . . ." He nodded wisely. "I believe he is not as healthy as he would wish to be, and this is why he takes me with him and teaches me more, from next week. I think it is a very wise decision."

"Oh, so do I, Abel!" Dorothea said immediately. "And what shall you do when you go with him?"

Since Abel had no idea at all, he said brusquely, "Oh, that is enough for one day! I shall tell you some other time! For now, it is enough. And I must study. Please to leave me in peace, Dorothea, for I am really very busy."

And Dorothea had settled happily to her beadwork (she was making a pair of slippers for Abel) and watched him over her flying fingers as they sat in a comfortable silence before the fire crackling and hissing in the grate. With his head bent over his books and his cheeks outlined with the light, he looked quite achingly familiar, and yet so desirably strange. She did love him so very dearly, she thought, curving her lips as she bent her head over her work again.

Remembering this now, she smiled a little and wondered

whether Abel would tell her what he had done this week if he were here now. To have to wait another two whole days until Sunday to talk to him was dispiriting indeed.

And then, quite suddenly, the idea came to her, and her pulse beat more rapidly at the temerity of the thought. Why should she wait until Sunday? Was she not a young lady now—indeed, past her twentieth birthday? Had not Mama agreed that she could go upon her own shopping expeditions as long as she was properly chaperoned by her maid? There was no need to sit here forlorn and lonely another moment if she did not choose to; she could set out to do some shopping in Piccadilly. A most fashionable quarter for shopping, even more so than Oxford Street or the Strand, and expensive, of course, but there were many shops there, after all, that she could legitimately visit. And if by any chance she should happen to enter Mr. Witney's and see Abel, surely he would not be displeased, while she for her part would ask nothing more than to see that splendid place about which she had heard so much.

She hurried to her room in search of pelisse and bonnet and reticule, to pinch her pale cheeks to a becoming color before summoning her new maid, Susan, to accompany her. As she looked at herself in the mirror, and tweaked her curls into fashionable disorder under the brim of the feathered bonnet, she felt the rustle of anxiety within her breast settle down to a steady heaviness, and knew that her greatest fear was that Abel would not be pleased to see her, but would be angry with her for invading his working life. But knew, too, that this fear was in part the attraction she found in the planning of her visit to Mr. Witney's shop.

It had been a long time since she had enjoyed herself so well, found so much agreeable anticipation in an outing. With Susan beside her, she hailed a hack (and the maid rounded her eyes with delight at so sophisticated an action) and dismissed it at the most western end of Piccadilly, preferring to walk back toward Mr. Witney's shop rather than risk being seen alighting too near. With Susan the approved couple of paces behind her, she walked along the crowded street, feeling the thin spring sunshine on her shoulders and peering with every semblance of interest at the shop fronts they passed, actually stopping sometimes to handle with simulated attention the pieces of stuff that draped the doorway of a mercer's shop, to ask the cost of some gewgaw and then reject it loftily, but aware all the time only of the nearing bulk of St. James's Church and the thick beating of her heart as she thought of Abel's possible reaction when he saw her.

She came upon the shop by surprise—had almost walked past it before she realized what it was. Then she saw the heavy door half open beside the wide glass windows filled with great flasks of purple, green, and crimson liquors; the discreet card in front of them announcing that Mr. Josiah Witney could be Called upon in Any Sickness and Would Endeavour to Give of His Best Services to All Afflicted with Disease; the gleam of mahogany and gilt on the shop front. She stopped so sharply that Susan nearly ran into her.

"Susan!" Dorothea said as casually as she could. "Please to go back to the bazaar. I had forgot I wished to match my silks. Here are the pieces"—she rustled in her reticule—"and see to it that they match well, do you hear me? You need not hurry. I shall be here when you return, and waiting for you."

"Oh, Miss Dorothea! Your mama said as—"

"I know what Mama said, and I know what I said! If you do not do as I bid you—and keep your tongue between your teeth into the bargain—then I shall have you turned off without a character!" And she glared at the girl so ferociously that she whimpered, and Susan took the silks and hurried away up Piccadilly; Dorothea had learned much about the handling of servants since the days of her childhood.

She hesitated a moment before walking into the shop, feeling the fear thick in her throat. Suppose he were to be angry with her, spoke scoldingly before his Mr. Witney. Suppose he were to tell her to go away, and were to turn her out of the shop to stand in the street and wait for Susan's return and her own ignominious flight back to Gower Street! For a moment she almost turned to run after Susan, ready to abandon the whole idea. But then an elderly man came out of the shop and, seeing her standing hesitantly there, courteously stepped back to hold the door, and, confused, she bobbed her head and muttered her thanks and went in.

It was not very bright inside, the whole shop being filled with purple, green, and crimson bars of light thrown from the window, and she stood blinking for a moment, accustoming her eyes to the newness of it.

"Good afternoon to you, ma'am. Why, bless my soul! Surely you are— Indeed you are! Grown to a young lady, but not out of all recognition! Jesse Constam's daughter, are you not? The last time I saw you, why, you were no higher than my elbow!"

She turned her head to look at the man who was standing beside her, and knew him at once from Abel's description of him.

"Mr.—Mr. Witney?"

"Indeed, Miss Constam, indeed! You remember me, then?"

"I'm not sure. I believe so, sir. But I am Miss Coombe, not Miss Constam, although Papa Constam is of course my step-father."

"Well, why should you remember me, to be sure? It's many years since I saw you—or you me. What do you here, may I ask? And all alone, besides?" His round face suddenly filled with a ludicrous expression of alarm. "I trust there is no trouble? That you have not come because—"

"Oh, no, sir, indeed! I just thought— I was shopping, you see, and—and my maid has gone to buy some silks—so tedious a task—and I thought, seeing I happened upon your shop, to wait here until— But of course, if . . ."

He looked at her for a moment and then beamed a wide and knowing grin. "Ah! So that's the way of it, is it! The sly young dog! And he never saying a word about it! Well, my dear, he wasn't to know that I should remain here this afternoon. I am usually out and about my business at this hour, and he was not to know I should fail to behave as usual today! But I am not one of your killjoys, so I shall not meddle—no, nor say a word to anyone! You shall see your young man. Abel! Hey, there, Abel!" And he went bustling away to the back of his shop, leaving Dorothea with her face scarlet. She could hear Mr. Witney's voice, jovial, rallying, teasing, and felt her heart sink even deeper in her chest. Oh, Abel would be so angry! He would say such things to her! Oh, why had she ever come?

And yet, somewhere even deeper inside her, there was jubilation. That Mr. Witney should think that Abel was *her* young man! That he should be able to look at her and see in her a fit person to be considered by Abel as— It was almost more than she could bear to consider.

When Abel came from the back of the shop, rubbing his powdery hands upon his heavy calico apron, his face creased with puzzlement, he did not know who was waiting for him, for Mr. Witney had been so arch about the assignation he believed Abel had made in full expectation of his own absence, had been so heavy-handed in his teasing, that he had not once given a name to the young lady who had called. For one glorious moment Abel had thought of Lil, and then dismissed it. That was not possible, for she had disappeared completely. But that gleam of hope had made him very receptive to what he saw.

She was standing in the middle of the shop, poised as though to turn and run, her pale yellow dress gleaming softly with bars of reflected light from the window and her shoulders heaving rather rapidly under her fur-trimmed pelisse in a way that made her figure look remarkably mature. Her face was a little flushed with her nervousness, and her eyes were bright; altogether she looked as pretty as Abel had ever seen her look.

He stared at her in amazement for a moment, and said blankly, "Dorothea! What in the name of God do you do here?"

"Oh, come now, sir, you shall not pretend to me a moment longer!" Mr. Witney cried, and gave the boy a sharp nudge with his elbow that sent him almost stumbling toward Dorothea. "I was young m'self, and I know what it is to be taken with a girl! Go on, boy, salute her as she should be saluted! She's come all this way for her assignation only to find me here as chaperon, but she shall at least have one kiss for her pains, and I'll not say a word!"

"Indeed, Mr. Witney, we made no assignation . . ." Abel began, as Dorothea reddened even more, but Mr. Witney laughed and slapped the boy on his shoulder and would not let him say another word. A man of intensely sentimental nature, he was completely enchanted by the scene of young love that he saw enacted here before his eyes, and would not be gainsaid. And Abel, ever practical, shrugged his shoulders in resignation and obediently bent to plant a perfunctory kiss upon Dorothea's cheek.

For Dorothea this was almost more than she could bear. She felt herself hot and then cold, and opened her mouth to speak and closed it again, and Mr. Witney beamed upon her confusion and was totally charmed by it.

"Master Abel!" he said. "I shall take myself to the back of the shop and complete some small task in my office. You shall have ten or even fifteen minutes here to speak to your young lady. But then, my boy, she must be on her way, for happy as I am to see the affairs of young hearts prosper, I have a business that must prosper as well, so—fifteen minutes!"

And he went bustling away toward the back of the shop, leaving Dorothea dumbly standing beside Abel while he stared after his master in blank amazement.

"The stupid old man!" he muttered furiously. "Where in the name of God did he get hold of so absurd a notion! To think that I should do anything so bird-brained as to make any such arrangement as . . ." He looked down at Dorothea then. "And what are *you* doing here, you great gull? To come here in the middle of the day like this! You must be clean out of your attic!"

"I—oh, indeed, I am sorry, Abel," Dorothea said breathlessly. "I meant no harm, indeed I did not, but I was so bored, you know, sitting in the schoolroom, and thought of you telling me of all your work here, and then I thought I could do some shopping, and if you were here, why, it would be no harm, and I did wish to buy some complexion wash, and—well, I thought no harm, Abel. Please not to be angry with me!" She looked up at him beseechingly. "I wanted only to see you—the shop, you know, and the great work you do here, and—and—"

"Foolish creature!" Abel said scathingly. "What is there here for you? I tell you all you are able to understand. You need no more than that."

He was surprised at his own discomposure; he had a most disagreeable feeling that in his tales he had given her to believe that he was far more important a member of the

Witney establishment than indeed he was, and it was difficult to face with complete equanimity the possibility that she would discover for herself his insignificance. But as he looked at her face, turned worshipfully up to his, he realized that this could not be; whatever he told her, whatever he did, she would believe him to be perfect, and his mood lightened, and his scowl relaxed.

Immediately she set a timid hand upon his arm. "Please, dear Abel, will you show me? The many things you use, the work you do? Mr. Witney said you might, after all, and—"

"Oh, very well," he said, and she smiled widely upon him, and let her hand slip into the crook of his arm, so that he could lead her about the shop. In her own timid way, Dorothea could be very determined.

She had never been happier than she was for the next ten minutes. He walked her along the shelves and read off the names on the great japanned tins that lined them: Valerian and Ipecacuanha; Belladonna and Sulphur; Senna and Linseed.

"What are they for, Abel?" she ventured once, and he frowned and said shortly, "You would not understand," and obediently she subsided and contentedly let him go on.

"These you will know of, of course," he said, when he paused before one shelf, "for many of them are your father's stock in trade as well as ours. Ginger and cloves and cinnamon, you know, and licorice and so forth. They have many properties as well as those of which you are aware, however." And again he swept her on without giving her time to speak.

He showed her the great pestles and mortars, the plaster irons and great marble slabs upon which pills were massed before being rolled, and she nodded and listened in total enchantment. And when the shop door opened to admit a frightened, bobbing Susan, and Mr. Witney came bustling out of his small back room, she sighed softly and regretfully but with intense happiness all the same.

Abel, much embarrassed by Mr. Witney's heavy winking and nudging, went back to his work with a curt nod at Dorothea, and it was Mr. Witney who escorted her to the door. She stopped when they were on the pavement outside, and with a jerk of her chin sent Susan out of earshot.

"Please, Mr. Witney," she said, and looked up at him for a

moment, and then away in confusion, "you said you would not say aught about my visit here—to Papa Constam or Mama, you know, and—"

"And neither shall I, you young minx!" Mr. Witney cried in great good humor. "For who am I to set rubs in the way of the young? Never let it be said that Josiah Witney—"

"Indeed, sir, I—I am not certain that . . ." She bit her lip. "Well, sir, I believe I should not mind particularly if you *did* happen to see Papa Constam and speak to him of—of my meeting with Abel. He, I think, would not be too angry, since he is like yourself, is he not, a merry and kind person?" Again she hooded her eyes, looking down at her mittened hands. "Of course, Mama would be most displeased if ever she thought that I wished—that I and Abel— Well, she would be displeased. But if Papa Constam should know of it first, and consider that it is—suitable, you know, and— Well, I believe he could persuade Mama."

She looked at him again then. "It is exceedingly difficult for me to speak alone with Papa Constam, you understand, Mr. Witney. In the normal way of the house, that is."

Mr. Witney had been blinking at her in some surprise, but now a slow smile began to spread across his face. "Well, Miss Dorothea! I should not have thought, from my memory of the shy little child you were, to find you so clever in your ways! Though to be sure, as they say, the way of a maid with a man! So, you would use my services, would you, in persuading your family? And why not, indeed? I know, of course, of the history of this young man of yours, and though I can fully enter into the feelings of a parent who would feel some disquiet at so unfortunate a start in life for a young lady's husband, I know him now to be a boy of such parts, of such ability, that I confidently believe he will become an excellent man of our trade! Indeed, my dear child, I will gladly speak to your papa in your behalf, and enlist his aid against your mama! We all know how the tender heart of a mother can obstruct the ways of the young. Well, leave this with me—I shall see your father in due course, no doubt."

Dorothea rode back to Gower Street in a haze of delight. She had never dared think before of the possibility of a future life with Abel, but now Mr. Witney had brought the idea to the surface from the deepest recesses of her secret heart, it fastened itself into her mind with all the tenacity of a limpet. To be Abel's—wife. There, she had thought it! To marry Abel. That was what she wanted above all things, and with Mr. Witney to speak to Papa Constam and set him against Mama, who would certainly oppose the merest mention of such an idea, almost anything could be possible.

It *had* to be possible.

· TWENTY-TWO ·

AT FIRST Abel tried very hard to disabuse Mr. Witney of
the notion that he had any affection for Dorothea, coming as
close as ever he dared to telling the older man with some
tartness that he was a fool. But then he realized that this
notion, so fast held in the romantic Mr. Witney's imagination, was redounding to his own advantage. Making heavy
jokes about the responsibilities of young husbands, the importance of a man's having a trade at his fingers' ends before
he could support a wife and offspring, Mr. Witney became
far more willing to allow Abel to learn more of the mysteries
of his craft.

He rapidly progressed from mere shopkeeping and ac-
counting and stock maintenance to dealing with customers
who wanted more than mere complexion washes. When a
man came in to demonstrate a skin eruption to Mr. Witney,
demanding advice, the old man would make a point of calling
Abel to look at it, asking him owlishly which salve he would
think most like to effect a cure; and Abel, after a few false
starts, soon learned to look knowing and suggest the most
expensive unguent the customer looked likely to tolerate. So
Abel bit his tongue and argued no more, patiently bearing
Mr. Witney's raillery, albeit with a tight-lipped smile.

It was in the visiting of patients that Abel learned the most.

Each day Mr. Witney would set out to cover his district, running as far north from his shop as Grosvenor and Fitzroy squares, east almost as far as Temple Bar, and west to Hyde Park Corner, the very edge of town. He was rarely called to see any patients in the huddle of buildings that lay behind his shop, however, for this was fashionable St. James's, and the aristocratic inhabitants of this splendidly important area were unlikely to call apothecaries to their ills. For them it must be a physician, no less, and though sometimes a servant would come with the physician's instructions written out to be made into a pet medicine of his own devising, by and large the apothecary's practice was with the middling sort of people of the town.

Abel would stand at bedside or sofa side next to Mr. Witney, holding the bag of salves and medicaments and listening to the patients' talk of their ills and pains. Most of them were women and children, and Mr. Witney's treatment seemed to be largely limited to offering linctuses of ipeca-cuanha and opium for coughs, the use of belladonna plasters for putrid throats and congested lungs, and the suggestion of laudanum drops for all other pains and distresses. There were many women who sent for him each month to be brought their supply of the pain-killing drops, and it was Abel's task to carefully fill the little tortoise-shell dropper bottles that so many of them used, or to give to new patients a small green glass bottle with a narrow neck.

He asked Mr. Witney once why so many people used laudanum and for so wide a range of symptoms, and Mr. Witney had said with an uncharacteristic sharpness, "My boy, there's much of human ills that is plainly not under-stood. The surgeons rush with their knives and bowls, and the physicians with their leeches and blisters, and inflict such pain and misery upon the poor patient that he is too took up with thinking of his new agony to recall the original one that put him into the hands of those devils! But I am an apothe-cary, and as such have a truer understanding of what the care of the sick is about. It is about—and hearken to me carefully, boy—it is about the relieving of suffering. If the knife or the leech or the blister ever cured any disease, I'd wish such trickery well. But they do not. My salves and medicines, on the other hand, *do* give relief, and much of it. And of all the drugs that give relief, laudanum is the best. There are none harmed by it, and many helped."

That this was true was incontrovertible, as Abel saw often for himself. There were many people who benefited from Mr. Witney's care of them. One whom Abel was long to remember was the small son of the mercer who lived behind Jermyn Street. They had been called hurriedly to the snug house one cold and dank afternoon, to find a distraught mother kneeling beside a couch on which a child, a stout and handsome little boy of some three years, lay in plain distress. His face was bluish in color, and his eyes staring, with tears running slowly down his streaked cheeks. He lay with his jaw thrust forward, and his lips pulled back in a grimace against his small teeth, as he tried to breathe. The sounds he made were agonizing, for the room was filled with the wheezing, raucous cawing he created with each attempt at inspiration. Below his jaw, his neck was strung with effort, so that it looked more like the throat of an old man than that of a child, and his chest heaved awkwardly, the ribs seeming almost to curve in toward the spine as he struggled for each breath.

Looking at him, and at the mother's staring, fearful face as she turned to see them come into the room, Abel felt a stab of fear mixed with his immediate response of pity. How could anyone help a child in such a condition? He was so clearly in a parlous state, so near to dying for want of air, that it seemed to Abel that he wanted to run, to be anywhere but beside this mother and her child when the moment of death came. But not so Mr. Witney.

"Another of these attacks of his, Mrs. Crosby?" he cried cheerfully as he hurried forward to set his bag down beside the couch. "Did you allow him to excite himself in some way? Well, let be, let be. He is of a busy, pushing disposition—are you not, young rascal of a Johnny that you are? Is the kettle ready, ma'am? Come, come, the kettle—you know by now, I trust."

The mother surged to her feet in a rustle of skirts and hurried to the door to call a maid, and Mr. Witney looked up at Abel and smiled crookedly at him.

"Nay, boy, don't look so fearful! This lad will thrive yet, I promise you! We're old friends, Master John and I. He does this often and often, whenever he is distressed, or the wind is in the wrong quarter, or when he feels in the mood for such matters. We'll have him right enough, I promise you."

His hands were busy in his bag as he pulled out bottles and powders, and then he turned to the child and with one swift movement, unusually deft in so plump and bustling a man, slid a cushion beneath his shoulders. The boy was still wheezing agonizingly, but seemed less tense now, as his wide eyes followed every movement of Mr. Witney's hands. He lay quite still as the apothecary began to rub some of the unguent he had seized onto his throat, and then opened his mouth obediently as the old man approached him with a familiar green laudanum bottle.

"Camphorated oil to clear his breathing," he murmured. "Laudanum to cool his anxiety, and now dried whole ox kidney in a decoction."

He spooned a foully black mixture into the boy's mouth, and the child grimaced and half choked, but the old man insisted, and eventually he swallowed it.

Abel watched, fascinated, feeling sorely useless as the mother came back with an anxious little maid in hot pursuit and clutching a large black and steaming kettle. They set this upon the newly stirred embers of the fire, and Mr. Witney hurried over to spill the contents of a packet into it and stir the fire even higher as the women rushed about closing the curtains and the door.

The room filled gradually with the steam from the kettle, fragrant and heavy and sticky to the nose, as Mr. Witney bustled back to the child and set his fingers on his pulse. The mother brought a pair of new-lit candles closer, and together they stood and stared down at the child, Abel and the little maid standing just outside the circle of light and watching too.

For a while longer the painful cawing noise went on, as the small chest caved in and curled out again in the child's battle for air. But then his eyes began to close, and the tight expression of anxiety that had mantled his blue and sweating face softened and gradually disappeared. His breathing became ever softer and more natural, and after a very little while he was fast asleep. Mr. Witney climbed, grunting, to his feet, and nodded.

"He'll do well enough now, ma'am. I shall leave for you a paper of the balsam for the kettle to keep the air hot and moist and saturated for the night, and some laudanum for his sleep—and again I must remind you, he shall not be made distressed! In such weather, too! It is bound to bring on his croups. No, ma'am, no need to be so effusive in your thanks—your good husband shall receive my account in due course!" And he hurried away down the stairs, back to the shop, with Abel hot on his heels.

"That, m'boy," he said, "is the chronic croup, and it has killed many a baby like that one. The surgeons would have bled him or blistered him, and what good would that have done? It would have weakened him! I use the natural way: the camphorated oil to soothe his breathing, the balsam in the steam to soften the air to his breathing, and whole ox kidney—well, I know not why particularly. 'Twas my master taught me so, and so I use it. It has some special property that makes the swelling of the tissues of the breathing passages subside."

"And the laudanum?" Abel panted, for they were hurrying full tilt along Piccadilly. "What purpose does that serve?"

"I've told you often enough, lad! It calms the nerves, and promotes sweet sleep, and takes the fear out of pain. The gift of the gods, is laudanum."

It was not long before Abel realized that Mr. Witney himself was very partial to laudanum drops, and often took them for the pain in his left breast and arm, the one that came when he was hurrying or tired and somewhat blue about the mouth. And understanding why he should care so much for this item in his stock of medicines, Abel said no more, though he felt convinced, deep in his being, that the man was often wrong, blinded by prejudice in favor of his own trade.

By tacit agreement, neither he nor Dorothea said anything more about the meeting at the shop. He told her, of course, that he was doing more with Mr. Witney, and learning more, and that indeed, another younger apprentice had been taken on to do the work that once had been Abel's, so that he would be more free to assist Mr. Witney. But he did not tell her that Mr. Witney believed that he was helping Abel toward husbandhood in teaching him as he did; to let her know that such a nonsensical idea had arisen would be foolish, he felt, for she might in fact believe it. And he had no notion of marrying anyone, come to that.

She, in her turn, chose not to tell him that she was well aware of Mr. Witney's belief. There had been a supper given at Gower Street to celebrate the anniversary of the founding of the London Ladies' Committee, whose affairs so occupied Charlotte, and Mr. Witney had attended. He had made an opportunity to speak to Dorothea, winking and nodding at her and telling her not to fret, for all was well—she'd find out in time what was to be. But not to fear her mama, who knew naught of her visit to Piccadilly, nor ever would for his or her papa's part.

And she had settled happily enough for that; there was plenty of time. Abel, when he was less preoccupied with his work, would be glad of her plans one day, she assured herself, and he, quite unsuspecting of the firm view she had of him as future husband and of the helpless way in which she loved him, went on busily about his own affairs, far too occupied with learning his trade and scheming in his mind about a way to arrange anatomy classes for himself to notice Dorothea much at all.

For still the idea of surgery remained strong within him. In some ways, being so close to it as to be doing the work of an apothecary made it harder rather than easier to be patient; whenever Mr. Witney gave out another bottle of laudanum, Abel ached to know *why*. Why did this one have a great swelling in her belly, though clearly past the age of childbearing? Why did that one have a great weeping sore upon her breast that would not heal and be growing thinner and weaker each day? What was the cause of the pain this child had, the cause of the sickness and pallor of that one? To simply soothe such states with laudanum seemed to him to be curiously wrong; he wanted to know what was happening beneath those skins, inside those bellies and limbs. And time and again he remembered the fascination of those opened corpses in Great Windmill Street, and yearned to go back.

He did not, for several confused reasons. For one, he was

afraid. He knew that he had acted criminally in working with Fitch, and could not be sure that even after so long a time he could not be taken up and sent to jail for it, should someone choose to inform on him. To return now to Mr. Wilson in Great Windmill Street would surely be stupid, remembering the man's twittering fear of discovery, and how he would behave when he came sneaking to the door to accept Fitch's newest consignment of goods. Could he not in such fear call the Watch if Abel came to him now?

And even when Abel managed to dispel this notion (which in many ways he suspected to be foolish), there was a curious pride that would overtake him. He wanted to return to Great Windmill Street indeed—but not as an object of charity. He wished, somehow, to go there as a true student of surgery, to learn the craft from start to finish because he had paid for the right to be there, and not because the principal of the school was in a mood to talk to a guttersnipe boy who hung about asking questions. He would, Abel swore to himself, become a true student yet, somehow. He remembered often the first corpse he had helped to raise, her pregnant belly and her helpless white hands, and would promise himself that one day he, Abel Lackland, would learn about such matters and even stop them from happening. And not with just a bottle of laudanum.

As time went on, Abel learned more and more that surprised him about the jovial and delightful Josiah Witney. He was, of course, as astute a man of business as any other London tradesman, and not averse to selling any potion or medicament that the customer could be persuaded to buy, however little suited it might be to his needs. But it was not until he had been apprenticed to Mr. Witney for some time that he discovered that he had another secret and most lucrative side to his business.

There had always been, from the first day he had come to the shop, a steady procession of women who patronized it, and he had learned early that some of these women had to be served by Mr. Witney himself, and only the silliest of servant girls in search of cheap cosmetics and such nonsenses could be dealt with by Abel. He had at first assumed that this was because the elegant women were ashamed to buy aids to beautify nature, but he had been disabused of that idea when one day one of the more regular customers, a handsome redheaded woman of some thirty-five years, came into the shop. As soon as he had seen her, Abel had turned to fetch Mr. Witney, but she had laughed and called him back.

"No, boy, I seek merely some oil for my face—the light almond with the essence of herbs. You can give me that. And some powdered alum and lanolin."

"But—d'you wish *me* to get them, ma'am?" Abel had said, almost shyly. "I thought you wanted always to consult with Mr. Witney."

She had smiled at that. "A discreet boy, indeed! No, today you may give me all I require. There will be other times perhaps, when you are a little older and wiser, when you can sell me—more interesting matters."

Abel had asked Mr. Witney to explain, and he had chewed his lip and looked sharply at the boy with his head down and his forehead creased. Then he had nodded as though some decision had been arrived at.

"Well, you'll know soon enough, if this is to be your trade. There are some matters that apothecaries sell that, shall we say, have a use that the moral people of this world would not approve. For my part, I care not what men and women do with the natures they were born with. For every one virtuous lady that can stay at her sewing, like your—um—benefactress, Mrs. Constam, there are many more like Miss Calthorpe, to whom you sold cosmetics this morning. A lady of heart, and warmth, and generosity, who has to make her own way in a harsh and cruel world. If she makes it by Haymarket means, well, that is her affair. And if I choose to help her through such occasions as she may need the aid of one learned in medicaments, why, then, that is my affair. You understand?"

"No," Abel said baldly.

Mr. Witney sighed heavily. "Damn the boy, so innocent as he is! And you grew up in the Dials! You know what I mean by Haymarket means, no doubt?"

"Oh, yes," Abel said easily; "the tails and whores. Is that what you say Miss Calthorpe is? She looks more the lady than the whore to me. I never saw her like in the Dials!"

"No, nor should you, for she is one of the Quality, and

never think otherwise. A remarkable lady, Miss Calthorpe, with her own house, and keeps her own carriage and pair. But she has her problems. There's not all as wants to have brats to feed, nor to die in childbed. And then, there's the matter of the pox."

Abel understood completely then. That there should be some apothecaries who specialized in providing the medical wants of prostitutes was obvious, now he thought about it; he had grown up with the processes of birth and death, had known of enough women that had died of their babies, just as the girl he had seen in St. Giles's churchyard had died. And of course he knew of the pox. What child of the slums could not?

So now, when prostitutes came into the shop, he could recognize them. He learned from Mr. Witney how to know which were the women who needed some of his Patent Female Pills, No Irregularity Can Resist Them, and which required his Potash and Mercury Cachets for the Removal of Afflictions of the Skin, Ulcers of the Mouth, and Similar Disorders of the Person.

He never thought at all about the morality or otherwise of this trade. He heard much talk of morality from Charlotte on Sundays in Gower Street, almost as much as he had heard during his four years at Mr. Loudoun's school, but he did not listen to it. He sat with an attentive stare upon his face and thought about the organs of the body and how they were arranged, and tried to listen to the beating of his own heart inside his chest, just for the interest of it. And when he was at the shop and sold abortifacients for Mr. Witney, he thought no more than that he had sold goods to another customer and sent her cheerfully away.

And then, on one damp evening in June—for it was a wet and heavy summer, dispiriting and unhealthful, and excellent for business—as he was about to put up the shutters, another customer arrived. He saw at first glance at her tattered silk dress and painted face that she was one of the cheaper sort of prostitute and raised his eyebrows slightly; Mr. Witney's trade was usually a little higher-quality than this. Perhaps, he thought for a moment, another apothecary had sent her away, and this was why she had appeared in Piccadilly in so obvious a pother.

"Hey—you. . . ." She was out of breath and anxious, and took hold of Abel's arm in her sharp little hand, and he shook it off irritably. "You keep your hands off me!" he snapped. "If there's aught you would buy, say so, and buy it and go!"—and then, ashamed of his bad temper, said more gently, "Well? What would you have of us?"

"There's a girl—got her in the greenroom, they have, and she's carrying on alarming, and Mr. Cole says as 'ow if I don't bring a surgeon to 'er quick I needn't come back—and she's fit to die, I swear it, and—"

"What's this? What's the girl asking for, Abel?" Mr. Witney came from the back of the shop buttoning his coat across his belly, clearly ready to be away as soon as he could. "We're no surgeons, girl, and never think it. Honest apothecary, that's what I am, and—"

"I *know*!" The girl almost wailed it. "I knows you ain't, but there's not a surgeon I can find as'll come, and 'oo else is there? An' she's fit to die, the way she's goin' on, and—"

"Who is dying? Where? Compose yourself, girl!" Josiah said soothingly, and came to stand beside her with one hand set in fatherly fashion on her shoulder.

"Young Nancy. She's not above thirteen year old, though she's billed as bein' only ten, and her playing Miss Peggy this week in *Country Girl* and a poor job of it she's doing, but they would have a child to play, with all the town running to Drury Lane to see Master bloody Betty, and—"

"Ah!" Understanding spread across Mr. Witney's face. "You're from the theater—is that it? In the Haymarket?"

"Aye—and Mr. Cole frantic about his precious Miss Nancy, for didn't he promise her parents she'd be as looked after as his own child, and here she is, screaming and shouting in her time, and—"

"Her time? She's dropping a brat, you mean? Then there's naught I can do for her, girl, and so you can tell your precious Mr. Cole, whoever he may be. I'm no man midwife! Find some other to aid her."

"I *can't*. There's been a midwife and she's run off for fear the girl'll die and she'll be held to account for it, for she says she can do no more, and a surgeon's needed to pull the child piecemeal from her, but I can't get a surgeon, and if you don't come the dear God knows as—"

"We'll have to go." Abel had said it before he knew the words were out of his mouth, and Josiah turned and stared at him, his eyebrows raised. "Oh, shall we? And what can we do if the midwife has taken to her heels? And what sort of woman would let men near her in such a matter, anyway? Man midwives! Such creatures! If you think—"

"She's not a woman," Abel said; "she's a child. And we can't do worse for her than's been done, from all accounts, and if there's none other— Please, Mr. Witney, you'll never sleep sound in your bed tonight if you don't! And I'll do all I can to help, and—"

"You! And what can you do?" Mr. Witney looked at the girl, still standing anxiously beside them, and then back at Abel. Sensing the uncertainty in him, the boy pressed his point home. "She'll be no worse if we do go than if we don't. And you may be able to help better than any surgeon, for you know of women's ills. . . ."

There was a moment's silence, and then Mr. Witney laughed, a short and embarrassed sound, but Abel knew he had succeeded, and turned to run into the office to fetch the visiting bag.

Mr. Witney bustled then, filling the small bag with medicines and loudly calling the younger apprentice from the back of the shop.

"James! You are to stay here until such time as I return! Set the shutters up, and then stay within doors and open to none but me, you hear? I'll return as soon as may be.

"Now, girl! Go back to your Mr. Cole and tell him we're coming. Tell him we're apothecaries and not surgeons or man midwives, but we're coming. Abel! We'll need some old linen, I've no doubt! I've no mind to get myself as blood-spattered as some damned barber, and they'll have naught of much use at the theater, of that much you can be sure. Hurry, now, boy! You were the one so anxious to help this child, so let's about it!"

· TWENTY-THREE ·

ABEL had never seen anything quite so confusing in his life before. He knew of theaters, of course, and had seen actors perform often enough in the streets and market places, giving their impromptu shows, but never before had he set foot inside a building such as this.

They had entered from the back, through the doorway in Suffolk Street, hurrying there purposeful and anxious through the strolling crowds of prostitutes and their customers in the Haymarket, Abel in particular filled with a sort of exultant fear. Why he had felt he could cope with such a dilemma as this he would never know, he thought desperately, and looked sideways at Mr. Witney, panting bluely along beside him, to feel himself filled with a deep gratitude at the sight of his round face. For all his prejudice against surgeons and his passion for the cure-all properties of laudanum, he was a good and caring man, and Abel knew it.

The theater seemed not to surprise Mr. Witney in the least. He plunged into the great building without a moment's hesitation, pushing his way past the pieces of scenery that stood about in disorderly profusion into the dim recesses beyond.

It smelled extraordinary, even to Abel with his nose accustomed to the heavy scents of an apothecary's establishment.

He was assailed by a fishy stink of glue and size and cheap tallow candles and mice and human sweat, and another, heavier reek lying beneath which made his throat tighten. Stumbling a little, he hurried along behind Mr. Witney, and then, as the older man turned a corner into what seemed to Abel to be an even vaster area, stopped short.

They were standing, obviously, beside the stage. Ahead of him, framed in a great towering structure that was held in place by the flimsiest of wooden struts and trembled a little in every movement of the air (although it looked, at cursory glance, to be the great, grim facade of a stone wall), was light. And such light! Abel blinked and looked and blinked again at the vividness of it.

Above his head were great flaring jets of flame, and spreading across the stage in front of him in receding perspective were more flaming jets, all hissing softly and giving out the steadiest and most sparkling light he'd ever seen. He could hear sound, too, echoing human voices, and for a moment he could not see where it came from until he realized that there, in the middle of all that light, stood human figures. They seemed minuscule against the scale of the stage on which they stood, with its soaring scenic flats painted to look like unbelievably leafy woodland, the dangling ropes and flapping curtains hanging high above in the remotest recesses of the roof.

Mr. Witney was talking to someone, a man in fustian trousers and a dirty white shirt who had been standing beside the stage peering anxiously round the edge of the canvas castle. He turned his head when Mr. Witney spoke to him and listened and then nodded and beckoned into the shadows beyond.

There was a sudden roar from somewhere, which made Abel start a little until he recognized it as the sound of laughter coming from a great many human throats, and the man to whom Mr. Witney had been speaking brightened at the sound of it and turned eagerly back to peer again round the corner of the scenery.

"Not so bad," he grunted. "They seem to be 'appy enough with what they're getting, damn their eyes! Thought we'd 'ave a bloody riot there for a bit, I did—and we 'ad enough o' that with all those bleedin' tailors when we did the Foote play last month. 'Ere's Lotty—she'll take yer."

He jerked his head over his shoulder, and Abel turned to see a girl standing beside him. Her face was so heavily painted, so very red and white and blue about the eyes, that it was almost as though she wore a mask, but then he saw the lines round her eyes, and felt the tension and fear in her, and smiled in as reassuring a manner as he could.

"You the surgeons?" she whispered, her face as taut as ever. "Do come, there's a good man—they'll hear out front soon if someone don't put the poor creature out of her agony as fast as may be."

"Not surgeons . . ." Abel began, but she was gone, disappearing into the shadows, and he and Mr. Witney had to hurry to catch her. They came up behind her at last as she reached a door set well behind the stage. She stood for a moment with her hand on the knob and her head raised, and then as another great roar rose from the distant audience she swiftly pushed open the door and shoved the two men through, closing it behind them just as the noise died away.

Standing there inside the cluttered room, Abel realized at once why she had behaved so. It seemed filled with sound—a steady, agonized moaning that from time to time rose in a shriek of greater protest, only to die away into an even more piteous wailing. Abel, with all his experience of life in the gutter, had never heard anything quite so dreadful in his life; had never heard a sound that was so physical, so capable of thrusting itself into his own belly, filling him with some of the same pain that had created it.

Mr. Witney moved first, marching purposefully across the big room to a cluster of people on the far side. They turned their heads as he came up, with Abel following him, and fell back a little to expose a couch on which a girl was lying.

Her face too was painted, just as were those of some of the people standing around her, but the paint had slipped and merged and spread itself so that she seemed a caricature of a human being, with a great red rictus of a grimace, black-smudged eyes and caked white cheeks beneath tumbled yellow hair.

She was lying on her back with her knees drawn up, and

her skirts were thrust up about her waist to show her trunk and legs. She was quite bare beneath the heavy scarlet satin of her dress, and her legs, chunky and well rounded, were blotched with the faint purple markings of adolescence.

They were set wide apart, with the knees slightly flexed, and there where the thighs merged into the curve of buttock behind and met the line of softly curly blond hair in front was a most pitiful object: a soft, round baby arm, a small, plump hand with curling fingers, lying there between those blotched thighs on a dirty gray shirt someone had thrust beneath it. The hand did not move at all, but lay with a laxness that was so exactly like that of the corpse Abel had uncovered in St. Giles's so long ago that it seemed to him for a moment that he was there again in the dark coldness, smelling the heaviness of disturbed earth and rotting leaves and grass. But he blinked and was again in the brightly lit greenroom of the Theatre Royal in the Haymarket as the girl writhed and shrieked and two of the women standing beside her bent forward to grasp her shoulders and hold her down.

Staring with a wide-eyed fascination at the girl's belly, Abel could see it, the wave of contraction that moved across it, saw the flesh that was surrounding that small emergent arm tighten and then seem to swell forward. The movement of the girl's body made the small hand move and lift a little, quite lifelessly, but for all the world like a beckoning invitation; it was to Abel's eyes the most terrifying thing he had ever seen in his life, and he wanted to turn and run shrieking away, back to the normality and reality of the Haymarket, Piccadilly, Gower Street, anywhere—anywhere at all as long as it was away from this screaming creature that had once been a human child, and the dead doll-like limb protruding so horribly from her body.

But then he saw it, the faint trickle of blood that ran down to add its stain to those already streaking the girl's legs and the infant arm and hand, and somehow that brought it all into focus again. The baby's arm might be dead, was obviously so, but the girl wasn't. She was still lying there, crying and moaning and desperate for help. Any help, to live or die, but help.

Abel looked up and saw Mr. Witney standing at the top of

the couch, his back resolutely turned on this exhibition of naked female body, holding a bottle of laudanum in one hand and trying with the other to prise apart the girl's clenched teeth so that he could pour in some of the contents.

"Mr. Witney!" Abel said, and his voice sounded cracked and hoarse in his own ears. "I— Please, I know what I should do for this. Shall I just do— Shall I try?"

"Aye, if there's aught can be done," Josiah grunted. "She'll hardly live much longer like this. How long has she been so?"

A man came pushing his way forward through the little knot of people still standing beside the couch. "Since before five o'clock," he said, and his voice was thin with anxiety. "She'd got herself dressed for the performance—was due on stage at half past five—and then—well, then she shrieked, and the women came and looked. I'd no notion of her state, none at all, and if I had I'd've sent her packing long since, for I've no wish to be running a bawdy house here, and so I tell you."

"He knew, sure as eggs." One of the women, middle-aged, sharp-faced, and wearing a stage costume and paint, had spoken unexpectedly, and when the man turned on her, his teeth showing white as he produced a glare of pure hate, she said more loudly, "Don't you go on at me, Cole, not if you values your eyes, for I'll scratch 'em out o' your head as soon as spit at you! You brought the creature here to put such as me out o' work, and to try to make the sort o' money they're makin' at Drury Lane, the like you'll never make as long as you've an arse to sit on, for Kemble makes twenty o' you, and you used her—oh, yes, you did! Don't think we don't know what goes on!—and now she's at her time, you'd be as glad as you could be if she was to die. Well, if she does, I'll not keep quiet about it."

"I've no interest in your private squabbles." Mr. Witney spoke sharply and with a cold authority that sat oddly on his round little body. "She's been so for four hours? She could go on for long yet, then. A country girl, isn't she? Looks too well fed . . ." And indeed, the contrast between the girl on the couch, with her round face and plump breasts swelling above the low-cut dress, and the scrawny, hungry-looking creatures standing beside her was very marked, in spite of the state she was in. "What can you do, Abel, do you think, apart from give her such help to bear the pain as we can? She'll not live if the babe is held fast in her—it's dead, I imagine . . ."

Delicately, Abel put forward one hand and touched the skin of the curled infant fist lying there so still on the soiled shirt, and nodded. It was cold and waxen to the touch, and he knew well that this was what death felt like.

"But I could help her, I believe," he muttered, and moved forward to stand beside the couch looking down at the taut, round belly. It was quite extraordinary, the sense of knowledge that he had. It was as though he could see beyond the opacity of stretched skin and muscle and fat to the child beneath—could see precisely the position in which it lay. He let his hands rest on the belly gently, and the girl moaned and moved, though she had quieted a little under the influence of Josiah's generous doses of laudanum. He felt it start again, the hardening of the contraction, and turned his head to look at her face, waiting for the reaction to come. It came in another great shriek of agony as the muscle tightened again round the dead baby and tried yet again to thrust it out of the bottleneck of its mother's body and into the outer air, and again Abel could almost see it: the child lying across the outlet, the head turned awkwardly and cruelly to one side, the legs curled up round the cord springing from the belly, the one arm outthrust and lying in the safety of outside.

He moved, without knowing he had, to sit beside the girl, and leaning forward, slid one finger along the baby's arm until it was within the girl's body. He felt the curve of the elbow and the upper arm, and tried to lengthen his finger to reach farther, but it was impossible, and he bit his lip and pulled his hand back again. Then, very delicately, he curved his fingers tight against one another, tucking the thumb inside so that his whole hand became as small and as pointed as possible, and moving with great care, he slid it under the baby's arm again.

And this time nothing stopped him. The girl was lying relaxed in some sort of stupor, and whether it was due to sheer exhaustion or the laudanum he didn't know, and didn't care. All his sensation, all his concern, every atom of his feeling, seemed to be concentrated in that right hand. He closed his eyes and let his hand go on moving almost of its own volition, felt it slide in and upward, until he could feel the warmth of the girl's body about his wrist.

He snapped his eyes wide open then, for the girl moaned and moved a little as another tightening spasm moved across the muscle and he felt the strength of it curl cruelly about his hand and bit his lip with the pain of it. But it passed, and again the girl lay still, and this time he moved faster, letting his hand travel farther onward, letting his fingers open and spread wider.

It was as though his fingertips were his eyes. He sat there with his lids screwed close shut and saw what he could feel: the head indeed to one side, the body across the cavity—and setting the heel of his hand against the infant's armpit, he pushed, gently at first and then more firmly as the flesh moved beneath his touch.

In one corner of his mind he knew that soon there would come another of those tight waves of muscle movement clutching at him and the infant, was concerned that he would not move the child in time to meet it. But still he went on, and felt the shoulder give as the arm moved and knew the head had straightened.

The next time he felt the muscle try to work again he opened his eyes, and was not particularly surprised to see that the baby's arm and hand had gone, returned within the mother. He knew he had turned the child, and that there was room now for the birth, and gently, as soon as the muscle relaxed enough, removed his hand and looked wonderingly at it, at its blood-streaked skin and the soaking-wet cuff of his shirt. He did not know what he had done, or how he had done it, but he knew he had done what was necessary.

And so he had, for the next moaning shriek that arose brought with it a much more definite swelling at the entry to the girl's body, a swelling that moved on and down and made the girl grunt and push and grunt again between her shrieks.

And then, a few moments after that first hopeful swelling, the pain came again, and again she pushed and heaved to rid herself of it, and with one sudden rush, the baby's buttocks appeared in full, and then the rest of the body, the arms—one blue and swollen, the other still wrinkled and yellow-damp—and leaning forward, Abel tipped his fingers into her body, under the child's neck, and felt the chin, and hooked it forward under the crest of bone that lay beneath his touch.

And then it was all over. The dead infant lay sprawled upon its dirty shirt of a bed, looking infinitely old and tired, and the mother lay gasping a little, her head to one side and her mouth lax. The women moved forward then, one of them hastily wrapping the baby in the shirt and then standing arms akimbo, waiting beside the couch. The afterbirth came quickly, and there was bustle among the women for a while, and then one of them disappeared from the room, carrying the bundle of shirt, while the others wrapped the exhausted girl on the couch in her skirts, restoring her to some semblance of decency.

Abel had stepped back and was standing beside a dilapidated old sofa, mechanically wiping his hands over and over again on a silk kerchief one of the women had thrust at him, and Mr. Witney looked sharply at him as he packed away the last of his medicines in his little bag, and came to stand beside him.

"You behaved surprising knowing there, boy," he said after a moment to Abel's bent head. "Where did you learn of such matters? If you were country-bred, as I was, and cared for cows and sheep and the like, I'd know whence you got such understanding; but you are a slum boy, a gutter boy, one who—"

"I don't know." Abel said it softly, still staring down at his hands. "I don't know, Mr. Witney. It was as though I were not here at all. I could see, you know—see inside her to the way the baby lay. I saw his arm, and it was so clear and easy to see the rest of his body, and it was just like—like turning a cork that's got thrust inside a bottle. To get it up the right way was all that was needed, and my hand just set it the right way."

"Hrmph! You'll be setting up independent, soon, as a healer or a bonesetter, if you've hands that think so well for you," Mr. Witney said, and Abel looked at him sharply.

"Aye, don't look at me like that, boy! There are some that have such gifts—that can set broken bones so that they heal, without need to chop off an arm or leg and kill the rest of the body, the way the surgeons do! Without need of my medicines either, come to that. Well, just to remember, boy, you're apprenticed to me for more than three years yet. If you've a mind to—"

"I've a mind to nothing but learning, Mr. Witney," Abel said quickly, wanting to reach out and touch the other man, for he was looking at him with so bleak an expression on his face, looking so tired and so much older, suddenly, that he was in his way as pitiful as the girl now sleeping noisily on the couch behind them. "I won't hide from you that I've still a notion to learn the art of the surgeon, much as you hate 'em, but I stay with you till I complete my indentures, if you'll so have me." He put his head to one side for a moment and smiled his wicked little smile. "Is it not possible that both apothecaries and surgeons—aye, and physicians too—have much to offer people in need of aid? Like this girl here—my hand, but your laudanum—and she needed both, didn't she?"

Mr. Witney stared back at the boy for a moment and then laughed his usual fat and ridiculously jolly laugh. "Aye, lad, you could be right. I'm not so old yet, nor yet so young, as to deny there's some may know better than their elders. You could be one of them."

"Can we move her away from here?" The voice came sharply, pulling them out of their preoccupation with each other, and both turned to look at the thin-faced man in the black coat who was standing looking dourly at them. "Well, sir, may we move her without risk of damage? She can't stay here, that much is certain. With the performance over in less than an hour, the audience'll be coming round in their droves, I've no doubt, wanting to nose out all that's happened and why we changed the program so sudden. We must get her out of here to somewhere she'll be—"

"And where'll you take her?" the jeering voice of the woman who had taunted Cole before came cutting across. "She's been sleeping here, where you could get use of her whenever it suited you. Do you plan to send her back to her parents in this state? God help you if you do! They'll horse-whip you, have you hanged, God knows what they'd do to you."

The man whitened a little, but he turned his back on her and said again, urgently, "Well? Can she be moved? I'll find somewhere for her, one way or another."

"Aye, bottom of the river if you have your way," the hard voice came again. "You'll have to do better than that."

"She could come with me, if so be she's fit," the other woman said, and her voice was not much softer. "Leave him be, Mary! There's no use in shouting the matter to him. He's treated you bad and so we all know, but there's an end of it. He'll not hire such children again, no matter what Master Betty may be doing to steal all the custom—not when they've no sense to look after themselves. So—"

"By Christ, I won't! Next child I get'll be a child in every way—not one of your half-grown dollymops like this one. Spent all her time telling me she was sixteen and gone, and ready for such a man as I. How was I to know that—"

"You're a stinking dog of a liar," the woman called Mary said, but without real rancor now, just a weary knowingness that was somehow much more painful in its acceptance. "You knew her to be thirteen—you've been selling her as ten to the audiences—and spat me out so's you could seduce her in your dressing room whenever you felt the need. D'you think the whole bloody theater couldn't hear her shrieking to be let go? You make me—"

"She can come with me, and there's an end on it," the other woman said peaceably. "I've said I'm willing to take her, and I daresay Lucy'll welcome her and care for her well enough. She's a heart as big as she is, and—"

"Lucy?" Abel asked sharply, and the woman turned and looked at him.

"Yes, Lucy. You know her? Well, it's not surprising. Everyone knows Lucy."

"In Panton Street?"

"Yes! I told you! So, young surgeon or whatever you are, is she fit to go there? For if she's like to die of her state, then I'll not put her on to Lucy, who's willing enough to help but like to murder me if I land her with a corpse. Can we take her there?"

It was Mr. Witney who came and looked at the girl, now lying curled up on her side and fast asleep, and after checking her pulse with a fine judicious air nodded cheerfully enough.

"Yes, she can be shifted. She's young enough and tough-bred enough, with all the good flesh she has on her, to survive worse than this. If you can wake her—for she's fast sleeping with the drops I gave her—you can shift her."

"I'll carry her there," Abel said, and moved toward the woman standing beside the girl. "It's not so far to go, and—well, I'll take her to Lucy's place for you. Gladly."

· TWENTY-FOUR ·

IT CAME upon him so suddenly and so alarmingly that it was as though it were happening to someone else—that he was standing aside in one corner, watching.

They had arrived at the house in Panton Street, and his heart had lifted as he realized it was indeed the establishment at which he had experienced his first bath, and there had been a great fussing and excitement as Lucy was fetched (looking, to Abel's delight, much the same as ever, though markedly fatter) and told the plight of Nancy. She had sworn as fruitily as only Lucy could swear, had clouted the woman who had so confidently brought Nancy to her, and carried the girl up to one of her rooms within a matter of minutes.

Waiting for her to come down again, Abel had sat with the younger actress from the theater, whose name was Bess and who seemed to be a friendly enough soul, and asked questions. How could a child as young as Nancy be working as an actress, when she had parents to care for her? How could it be she was so far gone in a pregnancy and still appearing on the stage? What sort of life was it they led there? What were the incredible lights he had seen? What . . .

Bess had laughed but answered him cheerfully enough, telling him of the people of the theater, who lived most haphazard lives—who worked together and played together, drank together and fought furiously together, shifting their allegiances as often as they ate a hot dinner; who lived in a confused world where stage merged with street so imperceptibly that out-of-work actresses thought little of making up the deficit in their purses with a little easy prostitution (even living in a brothel, as Bess did, for the convenience and company); where actors thought even less of accepting money from their whoring colleagues when times were hard for them; where babies were as likely to be born in a dressing room as anywhere else. He heard of gaslight—the marvelous illuminations that had so impressed him and whose smell had so surprised him—and costumes, stage paint and properties, benefit nights and audience riots, and was fascinated.

And then Lucy had returned, scowling, to ask tartly why Bess hadn't sent that fancy boy back to the theater instead of keeping him sitting around in her parlor, and Abel had laughed, childishly pleased that she had not yet recognized him, and reminded her of their past acquaintance.

And then such shrieks of delight from Lucy, such hugs and kisses, such an outpouring of hot chocolate and little cakes, as Bess was sent roundly about her business so that Lucy could settle down with her "likely lad" to talk and exclaim and ask questions and exclaim again.

And then it happened—without any warning, and so violently that the cup of hot chocolate he had been holding spilled painfully down his leg and his teeth rattled noisily in his head. He had been telling Lucy of his apprenticeship with Mr. Witney, of how he was starting to learn more about looking after people instead of just mixing up stock medicines; had begun to talk, a little shyly, of his other ambition, when the shaking began. It was as though a wave of ice had come rapidly welling up inside him, from the soles of his feet to the crown of his head, and as it receded it took all his strength with it, for he was shaking and shaking and shaking.

Lucy seemed to him then to be the most understanding person in the world. She needed no telling of what was happening to him, asked no questions, but reached for him and picked him up almost as easily as she had when he was a child, and wrapped him in the heavy shawl from her own back, and settled him upon a couch. She fetched a glass of brandy from her cupboard, forced a few drops through his clenched teeth so that he coughed and spluttered, and then plumped herself down beside him to enfold him in her vast arms and hold him tight.

He sat there smelling the heat of her body and feeling the weight of her chin as she rested it on his head, and relaxed into the dark, warm safety of her. Slowly the shaking subsided, gradually the chill left by that wave of ice was dissipated, and he could sit up and take a deep breath and smile at her, still rather tremulous but with some measure of control of himself.

"I'm sorry," he mumbled. "Don't know what happened."

"Had a shock, did you?" She was still sitting beside him, one arm about his shoulders, and she bent her head to peer into his face. "Want to tell about it?"

He rubbed his face with both hands, wanting to rid it of the numbness that still lingered there. "Don't understand," he said after a moment, "unless it was— Well, I never did it before, did I? And though it seemed so right and easy, as if I knew exactly how, it was—strange."

Haltingly he told her of the delivery of Nancy's baby, explained as carefully as he could the way the baby had been lying, how he had turned it and made its birth possible, and she sat and hugged him and let him talk it all out.

"You should be pleased with yourself, after such a piece of work," she said when he stopped. "Not so . . ." She shrugged. "Can't say whether you're scared or just plain in a rage. You 'ad a lively temper as I remember you, though I 'ad you with me no more'n a week; you was a lively one, not given to biting your tongue about things you don't care for. Not you! So did you shake because you was scared, or because you was mad angry?"

He turned and looked at her, considering carefully, trying to arrange his thinking, for he was still confused by the reaction he had experienced. Angry? Why should he be angry? Scared, yes. He could understand that, for thinking of it now in cold blood, it had been a terrifying thing to do, to set his hand to such unknown territory, to try to help a screaming, agonized child without knowing how to, only by guesswork and a sort of inspiration. But why angry?

"Because I didn't know what I was doing," he said, talking more to himself than to her. "I didn't know what I was doing, and I want to know. I did it not knowing, and it's all wrong like that. There ought to be people who *know* what they're doing, always, for everybody. She shouldn't have been brought to such a pass. If someone had got to her sooner, and turned that baby, it'd not be dead, and I want to know *why* it was dead, and—"

"You'll get yourself into a right pother again if you don't quiet yourself," Lucy said calmly, and he realized he had started to shake again, and took a deep breath and quite deliberately let his shoulders sag and flop. The shaking stopped, and he sat, for a while, staring at his hands on his knees and trying to think.

When she spoke again it made him jump, for his mind had wandered, was cloudy and confused.

"You're tired out, ain't yer? You ought to get back to your fancy ken in Gower Street and sleep it orf. I'll get a hack for you. No, don't fret; I'll pay. Got enough and to spare."

She had reached the door, but then she stopped and turned to look at him. "You was startin' to tell me of this business in Windmill Street—where they teach the surgeons. Is that what you mean about knowing?"

"What? Oh. Well, yes, in a way. You've got to learn, do you see, find out what really happens, before you can—before you can . . ."

"Before you can what?"

He looked up at her with a sort of helplessness. "I'm not sure I know what it is I want to know—what it is I want to do. But it's all wrong, isn't it? Gower Street and all round here"—he waved his hand in a vaguely comprehensve way—"and Nancy and—all sorts of things. It's all *wrong*."

She grinned her great gap-toothed smile. "And you can put it right?"

"Me? I don't know. Not till I've learned more, anyway. Maybe I can do something—better than selling fancy useless ointments and mixing up plasters."

"Why don't you go to this place in Windmill Street, then? Will it cost you?"

He grimaced. "It'll cost. I don't know how much, but it

won't be counted in ha'pence, I'm sure of that. I'll do it though, one of these days."

"What about your indentures?" She was leaning against the door now, her arms folded heavily against her great breasts, which bubbled over the top of her brawny forearms like dumplings in a pot. "Can't go studyin' at some other place when you're 'prenticed, can you?"

"I never thought about that," he said, and suddenly yawned hugely. "I daresay I'll be through my time and long gone past it before I get the money to arrange anatomy school." He struggled to his feet, unwinding the shawl from his arms. "I'll come and see you again, Lucy, and Nancy—I want to know what becomes of her; but I'll have to go now. It's long after midnight, and I've to be back at the shop by seven tomorrow—this morning." And he yawned again, and she nodded and went away to find a hack for him.

She insisted on coming out to see him into the small carriage, and shoved a handful of coins at him, refusing with most choice language to take it back, insisting on her right to pay the fare. He didn't argue much, for he was now far too tired. And she was Lucy, and there was no need to feel shame of any sort with Lucy. For all the years that had passed since that last meeting, he felt as comfortable with her as though their relationship had continued without any break at all.

Just before she closed the door on him, she thrust her head inside the carriage and said in a matter-of-fact way, "If your master—what's'isname—Witney—if 'e'll give you leave to study at this school in Windmill Street yer fancies, maybe I'll give a bit of thought to the possibility I'll pay your way. I'm not making no promises, one way nor the other—except to say as I'll think about it. No, don't say aught about it. I've me own mind to make up, and it's my affair what I does with me money—an' I've plenty of it—an' you never know: I might be glad of a surgeon of me very own before I'm that much older! Get on your way, then." And she slammed the door on him, to send him swaying back to Gower Street in a very bemused state.

Abel thought a great deal during the next few days about what Lucy had implicitly offered him, and they were difficult days indeed as he pondered and plotted, discarded new-made plans to make fresh ones, thought out conversations with Jesse and Charlotte as well as with Josiah, and still came no nearer to finding a time and way in which to broach the subject. Knowing as he did how Josiah felt about surgery, it was clear he would be hard put to it to get permission to spend some of his working hours in Great Windmill Street; knowing of Charlotte's views on "nasty, brutish surgeons," it was equally clear he would find no useful allies in Gower Street. But how he yearned to seize on the possibility of Lucy's offer! He would think of that big, cool cellar room and the tables with their stripped and staring cadavers and long for it with all the urgency that was in him.

He still had not solved his dilemma when Sunday came, and was sitting gloomily in the schoolroom staring at the rain pouring down the window—which it seemed to have done every day of this miserable summer—when Dorothea came in, as she always did on such afternoons, to sit silently and confidingly beside him on the old sofa.

Dorothea too had been spending a great deal of her time in thinking and planning. She had been content enough to let time ride on without making any further push to settle her future with Abel, but she had been for so long buried in her dreams of this hopefully golden future that she paid too little heed to the present, and this dreaminess had not escaped Charlotte's eagle eye.

On the previous Tuesday, Charlotte had chaperoned Dorothea to a party of young people; it had been planned as a picnic, but because of the weather had become an indoor affair at a house in Bedford Square to which Charlotte, much to her delight, had recently gained regular admission. Her delight was compounded of two parts: one, that the lady with whom she had struck up this new friendship was just that, being Lady Field, the wife of a newly created City knight (rather vulgar but titled, and that was what mattered), and the other that she was the mother of two likely sons neither of whom was married.

So Charlotte had been pleased when the rain had driven the party indoors, for it was a small and select young group, and she had greater hopes in such circumstances of Dorothea's attracting the attention of Mr. Peter Field, the older of the brothers.

To Charlotte's chagrin, Dorothea had indeed attracted the young man's attention (he was a rather simple boy, but biddable, and his mother had told him to pay attention to the rich Mr. Constam's stepdaughter, so he did) but been totally unaware of it. When he spoke to her, she answered him in vague monosyllables; when he invited her to take an ice with him, she seemed unaware of the particularity of his attention and murmured, "No thank you," and eventually drove the young man from her side to livelier company. Biddable and simple though he was, not even he was able to maintain conversation with someone quite so unresponsive. And how could Dorothea be other than unresponsive? With her heart and mind so filled with Abel and his effects on her, every other young man seemed insipid, to say the least. She had, indeed, hardly noticed that young Field had spoken to her.

When they returned to Gower Street, Charlotte stripped off her gloves with a controlled anger that Dorothea did not notice; and when her mother said icily, "Dorothea, you will come to my boudoir, if you please, after I am rested. There is a matter I would speak to you about," she still did not worry in the least, although usually she would have quaked at such a note in the maternal voice.

The reason for her more than usual absence of mind was her concern for Abel; she had fallen into the habit of listening for his return each night, not willingly going to her sleep until she was sure he was safe within doors; and last night he had returned at gone midnight, having to call Frederick, the footman, from his bed to let him in.

All day she had been puzzling and worrying about it, for at the back of her mind was the fear that Abel would return to Seven Dials and leave her alone in Gower Street. He must not be allowed to do such a foolish thing, she had been crying inside herself all day. The time had come to be open with Abel and tell him, somehow, that all was well, and they *could* be wed—one day, if not quite yet. In her own mind, she had decided that of course Abel cared as much for her as she for him, and was kept from speaking to her only by his pride, his awareness of his inferior station. Dorothea had been doing an immense amount of dreaming these past months—immense even for her, who had dreamed and made fantasies all her life.

So she went to her mother's boudoir calmly enough and totally unready for the storm that was unleashed about her head. How dare she, demanded Charlotte in that painfully controlled voice of hers, behave so ill to a young man who did her the honor to address her? Did she believe herself to be some great beauty, one of the Town *On-Dits*, who had but to raise a finger when she was ready in order to find a husband panting at her feet? She had best think again, said Charlotte cruelly, for though she had some advantages which would make her desirable to some respectable young men, she would have to make some push for herself if she was to contract the sort of marriage that was a cut above the ruck, for she lacked the great beauty, the sureness of address that would commend her and enjoyed possession of only the most meager of accomplishments, despite the years of her mama's devoted teaching.

Dorothea blinked, and wept, and protested, but it made no difference. For a full hour her mother told her precisely how she was to behave in future, warning her that unless she made far better use of her limited gifts and set her mind to establishing a suitable marriage, she could resign herself to a life of spinsterhood.

"And do not think," she added with some spite, "that you will be a spinster of means, for your stepfather, while a rich man, is not one to consider his duty to his wife's child as paramount. I cannot be sure that there will be any estate of worth for you from him, although as long as I am alive I can intercede for you for a decent marriage settlement. But don't think he will leave you money to keep yourself alone, for I have no doubt that he would not!"

Charlotte and Jesse had been passing through one of their stormier periods, with each fighting ever more furiously with the other, and each seeking ever more cruel ways in which to taunt. Charlotte's anxiety about Dorothea stemmed largely from this, in fact, for Jesse had, during one of their bitterest quarrels, told her he would as lief let the beggars have all his money as leave it to her and her miserable rag of a daughter

—oh, the words and feelings had been running very high! And now Dorothea reaped the harvest.

She had escaped at last, drooping with the exhaustion of tears, feeling as though she had been physically whipped, sure of one thing only: if she did not soon make sure that Abel and she were truly betrothed, then her mama would see to it she was betrothed to someone else—anyone else who would have her. She spent the rest of the week wondering and weeping and planning, and at length made up her mind. Abel must be brought to understand that he need no longer keep silent.

"Abel," she said now, sitting there beside him on the sofa. "Abel? I must speak to you of . . . It is most important, and . . ." she stopped and reddened, for he had turned impatiently on her and was frowning. "Oh, please, don't look so, Abel! I am so miserable!"

"You're miserable?" he said, his voice thick with scorn, as he looked at her careful curls and fashionable dress and soft white hands. "What right have *you* to be miserable when out there"—he gestured toward the window— "out there are people who are so starved, and sick, and helpless, and . . . You miserable? *I'm* miserable! What do you say to *that?*"

"But you must not be, dear Abel! You must not be," Dorothea said eagerly. "I am sure we can solve our problems easily enough if we put our minds to it."

"Are you?" demanded Abel savagely, and he stood up and went to stand by the window to stare out at the pouring gutters below. "I wish I could be so certain. Here I am, with a chance such as I have wanted these— Oh, what's the use? I cannot do as I wish, so why should I try?"

He was talking as much to himself now, as he so often did when with Dorothea. "If I speak to them about it, they'll say no, for all sorts of stupid reasons. If I do not speak to them and try to arrange it alone, they'll be sure to find out, and then where am I, for if I am turned out of my indentures, what can I do? I must wait this five years out and try again. Maybe she'll wait till then and still wish to provide the cost of it."

Dorothea had picked little out of this stream of words, but of one thing she was sure: Abel was yearning, aching, longing as much as she was. She could hear it in his voice, see it in his posture, even if she was not certain precisely what it was he was saying.

She went running across the room to stand beside him, with one hand set beseechingly upon his arm, and peered up into his face.

"Dear Abel," she said breathlessly, "I have given it all so much thought. I think I know how we can make a push to gain our way! I have spoken already to Mr. Witney"—she blushed a little at this confession—"and I know him to be in full approval of our—our wishes. If you will speak to Papa Constam, I believe you will find him—willing. And if you will tell him that Mama says she—she will make me marry any person she can find, for she wants to be rid of me, and says she will tell all the town that it is *his* fault she did it, because he threatened to cast me off—why, then, I am sure he will allow it! And once we are—are betrothed as we should be, then none will stand in our way! And you have said that Mr. Witney cares for you, and if you show yourself to be settled for your future with me, why, perhaps when you are free of your indentures he will make a partner of you! And it will all be . . ." She faltered and stopped, staring up at his face, for he was looking down at her with so blank an expression on it that she could not tell whether he was pleased or angry, approved her plan or rejected it out of hand.

"Abel?" she said timidly.

"Let me understand you," Abel said carefully. "You wish we should be betrothed? And you say Mr. Witney has already spoken to Mr. Constam of such a matter?"

She nodded dumbly.

He looked at her for a long time, trying to rearrange his thinking. That Mr. Witney had fallen into the error of thinking there was more than the friendship of propinquity between himself and Dorothea was one thing, but that she should share this misapprehension was . . . He shook his head sharply and opened his mouth to speak, and then, looking at her face, closed it again.

She was staring up at him, her chin tilted upward, and it was as though he were seeing her clearly for the first time. A soft and fragile face, with its delicate coloring, the china blue of the eyes, the pale arched brows under the spun fair hair. For a moment he tried to superimpose Lil's remembered face over it—the wicked green eyes, the intensity and color of them—but that vision faded as soon as it had come, for Lil was part of the dead past now.

Looking again at that pleading face, he saw more: the face of the only person in the Gower Street household who had accepted him unquestioningly, who had never criticized him, had tolerated his sharp tongue, his self-absorption, his misery-bred surliness, and still remained his friend. He seemed to see, as at a vast distance, a picture of her feeling and concern for him, and without thinking, he bent and kissed her cheek with a friendly roughness, a grateful kiss meant to express as best he could his awareness and appreciation of the interest in him she had displayed over the years.

"They'd never even consider it," he said, unwilling now to say what he had been about to say: that the idea was ludicrous and that he wanted no part of it.

"Indeed, believe me, Abel, they would. Papa Constam and Mama are at such odds with each other that I am certain we shall fall between them into the situation we most want! I do not enjoy being so devious, Abel, but sometimes one must shift as best one can. When one has such parents as I."

He looked at her again, at the way she stood there before him, still invested with a personal dignity despite the pleading she had expressed, and suddenly saw her as vulnerable, as a real person in her own right, rather than as the cipher member of the household she had always seemed.

"You really wish it, Dorothea? To be—betrothed to me? It is not just a—a device to free yourself of your parents' controls?"

There was a short silence and then she smiled, a sudden wide smile that showed her small teeth, and lifted her face into a strange sort of gaiety that overlay the expression of anxiety that seemed always to invest it. "I really wish it," she said simply. "I—I bear a great affection towards you, Abel."

He moved away from her and went back to the sofa, to sit with his head thrown back and his eyes closed, trying to think. If he were in fact to be betrothed to Dorothea, that idea of Mr. Witney's which he had never before taken with any seriousness, what would come of it? First, he must surely become more—important in the house. They could no longer —could they?—regard him as almost one of the servants. And if he were to have this new status, what else? As the soon-to-be son-in-law, surely they could not refuse to allow him to better himself in any way he saw fit, whether or not they approved of what he chose? And if Mr. Witney saw him as a future partner, could not he be persuaded that a knowledge of anatomy could be of use to an apothecary? After all, Abel told himself, when he thought we were but considering betrothal, look how he relaxed and taught me more, and let me go with him on visits; if we were to be betrothed in fact . . .

The thoughts ran and twisted in his head and he tried to pin them down. Married to Dorothea. An extraordinary prospect! But he would have to be married one day, he supposed, and why not to Dorothea, who liked him so well, and for whom he felt such friendship? Not since his childhood and Lil had there been anyone he really cared about . . .

Lil had nothing to do with this again. He pushed the memory of her away, angered that it chose this moment to come up. No, she was dead and gone, part of yesterday. It was now, tomorrow, that mattered.

So, again, if he were to be betrothed to Dorothea, what then? It would change his prospects, and all he would have to do in exchange would be to be a good and gentle husband to her. And it would, after all, be pleasant to be cared for and loved by such a wife as Dorothea would certainly be. Why not? Accepting this plan of Dorothea's seemed to offer the answer he had been seeking, seemed to offer much indeed. Not least, the fury that Charlotte would experience if it were arranged against her will. . . .

His lips curved at that thought. He remembered in a sudden muddled blur the things she had said to him, the sneers she had heaped upon him, the sharpness of her tongue, and those memories overlay the better ones, of the hours of teaching she had given him, the unexpected softness in her look when he had come back from school, the way she seemed to want him to live in her house now. Indeed, he thought, with a malice that was unfamiliar to him, there were many benefits to this plan, and few drawbacks. And it would be pleasing to set himself against Charlotte and win.

He opened his eyes, and looked at Dorothea standing by the window with her hands clasped in front of her in unconscious supplication, her face creased with anxiety.

"You truly believe Mr. Constam would agree to such a plan? You are quite sure he will?"

"Oh, yes, Abel, quite sure! Mama will be very angry. But if Papa Constam gives his consent she cannot say anything, and . . ."

He smiled then—a long, slow smile—and nodded. "So be it, then," he said simply.

· TWENTY-FIVE ·

"SHE says," Jesse said thickly, "that she'll not speak to you again. Not one word. How do you say to that, hey?"

He looked owlishly at them over the rim of his glass, and Abel looked back at him with a faint distaste, for he was unappetizingly blotched and sweating with the brandy he had been steadily swallowing, and his eyes were congested and moist.

"Well, boy, what do you say to that? And you, miss? Does it fill you with tears to think your mama is so bitter angry?"

Dorothea sat with her head bent, staring down at her hands folded in her lap. She was frightened of Papa Constam's state, disliked the smell of him, but was so thick with happiness that it did not matter in the least. She had but to sit here quietly until the chance came for them both to slip away, and then she and Abel . . . Her mouth curved into one of her secret smiles.

"Well, I'll tell you what I think. I think you're as fortunate a pair as ever I came across. You've got your way, and in getting it saved yourselves the tedium of listening ever again to all the . . ." He belched suddenly and noisily, and Dorothea gave him a quick scared glance, and then looked appealingly at Abel.

"Dorothea, you should go to your room," Abel said curtly. "Your mama would wish it. Good night."

"Her mama don't care what she does any more. You heard her say it, boy, heard it with your own ears! She don't care."

"Good night, Dorothea," Abel said again, and obediently Dorothea stood up and came across the room to stand before Jesse. She stood hesitantly for a moment, and then bent to kiss his cheek, and he looked up at her and produced a drunken leer that made her redden without knowing why; and she turned quickly to come back to Abel.

"Shall you be—shall we talk a little, Abel, in the school-room?" she asked softly and urgently, and behind her Jesse laughed his coarse laugh.

"I don't think so," Abel said, more sharply than he meant to, for he was controlling his irritation as much as he could. But the last week had been so dreadful—filled as it was with Charlotte's fury, Jesse's knowing leers and guffaws and maliciousness, and above all Dorothea's freely expressed lovingness. Ever since Jesse had roared at Charlotte that he'd made up his mind, dammit, and they *should* be betrothed, and she could bite her tongue, for that was all about it, Dorothea had been so clinging, so affectionate, so filled with a need to talk and touch and talk again, that Abel had been driven almost to despair. She would have to learn to be more circumspect, indeed she would, and he would have to teach her. He could not bear the thought of the years of such possessiveness that would lie ahead if he did not check it now. But still, he should not have been so sharp with her, he thought guiltily, looking up at her face suffused with color and her eyes brimming with tears. She was little more than a child (he quite ignored her seniority in years), and she had had a cruel enough time at her mother's hands.

"Good night," he said more gently, and smiled at her, and immediately her face lifted and she smiled back at him through her tears, and bent and kissed his cheek.

They sat in silence for a while after she had gone, and then Abel stirred and said carefully, "You know that Mr. Witney has given me consent to attend anatomy school, sir, as long as you are willing to permit it. You paid for my apprenticeship, after all, so the decision is with you. I wish you would say one way or the other which it is to be. I've spoken of it these many times this week, but—"

"Hey? What?" Jesse grunted, and moved heavily in his chair. He had been almost asleep. "Anatomy—what for? You must be clean mad! Here you are, got yourself well set up with a master apothecary who's taken a rare fancy to you, man with no sons of his own and a warm business—what do you want anatomy school for? You'll do well enough and keep a wife in great style, you wait and see." He laughed then. "Keep a wife! Must be madder still to want that! What you want to—"

"I believe we shall not speak of Dorothea, sir," Abel said, and his voice was very flat. "I wish to speak only of my desire to attend the school. May I tell Mr. Witney you are agreed?"

There was a pause, and then Jesse stood up and started to prowl about the room. Suddenly he did not seem quite so drunk.

"Oh, boy, why can't you let well alone? I've let you have the girl, and that's driven her mother near demented! Oh, don't fret you, I won't go back on my word to you, though I have it in me to wish I had not been so angered by the tears and the arguments. I'd not have agreed as I did if she hadn't been so damned— Well, let be! I've said it now, and there's an end to it. But why compound it? She'll clean lose her mind if she thinks you spend your time with corpses—you've heard her on the subject! You've a better life than you could ever have hoped for, better than any I planned for you when I brought you here, and I cannot deny it—so why make more difficulties? It's a foolish notion that's got into your head, no more."

"If it's because Mrs. Constam won't have a surgery student near her that you're refusing me, then I'll find elsewhere to live. I've lived on my own before now."

"No!" Jesse was standing still now, and looking at Abel with an expression that was almost alarm on his face. "No need for that. This is your home now, dammit!"

He could not have explained aloud why the thought of the boy's departure so perturbed him, but it did. He saw little enough of him, in all truth, for he spent the largest part of his day in his own countinghouse and warehouse, and most of his hours of leisure with his cronies in the coffeehouses or away on expeditions of his own, yet he had come to find pleasure in seeing that dark head and long white face with the extraordinary green eyes about the house when he was in it. And now, having dealt so grievous a blow at Charlotte as he had in disposing of her daughter's marriage against her will, he would find life in Gower Street intolerable if the boy went.

"No," he said again; "it is my wish you remain here, whatever you do."

"Then you will allow me to tell Mr. Witney I may attend anatomy school," Abel said, and looked very directly at Jesse, his chin up and his mouth set in a straight line. This is what the whole betrothal business is about, he was thinking. If I cannot take up Lucy's offer, then I may as well end the whole thing now. Perhaps Lucy will let me live with her and study, and leave Mr. Witney and—

"Oh, God damn you to hell and back!" Jesse roared, and now he looked as deep in drink again as he had been earlier, although he had taken no more, for his face was red and his eyes blotched and heavy. "Do as you wish! Just leave me in peace, the whole damned boiling of you!"

And he slammed out of the drawing room to shout for Frederick and his coat, leaving Abel feeling curiously flat. He had at last won his way, and he should be exultant; and indeed, in part he was. But another part of him was filled with doubt, and he knew why. It was all involved with too many people, this success of his. Dorothea and Charlotte, Jesse and Mr. Witney and now Lucy. All embroiled in his affairs, just because he wanted to *know*. "I hate them all," he said aloud, his voice vicious and his fists thumping down against the arms of his chair. "I hate them all!"

And then, startled at the intensity of his feeling, he took a deep breath and fell to planning the future that was now within his reach. To spend time and effort being angered about the behavior of other people was wasteful, and Abel was becoming, as the years passed, ever more practical.

He stood at the top of the familiar stairs, filling his nose with the remembered smell, and felt his hands trembling. It suddenly did not seem possible that he was truly here, on the first morning of the first term of his first year, that it was all actually going to happen.

Behind him there was a rattle as the door from the street opened, and a rush of footsteps, and he shrank back against the wall as a tall figure, outlined against the light from the door he'd left swinging open behind him, came hurtling toward him.

"Well, lad, well—and for why are ye standing there gawping? If you're here to work, then come away down the stairs and set about it instead of lurking up here in a dream. Who is it, anyway?"

"Ah—uh—my name is Abel Lackland, sir," Abel stammered. "And—"

"Lackland? Lackland? Never heard of ye! Who are you? New student? Where from? University? Surgeon's son? Hey?"

"Yes, sir. No, sir. I mean, I'm new, and I'm not a surgeon's son. I'm apprentice to Mr. Witney the apothecary, and he gave me consent to—"

"Well, well, well! There'll be no work done standing here." The man was gone, clattering away down the stairs, and Abel hurried after him, breathless from the speed with which he moved and talked. Whoever he was, he was clearly someone of great importance, for at the foot of the stairs an old man in a heavy calico smock was standing obsequiously waiting to help him out of his coat.

Now they were in the well-lit cellar, Abel could see more clearly what sort of man he was. Tall, he had already noticed, and handsome too, with a square, firm jaw and very large dark eyes. He was well dressed, completely the gentleman from the quality of his heavy broadcloth coat to the white tops of his beautifully polished Hessian boots. As he shrugged out of his coat and into a much older black one that the servant was holding ready for him, Abel saw his hands, long and white and with fingers very flexible as they moved, and dropped his eyes to his own square-fingered hands and felt a heavy twinge of doubt.

"So what's worrying you, lad? Smitten by the myth of a surgeon's special hands, are ye? Well, it's so much nonsense, and never fear ye can't make a surgeon o' yourself unless you've hands like a woman." He stretched his own fingers wide and looked at them consideringly. "'Tis purely an accident that I've such long fingers, and they're more use to me in the painting and drawing than in the cutting. A surgeon needs a good eye and a clear head more than he needs fancy hands, and so you'll find out—hey, Davy?"

The servant grunted and went shuffling off across the room with the coat held reverently over one arm, and the tall man laughed and went over to one of the tables in the middle of the room, to pull the covers off the cadaver that lay on it.

"So, you're Lackland, are you? 'Pothecary's apprentice. Hmph. Well, I'm Charles Bell, late of Edinburgh and for my sins one of the people who will be teaching you your business here."

Abel was standing very still, letting his gaze roam about the room, resting on the tables, the rows of instruments, the shelves and rows of benches, and his mouth curved delightedly. "It's all just the same," he murmured.

"Hey? Same as what? Did ye not say ye were new this term?"

"What? Oh, yes, sir. Sorry, sir. It's just that . . ." Abel felt his face go crimson. "I—I've been down here before. Not as a student, of course, but . . ."

Charles Bell looked at him, his head on one side. "Have ye, now? Well, that's no concern of mine; as long as you're a registered pupil and ye've paid your fees, I'll teach you. And since you're the only one who's made the effort to get here in good time the first day o' term and thus impress the dominie, ye can have the privilege of handling my instruments for me. And we'll see how much ye noticed when last ye were here, for whatever reason that was. Give Davy your coat, unless you've a mind to spoil it, and come here."

It was, Abel felt, what he had been waiting for all his life. There in the circle of light thrown by the oil lamps from the shelves beside them, with the rows of instruments spread gleaming and cruel before him, he watched those long white fingers move with great speed but perfect control over the waxy yellow flesh, watched as the knife parted a way along the belly, sliding smoothly and with delicate energy through the layers: yellow bubbles of fat; red streaks of muscle; the pearly gleam of the peritoneum, the last layer to be split before the belly contents would be revealed.

As the knife moved on, sweeping round in a great curve to widen the opening into the belly, Abel reached automatically for the long dissecting pins that would be needed to hold back the flaps of abdominal wall and leave space for the students to work, and Bell looked up and said sharply, "You've seen a cadaver dissected before today, then?"

Again Abel reddened. "I used to be allowed to help Mr. Wilson sometimes," he muttered. "Just because I was interested, and—"

"Mr. Wilson? How d'ye know him? Friend of the family?" Abel shook his head.

"Hmph. And you say your father wasn't a surgeon? So that wouldn't . . ." He shook his head then. "Rather not say, lad, is that it?"

"If you please, sir," Abel said, "it was a long time ago."

"Ah, well, it's none o' my consairn, I suppose, though it's rare enough to find a new pupil with some useful experience behind him. I was merely curious, but I'll ask no more, if ye so wish it."

They worked on in silence for a while, with Abel handing instruments as memory came surging back of the times he'd spent in this cellar with Mr. Wilson long ago, until the body was ready for demonstration, and they moved on to the next. There was a clatter from upstairs, and Bell raised his head and grimaced.

"Ah, here they come, the hope o' the future! Such a crew! Well, let's aboot it." And he moved toward the end of the room and the lecturer's podium.

"If you please, Mr. Bell," Abel said nervously as he too moved toward the row of pupils' benches. "Can you tell me when Mr. Wilson will be coming here?"

"Wilson?" Bell said, his head down as he leafed through a pile of papers on the desk. "Not in this world, lad. Died of a ruptured aneurysm, day of Lord Nelson's funeral, a twelve-month ago. We taught on him and buried what was left when the weather changed." He looked up then and saw the stricken look on Abel's face, and spoke more gently. "I'm sorry, lad. I had not thought perhaps you cared specially for the man. He was a good anatomist, for all his fussy ways, and he taught well. And ended as he would have wished, teaching anatomy from the grave. But I'm sorry if the news has distressed ye."

"A little, sir," Abel said woodenly, and then, as a rattle of footsteps came down the stairs, moved away into the corner. He needed time to observe his fellow students, he felt obscurely, before they observed him. And he needed time to recover from the undoubted shock Bell's casual announcement had created in him. He had not realized how much he had looked forward to once more seeing the dry old man who had given him his first lessons in anatomy.

Long before the end of that first morning, he had recovered from his distress. At first just to be part of the class was enough, and he was content to look at the other seven students and assess them. Two looked pale and positively sick as they stared at the naked corpses spread awaiting them, and he marked them down at once as new men like himself. The other five were clearly old hands, for they swaggered and shouted and generally performed a good deal, and Abel remembered the two young men who had so impressed him years ago in Jesse Constam's countinghouse, and his mouth quirked at the memory.

Bell allowed the noise to go on for a little while, even joining in the ribaldry on occasion (and indeed, Abel had heard no language like it since he had left the gutters of the Dials behind him), and at first he wondered about that. He had been so impatient to start work when he had been alone with Abel; why now should he so willingly exchange dubious jokes with the students, and join in the laughter so loudly and rumbustiously?

Catching a glimpse of the expressions on the faces of the other two new men, he understood. The sick pallor was receding a little as the raucous laughter went on, and they seemed less poised for flight than they had when he had first noticed them, and he turned back to the tables, looking consideringly at the corpses and trying to imagine how he would feel if he had never before seen such a sight as a flayed human being lying ready to be cut to minute pieces.

But although he could in part understand the revulsion and

disgust that so filled the raw young men now trying weakly to cap the jokes the more experienced were bandying, he could not enter into it. There they lay, full of the promise of knowledge. How could anyone fear them, or be sickened by them? "Only so much dead meat," he thought, and for a moment couldn't remember who had said it. And then, as a faint picture of Lil rose before his eyes, remembered and deliberately forgot again.

At the end of the morning, which, once they had settled to work, was spent discussing the arrangement of the main parts of the body, he felt as though he had been a student all his life. Despite the fact that there were five people in the class who had already done a year's work in anatomy (three of them, in fact, were also walking the wards of St. Thomas's Hospital), he did not feel as raw as he might have felt, and certainly not at all as stupid as the two other new men. He had learned more than he had realized in the years of school, of observation and growing fascination with all matters pertaining to the natural order.

He left Great Windmill Street at half past two o'clock in search of food (and found it in Lucy's comfortable kitchen, where she was waiting for news of his first day), content and happy as he had never been before. He was, at last, a true student. Life had little more to offer.

▪ TWENTY-SIX ▪

BUT IN fact it did. While the next three years moved over his head, Abel was as happy as he could ever have hoped to be. Not all around him were so happy, as the French Wars dragged on and on and money became ever shorter and fears of Boney ever stronger, but he was unconcerned with such matters. When Mr. Witney puffed and muttered about the price of his raw materials, the shortage of glass for bottles, and the general difficulty of finding all he needed to make his business run as it should, Abel would close his ears, leaving lugubrious James, the tall and skinny junior apprentice, to nod his head and murmur platitudes back; Abel would remove his mind from them to recite silently the names of muscles and arteries, organs and bones.

When at Gower Street the atmosphere became almost intolerable to Dorothea, for Charlotte had kept her promise and spoke not a word to any member of her household except the servants, emerging from her room rarely and then only to attend or arrange meetings of the London Ladies, and Jesse spent more and more evenings drunk and snoring, Abel did not notice. Dorothea would come fluttering from the schoolroom as Abel came into the house at the end of his exhausting day, timidly to kiss his cheek and eagerly to help him with coat and boots, and he would speak to her in his usual offhand manner, his mind still filled with the day's doings, and not even see the tension on her thin face, the gratitude for his appearance that filled her. He simply never thought to wonder what she did all day, how she occupied her time, or to consider how she felt about her mother's refusal to have any contact with her. Such matters were, to Abel, totally irrelevant.

What was relevant, exceedingly so, was the way he spent his days. Each morning he would open the shop for Mr. Witney, and set James (who was proving a capable enough boy) his day's tasks. Then Mr. Witney would come puffing along Piccadilly, bluer than ever about the mouth but refusing as always to pay any attention to his breathlessness, and together they would set about the daily visits to patients.

For Abel this was becoming ever more fascinating, for he was beginning to be able to understand the nature of some of the diseases they saw. Now, when Mr. Witney had given a bottle of laudanum to a patient with a cancerous lump upon her breast, or a bottle of his special Dissolving Mixture to a man kept up all the night with the pain of a stone in his bladder, Abel would slip back after he had gone to suggest earnestly a visit to a surgeon—"for a surgeon could do much to relieve you"—pressing Mr. Charles Bell's card into their unwilling hands.

Then, during the afternoons of the winter months, there were the classes at Great Windmill Street, where he rapidly progressed to being Mr. Bell's most favored pupil. That this made him less than popular with his fellow students deterred him not one whit. Abel had no need of friends, and when the others went rollicking off at the end of the class, arm in arm and singing and shouting their way toward the nearest tavern, caring not at all that they blocked the entire street with their passage and frightened the women and children they passed half out of their minds (for everyone feared medical students, and rightly enough, for they were indeed a rough and noisy lot), Abel felt not at all put out that they excluded him. He would have found no pleasure whatsoever in such activities.

Much the same applied to the students he met in the summer months. This was when he walked the wards at

Guy's Hospital. It had been Mr. Witney who, to Abel's delighted surprise, had arranged this shortly after his eighteenth birthday. "If you're going to study with the damned anatomists, boy, you'd best make a full job of it and see the work they do on the living. If seeing the state of the wards at the hospitals and the cruelties of those bloody surgeons doesn't put you off surgery for good and all, and bring you glad and grateful back to the decencies of the apothecary's trade, then, goddamme, nothing will." And he had paid the fees for two years at Guy's and went to considerable trouble to ensure that Abel got there as often as was possible for him, allowing for the exigencies of his shop duties.

Abel's gratitude for this action of Mr. Witney's ran deep. He knew the older man had still the same dislike, even horror, of the surgeon's craft, had nothing but scorn for the lordly physicians, but he was an honest and a caring man, and open-minded too, able to comprehend the importance to Abel of learning his matter thoroughly even though he himself so disliked it.

So Abel would make the journey east, hacking along the Strand to Fleet Street, on to St. Paul's at the top of Ludgate Hill, then turning south to push through the narrow streets and bewildering cluster of buildings and alleys that lay between the Cathedral and London Bridge, clattering eagerly across the river toward Snowsfields. And there he would put on his ward coat, a shabby black thing that was all that was fit to be worn in such surroundings, and sally out among the patients in company with the other students.

They soon learned, as had those who went with him to Great Windmill Street, that Lackland was no fun, no fun at all. They used horseplay and noise and wild oaths and heavy drinking to prepare them for the horrors of the wards, but not Abel Lackland. He would stand against a wall, his head bent over a book in his hand, waiting quietly for the surgeon or physician who was to teach them, ignoring all else.

At first his aloofness had been interpreted as weakness, and one of the biggest of the students, a hefty Yorkshireman, son of a country surgeon who doubled, it seemed, as a horse doctor in his parish, had set upon him. But Abel, as wiry and swift and cunning as he'd ever been, had the man flat on his

back and almost weeping within a matter of seconds. There-
after they all treated him with a chill respect and kept their
distance.

Not that, at first, Abel did not equally feel the need for
some way to relieve the emotions called up in him by the
things he saw at Guy's. The vast rooms with their rows of
heaped and shabby beds were dispiriting enough, so imper-
sonal and lacking in any human warmth as they were, for all
the sea-coal fires that burned heavily in the grates and the
amount of human life that existed between those bleak walls,
but it was the sounds and smells that assaulted his senses that
disturbed him most in these early months.

The stench of the place, with the windows kept always
tight shut, was indescribably revolting, a nauseous mixture of
pus and human excreta and vomit and the thick reek of
blood, and underlying it a heavy scent that Abel knew at
some very deep level of his consciousness to be the smell of
fear. It could only be that, for it drew from his own depths
so intense a surge of anxiety that sometimes it was all he
could do not to turn and flee, and he knew why his fellow
students roared their raucous jokes and wrapped themselves
in a shell of careless joviality. But no such carapace was available to him, or ever would be, not to him who had spent his
infant years in the Dials, to him who had already seen so
much of human misery. He had to tolerate the stench with all
the stoicism he could muster, forcing himself not to retch
and heave while the other men laughed and smoked and
swigged brandy from hip flasks. He had to close his ears to
the sounds that filled those high wards, the moans and wails,
the shrieks and despairing prayers, the pleading with God for
an end to misery, be it death or whatever, just let it end. . . .

Once the physician or surgeon who was teaching them
arrived, matters were less difficult. Then, as they walked
about the wards listening to the words of wisdom falling
from the great man's lips, there were matters to look at,
things to be learned. Abel would stand with his fellows at the
foot of a bed as one of the slatternly women who were the
nurses pulled back blankets to reveal a putrescent stump
where once had been a leg, trying to visualize how the operation had been performed, considering how he could do the

job himself on the basis of his own knowledge of the anatomy of the limb, garnered so carefully and eagerly at Great Windmill Street.

The chance to apply his knowledge a little more directly came at the end of his first year at the hospital. One of the more senior students fell sick and died of a ward infection just after he had paid his fees to act as assistant to Astley Cooper, the pride and joy of the whole of the hospital. There were none who did not speak his name with a very special sort of tone in their voices, a combination of awe and admiration, jealousy and amazement that one man could be so gifted, so swift a surgeon, so attractive a creature in face and physique, so well liked by so many people. And so rich and successful.

He was also a perspicacious man, and one with an eye for a likely pupil; when, after the loss of his assistant, he cast his eye about the group of available men, he saw Abel, with his eager face and thirst for knowledge, and made inquiries about him, and then sent out his summons.

"Since the family of the defunct Robinson appear unconcerned about the return of their fees, I am free to select another to take his place, gratis, as it were," he said in that flutingly clear and slightly condescending voice that was so well known to all the hospital, from lowliest porter to the Secretary himself. "And since I understand from my friend Mr. Bell that you show a certain aptitude in your work with him, and you look a spry enough young man, then the offer is there for you."

Abel had accepted with alacrity, aware that this particularity was likely to make him even more loathed by his fellows and quite untouched by that. To be allowed not simply to stand peering over others' shoulders in order to watch Astley Cooper operate with that famous and incredible deftness of his (an amputation of the leg below the knee in three minutes flat, they said! Incredible!), but to be there handing instruments, *assisting* . . . ! Abel was indeed in a seventh heaven.

The first operation at which he was called to assist was in fact a particularly difficult one. A porter from the meat market at Smithfield had been pulled out from under a dray with his left upper arm looking like chopped beef. They had brought him to the hospital shocked and sweating, his face green with pallor, and clearly not expecting much chance for him. Big and strong and young though he was, the injury was so frightful, with shattered pieces of bone protruding through the torn biceps muscle, that it seemed unlikely in the extreme that he could survive.

It was for this reason that Astley Cooper decided to operate on him, attempting an amputation of the arm through the joint with the shoulder blade—a most heroic piece of surgery, and one that would deter all but the surest and most arrogant of surgeons. But not Astley Cooper, who never set limits on his ambition to perform the unperformable.

The man had arrived at the hospital at a few minutes past one o'clock, while the students were still in the surgical wards, which was why it fell to Abel to assist: he had the fortune to be there when he was needed.

He hurried to the room set aside for operations in a state of high excitement, both frightened and exhilarated, knowing it would be a harrowing experience, yet so filled with interest that it would teach him an immense amount; and he was not wrong in his expectations.

The man was shouting and swearing with monotonous agony when Abel reached the room, sitting there in the operation chair, with its high back, and struggling feebly against the restraining hands of the two brawny porters who were in charge of him. At the far side of the room was another student, a very senior man, who, after one sharp stare over his shoulder, ignored Abel completely and turned to setting the instruments out in rows on the table. There were saws and chisels, large knives and little bistouries, needles and ligatures and piles of charpie, the soft grayish teased-out linen threads that were used for packing and dressing.

There was a flurry at the door as Astley Cooper arrived with his train of students behind him, and Abel nodded his head a little shyly and stood waiting a shade awkwardly, not sure what was expected of him.

"Now, Lackland, your task shall be the holding of the arm." Cooper was already standing beside the chair, running his fingers along the course of the shattered limb while the man rolled his head against the back of the chair and moaned pitifully. But Cooper seemed unaware of the man as a man, only of his arm, and the joint at the shoulder where it met the shoulder blade.

"Mmph," he said after a moment. " 'Tis fit enough. Cover the face, man, cover the face. Has he had the brandy?"

"Aye, sir," grunted the porter. "Not that it's made a great deal o' difference, on account e's as—"

"Well, well, there is no other way about it—whether the spirit aids or not, God help him, the work's to be done! Lackland!"

Abel hurried forward and found himself, under Cooper's direction, clutching the injured arm, with one hand holding the bent elbow and the other grasping the lower part of the upper arm; and adjured to "Hold hard, pull hard, and pray hard!" he set his teeth and prepared to do just that.

The other student pulled the table of instruments nearer, and Cooper shot his cuffs under the black coat sleeves, which were thick and hard as a wooden board with the dried blood from the myriad operations he had performed while wearing it (and smelling almost as bad as the wards themselves), and seized a scalpel in his right hand.

Abel watched, fascinated, never once letting go his grip on the arm, and with one foot set firmly back and braced against the floor to give him a stronger pull and to steady him. The knife slid through the undamaged tissue under the arm, while with his other hand Cooper felt, as Abel realized with the knowledge gleaned from his anatomy classes, for the brachial artery. The man on the chair shrieked, and the porters held his other shoulder hard, one of them almost lying across the chest in an attempt to hold him still.

Seemingly totally unaware of it, Cooper worked serenely on, finding the artery, sliding curved needles bearing eight threads under it, and tying a series of surgeon's knots, so speedily that his fingers looked to Abel's eyes to be a blur. They moved again, then, lower down, seeking for a pulse below the level of the ligature. Finding none, Cooper nodded, satisfied.

"Lower the arm, Lackland, to ease the skin," he ordered crisply, and immediately Abel did so and the man shrieked louder than ever.

"Now," Cooper said, through his teeth and with a curious relish, and reached for another scalpel, longer and gleaming cruelly bright. He stood there with it poised above the shoulder for a brief moment, and it was as though the whole roomful of watchers held their breaths together, waiting for it to descend; for that moment even the man in the chair lay still and silent, sharing the watchfulness and sense of intense anticipation.

The knife came down in a movement so direct and sure and convinced that it seemed to Abel to have been pre-ordained by some other agency, as though there were some invisible power that had drawn that line in the air and the knife had been irresistibly pulled to follow it. It moved across the shoulder, splitting the muscle easily; crossed the deltoid with such coolness and elegance that the movement of the flesh behind it looked like a lazy opening of a two-petaled flower, blushing redly as it met the light of day. Cooper worked swiftly and easily on, reaching for compresses, plug-ging bleeding points with charpie, once stopping to apply a ligature to a stubborn bleeding artery.

Again the knife moved on, round the joint, and suddenly, as it slid through the tissues that held the pearly globe that was the head of the shattered bone, Abel felt the pressure against which he had been pulling slacken and ease, and instinctively relaxed his hold to match to avoid tearing the cartilage. Cooper glanced at him for one moment and with the briefest of movements of his eyelids signified his approval, and Abel felt his face redden with pleasure.

The knife moved again, creating a triangular flap under the armpit, and then with one last movement through the shat-tered shoulder, it was over, barely five minutes after it had been started. Abel was standing holding the dead arm in his hands, while the other student coated the open wound with caustic and Cooper applied pledgets of lint to the arteries he had ligated.

Someone took the arm from him, and Abel did not even turn his head to see who, for Cooper had beckoned him with a jerk of his head, and he moved nearer, his hands out and ready for whatever was needed of him.

"Compresses. Plaster. Lint," Cooper said succinctly. "The wound must be packed, so—you see? To prevent a fatal hemorrhage. Not, sirs, that I expect great gains from this operation"—he was speaking to all the students now—"for a man must be in good general condition to survive the shock of the loss of so large a part of his being, and this man, as you observed, was deep in shock from the injury he had suffered before he reached us. I doubt he'll live another twenty-four hours, to be honest on the matter, but I was glad enough of the opportunity to perform so complex and difficult an operation on a living man. I have no doubt it is one I shall shortly wish to perform on one with a better chance of survival. There are in the wards, you will recall, a man with a spina ventosa, and a woman with a gross enlarging tumor of the humerus that I would wish to deal with. We have here today gained most valuable surgical experience, gentlemen, and I trust you will long recall all you have seen and learn from it. But do not attempt to perform any such operation yourselves until such time as you are at least half as experienced a man as I am. Mr. Lackland, that is a tolerable bandage, but it could be better. Observe. . . ."

He applied the bandage with deft turns of those supple wrists, and Abel watched, humbled. To be as expert with bandage as with knife: it offered almost too much of an example to follow, he thought, suddenly dispirited.

"So. Return him to the ward." Cooper stood back, and the two porters hefted into their arms the now unconscious man, who, to his own good fortune, had swooned away completely, and bore him away, and the students turned and followed, leaving the other assistant wiping instruments on pieces of old linen and replacing them in their case ready for their next use. Cooper took off his hideous black coat and hung it on the door before turning to wash his hands in the bowl of water held for him by a woman in a soiled print dress who had come in as the last student left.

"So, Mr. Lackland, you too have your operating coat now!" he said jocularly, and Abel looked down at his own black coat and felt his cheeks crease with pride. There, across the front, was the heavy deeper blackness that was a broad bloodstain, and the sleeves too bore sticky evidence of his morning's work. He looked up at Cooper, his face still bearing its smile, and Cooper laughed indulgently. "Aye, boy. You'll make a surgeon yet, don't fear. Tomorrow at two, if you please. I shall be cutting for the stone. Good day to you!"

Abel left the hospital that afternoon on his way back across the river in a state of happiness that was as intense as any he had ever known. It was a hot day in June, as warm and agreeable as any that year, and he walked across London Bridge filling his eyes with the lines of the buildings on the north bank (and ignoring the smells that filled his nose from the rotting wharves below), at the way the sun glinted, upriver, on the great dome of St. Paul's, and wanted to jump and sing. He had assisted at his first operation. Everyone ought to know of it, rejoice with him, and be happy with him. For the first time he could see the end of his road, see himself as a surgeon practicing upon his own patients, performing his own operations, deciding his own decisions.

He hesitated only a moment when he reached the other side. He had intended to return, as he usually did on his Guy's days, to Gower Street to make notes on his day's work and observations, to fix in his mind the knowledge he had gained. But today he did not need to do that. He would never, he knew, forget any detail of the operation. It was all engraved upon his eyes and brain forever.

So he hailed a hack and gave the address of Lucy's house in Panton Street. He would give himself the pleasure of an extra visit this week to his friends. He imagined the greeting he would get from Lucy, who would not expect him until Friday night, as usual, and wriggled comfortably into the corner of the carriage with a grin on his face. It would be a great greeting, and he had earned it today.

· TWENTY-SEVEN ·

IT WAS because of Lucy and her girls that Abel could tolerate the sterility of life at Gower Street, and had no need of any friendships with the men among whom he studied. Beside these women in whose company he found so much pleasure, Gower Street was a half-dead place, and the other medical students were boring, gross, thick in the head. Lucy, after all, chose her girls with a great skill. She knew that most men love a pretty face, a pert bosom, fluid hips, and plump, round buttocks, and are satisfied enough with that, but add the dimensions of wit and charm and sheer force of personality and the possessors of such attributes become formidable bed partners indeed. So she looked far and wide for her girls and chose them from the head down, consequently making a great deal of money for them and even more for herself.

"I'm a warm woman, Abel," she would say to him on one of her discursive evenings, when they sat at her kitchen table (which she much preferred to the parlor), she in uncorseted freedom, her feet thrust into old slippers and her fat bulging comfortably in all directions, he with a glass of beer and a plate of good bread and meat before him. "I could buy up the whole of Panton Street—aye, and the bleedin' 'Aymarket besides—if I 'ad a mind to. Not that I 'as. I've tucked it all away against the day when the girls get uppity and set up on their own, and leave poor old Lucy to starve. Only I won't, because I'm a warm woman." And she would swig her gin and water lustily and wipe her hand across her mouth with great gusto and grin her hideous and loving gap-toothed grin at him.

Not, it was clear to Abel, that Lucy would ever be left on her own. Although her girls were sometimes frightened of her, and learned early to dodge that great meaty hand aimed so accurately at their ears, and knew to their cost that she could be harsh, they knew too that when occasion arose she could be infinitely good. Bess had known what she was doing the night she had brought Nancy to Lucy, and Nancy had known what she was doing the night she had begged Lucy to let her stay, refusing to go back to her parents—who would kill her anyway, she swore, for what had happened to her.

And Lucy, of course, had agreed she should stay, but not as one of her girls; Lucy did not need to recruit her girls that way. For her customers she wanted only girls who were whores of their own free choice, who opted for the life because of their unbridled enjoyment of their own sexuality (a privilege not accorded to respectable married ladies) rather than for want of a better career. Since Nancy had clearly not enjoyed her encounters with Cole of the Haymarket theater, then she was not to be a whore. Instead, Lucy decked her in the frills and clean print of a parlormaid, and settled down to hugely enjoy the comfort of having personal service of her very own. And comfort certainly she had, for Nancy adored Lucy, more than anyone else in the house. The girls would often swear about Lucy, cursing her heavy hand and sharp tongue, but never round-faced little Nancy. For her, Lucy was all that was perfect, and Abel often wondered how it had been in those days after the birth of her baby, about the sort of care Lucy had provided. Clearly it had been something very special, to so enslave young Nancy.

Not that he wasn't enslaved himself. He adored his Lucy, adored her for her warmth and wickedness, her gentleness and her vicious, fluent swearing, her sluttishness and the basic beauty of that broad, fat-blurred face. She must once have been very lovely, when she was young and slender; to Abel she still was, for she gave him unstinting praise and approval, and made him feel as he never felt with anyone else. He did not know that her gift to him was self-esteem, but so it was. And he loved her dearly for it.

Tonight she sat beside him in the kitchen, watching him stuff himself greedily with hot mutton pies and caper sauce, approving the brightness in his eyes and the hectic flush of excitement on his cheeks as he told her, with a wealth of graphic detail, all about *his* operation. It never occurred to him that Lucy might be in any way repelled by his talk of bleeding arteries and shattered bones. But that was part of her charm: nothing ever repelled Lucy.

She laughed and exclaimed and applauded and gave him plum tart and thick yellow cream brought fresh from the cowkeeper's shop in Endell Street, and a pint of good ale, and he chattered on happily and ate until he was as full as he could be, and then leaned back and grinned at her.

"So there you are! I'm set as the great Astley Cooper's man, and will be so for another year. And then—why, shortly after that my indentures will be finished, and I can set up in practice for myself!"

She sniffed at that. "Sounds good. But 'ow's yer proposin' to do that? Will yer just walk out on that there Josiah the day you're free, and never look back? From all you've said of 'im, 'e'll not let yer go that easy." She nodded sagely. "Nor would you be clever to do it. For apart from whatever you might feel about the man—and as I understand the things you say, you've a deal of affection for 'im—remember there's that Miss Dorothea. As I reckon it, you only got yourself betrothed to 'er on the understandin' you'd 'ave that there shop to work in and provide a livin'. 'Ow will old Jesse be'ave if you goes cavortin' off to set up as a surgeon? I've known 'im these dunnamany years, and I tell you, 'e won't like it one bit. So if you wants to marry Dorothea . . ."

"Marry her?" Abel frowned, some of the pleasure of his day dissipating. "Oh, God, Lucy, I never think about *that*! Anything can happen!"

She looked at him, her head set to one side, birdlike and sharp with curiosity. "You don't want to marry 'er? Only got yourself betrothed for convenience, was it? Well, you ain't the first, nor yet won't be the last. But—"

"No!" he protested. "You make it sound so— It is not alone a matter of convenience, though I cannot deny that in many ways it falls mighty convenient for Dorothea as well as for myself. And she's a good girl enough, and kind to me, and seems to bear a goodwill and affection toward me. . . ." He grimaced again. "Damn it all, it suits me well enough to be a betrothed man. But I cannot think much beyond my work, at present, and as for marriage—well, there's time and to spare."

She shook her head a little, and uncharacteristically dropped her glance, a little embarrassed. "Tell me somethin', young Abel. You can tell me, yer know, on account I'm your friend and always will be. This not wantin' to marry—you've never wanted none o' my girls, neither. And yer a likely lad, as I've always said, and there's plenty of 'em's given you the eye, many's the time I've seen 'em, but you don't pay no nevermind, not once. 'Ave you ever 'ad a girl?"

Abel looked at her blankly for a moment, and then went scarlet. "Goddam you, Lucy, what the hell do you mean by—"

"Oh, stow yer noise," she said equably. "This is me, old Lucy, remember? I can say what I likes to you and anyone else I fancies. So answer me somethin': Are you one o' the boys? Is men your lay? It don't matter to me, not a groat, but I'm interested. Seeing as 'ow you could say it's my business to be . . ." And she laughed with great coarseness—a guffaw that was so hugely bawdy that it was totally inoffensive.

Abel shook his head, and grinned unwillingly back. "No! I'm just . . ." He shrugged. "Never been interested. Never had the time for any girl. And I keep my head busy enough with other matters not to concern myself unduly with what goes on beneath my belt."

She grinned then. "Garn! Tell your Banbury tales to some other gull! Don't care what a man's got goin' on in 'is 'ead, 'e's got plenty o' time to be interested in what's going on in 'is trousers too. You can't bamm me, you know! Not Lucy as provides the necessary for the 'ole damned House o' Lords and 'alf the Commons into the bargain! There's a better reason than that. Fancy someone, do yer? Got no eye for none but one? That's 'ard on a man, that is, when it 'appens. Though it shouldn't cause you no troubles. Can't see any girl as'd turn you down, you with your pretty face. . . . Garn, look at 'im blush! But it is, and the girls fancies yer, as none knows better'n me. If I was twenty years younger, my boy, why . . ." And again she launched into that bawdy shout of laughter.

"If you was, Lucy, I'd knock you on your back here and now!" Abel said promptly, and grinned at her, but she was not to be so easily led aside.

"Come on, boy, am I right? Some girl you wants? Can't you get her?"

He tried to prevent it, but he couldn't. The sight of her rose before his eyes for all the world like a theatrical show: Lil parading in one of the dresses stolen from Dorothea; Lil laughing at him from beneath a hat stolen from Dorothea; Lil skipping along beside him with her hair bouncing on her neck, her eyes sparkling green in the dimness, her laughter in his ears. And he felt it, that physical response stirring in him, and pushed the thought away, willing the sensation to fade as well, hating himself for it.

Watching him shrewdly, Lucy knew she had hit home, and sighed sharply. "Stupid boy! Let me give you young Jenny for the night. She'll make you forget whoever it is, *and* give you something better to think about. A man needs entertainment as well as work, 'owever well 'e loves 'is tasks. She's a clever girl, and one that follows you with 'er eyes all the time you're 'ere. Don't be so foolish, boy! Get yer pleasures where yer can; marry your Dorothea and get yer children on 'er, and go on comin' 'ere to Jenny or one like 'er, and you'll not do so badly. Then you can concentrate on your operations and your blood, and never give—"

"Lucy, you're a great friend, and I care dearly for you," Abel said, and his voice was crisp and rather loud, "but I ask you not to talk so. I have no interest in these matters. Any bull in a field can couple with a cow. For my part, there's other and better matters with which a man should concern himself. As for Dorothea—well, we shall see what we shall see. And don't fret yourself about my finding entertainment, for I find that, as well you know, at the theaters. If I can watch the play for a few hours, I need no more, and return to my work that much refreshed. Now"—and his voice lightened—"give me some more ale, you old bawd, and tell me the gossip. What's news among the girls this week?"

And Lucy sighed and gave him his ale and shut up. She knew when she was beaten and had no notion ever of flogging a matter beyond endurance. She was glad enough that her boy, as she thought of him now, was no man's fancy-piece, as she had begun to fear, sorry he was so clearly enamored of a girl who did not care for him. She could not for the life of her imagine any girl's not adoring her likely lad, but there it was.

One day, she thought, as she drew his ale and gave it to him, I shall find out who it is, and get her for him. He's a good lad, and there's nothing he shan't have that Lucy can get him. And nothing Lucy can't get for any man if she decides to.

He had spoken very truthfully when he told Lucy that as long as he had the theater he needed no further entertainment. With Mr. Witney's shop and patients, Charles Bell at Great Windmill Street, Astley Cooper at Guy's, Lucy at Panton Street, he had enough to fill his life and more. But when he added his newfound passion for the theater, his cup truly ran over.

It was Bess who had started it, casually giving him a seat for the play the night he had come back to see Nancy just after her baby was born.

"Grateful, see, Cole is, that you got it all fixed like you did," she said. " 'E said as if I saw yer, I was to give yer this, and say you was welcome and to be sure to come. Give it a go. It's a good show this week."

And with Lucy deeply occupied with caring for Nancy (who ran a fever for several days after the birth), he had had time and to spare, and went. And had fallen almost as deeply in love with what he saw as he was with his own work.

He was bedazzled by it all, bewitched and beguiled and enchanted. When the curtain rose on those vast glittering lights, revealing scenery that he had seen backstage and knew to be mere lath and linen and glue size but that now looked so completely real and solid, he was lifted out of himself. He saw the people he had seen backstage and knew to be tired and worn out, with heavy gaudy paint over their lined and hungry faces, and believed totally in the images of youth and innocence, wisdom and grandeur, wit and jollity that they offered him. The theater was a special heaven, and he, Abel, had the freedom of it.

As time went on, he did in actual fact gain the freedom of it. The company then at the Haymarket took to calling him to advise on their aches and pains and problems, so impressed had they been with his care of Nancy, and Mr. Witney had been content enough at this extension of his practice, but glad to let Abel handle it, for they paid erratically if at all (though lavishly when they had any money) and were not people to his taste anyway. Abel could handle them well enough, Josiah said wearily, and for his part, businessman though he was, Abel could pocket such fees as he earned from them with no entry in the shop's books, although of course they did have to pay for any drugs they needed.

So Abel had become a sort of unofficial apothecary in residence to the Haymarket theater, and loved it, being as welcome backstage as before the curtain. They all knew him and he them, and they liked each other, for the actors, for all their warmth of manner and instant friendliness, had one thing in common with Abel: intensely private persons in many ways, they projected an image of themselves to others while living their private lives secretly and truly in private within their own heads. Abel, so much the same, recognized and respected this trait, and was grateful for the peace it gave him. Superficial friendships, with no demands made either side: what more could a man ask for who was a student with so much to fill his head?

So he dosed their pains and dressed their wounds, and there were many of them indeed. People would fall over stage braces in the ill light of the backstage area, or singe themselves cruelly on the sticks of lime that were burned in the wing gas jets to throw a brilliant illumination on special players in special scenes, or get involved with difficult customers who thought nothing of battering the heads of the actors when they did not like their performances. And while he dealt with such matters, the theater people would tell him much—of past performances, past great actors, past hazards—thus increasing imperceptibly but considerably his affection for and new fascination with this strange world into which he had stumbled.

"This ain't aught to fret about," the old man who guarded the stage door told Abel the day he fell down an open trap and caused his old nose to bleed copiously. "You should 'a' bin 'ere the day them tailors turned out; they was really pricked in their pride, they was. . . ."

He guffawed heavily at his joke, which made his nose spurt another small jet of blood, and Abel pinched it hard to stop it. But the old man was undeterred, and rambled on in his muffled nasal voice telling the story of the way the tailors of London had been most ill pleased at a revival of Foote's satire *The Tailors* and had come storming up to the Haymarket theater to riot and rampage at its doors until the troops had to be called out to disperse them.

"Got a shrewd smash o' me nose then, I did, just like this. Looked like I was painted up more than them actors, and that's the truth of it. Cor, this ain't nothin' after that."

But it was always what went on before the stage rather than behind it that gave Abel most pleasure. He would sit wherever there was a space for him, never paying for a seat, and depending on the popularity of the play might find himself ensconced in great splendor in a stage box, tucked neatly into one side of the great square proscenium arch and near enough to the actors to touch them when they came out onto the apron that jutted out so arrogantly into the auditorium; or would have to fight for a seat with the pittites as they came bursting in when the doors were opened at six o'clock to go leaping over the rows of benches that were packed tightly into the pit of the auditorium, screeching and elbowing their way to the best vantage points and caring not whom they damaged in their headlong dash. He had his favorite seat, of course, and most of all liked to sit in the very center of one of the great sweeping balconies, seeing on either side of him the other boxes, filled with elegantly dressed people, expensive prostitutes and men of the town, go sweeping away into the shadows.

And before him the stage, with its great heavy curtains and the excitement as they parted to reveal the scene within. Sometimes there was the green carpet of tragedy spread on the floor, and he would settle down to see deep suffering and agonizing heartbreak sketched out with great gestures, thrilling and reverberating tones of voice, and floods of tears—real tears, for the actors of the Haymarket were very skilled in their craft. Or the orchestra in the pit would strike up a sprightly tinkling tune as soon as they had completed the obligatory "God Save the King" that opened every performance, and he would lift his shoulders with the pleasure of anticipation, waiting for the delicious comedy that was coming.

But whether it was during the play or before it, he loved most of all the atmosphere of the theater. The cries of "Bottled porter and cider!" "Choice fruits and bill of the play!" and "Watch your pockets!" that rose above the hubbub of chatter before the performance started; the hilarious if sometimes infuriating interruptions that came at nine o'clock when the half-price customers could come scrambling in; the occasional fights that broke out in the pit when a couple of the overpainted ogling prostitutes tried to pick the same customer—it was all a special and wonderful world to Abel.

Within a few months he had become as much a part of the scenery as the actors at the Drury Lane Theatre as well as the Haymarket. One of the women leaving the Haymarket to join Mr. Sheridan's company at Drury Lane took the news of the young apothecary of Piccadilly with her, and the company there were soon as enmeshed in his life as the Haymarket one. He gained even less profit from the work he did at Drury Lane—opening boils and dressing small wounds and dealing with the pox and congestions of the lungs—for Mr. Sheridan, the lively, outrageous, fascinating and totally unreliable Mr. Sheridan, paid his actors on inspiration as it were, and they rarely had any money for the young apothecary. But they were rich with promises, and he was content enough with that, for they were pleasant people—and there were the plays. He would drink them in—the burlettas, the comedies, the tragedies and masques—and loved them all.

And so his life went happily on, split between studies of anatomy and ward work at Guy's, and Lucy's brothel and the theaters, and he grew even more, and his chest filled out and deepened so that although he remained spare-framed, he was most palpably a man, and a most handsome one at that. He was unaware of it, but many were the female glances that followed his square shoulders and deep chest and admired the curly head and the fascinating green eyes and long white face when he went hurrying about his business.

Certainly on the rare occasions when Dorothea walked abroad with him—for betrothed as they were, Abel must sometimes play the gallant for her, much as he would have preferred to stay within doors studying his books, and they walked out on perhaps one Sunday in seven, to please her— she would almost die of pride as, hanging on his arm, she felt the envious, startled gazes of other women.

He was two months from the end of his indentures, had ended his studies at Great Windmill Street (though still visiting there to assist Charles Bell, for the interest of it), and was the most senior of the students at Guy's, with less than a month to pass before he should be ready for admission to the College of Surgeons, when there came that event that was to shatter the peace of the past five years. And he was totally unready for it when it came.

· TWENTY-EIGHT ·

THAT Charlotte had become decidedly strange was known to very few people indeed. Her own private maid, a rather simple woman who had been with her some five years or more, knew how often Charlotte talked aloud to herself, how commonly she would lie awake half the night arguing and hurling epithets at the ceiling, but as long as she was paid regularly gave little attention to it all. She did, on occasion, drop dark hints in the kitchen, so that some of the other staff were aware that the missus was a bit odd, but since the doings of their employers were naturally regarded as odd by servants, this meant little.

Jesse too had his suspicions, for although Charlotte had steadfastly kept her word and had not once spoken to him directly since Dorothea and Abel had become betrothed, he spoke to her often enough. He had taken more and more to the brandy bottle during these years: in part because of the disagreeable nature of his home life; in part because the affairs of the business were becoming ever more complex as the French Wars dragged on, and the troubles with Boney inevitably affected the shipping routes and lost him much of his legitimate as well as his less legal trade; and in part because of his awareness of himself.

Never a fool, he had been made to face the fact that many

of his hopes for his own happiness were finally blighted, and that he himself had been the instrument of destruction. He had hoped, all through those early years of this marriage, that one day she would understand, would soften and come to see that he was a man in need of affection, *her* affection, and would stop hating him for the form his physical loving sometimes took. He had earnestly hoped one day to have a son of his own. But bringing Abel to her, he now knew, had killed that son before he was conceived. Abel's presence had run through their relationship like a curtain—sometimes black and grim, sometimes lightened with a sort of fascinated affection, but there all the same. Jesse had come to realize that adopted Abel was the only son he would ever have, and hated his own body for the fact. And turned to the brandy bottle to make his hate bearable.

So that when he went lurching into her boudoir in one of his maudlin drunken moods, as he sometimes did, and she sat there staring at him with her eyes glittering and her lips steadily moving to shape silent words, he knew at some deeply buried level that her behavior was odd—that his Charlotte, the one he had married, should have sneered at him, shown him her rejection and anger in clear terms; but he dismissed the knowledge. Even in his sodden state he was aware that he was sodden and made allowances for it, so, he reasoned drunkenly, if Charlotte seemed odd it must be because he himself was odd, brandy-odd. And he would laugh and snort and weep a little and then go back to his own bed to sleep it off in time to go to the countinghouse next day, to drive fat little Hunnisett (looking not a day older than he had looked the day Abel had first seen him, ten years before) into a state of muttering, worrying tutting. The business indeed was suffering, and not merely from the influence of the far-distant Boney.

Certainly Dorothea did not know of the change in her mother. At first she had fretted a little about Charlotte's refusal to speak to her or even see her, had sent dutifully affectionate messages to her via the maid, but as time went on and she became ever more wrapped up in her dreams of Abel, her concern waned. Now, after four and a half years, she hardly noticed her mother's presence in the house.

Indeed, she had gained a good deal from Charlotte's withdrawal, for now it was largely Dorothea who ran the house. Charlotte still gave orders to cook and housekeeper, still controlled the household budget (for Jesse, however drunk, could never forget to bring money to Charlotte each month), but it was Dorothea who moved about the house scolding the maids if the drawing room was not cleaned properly, complaining about the service at table, and generally playing the chatelaine.

She enjoyed this very much indeed, for she could pretend, throughout her housewifely operations, that this was not her parents' house but her own; that she was the true mistress, married to Abel, and preparing each day for his care and comfort. In many ways Dorothea was enjoying all the pleasures of marriage, as she saw them, and none of the problems.

As for Abel himself, he noticed nothing about the Gower Street household. He had won his way, was living his chosen life, and with his essential economy gave no attention at all to the people with whom he lived and shared a house. When he left Gower Street each morning it was as though it disappeared, only to re-form when he was ready to return there to eat, or sleep, or read. Which was why the shock of involvement, when it came, was so intense.

It was a Sunday in late October, grim and dismal, for the town had been for four days in the grip of a heavy fog which showed no sign of lifting. Street sounds were muffled, the smell of sulfurous gritty smoke was in every nose, and whatever was touched was thick with greasy soot.

In the drawing room at Gower Street, Jesse was snoring heavily, slumped on the sofa, and Dorothea was sitting on a small gold chair sewing a pair of slippers for Abel, while Abel himself was sitting with his back to them at the occasional table in the corner, two oil lamps beside him so that he could see his book. He was making anatomical drawings in the style of his mentor, Charles Bell, and did not appear to have noticed that his appropriation of two lights meant that Dorothea had to struggle to see; and she, of course, would not have dreamed of telling him.

When the screeching started, Abel ignored it at first. If one of the maids was having a fit of the hysterics, it was

Dorothea's affair, not his, and he went on happily working, brushing red ink gently onto the line of the cranial nerve he was delineating. But then the door crashed open and the woman was standing there shrieking, her head thrown back and her mouth a great black gash in her face, producing wave after wave of noise, and Abel's hand jerked and the ink splattered, to ruin his drawing, and he jumped up in a rage.

But even his own shouts of anger could not be heard above the din the woman was making, and he moved across the room to take her by the shoulders and shake her, and then hit her face hard with the back of his hand. She stopped shrieking then, and gasped, and pointed behind and above her, and gasped again, and then turned and ran in terror down the stairs and across the hall toward the kitchen, weeping noisily all the way.

"What in the name of God's good . . ." Jesse was on his feet, swaying a little and blinking his reddened eyes in bewilderment, and Dorothea was the color of dust, her face filled with alarm.

"Abel, what is it?" she cried, running across the room to hang on to his arm. "Abel? What is it? Is she run mad?"

"How the devil should I know?" Abel said roughly, and shook her off before returning to his table to stare at his ruined drawing. "Look at what the goddammed woman did! A day's work, destroyed! Does she always run crazy in such fashion?"

"I don't know—she's Mama's maid—I hardly ever see her . . ." Dorothea said, and clutched at her chest in a theatrical way. "Oh, Abel, do you suppose— Is something— She is the only one to enter Mama's room, you know, and . . ."

"How should I know?" Abel shouted. "Go see for yourself if you're so concerned!"

"Oh, Abel, come with me—please to come with me! I'm sure something has happened, for Jane to behave so, and— Oh, Abel, I'm so afraid! Please come and see if Mama is well. And if she is, and I go there, she will run mad anyway at the sight of me, and I shall need you. . . ."

The practical note taking over from the theatrical and half hysterical made Abel stop and look at her, and he saw for the first time how genuinely afraid she was, and after a moment he nodded brusquely, and picked up one of the oil lamps.

"You're making a great pother over a stupid female who's probably been drinking your father's wine and seeing ghosts on the stairs, but if you wish, we shall go and see. I might as well as sit here, for my work is destroyed anyway."

They were halfway up the stairs, Abel carrying the oil lamp high to illuminate the way, for the hall and staircase, like everywhere in these dismal days, were wreathed with wisps of smoky fog, and Dorothea hanging as ever on to his arm, when he realized that Jesse was accompanying them, moving heavily up the stairs behind them, clutching at the balustrade and grunting a little with the effort.

For the first time Abel felt a twinge of doubt, a sort of anxiety. He did not care much at all for Charlotte, had not given her a thought since he could not recall when; but the maid had been patently terrified by something, had pointed up toward Charlotte's boudoir before fleeing, and now here was Jesse, concerned enough to join them on a visit of investigation. . . .

Moving more sharply, he went on, and when they reached the door of Charlotte's boudoir, he pushed Dorothea back a little, almost protectively. The door was ajar, and he could see the light of a very big fire shifting and gleaming on the walls, could feel the scented heat coming out of the room at him, and his faint alarm increased. Charlotte had never been one to be extravagant, and clearly the fire that blazed in the grate of her room was almost twice the size of the ones that were usually permitted in the house.

He tapped on the door and waited; and tapped again, louder; and they stood very still, the three of them, and he could hear only Jesse's heavy, grunting breathing; and once more he knocked on the door, this time pushing it open with his other hand.

The shrieking started again, but this time it was Dorothea. He stood and stared for what seemed to be an age, and then, wheeling sharply, pushed Dorothea out the door and then turned and looked again, and felt the heat of sick embarrassment rise in his cheeks as he stared.

The light from the fire was clear and strong for all its

flickering, and he could see her clearly—swaying and turning a little, her head cocked awkwardly to one side and her shoulders a little twisted.

But it wasn't so much the fact that she was hanging there before the window on a rope torn from the bed curtains and now tied to the curtain rail above, or that the chair that lay on its side beneath her feet showed beyond doubt that she had died of her own decision, that was so sickening and obscenely frightening; it was the way she looked.

Quite naked, her scrawny shanks and skinny legs clearly displayed in the firelight, she had bedecked herself with wreaths of artificial flowers and feathers and pieces of net and gauze and fur—the entire contents, it seemed, of her frippery chest. The gaudy scraps of trimming sat perkily on her thin little breasts, flapped against her papery-skinned dome of a belly as the air moved across them, and seemed to laugh aloud at him. But worst of all, on her head and held in place by a narrow gold fillet, with graying curls peeping coyly out from beneath it, was a bride's veil.

It was Abel who took over; Abel who cut her down and removed the pathetic trimmings with which she had adorned herself; Abel who dressed her in a nightgown and put her in her bed. He was used to dead bodies, and she was not difficult to handle, for the heat of the room had prevented the onset of rigor mortis; and certainly neither Dorothea nor Jesse was in any fit state to deal with anything.

But it was later, when Charlotte lay tidy in her bed, with a high-necked gown to cover the weal on her throat, that he made his most thoughtful decision. Someone had to concern himself with the matter, and there was no one but himself who could.

He went down to the drawing room, where Jesse and Dorothea were sitting in a rigid silence, still apparently stunned by what had happened, and sat down beside Jesse.

"Sir, we shall need to take care if you are to avoid the trouble of scandal. Sir? Do you hear me?"

Jesse turned his head, infinitely slowly, and stared at him, frowning a little, and then his eyes cleared as he saw Abel, and he said thickly, "Charlotte? Mrs. Constam? Is she—"

"She is dead, sir." He said it loudly, and shook Jesse's arm a little trying to drive the fact in. "And unless we take care, there will be such a hue and a cry as will—well, I cannot believe you would wish it."

"Dead?" he murmured. "Is she dead?"

With a sharp sigh of irritation, Abel started again, repeating over and over the importance of planning carefully, that they must avoid scandal at all costs, and at last it seemed to penetrate Jesse's bemused mind, for he turned his face to Abel and said pitifully, "She's dead. Charlotte. She's dead, boy, d'ye know that? Quite dead. . . ."

"Aye, sir"—Abel said it almost gratefully—"quite dead. Now, sir, I believe this is how we should manage the affair. . . ."

Jesse nodded and listened and nodded again, and at the end of it closed his eyes wearily and said, "It is as you please, boy. You know better than I. As you please. I am too tired—I cannot— It is as you say, for you know best. . . ."

Abel sat and looked at him for a moment, for the first time feeling a surge of personal distress moving in him, a little akin to the way he felt when Charles Bell had told him so casually that James Wilson had died. To see Jesse quite so shattered, so bereft, so altered a man was much more painful to him than had been the sight of Charlotte's gaudily bedecked nakedness; he had found that merely strange, embarrassing, queer, but not sad. It was Jesse who was pitiful, and awkwardly Abel touched his shoulder and then stood up to set about his tasks.

He was at the door before he remembered Dorothea, and with his feeling for Jesse still thick in his chest, turned back, full of compunction. She was sitting there, her hands crossed on her lap and her head bent, and he went over to her and said gently, "Dorothea? Are you— Would it not be best to go to your bed, my dear, and sleep a little? I will deal with all that must be done, and you have had a great shock."

"Oh, yes, indeed, dear Abel, a great shock," she said, and looked up at him, and he frowned, a little puzzled, for her face was clear, showed none of Jesse's bewilderment—or, indeed, any expression apart from a calm acceptance.

"A great shock," she repeated. "Poor dear Mama! To

behave so strange . . . But she is at peace now, is she not, Abel?" And again she turned that limpid gaze on him, her eyes wide and innocent.

"Yes . . ." he said uncertainly, and they stood looking at each other for a moment, and then Abel said, a little brusquely, "Well, if you are feeling able to do so, it would be wise to help your papa to his bed, for he—"

"Papa Constam?" she murmured. "Indeed, dear Abel, if you wish it. Shall I call Frederick?"

He nodded and went away, feeling curiously alarmed by her reaction, and puzzled too, for had he thought about it he would have expected from her a fit of the vapors at the very least; he could not understand her calmness. But then, he did not know that for Dorothea the last rub in the way of her marriage to Abel had melted away in the heat of the fire in her mother's room; as long as her mother had sat there in her boudoir, brooding spiderlike on the state of affairs in her house, there was a possibility that she could, somehow, overset her stepfather's decisions. But not now, and it was with real solicitude and no remnant of the disgust he could usually arouse in her that Dorothea went to him, and spoke to him, and soothed and comforted him. For the first time since her mother's marriage to him, Dorothea felt a true affection for Jesse.

In the rush of activity with which he was occupied, Abel gave no further thought to Dorothea. He had first to deal with the maid and the rest of the servants, and he took himself down to the kitchens in some trepidation, but with his mind made up.

He had a less difficult task than he had expected. In many ways the servants were as anxious as he to cover up the facts of the matter, for to leave a house where there had been a suicide in search of a new place was an unattractive prospect; there were many employers who would not willingly associate themselves with such a situation.

They required little more than the assurance that they would not be turned away now that the mistress of the house was dead, and the most modest of pecuniary bribes to agree that Madam had been sick of a fever these many weeks, and died not at all unexpectedly. Even Jane, who had been so frightened by her discovery, agreed to remain as Dorothea's maid, and even began to find some enjoyment in her situation as sufferer; while the other servants were there to listen with breathless excitement to her account of how dreadful it was and how bad she had felt, she was happy enough.

Even the journey through the fog-heavy streets, muffled to the eyes with a thick scarf, was not as difficult as it might have been, for he knew the streets so intimately that even though he could see no farther than a yard or two before his face, and his eyes smarted and wept in the stinging coldness of the fog, he reached Mr. Witney's home in much the usual space of time.

And after sitting closeted with him for an hour, and talking, talking, talking, Mr. Witney agreed, for the sake of old friendship and his affection for his senior apprentice, that Charlotte had been suffering from the bloody flux these past three weeks and died of it. With such a story to tell Mr. Spenser and the gravediggers at the church, there would be none willing to look too closely at the dead body of Charlotte and discover that she had no right to be buried in consecrated ground.

Abel had wrought well that evening, and he knew it as he returned wearily to Gower Street, to fall asleep in exhaustion. Tomorrow there would be a funeral to organize, and after that the planning of life at Gower Street without Charlotte. Tomorrow.

· TWENTY-NINE ·

HE sat there at the rosewood desk feeling the information in his bones, in his skin, moving through his muscles. He closed his eyes and opened them again and stared at the paper in his hand, and took a deep breath, smoothing out the folds in the paper with slightly shaking fingers.

It had seemed so natural that it should be he who should go through Charlotte's desk the day after the funeral. It had been he who had arranged it all, he who had convinced inquirers that Charlotte's death had been expected, he who had paid (with Jesse's money) all expenses, he to whom they all turned. Even the matter of the selection of mourning clothes for Jesse and Dorothea and the provision of crape for the servants had been left to him.

He did not object to the responsibilities being heaped upon him, though chafing a little at the loss of time. He had his own work to do, his own studies to deal with; but Astley Cooper had understood fast enough when Abel had told him he must seek leave to deal with matters pertaining to his benefactress's death, and Mr. Witney of course did not object to his absence (and indeed had no need to, for James was proving an excellent assistant), so he had been willing enough to shoulder the burden. And here was his reward.

Much of the material in her desk had been old bills, old

letters—little that was of interest or value. But there were some papers dealing with the affairs of the London Ladies, and he had decided to turn all these over to the Committee, for the Charity was as active as ever it had been, and indeed had largely outgrown its founders. They would be glad of such material as Charlotte had, Abel felt, and was methodically collecting a neat pile from the haphazard collection before him.

And that was how he had found it: a single sheet of heavy paper upon which was written a clear account of the placement, made on behalf of the London Ladies' Society for the Rescue of the Children of the Profligate Poor by Officer Mrs. Constam, of one Lil Burnell, an orphan aged twelve, with Mr. Lucas of Carter's End at Edenbridge in Kent, for a period of five years from March 31, 1801. Indenture fee to be repaid from March 31, 1806.

He sat and stared and counted feverishly in his head. Nearly twice that five years had passed, and yet there was no note here of the return of Lil, no mention of any attempt made to recover the money the London Ladies had spent on this placement. So what had happened? Had she run away? His lips curved at that thought, for it would be so like what she would have done. Or had she, perhaps . . . ? No, he could not consider that possibility! Strong, lively, perky Lil, she would not, could not fall sick.

Or perhaps—and he felt suddenly certain that this was the true reason, the one that really fell into place—perhaps Charlotte had not cared at all about the repayment of that money. She had never wanted to hear of Lil ever again.

All Charlotte had wanted, he thought bleakly, staring down at the heavily creased sheet of paper, was to separate them. It had not been enough to send him away to school when she had discovered their friendship; she had had to send Lil away too, his Lil, the only person in all his life who had ever been truly important to him. He began to shake then, seized with a curious blend of rage—immense and towering rage that the acidulated woman had stolen from him so many years with his Lil, had caused him so much misery and bitterness in his unavailing search for her—and a vast exultation, an exultation based on the knowledge that Lil had not aban-

doned him of her own free will but had been forced to do
so. . . .

"Abel?"

Dorothea's voice came to him not from across the drawing
room but from across an aeon of time, and he looked up at
her, blank and bewildered as though he had never seen her
before in his life, and she stared at him in alarm, and her
voice rose a little shrilly as she said it again: "Abel?"

He blinked then, and turned sharply in his chair, ignoring
her, but speaking directly to Jesse in a voice as harsh and flat
as a corncrake's.

"Sir, you will recall the events that led to my departure for
Mr. Loudoun's school. The night I left the house and was
brought back by the footman—I forget the man's name—you
remember?"

Jesse looked up blearily and frowned and shook his head,
and Abel, moving with a barely controlled energy, threw his
chair aside and shot across the room to sit firmly beside him.

"I wish to know, sir! Did Mrs. Constam speak to you of
this?" And he thrust the paper into Jesse's hands.

He read it slowly and then shook his head. "Lil Burnell?
Who is— I know naught of this, boy. I cannot—"

"She is my friend. The girl that came here with me that
night when—the night I left the house and *she* sent after
me."

Jesse had been looking at him with blank eyes, but now,
gradually, they began to clear, and he nodded, almost smiling
as the memory moved into his mind.

"Oh, a pretty little madam, a saucy piece, that. Oh, yes, and
she thought—Charlotte thought—I had designs upon her, and
indeed, she was a child of such—"

"Did you know she had done this? Sent her away?" Abel
almost shouted it. "Or what became of her after? Did she
ever return to London? Or what happened?"

Again Jesse shook his head. "She took worms into her
mind, you know, boy. Would take a notion from such small
things, and could not be rid of it. And she took a notion that
both of us, you and I, had thoughts—such thoughts!—of that
pretty child, and said she would make— I misremember all
that happened. She told me"—his eyes clouded again—"she

told me that— I believe the girl went away, and did not come to—oh, I don't remember! Long ago now . . ."

"Abel, please, what is it?" Dorothea was standing beside them now, staring down at him, her hands clutching her eternal needlework at her breast and her eyes anxious beneath the faint creases between her brows. She looked sickly pale, but that could have been as much the effect of the heavy black of her dress as any emotion that was in her; but Abel noticed neither the anxiety nor the pallor. He was staring down at the paper in his hand, his upper lip caught between his teeth and his lower lip protruding and trembling a little as he concentrated.

Then, suddenly, as suddenly as he had left the desk, he stood up and went purposefully across the room to the door, and she went fluttering after him, and cried, "Abel! Where do you go? Have you completed the . . ."

He stopped then, and looked back at her, frowning.

"Dorothea, I shall be away for a few days, perhaps. If you will be so good as to complete the work at the desk there. There is none that is important, as far as I can tell. Send the Charity papers to whosoever is concerned, and for my part— I shall return as soon as I may."

"But where are you *going*? And so sudden, and—"

"I am going into Kent." He said it flatly, with no expression of anger, or joy, or anything else in it: a plain statement of intent. "I am going into Kent to fetch Lil."

And the door slammed behind him, leaving her staring blankly at its panels, her throat tight with anxiety and a queer foreboding.

After a moment she turned, and came back across the room to sit beside Jesse, and with an attempt at calmness began to sew again. But after a very few stitches, she stopped and raised her head to look at the old man.

And indeed an old man he seemed now, sitting slumped in his black clothes on the yellow plush of the sofa, his gingery head sunk between his shoulders—the powerful man he had once been seeming to hang over the shape of the man he now was like a phantasm.

"Papa . . ." she said softly. "Papa?" And he looked up and blinked at her.

"Papa . . ." She put down her sewing and leaned forward to take his hands in hers, and looked closely at his face. "Papa—this Lil of whom Abel speaks—what is she? I do not understand. And if I delay him with questions . . . Well, I wish you would tell me."

"Give me some brandy," he said suddenly, and she looked at him consideringly and then went across the room to fill a glass from the decanter that stood on a corner table. Abel had said he must not have so much brandy, that it was bad for him, but since Abel was not here . . .

He drank it thirstily, and she refilled it, and then sat quietly beside him, waiting and judging the time to start her questions again. And when his eyes seemed to glaze like a hawk's, she asked softly, "Who was she, Papa?"

"She took notions, you know," Jesse said loudly, as though he were hard of hearing and trying to listen to his own voice, "took notions. She said young Abel was my by-blow, you know that? Thought I'd got him on a whore and brought him here, and I said it was so—told her often, I did, for it made her sick, sick and angry—and so . . ." He shook his head suddenly, and tears sat on his eyelids. "She took notions," he said again, and drank the glass dry and gave it to her, and again she hesitated only a moment or two before filling it.

"Why should she think that?" she asked, and again her voice was soft, and gentle, and slow, quite unremarkable, and he answered her easily enough, for it was as though she were not there—just he, staring through a haze of alcohol back across the years. "Wanted a son on her, wanted and wanted. Wanted. But what could— There was— If she had been but loving enough, and caring enough, and— I could have done, many's the time I could have done, but she, she would not. On her I could— I nearly . . ." He was weeping frankly now, and she gave him her own handkerchief, and he mopped at his eyes and drank again.

"And Lil? The girl he has gone to Kent to seek? What of her?" Dorothea was being very careful, keeping that same soft wheedling note in her voice, but now it did not have the same effect. He stared at her, and shouted with a sudden spiteful fury, "Some bitch of the gutter, a guttersnipe like himself! That's who, some bitch of the gutter! Naught of mine, either of them! Be silent, you drab, you stinking drab, you're the same as your mother with your whining, grizzling ways—you make me puke!"

He was weeping copiously when she quietly left the room.

He should have been tired. There had been the hectic rush to reach Lucy and get money enough for the journey from her (and she in her wisdom had given it and asked not a word of explanation, for which he had kissed her warmly and hugged her close), and the panic as he tried to reach Charing Cross, absurdly sure in his mind that he would find a coach had left just before he had arrived if he did not rush. And of course when he reached the Golden Cross there had been a long wait, an interminable wait, for the next coach to that part of Kent. And the bouncing, rattling, slow, impossibly slow journey, south through London and then on through the villages of Clapham and Streatham, Purley and Godstone, with many halts at tedious country inns for the collection and disposal of old women with baskets, old men with pockets filled with dead hares and rabbits—he had wanted to scream, to fill them all with the urgency of it.

But now, the journey was in the past and the lumbering coach had gone rattling away farther south to Eastbourne, leaving him in this impossibly sleepy town at eleven o'clock in the evening, aching to complete the journey to Carter's End but knowing he could not. He would have to wait till morning as best he could, and uncharacteristically he ordered a glass of brandy to take with his meal, hoping it would help him sleep.

In the event, it did not, and he spent the night tossing in the unfamiliar bed, trying to imagine how she would look, how she would be, and then, in the dark small hours when the moon had set and there was just the deep black night with its dreadful silence—not even the cry of the Watch to break it, let alone the sound of human traffic with which he had been surrounded all his life—the bad thoughts.

She would not be here; she would have gone away long ago. She would be dead and buried in the small churchyard across the market square that he had seen dimly in the moonlight as he arrived. She would be there but would have forgotten him and have no interest in him. She would be married, the mother of a hopeful brood. She would be . . . And he turned and thumped the pillow and tried to sleep.

And now, standing in the inn parlor and staring out at the thin traffic of the square, he should be tired, but was not. He had washed and shaved and dressed with infinite care; had, unusually for him, examined himself closely in the mirror, trying to see what sort of person he might seem to her, and found little comfort in the reflection. Long green eyes—hers too had been green, he remembered with a sudden lift of pure exhilaration, and soon, soon he would see them again!—a white face, dark hair. He shook his head irritably, and went down to drink coffee and refuse cold beef and send a message to the landlord that he would speak with him. And now he waited, hoping and sick, almost, with fear of what he would be told.

"Sir? You wanted to speak to me?" A soft burring voice, hard to understand for Abel, with ears accustomed to the hard edges of a Cockney's speech, and he smiled awkwardly and said quickly, "Uh—indeed, yes, landlord, I would—uh—I need your help."

"Do you now, sir?" The landlord was a small man, thin and with a crest of white hair above a startlingly red face, but he looked friendly enough, even patient as he stood waiting.

"I . . ." Abel swallowed hard, and then with a strong effort of will composed himself. "I have come to Edenbridge in search of an old friend of mine," he said and his voice sounded remarkably strained in his own ears. "She came to live in these parts some—oh, it must be nearly ten years ago. She was a child, you understand, a very pretty little girl, a London child. She came to Mr. Lucas at Carter's End . . ." And then he stopped, to stare at the landlord with all the hope he had ever felt wrapped up in the reply he awaited.

The man stood staring consideringly at him for a moment, and then said slowly, "Ah, well, now. Mr. Lucas, you say? There be a Mr. Lucas, a very nice gennelman, though sick in himself, they say, lives up to Carter's End, and lived there these dunnamany years—afore my time, for I've not been

'ere above three year come Michaelmas. But as to a friend—
well, I cannot say."

"He's a widower, I believe?" Abel tried to sound casual.

The man grinned at that. "A widower? Well, that's not for
me nor no others to say, is it? That 'e *was* a widower is
suthin' I've heard said many's the time in my snug, but as to
that—well, the lady o' the 'ouse is a very fine young lady,
and one as no one'd want to look sideways at, not for one
moment. A real lady, she is, and such a . . ." He shook his
head, lost for words. "A *admirable* lady, 'er is. If she knows
of your friend, I've no doubt as she'll tell yer. They *calls* 'er
Mistress Lucas, anyways. . . ."

He almost wept with the relief of it. There was a Mr.
Lucas still in Edenbridge, and from all accounts Lil was
there, and . . .

It was at that point that some of his relief ebbed. *Mrs.*
Lucas? Could she have married her employer? Could this be
why she had never returned to London, why she had so
totally disappeared from his life? For one sick moment he
wanted to turn and run again, back to London, away from
Edenbridge, back to not knowing. But his common sense
came surging back then, and with it a faint whisper of doubt
as he thought of what the man had said: "They *calls* 'er
Mistress Lucas anyways. . . ."

And then he almost shook himself with irritation; he must
indeed be tired to be behaving in so absurd and shilly-shally-
ing a fashion. He must go to Carter's End and see for himself.
There was no other step to take.

He walked there, wrapped in his heavy coat, through
country lanes rimed with white hoarfrost, his boots ringing
on the frozen ruts left by laden carts, watching the birds
wheeling against the iron-gray sky and swooping behind the
naked trees standing startled and exposed along the horizon.
The cold bit his nose and ears, but his cheeks and hands and
feet glowed with energy and youth and hopefulness.

He was a little taken aback by the house he found at the
end of his long walk: set back from the road behind a row of
close-set chestnut trees, with a graveled carriage drive, well
raked and free of any weeds, curving through a half acre or

so of parkland, it was a long red-brick house, with black beams and white paint, and many mullioned windows. It had an air of richness about it, a sense of being inhabited by people of taste and wealth, and almost instinctively he looked along the front of it, seeking for a tradesmen's door. And then, annoyed with himself, he marched purposefully to the broad oak door that was set back under a stone porch and pulled hard at the iron-ringed pull beside it.

The maid who opened to him was small and pert and neat. The hall was broad and stone-flagged, with a great fireplace in which burned a vast log. The furniture was heavy and dark and well polished, and looked rich. Altogether, he thought nervously, staring round him after the maid had taken his coat with a curtsy and gone to seek her mistress in reply to his demand to see Mrs. Lucas, the house breathed rich. He was used to richness, for Jesse Constam's Gower Street house had always been equipped with all the most expensive and tasteful of furnishings (although matters had lapsed somewhat during the past four and more years), and Lucy's house, while vulgar in the extreme, yet lacked none of the richest comforts money could buy. But this sort of richness was different. It had an air of permanence about it, seemed to have been there forever, seemed not to care that it was richness. The house, the furniture, everything he saw and felt seemed to be saying to him, "Rich? Are we? I suppose so. But we never noticed it ourselves, you know."

"If you will wait here in the morning parlor, sir, Madam will come to you directly." The little maid led him to a small room at the back of the house, overlooking a garden, a room that was pretty and soft and filled with so many little decorations, so many china ornaments and pictures and flowers and nonsenses, that he felt as though he were as huge as one of the great horses that displayed themselves at Astley's Amphitheatre, and moved stiffly and awkwardly among the furniture for fear of breaking something.

But then the door behind him opened, and a voice said flutingly, "You wished to speak with me, sir? Have you any business with Mr. Lucas, perhaps?—for he is, you know, unfit to see any but . . ."

He smiled a long, slow smile at the sight of her, for there

she stood: undoubtedly his Lil. Taller, but as slender as she had ever been. Her dark, curly hair was caught up on her head in the most fashionable of styles, as he knew from his visits to the Panton Street girls, and her skin was exquisite, looking as though it had been overlaid with a fine layer of the most delicate porcelain. Her dress, a soft blue, befrilled and very pretty, from which her shoulders and arms emerged like the stems of flowers, looked costly. But above it all there was her face—the green eyes, the sensuous mouth, the fine cleft in her chin, and the shadow of the dimples. And he held his arms out and said very softly, "Lil . . ."

Almost automatically, she said, "Lilith"—and stood staring at him, her head on one side and her forehead slightly creased with a frown, and he could see the memory working in her, could see it rising in her as it had in him, wiping out the frown and filling her entire face with an expression of total delight.

"Abel!" she shrieked. "Abel, Abel, Abel"—and hurled herself across the room to hug him with the fervor that he had remembered all these years, and been longing for ever since he had lost her.

· THIRTY ·

THEY sat and talked and laughed and ate a fussily elegant luncheon from flowered china, waited on by the little maid and collapsing into absurd giggles whenever she turned her back, and talked yet again long into the afternoon. He questioned her eagerly at first, wanting to know of all that had happened to her, how she came to be apparent mistress of this house, but she smiled obliquely at him, answered his questions with a flood of chatter that held no true information at all, and turned her own questions onto him. So in the event, it was he who did most of the explaining, telling her of his years at school, of his new career, and she gasped and rounded her eyes prettily until he felt he would burst with pride; to be a surgeon was important enough to him, but that it should impress her too! It was as though he saw himself in a totally new and very splendid light.

He told her a little haltingly of Jesse and his drinking and of Charlotte's death, though not of the circumstances of it. It was not from any sense of prudery that he withheld this information, but because he did not feel it important enough to speak about.

But he did withhold some information for different reasons. He did not tell her of his betrothal to Dorothea, or of his friendship with Lucy and her girls; it was, he knew suddenly, important to him that she should see him as free, unencumbered, as much her Abel as he had been those ten years ago when he was a scrawny eleven-year-old charity child.

It was when he started to tell her of his visits to the theater that she really took fire, and lost her ladylikeness to become completely the old imperious, demanding Lil he had known. They were sitting before the fire in her frilly sitting room, she on a chair and he on the rug at her feet with his head against her silken knees, when he casually mentioned having been in Drury Lane the night the theater burned down, and how he had seen Mr. Sheridan in the Piazza Coffee House, watching the flames leaping through the roof of his theater.

"Mr. Sheridan? Of Drury Lane? You know Mr. Sheridan?" she cried excitedly, and he looked up at her and grinned lazily.

"Aye, Lil. And why should I not? I know the people at the Theatre Royal in the Haymarket as well as Mr. Sheridan's crew. They are at the Lyceum now, you know, since Drury Lane burned down—it is not so unusual a matter for such a thing to happen, of course. Why, last year it was the Covent Garden Theatre that went up in smoke—though there was none there to make so good a joke about it as Mr. Sheridan. They said to him that he should go home and not watch the theater burn, for it was his own, you know, and he up to his ears in debt as always, but he sat there with a bottle beside him and said he would not go, for could not a man drink a glass of wine by his own fireside? Oh, he's a rare man, is Mr. Sheridan! And . . ."

"You know many people in the theater, Abel? You have friends among the actors and the actresses, and— Oh, Abel, *tell* me! Tell me at *once*. What are they like? Are the women so beautiful? Did you ever see Master Betty? Have you ever seen Mrs. Siddons? And her brother—Kemble—is he as great as they say? And . . ."

He laughed then, indulgently. "How do you know so much of such matters? I would not have thought news of the theater in London would have reached so far into the dead country as this!"

She thrust him away from her in her frustration and

slapped at his shoulder with an angry hand. "You shall tell me! And at once, you hear me, Abel? I wish to know of the plays you have seen, and the way the actors and the actresses play them and—oh, everything! I shall not be gainsaid! Now . . ." And she jumped up and went with a swish of her skirts to the chair on the other side of the fireplace, to sit with her hands on her lap and staring expectantly at him, her eyes wide and her mouth half open with anticipation.

He gazed at her for a long moment, enchanted by the look of her, and said impulsively, "I never saw any three actresses together who could look as you do, Lil! You have grown up so lovely!" And she laughed then, and tossed her curls on her shoulders, and smiled at him, and demanded again that he tell her *all*. And obediently he did, for how could he not?

They sat there all through the long afternoon as the wintry October light grayed in the window and the logs coughed and spat in the grate. The little maid came softly to bring candles and an oil lamp and mend the fire, and set a tray of tea before them, and still she would not let him stop—plying him with questions, wanting to know every detail he could tell her, from the structure of the stage to the sort of paint the actresses used and the way they wielded the hare's foot to set it after they had applied it.

And at last, when he had exhausted all the information he had, could think of no further snippet of news he could offer, she sat back, far from contented but accepting the fact that she had drained him dry.

She said nothing, just leaned back in her chair with her curly head against the dark blue plush and her face turned to the fire and stared dreamily at it, while Abel for his part was content to drink cold tea and watch her, seeing the way the firelight played over her soft cheeks and lit the shadows under her chin to heartbreaking vulnerability. And he felt it then and could no longer argue with it: that sensation he had been so desperately controlling all day. He set down his cup and saucer with a sharp rattle and, moving a little clumsily in his eagerness, crossed from his own chair to hers to kneel at her feet and look up at her, his hands set protectively covering hers on her blue silk lap.

"Lil . . ." he said, and his voice sounded thick in his own

ears. "Lil? Are you . . ." He swallowed. "Are you pleased to see me again? As pleased as I am to find you? I searched for you—oh, so much, and so long! I went so many times to Old Compton Street to find you and walked the streets looking and looking, and I wanted you so bad! And now I have found you, and you are— Oh, Lil!" And he put his head down upon her lap, holding her hands hard, and felt the tears rising in his throat, needle-sharp, to reach his eyes and sting them with the sheer agony of his happiness.

She moved then, pulling her hands back, and immediately he raised his head and looked up at her, and she sat and stared at him, her eyebrows gently raised and a faint smile curving her lips.

"La, Abel, so intense as you've grown!" she said lightly. "You'll be weeping next, for all the world like some hobbledehoy caught ogling his master's daughter! You are a man of the Town, now, and should not behave so foolish!"

"Foolish!" He stared at her, and the tears dried on his cheeks as anger rose in him. "Foolish! To be glad to have found you again, when I have wanted you and longed for you these ten years and fretted that you might be ill, and had no way to— You call that foolish? Then indeed, if you regard that care for you so light, I must be a damned fool."

She clapped her hands then, with a childish delight. "Oh, Abel, now you are as I love you! When you get all red in the face and angry, why you are as splendid a man as any Kemble! But I cannot abide silly posturings." She stood up sharply, making him fall back to sit on his heels, and went swishing about the room, her hands flashing about as she spoke. "Oh, Abel, you should see some of them! The farmers and their stupid sons, they come sniffing about here like some damned fools of dogs chasing a bitch in heat, and they stand and mop and mow and droop at me until I could scream! If you were to do that, I could not *bear* it!"

She stopped then and stood in the center of the room, and it suddenly seemed to Abel that she had placed herself there in full knowledge of the effects of the lights on her hair, and was making conscious use of the illumination to demonstrate the planes of her face. But she moved even as he thought it, to come and stand beside him and hold out her hands to help him to his feet. And looked up at him through her lashes, and said lightly, "I must tell you as I tell all the stupid local fools who would talk lovingly to me—it is not fitting for one in my position!"

He stood there looking down at her and felt a chill rising in him, a sense of inevitability, a certainty that he was to lose her now, even as he had found her. "Your position?" he said woodenly. "You have not spoken of yourself at all yet. What position? Will you tell me now how it is with you?"

She flashed away from him again to flounce down into the fireside chair and peep up at him over her hands held clasped under her chin, her face bearing the same sort of roguish look he remembered on her child's face.

"What would you think, now, Abel, looking about you? You have seen the house—is it not a very rich one? The carpets, the curtains, the furnishings—all are of the finest quality and cost, you know, if not of the first stare of fashion. And I am dressed very fine, am I not, and behave not a bit the apprentice girl?"

"The landlord at the inn said they called you Mrs. Lucas," Abel said slowly, and she laughed aloud at that, opening her mouth so wide he could see her pink tongue and sharp little white teeth, catlike and lovely.

"Oh, but I am clever, am I not, Abel? For that is what they all say and believe! All of them! I live here and I eat my fill of the finest victuals and live the life of a complete lady, and wear none but the richest of silks sent down from London for me by the carrier, and have my own maid to send about my needs—and they call me Mrs. Lucas! Oh, it's a rare joke!" And again she laughed that shrill fluting laugh, and he stared at her, his forehead creased.

"So? What *is* your position, then? You do not make yourself as clear as you might." It was like talking to a butterfly, so confusing were her sharp and sudden movements, her changes of mood, and he watched bewildered as she jumped up again and went to kick the log in the fireplace with one blue satin-shod foot.

"Oh, a rare joke! For the poor fool has a daughter, a fat, stupid bitch of a daughter who gave no heed to him at all before I came!" She spoke over her shoulder, and her voice was filled with a savage anger now. "Never came near him nor budged away from her stupid oaf of a husband and her dim brats until I came, and she heard talk that he valued me! Oh, then she came fast enough, the greedy cow! Came and brought her husband. . . ."

She turned then, and produced a great crow of laughter. "Oh, Abel, it was so funny! We sat here in this room, and a sour room it was then, not near so pretty as I have made it since, and her stupid Charles sat one side of me and could not keep his eyes off me, and the old man sat the other and could not keep his hands off, and she sat fit to die of rage and hate of me! Oh, that was a rare night!"

"You still do not explain the facts of your position here," Abel said heavily. "Are you Mrs. Lucas or are you not?"

"Oh, Abel, do not be so foolish! Of course I am not! She made so great a fuss and threatened such terrible things if he wed me; she said she'd never let him see his grandsons again, and the poor fool cares for them—though I cannot understand why, for they are hateful brats and I cannot abide them—but he is as stupid as the rest of them, you know!—so he agreed he would not wed me so that all his property should be hers and the brats' in due course. And she was content enough with that. But he said he would not part with me, and would spend all he liked on me in his lifetime, and would put it about that we were wed like honest folk. She went away content enough—had to, for her great fool of a Charles would have stayed forever had she not taken him away when she did—and so it has been since."

Again she kicked the log in a rage. "Oh, I do well enough, never fear! I've all the honors of the mistress of the house and the respect of all, for none dare speak ill to me while Lucas yet lives, and I"—she looked at him sideways, then through her lashes—"I am no fool! I do not need to wait for any man's death to line my pockets as cozy as they deserve! I've had such presents of him these past ten years—why, Abel, it will take three trunks at least to carry all my clothes when we go to London!"

He blinked, and tentatively let the hope that rose in him have its way. "When we—"

"Aye," she said simply. "When we go to London. It was

meant I should do so, for why else are you here? I have been casting about these many weeks for a way to arrange matters, and here you are!" She came swiftly across the room again and stood close to him, curling her arms about his neck, to gaze beseechingly up at him. "I have had so dismal a life here, in so many ways! I have much that is good, I know—food and comfort and clothes, and I am treated as a lady, and have all the graces, for he got all the teachers for me I wanted, and I can sing and play on instruments—but, oh, Abel, I have been so dull these past months and needed you so much! And now here you are, and . . ."

She smiled up at him invitingly, and the tip of her tongue appeared between her white teeth, and she tipped her chin, and as though there had been a marionette string connecting him to her, he bent his head and kissed her, shyly at first and then, as need of her came welling up in him, with a barely controlled passion that left him breathless and desperate. But she pulled away after a while and said, with that same easy roguishness, "Enough, my dear, enough! You will be as stupid as the others if you do not take care! Remember you are a Town man, supposed to be one with polish upon you!"

She skipped away and sat down, her hands folded on her lap in mock primness. "Now, dear Abel, we shall make a plan, shall we not? We shall go to London on the stage tomorrow, and you shall arrange all for me."

Beneath the exultation that now filled him, the knowledge that he was not to lose her so soon after finding her, other feelings struggled. A doubt about the unseen Lucas. A doubt, much more important, about Jesse and Dorothea. He had a new status in the Gower Street house, and well he knew it; Charlotte's death had invested him with an authority that gave him much play to please himself; but could he bring Lil there to live? Could he tell Lil about Dorothea and his relationship with her? He bit his lip and blinked his confusion, and she laughed again, softly this time.

"Oh, don't look so put about, dear boy! I shall cause you no embarrassment! You shall simply take me to London and introduce me to the theater—we shall decide on the journey which will be best—and set me up in a respectable lodging until such time as I can look about and choose my own. I shall not come to your precious Gower Street—indeed, I should not wish to, for I imagine it insupportable dull, with people drooping about in mourning—and I cannot abide black, it is a horrid color!—and then . . ." She drew a great sigh of enormous luxuriousness. "Why, then, in no time at all I shall be the greatest actress in London and they will break down walls to come see me and they will forget every other actress there ever was! And it will be all perfect and heaven for me!"

He laughed then with true amusement, for he could not help it, and at once she was flickering with anger, launching herself across the room at him with her fingers curved into claws and her teeth clenched whitely between set lips. He caught her easily enough and fended her off, and she tried to reach his face and cried breathlessly, "You shall not laugh at me! I can and I shall, for I am decided upon it and when I decide a matter so it is! You shall not laugh at me, for I have said it and so it shall *be*."

"You said once you were no whore, too, and now look at you!" The words came out of him almost before he realized it, and she stopped her wildcat fighting at once and stood staring at him with her face white and stricken, and he put his hand out toward her, filled with a vast and painful remorse.

"Oh, Lil, I'm sorry. I did not mean that! But I am so jealous, so . . ."

She raised her chin, and the color began to come back into her cheeks, and she tossed her head lightly and moved away to sit down again.

"Well, so you said it! So I did not remain as prim as I might—like your stinking Dorothea, no doubt! But I am still no whore! Does my arrangement here seem to be like that of any Covent Garden drab you know? I'm class, Abel! I told you so years ago, and I tell you so now. It does not mean I should not bestow my favors without benefit of parson if I so choose, but that I shall choose *right*. And I have chosen right!"

Suddenly, she grinned—a sharp, pointed little grin of pure wickedness. "Not, I do assure you, that I have been anything but as virtuous as a nun these past two months! Ever since he got took of his apoplexy, he has not been fit for aught but to lie there half dead in his bed with his mouth open and his eyes all wet and—ugh!" She shuddered prettily. "He could be no one's fancy, and he knows naught of me, so deep in his coma as he is. There's naught to keep me here now, I promise you! I shall go to London and be famous, and you shall never laugh at me again! And I—"

"He is ill? Of an apoplexy?" Abel said sharply.

"What? Oh, yes, and very tedious it is. Lies there in his bed . . ." She moved then, her right shoulder drooping, her hand curving into useless paralysis on her lap, her face creasing up so that one side looked as lax and drooping as though it were quite dead, even her eye on that side seeming to sag and share the paralysis, and sat there for a brief moment, the perfect image of a person who had suffered an apoplectic stroke. He gazed at her open-mouthed, and then said softly, "Aye, you shall be the most famous— I should not have thought it possible. . . ."

At once she straightened, and the perfectly sketched image she had offered him was replaced by the sparkle and laughter that was all herself, and she came again to stand beside him, gazing up at him wheedlingly.

"So, Abel? It is all arranged, then? We shall go tomorrow? I can be ready by eight o'clock, and then we shall reach London in good time. I should prefer to arrive in the morning, so that we may have time for seeking a lodging and you may take me to the theater of our choice, but—"

"You have your plan ready-made, it would seem! You have no need of any help from me." He was almost laughing, but still there was that undertow of doubt. She was Lil, and he loved her, would do all he could to please her, and yet . . .
"What of Lucas? Your—uh—benefactor? What will he say to such a decision? You cannot leave him if he is ill and . . ."

She shrugged carelessly. "Why not? What can a man in his state want of a mistress? I told you—he has no knowledge of whether I am here or no. He is dead to himself, if not yet in reality. He has had my company these ten years, and there's an end of it."

"Perhaps he cared for you as more than a mistress." Abel said it diffidently, not wanting to prevent her from coming to

London with him and yet still disturbed by that uneasiness within him. "You are a person who makes people— you are easy to love, Lil. I have loved you as long, it seems, as I can remember. Perhaps he too . . ."

She laughed delightedly at that. "Am I? Dear Abel! And you doubted I could make the Town my own in the theater. Funny Abel, silly Abel! I love you too." But she said it lightly, touching his lips with one fleeting hand, and his heart lifted and almost immediately sank, for she was away from him again, flitting about the room restlessly and eagerly.

"I shall take this and this . . ." Her fingers drifted across ornaments and objects, darting about busily, and he watched her, letting the sheer pleasure of looking at her fill him, and had to pull himself back to reality with a conscious effort.

"Would it help you if I spoke to your Lucas, and told him—oh, that you had friends in London who had long sought you and now that . . . He may not be so deep sunk in coma as you believe, you know."

She looked at him over her shoulder, and now there was a spark of irritation in her voice. "No, Abel! It is not necessary, I assure you! I shall deal with him as far as it is possible, and you need not concern yourself! Now, you must go to the inn, at once. I shall send the wagonette round for you— unless you can ride the cob? No? I thought not, townsman that you are! And you shall book two inside seats for us on tomorrow's coach, and I shall stay and set about my packing."

She flew across the room to hug him again—the same impetuous hug with which she had greeted him. "Oh, Abel, it will all be so wonderful! Will it not?"

· THIRTY-ONE ·

THE trunks sat in the hall below, and he stared down at them, at their squat shapes outlined in the faint flickers that remained from the wood fire, and smiled a little. That she could have packed her belongings so fast! . . . It was very typical of her.

He had returned from the inn in the heavy dark, the wagonette swaying a little behind the horse clopping softly along the frost-hard road. He had discovered within half a mile of the house on the journey to the town that the driver, a sour-faced man wearing heavy calico and smelling overwhelmingly of the stables, was totally uncommunicative, making no response at all to any comment Abel might venture, and Abel had been glad of it. He had enough to think about without conversing with this yokel, and think he did, with a sense of almost luxurious freedom.

Lil. His Lil. He had found her after all these lonely years, and it was as though he were complete again. In a curious way he had been only part of a person, and now she had come, she had filled the gap, and he could be all of himself. He moved contentedly in his seat, and let his mind drift happily away, seeing himself in his own surgical practice, visiting his own patients, coming back to his own home to find Lil waiting for him . . .

The dream faltered, shivered, would not take shape again. The thought of such a home brought a vision of Gower Street, and that brought a vision of Dorothea, standing clasping her needlework to her chest, her face white and pathetic as she stared beseechingly at him. Dorothea. He shifted awkwardly in his seat now, all his pleasure tarnished. She would have to be told. Would have to understand that now there could be no question of his marrying her, that he was obligated to his Lil, that there could be no other wife for him, and she must face up to that fact.

And it would not be so bad now, he had told himself optimistically, staring out at the darkness of the winter's night, at the bare trees with frost-crisped stars tangled in their stark branches, and seeing none of it. Now Charlotte is dead, he had thought, it will be possible for Dorothea to live a much easier life. She had been much constrained by her mother's presence in the house, but she was a grown woman now, and free of her, could look after Jesse and then, when the mourning period was over, could start to go about in society and meet some young man who would be glad to wed her. Perhaps his Lil would help her, would arrange parties for her to meet people and . . .

But his invention failed at that, and he grinned in the darkness at his own absurdity. The thought of Lil in the same room as Dorothea was ludicrous; as if anyone would consider giving poor, dim Dorothea a second glance when Lil was there!

He smiled again at the unseen cold fields and hedges. He must stop calling her Lil. She had told him that firmly when she had sent him off to the town to book their seats.

"I am called Lilith Lucas," she had said, "and that is how you shall book it. Not Lil. Lilith." He had asked her why, and she had laughed, her eyes glinting at him in the dimness of the dark hall as she pushed him out of the door upon his way. "Never mind why," she had said, and laughed. "I like it. Let that be enough for you. I like to be called Lilith." And she had shut the door on him, and he had climbed obediently into the wagonette.

She had had a snug supper ready for him upon his return, and they had eaten it in companionable silence, she staring into the fire and absorbed in her own thoughts, and he watching her over the rim of his glass, above every mouthful of his meal, eating roast partridge as though it were the toughest and stringiest of mutton, and swallowing a crême brulée with as much relish as though it were oaten gruel. It was she who gave savor to his life now, not the taste of mere food, and he ate only to satiate a simple hunger.

She for her part had not eaten at all, being clearly too excited about the life that lay ahead of her, and when the dishes had been cleared and the maid had gone they sat beside the fire again, and now she chattered and exclaimed and sparkled happily at him about it all.

"I wish you would not set too much store on this theater plan, Lil—Lilith," he had said after a while, disturbed by the sureness in her voice and hating to think of her suffering any disappointment. "I have my friends in the theater, I do not deny, but I cannot promise you shall be accepted just at my request. And even if you are, you may have to wait some time playing mere supers before you can show to any advantage in any larger part."

"Oh, never fear, Abel! You have but to take me to the theater!" she said with sublime confidence. "Once I am there myself and can speak to them, and show them what I can do, there will be no difficulties, I promise you! I ask of you only your help in taking me there, to get me to the people who matter. To Kemble, perhaps, or Mr. Sheridan. His company is at the Lyceum, you say? I think I should be content enough to go there—although perhaps . . ." She looked at him sharply then. "You will not refuse me, will you, Abel? You will take me to the theater, as you promised?"

He smiled then, a little lazily, aware for the first time of having some small power over her.

"I made no such promises, you know! It has all been you, not I! You decided that this is what shall be done, and I, poor fool, have been dragged along behind you like a fish on a bargee's string. You have not yet even asked me to make you any promises, so certain of me are you! You should not be, you know, for love you as I do and always have, I am still a man with a mind of my own!"

She had looked at him sideways and then smiled a long, slow smile, and laughed softly and yawned prettily.

"Well, I shall not worry myself more now, for it is late,

and we must rise early to meet the coach. There is a bed for you ready and warmed—I shall show you." And a little startled, he had agreed to go to bed, although it was still early, and followed her out into the hall. Now, standing at the top of the stairs and looking down at the trunks below, he was amused. For all her airs of being the grown lady, for all her pride in her silk dresses and her arrangement of the house, and her control over the daughter-ridden and invisible Lucas (What *was* he like?), she was still in many ways a child—impulsive, totally unconcerned with any but her own needs and desires, and utterly delightful.

"This is your room, Abel." Her voice came muted across the dim passageway, and he turned and followed her into a pleasant room with a half-tester bed and a fire burning cheerfully in the wide grate.

"I trust you will be comfortable, Abel," she said prettily, and set the candle down on the table at the foot of the bed, and turned to go. She stopped at the door and looked back over her shoulder and smiled at him—that long, slow smile again—and said very softly, "Good night, my dear. I go to my own room, across the way. I hope you sleep well and comfortable in here. And tomorrow . . ." And then she was gone, leaving him standing there with a smile cracking his face. He could not help being amused, for her pose at the door there, the pitch of her voice, the look she had thrown at him had been so very much of the theater; he knew from all she had said that she had seen little but the most ramshackle of strolling companies, playing their noisy shows in fairground booths and in the market square on quarter days, but for all that, she had the tricks and mannerisms of the complete actress, the ones he had seen so many times on London stages, and he found her irresistible. Indeed, she would do very well, he thought comfortably as he prepared himself for bed and slid between the lavender-scented sheets. Very well.

He had not expected to sleep easily in so silent and strange a room, accustomed as he was to the constant background sounds of London streets and the cry of the Watch, but he must have sunk into slumber faster than he realized. Certainly he woke with a sense of its being early, as though he had been asleep a very short time indeed, and lay startled, staring at the light and trying to recall where he was. He had been dreaming—a dream that had filled him with a faint alarm, though he could not recall what it was—and he turned his head, trying to establish the place he was in. And saw that the curtains had been drawn open, and she was standing beside him, a candle in her hand so that it lit up the hair lying tumbled on her bare shoulders, holding her nightgown to her breast with the other hand (and he was reminded suddenly and irresistibly of Dorothea and her needlework), but not very successfully, for the swell of her breasts could be easily seen above the frilled white cambric.

She was looking at him with a mournful expression on her face, her eyes glinting in the candlelight with sparks of fire, and he blinked and rubbed his eyes and said thickly, " Is aught amiss?"

She sniffed and swallowed, and to his horror, for he was fully awake now, a tear came trickling down her cheek and he sat up abruptly and put his arms out toward her.

"What ever is it?" he cried in alarm, and immediately she shook her head, and set her candle down on the table beside the bed, and wiped away the tear with the back of her hand. She looked infinitely vulnerable and infinitely lovely, and it seemed to him as though something in his chest began to swell and grow so that it filled every atom of him, making it hard to breathe and tightening his throat painfully.

"You— I thought perhaps you would come to me and tell me—say you were only funning," she said piteously. "That you *would* take me to the theater and help me and be my kind and dear Abel, and not a bit the cruel, unkind creature you sounded when we were downstairs. But you did not come, and now—now . . ."

Now she was crying in good earnest, tears spilling down her cheeks in a steady stream, but she showed none of the red-nosed, red-rimmed-eyes look that Dorothea always displayed when she wept; her eyes were as clear as ever, and only the tragic downward droop of her mouth altered the contours of her face, unlike the ugly grimaces that pulled Dorothea's face into a tangle when tears overcame her.

"Oh, my dear," he said softly, "as if I could ever— Please, don't cry! I can't bear it if you cry! My Lil never cried. Do stop!"

She slid into his arms as though she belonged there, and

curled up against his nightshirted chest as comfortable as a kitten, twisting one of the ties on the shirt with one hand, her head down so that her voice came muffled and still pitiful.

"Then you will take me, for certain, and are not just playing tricks with me? For I could not bear it if—if . . ." And she produced a heart-rending little gulping sob that made the swelling in his chest seem larger than ever.

His arms tightened around her, and he said thickly, "I shall take you, my little love, of course I shall. Whatever you want, that is what you shall have, for you— Oh, Lil, I missed you so, all these years!"

It was rising in him again, that urgent need of her, and he knew it was even greater now than it had ever been, that any sense of desire he had had for her before was a pallid shadow of what he felt now. And it seemed to him that she knew and understood and would not be angry, and he took her chin in his hand and lifted it and kissed her, and this time she seemed to return his passion, for suddenly it was to him as though he were floating, lying in a sea of warm silken oil with ripples of sensation curling across his back and down his loins, across his belly, making him feel as though he were a giant of a man, all man, the only real man who had ever lived.

He did not know how it happened, but there it was, quite suddenly. She was lying back against his knees, staring up at him with wide eyes, and her untied gown had slipped down her shoulders so that she was almost completely bare, only a fold of the fabric lying across her thighs, and he stared at her, and stared at her, and closed his eyes with the agony of it.

And then she was beside him, and he did not know if he had pulled her there or if she had floated there, but there she was: beside him in all her warm nakedness, her body curling to fit the curves of his, her skin laying its soft unction against his need, and she was above him, beneath him, part of him, and he wanted to shout it to the world, to shriek the suddenness of the feelings that were rising in him, still rising in him, and then engulfing him—to leave him sprawled in breathless, startled, exhausted amazement across her.

There was a long silence, and then, "Oh, Abel!" she said softly, equally breathless and with a moment of laughter in her voice. "Abel!" And she was gone, almost as suddenly as she had arrived, grasping her robe about her as she crawled across him and off the bed and seizing the candle as she went, without looking back at him.

And the door closed behind her and he was left in darkness again, feeling cold air move across the sweat-damp skin of his bared chest, and filled with a huge and absurd lassitude that was carrying him, almost against his will, into sleep.

He almost wondered whether it had happened at all. He had awakened abruptly, moving from deep sleep to total wakefulness with no transitional drowsiness at all, and found himself filled with an extraordinary mixture of exultation and sick guilt. Had he treated her as he thought he had—seized her, used her, poured out upon her softness all the dammed-up needs and drives of his twenty-one years? Was he now one of the sort of men about whom Charlotte had so darkly hinted in her moralistic teachings? Was he just a bull in a field, a less-than-a-man?

Or—and now the memory of that exquisite, extraordinary, exhilarating, and totally overwhelming sensation swept over him, making him shiver with a shadow of its delight—was he not now a true man, a complete man, a man who knew a woman, and understood the realities of living? A vast smile that seemed to come from the deepest part of him lifted his mouth, stretched his cheeks with self-admiration, to be replaced almost at once with a sick sense of revulsion, a certainty of his own hatefulness.

As he had shaved and washed (with a painful and unusually pernickety care, scrubbing at his buttocks, his thighs, his genitals as though he would somehow wash away the guilty aspects of his memory of the night), the swings in his mood continued. By the time he left the bedroom, venturing to seek the breakfast parlor and quaking inside at the prospect of having to face her, he hardly knew how he felt any more.

And was even more bewildered by her behavior. She was dressed in a most beautifully cut green merino traveling dress, fur-trimmed, and with a matching hooded pelisse set ready by the trunks, flitting busily about as she remembered yet another something she had forgotten to pack. The sitting room, he noted, was fairly stripped of its ornaments and prettinesses, and he wondered briefly whether the hidden Mr. Lucas knew of it, and then shrugged; it was none of his concern. He was more worried about how she would feel this morning after the way he had behaved to her, and he stopped her in her headlong rush from one room to another by putting his hand out and saying tentatively, "Lil—Lilith?"

"Good morning, dear Abel!" She flashed a brilliant smile at him and stood on tiptoe to bestow a swift kiss upon his cheek, and then slipped away past him, calling over her shoulder, "Do take your breakfast at once, dear Abel, for the wagonette will be round very soon, and we must be away—it is all ready in the parlor."

He blinked and opened his mouth to speak again, and then, puzzled, went obediently to eat his breakfast. She did not seem to be at all perturbed in any way, so perhaps it had indeed been a dream, the effect of the feverish excitement that had filled him ever since he had found that piece of paper in Charlotte's desk; perhaps he was suffering from an irritation of the nerves that was giving rise to such fantasies that seemed so real. But even as he thought it, he knew he deceived himself. It had been real: of that there was not the least doubt.

She came and flurried him out of the breakfast parlor almost before he had swallowed a half dozen mouthfuls, chivvying him into his coat and pushing him eagerly toward the front door, which lay open to the early frostiness of the morning. The wagonette was already laden with her luggage, and the horse and the driver stood side by side waiting, both with their heads bent, both producing wafts of steam with every breath; in their still heaviness, they seemed to Abel to be cut from the same piece of dead wood.

He helped her into her seat, and she settled herself with a flurry of fur, her face, rosy with the chill of the morning, peeping eagerly out of the frame of her hood, and he smiled at her with enormous pleasure; whatever happened, whatever he or she felt, just to look at her was a benison.

He was about to climb in beside her when he looked back, to see the little maid standing at the door with her apron up to her face and her shoulders shaking, and he frowned and said, "What ails the girl?"

Lilith was settling her skirts about her booted feet, smoothing the folds of cloth to her satisfaction, and she looked up only briefly at his words.

"Oh, silly piece! She does not wish to be left to care for him till his daughter comes—doesn't wish to face the old bitch. Well, that cuts no butter with me—*I* faced her, and she didn't eat *me*, and so I told the girl! She'll be over her tears before we're safely down the drive. Do come on, Abel, for we shall miss the coach, and that would never do." And she tugged at his sleeve with an impatient hand.

But still he lingered. "Have you told his daughter? Is she content that he be left with the girl there till she comes? And when will she come?"

"Oh, Abel, how you do prose on!" she cried irritably. "I sent a message yesternight. I don't know when she will come; how could I? I told her I was leaving, and she could have her father to herself, and he waited her arrival. For the rest—it is no concern of mine. Now, will you *come!*" And she pulled at his arm again so that he had to climb up beside her, and immediately the horse started moving, in response to her imperious gesture at the driver, now sitting ready in his seat.

Abel looked back once to see the figure of the little maid standing forlornly by the open door of the house and felt yesterday's doubt creeping up in him again; Lil had always been very much a child of the slums, like himself, and that meant she was practical, hardheaded, with a strong sense of her own needs and how to satisfy them; but was she not even more indifferent to others' needs than she had ever been? He shook his head slightly and tried to see her as he saw other people—as real, clear-cut, ordinary—but he failed. She was so uniquely herself, so wrapped in the glow of her own loveliness and so shining with the sparkle of her character, that it was not possible to see anything but that loveliness and sparkle. So he forgot the maid and he forgot Lucas, and turned his attention to his companion. Last night's experience had to be talked of, had to be understood and explained. That was what mattered now.

But she would not talk of it. He tried, haltingly and in whispers (for he was very much aware of the heavy back of the driver sitting hunched in front of them), to tell her of his guilt, his distress, his fear that he had harmed her. And tried too to talk of his joy and satisfaction and even greater need of her. But she turned her rosy cheek away and looked out at the passing scenery and exclaimed prettily at what little there was to see—a few cows desultorily chewing grass and staring at them with bored and lustrous eyes over dripping, drooping hedges; a red-armed woman pinning sheets and shirts to a washing line in a cold cottage garden—and seemed not to hear a word he said.

They boarded the coach in a flurry of excitement, and he was half amused and half irritated by the effect she had. People moving about the market square drifted over to watch, and men came out of the warm snug of the inn, their pewter tankards in their hands, to stand stamping their feet in the cold air and stare at her with their eyes filled with lascivious admiration. The people in the coach reacted powerfully to her too, the women narrowing their eyes and then sitting woodenly looking at everything but her, the men fussing to see she was comfortably seated and looking at nothing but her. He sat close beside her knowing himself to be the butt of the men's envy and the women's scorn, and did not know what to do at all.

The only notice she appeared to take of the attention she attracted—for she had moved throughout with a calm and sweet smile upon her face, apparently quite unaware of the interest taken in her—was to whisper in his ear as the coach went trundling noisily over the wooden bridge that led to the London road, "You need have no further fears for Mr. Lucas's welfare, you know. Half the town will have called upon his daughter by noon to tell her I departed in the London coach with a splendid young man and all my luggage. She'll be at the house before nightfall."

The journey was long, tiring and dirty, but she seemed quite untouched by any fatigue. They took a luncheon at Croydon, where the horses were changed, and again she attracted a great deal of attention, and now he found it totally irritating, discovering little pleasure in being the object of every man's jealousy. Then, as they rattled on through the rolling Surrey countryside toward Mitcham Common and the fear of highwaymen and she chattered of nonsense and exclaimed over sights seen through the windows—ordinary enough sights, in all truth—he felt depressed and angered by their inability to talk of the matter closest to his heart. It was important to him—quite desperately important—that she let him apologize, accept his guilt and absolve him; but how could they in these circumstances? Even if she were willing to talk to him on such personal matters, in this company it would be impossible.

But he had time to think. By the time the coach was rattling through Kennington on its way to Southwark and the river, he knew what had to be. They must be married as soon as possible—as soon, in fact, as he had completed his indentures, in two months' time. Somehow, all of them—Jesse and Josiah as well as Dorothea—would have to see the inevitability of it. She was his, totally his now, and that was all about it.

And she, staring with happy nostalgia out the coach windows and exclaiming with equal delight over the differences she recognized and the familiar, unchanged contours of other city sights, sat unconcerned with his plans for her future. He looked fondly at her, a smile of deep pleasure curving his lips. Oh, they should be so happy, he and his Lil. So happy!

· THIRTY-TWO ·

BUT somehow that sense of happiness seemed to elude him once they arrived. He settled her in a respectable pair of rooms at the Golden Cross, depressed both because he could not pay her score (for his borrowed money had run very short) and because she so patently could. She was secretive and careful about her possessions, but he had seen the purse she carried on her wrist, and the weight of coins in it, and was chilled. That she should have obtained so much from her sojourn with Lucas, lying alone in Edenbridge and waiting for his formidable daughter, disturbed him.

It was agreed that he would return next morning to take her to meet John Philip Kemble at Covent Garden. He had warned her that his acquaintance with the company was but slight, since he knew only two of the people who had been with Sheridan until his disastrous fire and who had chosen afterward to go to Kemble instead of the Lyceum, but she had still decided that she would like to try there.

"For Kemble, you know, is very remarkable. And the theater is new, is it not?—all rebuilt—and I should like that above all things. I shall be waiting for you, my dear Abel, at nine o'clock, so do not be late." And she had kissed his cheek so sweetly and kindly yet so dismissively that he somehow could not do as he wished and seize her and kiss her breath away and then talk of last night and his feelings.

Instead he went humbly and wearily away, and decided to call upon Mr. Witney, late as it was, to tell him of his news.

Josiah was sitting nodding over his books when Abel reached the shop, the shutters up and young James long since gone to his bed, and he looked sharply at the boy's tired and rather grimy face when he answered the sharp knocking at the door, and led him into the office and gave him a cup of hot chocolate (a drink to which he was much addicted) before letting him speak a word. And then he listened carefully, his round face cocked to one side and his little mouth pursed, to Abel's account of all that had happened. It took a long time, for he had to understand the past, to be told of the way Abel had first known Lil, before he could understand the present situation.

"So now you must tell one young lady that you no longer have a desire to wed her, since you have chosen to wed another. Hmph!" Mr. Witney looked at him with a quirk of his eyebrows that was humorous enough but still had an underlying seriousness that Abel could recognize. "How does this young lady—this Lilith—such an—ah—a quaint name, is it not?—how does Miss Lilith consider you should behave?"

"I have not spoken to her about it," Abel said stiffly. "I must of course settle this—this other matter before I can tell her the plans I have made."

Josiah made a small grimace. "You should not throw away your dirty water until you have clean in your bucket, boy. You may believe the well is full, but when you go there it still may not be full enough for you."

"Eh?"

The old man sighed sharply. "Oh, the *youngness* of you! Has it not struck you she—Miss Lilith—may not wish to wed you? That she may have other fish to fry? You say she's set on the theater—and you should know enough of theater people by now to know they are not greatly concerned with parson's blessings and settlements and the rearing of hopeful sons to their names! She may not wish it."

"Oh, she will—of course she will!" Abel said quickly. "She cannot believe otherwise after last night." And suddenly he flushed a dusky brick red, and his eyes filled with sharp tears of mingled embarrassment and fatigue and memory.

After one sharp glance, Mr. Witney looked down at his

desk and began to fiddle with papers, apparently searching for something, and did not raise his head again until Abel had quite recovered his composure.

"I think, my boy, that the time is ripe for me to speak to you of—of some matters I had meant to discuss with you when your indentures are complete, at the end of the year. But as matters are falling out, it will be as well to talk of them now." He sighed sharply, leaning back heavily in his chair. "I am not as well and strong as I was, and I cannot pretend otherwise to you. I believe I shall last your time out and some besides, but we cannot be sure. And now, with this matter . . ."

He stopped and looked at Abel, his expression almost ludicrous in its hangdog sadness, but Abel knew the reality of the feeling behind it and saw no amusement in it. Instead, he frowned sharply and said, "You will do well enough yet, sir. While there are foxgloves available to you, you need not be too concerned about yourself, I believe."

Witney gave a little crow of laughter at that. "You're a knowing boy, a knowing boy! Too good to have wasted so much of your efforts with those damned bloody surgeons! Such an apothecary as I've made of you—oh, indeed such an apothecary! I've told you none of my disorder, yet still you saw and understood—indeed, you're a credit to me!" And he beamed on Abel with so natural and sweet a pride and affection that the boy felt his spirits lift, and smiled back at him.

They sat in a companionable silence for a few moments, and then Abel stirred and produced a sudden jaw-cracking yawn, and Josiah shook himself a little and said briskly, "Well, I shall not keep you long! Listen, my boy. I have no sons, no kin I would cross the road to speak to—a rascally cousin, I believe remains alive, no more—and until you came to me, I had no notion how I should bestow my affairs. But I decided some while ago—after you had been with me but a short time indeed—that you had the makings of a man in you, my sort of man. So I have told my attorney that you shall be my heir. No, don't say a word. It is my decision and my desire, and has naught to do with you! Once I am dead and gone, I care little about what happens to such possessions as I may have amassed; but you—you are young, and you can have some joy of them."

He stopped and sat silent for a moment. "I used to have great pride and pleasure in my establishment, Abel," he said with touching simplicity. "To stand inside my shop and look about, and see the shelves and the mahogany and the glass and all the— Well, it gave me much delight, and I would wish one day that you will feel it too, though with this worm you have in you for surgery—well, enough of that. You have wrought well with your teachers, and times change, times change. Perhaps one day the surgeons will learn as much as the apothecaries, and you as one with a leg in both camps perhaps will— oh, damme, boy, I wander in my mind like some old pantaloon! It is the luxury of the old and foolish to prose on so, but I am not yet quite so foolish as I'm old, so I must stop it. So there you have it, my boy! You shall, on my death, become the owner of this establishment, and when at the end of your time you are admitted to the Society of our craft, why"—he smiled again, a little crookedly—"why, you are Mr. Abel Lackland, a man of property and established practice, worthy to wear the hat of Mr. Josiah Witney!"

Abel had been sitting throughout with his mouth half open with shock. Of course there had been times when he had wondered what would happen after Josiah's death, had realized the fact that Jesse believed that his master had a special affection for him that would be reflected in his will; but to be told in this way, at this time . . . He swallowed, blinked, tried to speak and failed, and simply shook his head. Josiah watched him in high good humor, clearly delighted with the response, and then leaned over and patted Abel's knee.

"You understand what I am telling you, dear boy? You are a man of prospects and expectations. You can throw away your dirty water if you so wish—and poor little Miss Dorothea! I fear she will take it poorly, for she has a deep and abiding affection for you or my name's not Josiah Witney— and the most you will lose is a good and loving wife, if so be your enchantress spurns you. Though I doubt she will once she knows you are a man of substance and no longer the— well, enough of that. But do as you wish in the affairs of your heart, Abel." He seemed to become suddenly very serious, and looked at Abel with his eyes a little blank, seeming to stare through him to some hazy vista far beyond. "I married as my father bid me, not as I wished, and still recall—well, well."

He laughed then, and twinkled at Abel. "The good God was on my side, for my wife died after a very short time with me, so I cannot complain too hard! Now, my boy, you must away to Gower Street. Tomorrow you had best leave the shop and the visits to James and to me. We've handled it all well enough this past few days, and one more day or so will make no matter. You have other affairs to settle." And he chivvied Abel out of his office, rattling his great keys as he opened the door.

Abel tried to speak properly, to thank him, to wish him a long and happy life yet and a tranquil antiquity, but he could not, so churned up was he with fatigue and confusion and the emotion of it all. So he shook the old man's hand with painful intensity, and disappeared into the darkness of Piccadilly to seek a hack to take him back to Gower Street.

It seemed to him sometimes that he was tied with invisible ropes, for however hard he tried to arrange matters to his satisfaction, however often he tried to talk about his plans, he was scotched. Lilith had no interest in any matter but her theatrical career, and simply ignored anything he tried to say that did not bear upon it.

He took her to Covent Garden, and with the aid of one Mr. Daniel Fletcher, a young actor he had known for some time (and who was clearly quite bedazzled by Lilith's bewitching smile and confiding ways), saw to it that she was introduced to Mr. Kemble. That was on her second day in London, and to his intense chagrin he failed to see her again for more than a week. Mr. Fletcher told him that Mr. Kemble had agreed to accept her in his company and that she was to spend all her available time at the theater to learn and observe and be "taught her trade," and Fletcher had laughed lightly when he said that in a way that filled Abel with foreboding and the heavy pull of an emotion he could not quite recognize, but which he was soon to know very familiarly indeed. He was to experience it much before he could name it as the jealousy it was.

But he accepted her absence with as good a grace as he could, glad enough that he had been able to bring her the gift she most wanted, a place in a theater company, and turned his mind to other matters. He had work to do at the hospital as well as at the shop, and pressing though his private affairs were, these had to come first. But as soon as he could, he went to see Lucy, feeling obscurely that it would be easiest to settle all other people before he faced Dorothea and Jesse with his decision.

Lucy, to his surprise, was not nearly as amazed at his various pieces of news as she should have been. He told her first of Josiah Witney's announcement and she merely nodded calmly, and said, "Aye, well, that was clearly to be expected. 'E'd 'ave to be clean out of 'is attic to do otherwise, for 'oo else is there? I've known this'd turn out so right from the start. So what'll you do? Give up your surgery after you worked so 'ard to learn it, so's you can run the shop and the apothecary side? Or—"

"He's not dead yet, for God's sake, Lucy!" Abel said sharply. "No need to rush the man into his grave for me! I am glad and happy to wait. I shall practice my surgery along-side him for years yet, unless I miss my guess. He's been ill of his heart these many years. He'll last a long time yet, so long as no fool angers him out of his peace and causes an apoplexy to destroy him!"

"If you say so," she said equably, and looked sharply at him. They were sitting, as usual, in her kitchen, she in her old red wrapper and he in shirt-sleeved comfort, drinking ale and eating cold meat for their supper. "But that's not all you came to tell me, is it? You're bustin' at the seams with it! What else you bin up to?"

He set his tankard down carefully and looked at her for a moment, and then away as a slow tide of color crept up his cheeks, and she raised her eyebrows a little but said no more, just sitting with her elbows planted on the table, propping up her head with a huge hand set either side of her face so that it looked ridiculously creased and misshapen. But in the middle of the rolling contours of flesh, her eyes were bright and knowing and very watchful.

"I'm going to— I'm not going to marry Dorothea," he blurted at length, not looking at her but fiddling with his tankard. "I have not told her yet, but I shall have to."

"Not because you got expectations," she said, and it was

not a question but a clear statement of knowledge. "Not because you don't need 'er influence no more."

"No."

There was a longer silence, and then, with an effort, he started to tell her, right from the beginning, of Lil and what she meant to him, of the overwhelming effect of meeting her again, of his bringing her to London—and as he spoke his confidence increased, and the words came more and more easily, and even fluently, and she watched him, never shifting a muscle.

It was when he told her he had taken Lil to Kemble, and that she had not had time to see him since, that her eyes narrowed a little and she said, "Kemble? Um. You've found yourself something very special, then."

"How do you mean? Because Kemble took her so quickly? Well, she is, after all . . ."

Lucy shook her head. "Not that. Because of what they're saying of her."

He snapped into a frown at that. "Who is saying? Saying what? What is there to say?"

"Oh, don't fly into your high trees, boy! There's naught to be got in a fit! There's talk about. Last night, there was some 'ere from Covent Garden, and they was tellin' me the women there are fair turned on their arses with rage and jealousy, for Kemble 'as this new girl oo's as clever as she's pretty, and got him round her finger like a leading string already. 'E's re'earsing 'em all for some new confection—I don't know what—and she's to play a showy part: not big, you understand, but showy, or so they said 'ere last night. She'll be the talk of the town, from all accounts, before too long."

She watched him shrewdly under her scrubby little eyelashes, saw the confusion in him, the amalgam of pride and jealousy—delight in his Lil's prowess and rage that others should admire her—and sighed sharply.

"Is this the one, Abel?" she asked gently. "The girl you didn't tell me of, but that—well, *the* girl? Is it, my likely lad?"

He nodded, looking up at her with a curious shyness, and she put out a hand and engulfed one of his in it.

"Try not to love her too much, Abel," she said earnestly. "D'you 'ear me, boy? Keep part of yerself for yerself, and don't give 'er all of yer needs. You'll break yer 'eart if you do that. Be she the kindest, truest creature that ever breathed, if she 'as this sort of effect on men, then you're going to 'ave a life with 'er that— Oh, Abel, try not to!"

But she said it with no conviction, staring at him with a wealth of pity in her face. Lucy knew women as well as anyone could ever know them, and knew above all that a woman who has the effect of enslaving every man who sees her does so not so much because of her looks, however useful good looks might be, as because of something else: a knowingness, an intention to enslave, a self-consciousness and calculatingness that never falters for a moment. Knowing this, and thinking of the expressions on the faces of the men who had talked so gloatingly in her glittering rooms last night of the new *On-Dit* at Covent Garden, she could have wept for her likely lad.

But she did not, being a practical person and not given to wasting tears or fears until she had to. She sent him briskly about his business duly filled with meat and ale, hugging him and bidding him not to consider his Lucy in the next few weeks. "You'll be a sight too busy for me for a while," she said equably, "or I miss my guess. Don't fret if you can't visit. You'll 'ave enough to worry about without worryin' over me. But I'll be 'ere as and when yer needs me."

Watching him go, she thought somberly, 'E'll need more'n me to get 'im through this, or I'm the Queen of Sheba," and went back to her kitchen as dispirited as she could ever remember being.

And now there was nothing for it. All that lay between him and his Lil was Dorothea. He had, for a little while, played with the idea of speaking first to Lil and taking her with him to Gower Street, feeling obscurely that Dorothea must, once she saw Lil, understand and gracefully accept the situation as it was. But he had rejected that almost as soon as he thought it, for he could not bring himself to speak to Lil of his serious intentions and plans for them both without first being sure there would be no disagreeableness for her. And anyway, his thoughts had added bleakly, until we can speak properly and privately, how could I?

He had seen her briefly on one afternoon at the end of her

first week in London, when he had been able to get to the theater to seek her backstage. That she was clearly in a state of total bliss comforted him a good deal. She was glowing with it and threw her arms about his neck as soon as she saw him and cried her gratitude and happiness, but then she was called to her rehearsal again, was swept away by several of the young men of the company, and he had to stand in the wings and watch her, surrounded by other people and aching to reach out to her.

That she was a natural and highly gifted performer was clearly apparent, even in this, a rehearsal of a most indifferent play (as his experience of the theater fast told him it was) in the early days of work before the characterizations had had any chance to be formed. She moved about the stage with such an awareness of her own body in relation to it, so naturally placed herself and tilted her head, so elegantly timed her speech, that even under the thin working lights thrown by the dimmed gas jets and in ordinary clothes with fit-up props, she wove a spell of enchantment.

He heard Kemble praise her, saw him move his spare and elegant frame about her in a way that showed her to even greater advantage, and knew that he must always share his Lil with all the world. Once she appeared in a public performance, it was clear to him, she would be adored by all the town, might even rival Kemble's autocratic sister as a draw. He smiled a little at that fantasy. Mrs. Siddons toppled from her throne by his Lil, his guttersnipe Lil! A delicious thought. But underneath his pride and pleasure lay a cold chill of fear.

But he put that down to his distaste for the coming interview with Dorothea and Jesse and set about remedying that situation. Now.

He came to Dorothea in the schoolroom, in which she had taken to sitting in the afternoons since her mother's death. She would have been hard put to it to explain to herself why she found such a curious satisfaction in the ugly, shabby room. In her mother's lifetime, while she had still been in control of her, Dorothea had hated it, forced as she had been to spend so many of her most boring and tedious hours there. After her mother's withdrawal from life and company,

Dorothea had taken to the drawing room with all the relish of a newly released prisoner; but now she found her comfort here. Perhaps it was a retreat to the past, perhaps a gesture of defiance against her fears, for it was here in the schoolroom that her relationship with Abel had first flowered and reached such fruition as it had. Whatever the reason, she used the room much.

That she had fears now was undoubted. In the days between her mother's death and the funeral, she had been deeply happy. It had all seemed so pat, so right, so *meant*.

But the small cloud of doubt that had risen over her horizon on the day when Abel had sorted through her mother's desk was becoming bigger and darker. Since his return from Kent, unaccompanied but quite silent and offering no word of information, she had watched him and listened to him and felt the doubt gnawing caterpillar-busy deep in her mind. Was he ill, perhaps? She watched his expression, the way he ate, the hours he kept, and fretted sorely.

For he certainly was different. The brusqueries of absent mind to which she had long been accustomed, and indeed accepted as an index of his masculinity, positively glorying in the strength of his character and his fearless sharpness of speech, had dissolved. Now when he spoke to her he was totally abstracted; chillingly, terrifyingly polite. He spoke to her now like a stranger, not like her Abel.

All her life Dorothea had known that people to whom you are attached often speak sharply and disparagingly to you, correcting your faults, pointing out your stupidities, indicating ways in which you could improve yourself. That was how her mother had spoken to her, how Jesse behaved to her, how Abel himself had often been. But not now. Just that distant politeness, that remote courtesy. In the loneliness of her bed at night she shivered in her dreams.

She had even considered speaking of her fears to Jesse, to ask him to pin Abel to a date for their wedding, now that no rub stood in their way, but she rejected that idea—for the time being, at any rate. He had deteriorated quite dreadfully in the weeks since Charlotte's death, drinking ever more and eating ever less, and not going at all to his countinghouse or warehouse.

Twice had Mr. Hunnisett and Mr. Nidd come to Gower Street in some despair, trying to get some sense out of their master in order to run his business as it should be, but to no avail. He had stared owlishly at them and turned his head away. Dorothea was a little surprised, as indeed were Hunnisett and Nidd. None had ever thought that Jesse had so dearly cared for his Charlotte, or that he would be so bereft of happiness at her death. But so it was, and so she accepted it.

When Abel came into the schoolroom that afternoon, she put down her sewing immediately. She knew, now, quite suddenly, that her fears were justified. He had come to tell her something she would not wish to hear, and she looked at his face, at the expression of discomfort that invested it, and for a moment wanted to close her eyes to hide the sight of it. But she did not, simply folding her hands upon her lap and looking quietly up at him.

He saw her clearly for the first moment in a long time. Slight, pallid, seeming rather faded against the darkness of her clothes, which made her pale eyes look so much paler, somehow, under the light eyebrows which were so unobtrusive that she seemed to bear a startled look. He wondered for one brief moment if she could possibly love him as deeply as he loved his Lil and then dismissed the idea. It was unthinkable on many counts; he was not himself in any way as lovable as was Lil, Dorothea was not the sort of person who could be consumed by emotion so strong, and above all, he could not bear to think that she could entertain such feelings. If she did, it would make his task much harder. But she did not, he assured himself, and knowing he sounded stiff and uncomfortable, launched into his prepared speech.

She would, he hoped, understand. Their friendship had become a betrothal not because of any great affection between them but because at the time it was politic. She would remember, no doubt, that her mama had threatened her with a disagreeable match, and that she had wished to be betrothed to him in order to escape such an experience. He, for his part, she would no doubt call to mind, had been in need of a way to persuade those with power in his life that he should be permitted to study as he wished. But now, with her mama sadly demised, and he himself set upon the road to his career, the convenience of their betrothal lacked force. He was sure, he went on, with his voice gathering certainty and strength as his words began to convince him too of the power of his argument, he was sure she would be happy indeed now to be released from her promise of so long ago, to be freed to live her life to her own satisfaction. He wished to say no ill of her dear mama, but he knew Dorothea had suffered some distress at her hands. Those days were over for her, and he, Abel, would now free her completely. He had no doubt her eyes would shortly fall upon one much more worthy of her than himself, one to whom she could give her wholehearted affection, one of better family than he (and he felt he dealt a shrewd hand of cards here), sharing her breeding and background. He himself—and here he coughed and walked a little about the room, feeling embarrassment rising in him—he himself had, as it were, reverted to his own background, being set upon marriage to a girl he had known for many years, who had been a guttersnipe and an orphan like himself and who was so well suited to the life of a surgeon's wife (and here he hurried on, hearing the palpable untruth in it as clear as a bell). In short, he finished, it was—he hoped she was as content—he trusted that . . .

He faltered to an end, and she sat and looked at him, her face tight and gray as dust, and he looked back at her and said with a sudden impulsiveness, "You did not really care for me, did you, Dorothea? Not really? How could you, indeed, knowing the sort of wretch I was when you first set eyes on me?"

A little to his surprise, her lips quirked at that, but still she said nothing, and he threw his hands out in a curiously stilted gesture.

"I know you will be glad of this when you consider it," he said, and went over to her and bent to kiss her cold cheek. "You will see. It will all be for the best."

She opened her lips to speak for the first time, and even to him they seemed stiff and cold.

"You have not spoken yet to Papa Constam?" Her voice was as stiff and cold as her expression, with no inflection in it at all.

"No." He moved uncomfortably. "No. I thought—it was

right you should know first, that you should agree with me that this was the best plan for both of us, for you as well as for me."

She seemed not to hear the appeal in his voice. "I would wish you not to speak to him yet."

There was a long silence, and then he said sharply, "It will make no difference, Dorothea. My mind is made up. I am quite set upon it. I shall marry Lil—Lilith, and—"

"Would you so kindly have bid me find another husband had she not returned?" she asked with a sudden harshness, and he stared at her, startled. He could not remember ever hearing such a note in her voice. And then, as the import of her words sank into his mind, he knew his speciousness had been recognized, and he reddened painfully, and could not look at her.

"You will not speak yet to Papa Constam," she said again, and now the harshness had gone from her voice, that flash of knowingness had vanished, and he looked at her again and saw only the flat, expressionless face, the faded pallor of her, and nodded, some of his confidence returning.

"If you wish me not to yet, then I shall not. But once I have completed my—once Lil has— I shall have to tell him at some time."

"Not yet," she said, and once more he nodded, and this time turned and hurried from the room, to stand outside the door in the familiar dark passageway with its smell of beeswax and the chalk used to polish the floors, the scent of dusty carpets and curtains, to take a deep breath of relief. He had done it.

His conscience was surging painfully below the surface of his mind, the vision of Dorothea's stricken face still clear before his eyes, but that was something that would ease with time. He had meant no ill toward Dorothea, and never would; there was no need to feel so ashamed of the way he had behaved, was there? So he argued with himself, out there in the dark and quiet passageway, and then, with a sense of almost luxuriant self-indulgence, he let the picture of Lil rise in his mind, a picture that effectively banished all thoughts of Dorothea and guilt and anything else but Lil herself. Now, at last, he could tell her of their future together. There remained no rub at all in their way.

In the schoolroom, Dorothea sat for a long time staring at the faded yellow paper on the walls, her face quite expressionless. Then, moving with a particular tidiness and economy, she folded her sewing and put it neatly away in her workbasket and went to the drawing room.

Jesse was sitting, as ever, sprawled on the sofa with the brandy decanter beside him, half asleep, half stuporous. She stood at the door looking at him for a moment and then said in a clear voice, "Papa! Papa Constam! There is a matter about which I must talk to you. Immediately. About Abel and the girl in Kent. *Immediately.*"

· THIRTY-THREE ·

HE moved about the greenroom in a long, loping prowl, barely containing his feelings and aching for the whole thing to be over and settled. There was more than a little of irritation in him these days, for she was coming between him and his work, and there should be room for both in his life; but he told himself it was not her fault, and tried not to blame her for it. She could not help being adored by all as she was. Could she?

He looked about him bleakly, and sighed sharply. The play had been running fifty-seven nights now, and generally in a theater where so long a run was being enjoyed, the greenroom would be full of people all through the performance. Actors not presently involved in the action, regular playgoers who had already seen the piece would be lounging about, drinking and talking. But not when Lilith Lucas was on the stage. Then everyone who could be was in the wings, from scene shifters and painters to hot-chestnut sellers from the street outside; all stood and watched and shared in the intoxication that was Lil. His Lil. Everybody's Lil, God damn it, he thought viciously, and flung himself about the room again.

He could hear them from beyond the closed door, the shouts and roars of laughter and approval, and wished with all his heart she had not demanded a career in the theater, and that he had not made it possible for her. He loved her dearly and deeply, and asked no more of life than to set up a household for her, to furnish and equip it for her as it should be, and then to do his work all day and love her all night. What more could any man ask?

He was qualified now, and only last week, as 1811 moved into a hard, frozen January so cold that the Thames had frozen over and there had been talk of a Frost Fair on the ice above London Bridge, Astley Cooper had offered him a post at Guy's.

He had thought carefully about it, and decided not to take the chance, for many reasons. For a start, he had no wish to live a life always second to Astley Cooper, and knew that Guy's had no room for more than one star of surgery. Astley Cooper was too firmly fixed in that firmament for a Lackland ever to enjoy either opportunity or reputation there. And then, there was the shop. For all his brave attempts to cover his gradually increasing infirmity, there was no doubt that Mr. Witney was not the man he had been, and his need of Abel to run his affairs was considerable.

So Abel had compromised. He saw the patients and dealt with the visits, and left it to Mr. Witney to stay in the shop and supervise young James in the remainder of the necessary tasks. Sometime James would have to be taken on visits, to be taught his craft as Abel had been, but not yet. At present, with his work among his own patients and his continuing regular visits to Charles Bell at Great Windmill Street (for he still liked to dissect a cadaver whenever he could), there was more than enough to occupy him.

And if only he could pin Lilith down to a decision about their future, all would be well and he would be free for other matters. There was at the very back of his mind, in the deepest recesses of him, a wriggling worm of an idea, a desire, a sharply pointed ambition. He had seen the care the people of Southwark enjoyed at Guy's, knew that St. Thomas's cared for many of the same people of that crowded, dirty corner of the city, and felt it deeply wrong that there was no such care for the people of his own part of London. He would think of the teeming thousands who swarmed through the ugly, dirty, pulsating alleys and hovels of the Dials, the Bermudas, the Caribee Islands and the other warrens, and try to see a hospital there, for them. Why not? he would ask himself in the darker watches of the night when aching need for Lil kept him awake; why not? And he would try to exhaust himself, to lift himself above the clamoring in his loins and belly by planning it all, the dispensary and surgery he would open for them, with the help of Mr. Witney's money. One day.

But it could not be more than a remote dream at present, and certainly until she would settle matters life was not as sweet as it should be for a newly qualified young surgeon and apothecary with expectations such as his. He went about remote and abstracted, and worried about it.

Dorothea watched him covertly, at first doubtfully and then hopefully. She could not imagine that any woman anywhere would refuse the love of a man as desirable as Abel, but from all appearances that was what this girl was doing. Even Dorothea had heard about her now, knew her to be the talk of the town, a raging beauty and the idol of all playgoers, and hope was rising in her. If she were to refuse him of her own free will, there would be no problem. But, she would tell herself, even if she does not, I need not distress myself. Even if she accepts him, with all her loveliness and success and money, it won't make any difference. Not when Abel knows.

And she would smile to herself, and go to sit with Jesse and talk to him, and whisper to him, and murmur to him in his half-sleeping drunken state, and he would listen and nod, bleary-eyed, and sometimes, under her prompting, repeat her words. And the rest of the time she went serenely about the house, doing her daily tasks and waiting. She need do no more.

And Abel too waited, and fretted, and then decided that he had waited long enough. The time had come to force her decision upon her, and make his arrangements. He would no longer tolerate her laughing teasing, her sweetly mocking flirtations and jokings with her followers ("It is not important, foolish Abel! But a necessary part of my work, for an actress must have her special following, must she not?"), nor her arm's-length treatment of him. The time had come.

But even when the performance was over, and the greenroom filled with a surging crowd, it seemed he was to be balked. There was talk of sending out to a cookshop to bring in victuals for a few chosen spirits who would remain late, but to Abel's intense relief that was decided against by Kemble, who had drunk his fill that afternoon and now was feeling far from well.

Abel cursorily examined him and advised rest and quiet (for he had become as much the doctor to the Covent Garden company as to the Haymarket and Mr. Sheridan's actors), and at last, people began to go away—unwillingly leaving the bewitching Lil behind, but going.

At last, hours after the curtain had come down, it seemed to Abel, the bulk of them had gone—Kemble home to his wife and family, the others drifting away to God knew what stews and sinks, leaving just Lil, himself and one other.

He scowled heavily at the way Sir Richard Crale sat on and on and on, apparently oblivious of Abel's simmering anger, just lounging with his elegant booted legs outstretched and slowly turning a quizzing glass in his long fingers.

"You become ever lovelier, my dear Lilith," he was saying lazily, watching her as she deftly wiped the paint from her face and brushed the powder from her hair (for the play was a period piece, and Lil would not wear a wig). "There must surely be an end to it! It is not mathematically possible for one incredibly beautiful woman to increase her beauty each day as you appear to, but so it is. I must try to discover the formula."

Watching him, feeling time running out between his fingers, listening to the silly, flirtatious, childish words and Lil's fluting giggle of delight as one more stupid and absurd compliment was piled on another, he felt anger rising in him as strong and as urgent as the desire for her that so often threatened to overcome him. That he, Abel Lackland, the only man with a true claim upon her—for was she not *his* Lil?—should have to stand waiting for such a one to go his way before he could speak—it was intolerable.

"I would take it kindly, Crale, if you would depart." Abel heard his own voice come louder than he had intended, and clamped his jaw hard shut as both turned and stared at him— Crale with a superciliously raised eyebrow above the ridiculous quizzing glass, and Lil with a glint of anger in her eyes.

"Really, Abel, you take too much upon yourself!" she said sharply. "Why should my friends go at your bidding, indeed? Do be silent, and go home yourself if you're so inclined." She tossed her head then with that familiar gesture that was well known all over London now. "I can't abide to see you drooping there another moment! Do go home to your books or your corpses or whatever it is, and leave me in peace!"

"You will gain nothing by displaying your temper to me, Lil!" he snapped, and she looked up at him again, for she had returned her attention to the mirror, and gave him a curiously calculating stare, and a faint smile appeared on her face and she opened her lips slightly so that he could see her tongue peeping redly at the corner of her mouth; and he felt that damned urge rise in his belly again.

"If anyone is displaying infant temper, dear man, it would appear to be yourself." Crale spoke with an ultrafashionable drawl, so flattened and drawn out as to be almost incomprehensible. Almost, but not quite. "Shall I turn this impudent sawbones out of doors, my queen? Shall we drop the leech into the gutter where it belongs? Shall I . . ."

All the anger of the past weeks, the frustration and the need, the delays and the irritations came bubbling up in Abel then. With a sense of luxurious enjoyment in his own strength the like of which he had not enjoyed for many years, he launched himself across the room, and seized the foppish Crale by the ribbon that held his quizzing glass about his neck, and tugged. It broke and fell to the floor, and deliberately Abel lifted his foot and ground his heel into the delicate little object, crushing it to splinters.

Crale had come half to his feet, his mouth open with rage, but he had no chance to say anything. Abel seized him by the shoulders and shook him so that his head rattled on his shoulders, and then, with a movement learned long ago in the gutter and never forgotten, brought up one knee with a sharp and twisting action. It hit the other man first in the crotch, making him shriek in agony and double up, and then, traveling on, hit him hard in the belly below the ribs, cutting off the shriek in mid-breath as it connected.

With the same economy of movement, he hauled Crale over his shoulder—and it was not difficult, for he was slight enough of build, so aristocratic a type was he—and dragged him to the door, to thrust him out and shout for the doorman, who came running.

"Get him out of here," he said shortly, shoving the now fainting Crale into the startled man's arms. "He insulted Mrs. Lucas, and should not ever be permitted to return. If he ever does and I am here, I shall kill him in good earnest." And then he turned back into the room, slamming the door behind him.

She was sitting at the table, staring at him with her eyes wide and her lips parted, and he came and stood beside her, his hands clenched at his sides and breathing heavily.

"Well, Lil, you devil cat! What do you say to that?"

She began to laugh—a soft easy trill at first, and then it became louder, more free and genuinely filled with amusement—and she stood up and threw her arms about his neck and rested her head upon his shoulder and laughed and laughed and laughed. And he stood there in stunned surprise at first, holding her close and glad to do it, but not understanding at all.

She caught her breath at last, and pulled back to look up into his face, and her eyes were creased still with the laughter, still wet with the tears her hilarity had created.

"Oh, Abel, Abel!" she cried; her voice was still thick with it. "You are the outside of enough, and I adore you! It will be all over town by tomorrow that you nearly killed a man for me, and I love you, I love you, I *love* you!" And she hugged him again and planted a great kiss upon his mouth, a noisy, affectionate kiss that he seized on hungrily.

"So you keep saying!" he said when he raised his head and looked down at her, holding her firmly by her upper arms. "You say you love me, you kiss me, you hug me, but whenever I come here you are surrounded by such fops and idiots and men of the town that I must near make an assignation to come close enough to talk to you—yet when I try to speak to you of our plans, of settling matters, you laugh, or cry you are tired, or must rehearse, or some such nonsense! And tonight I'll have no more of it, you hear me? We shall settle it for all! I've told you these many times that I would wish you to be my wife, that I want no more than to devote my love to you for always, yet you will not . . ."

She was slipping away from his grasp, turning in his hands, and he knew she was doing it yet again. She did it constantly, playing the little girl one day, pleading weariness another, and looking at her face now, he knew she was going to tell him some tale or other—not enough to send him too miserably away, but not enough to make him contented either.

And in his rage and frustration and remaining unexpressed anger, he raised his hand and struck out at her, so that his palm hit the side of her jaw a shrewd blow which snapped her head back with an audible click and left a red mark clearly outlined on her skin.

Horrified, he let go of her, and they stood in total silence staring at each other, she with one hand up, barely touching the ugly red weal that was rising on her jaw, he blank with the shock of what he had done. The second time, he was thinking confusedly, the second time I have used her so, the second time . . .

And then she smiled—a long, slow smile, just like the one she had offered him at the door of his room on that night in Edenbridge—and spoke softly, her hand still caressing her cheek.

"If you feel so violent about me, dear Abel, then I think I must tell you yes now, must I not? For if I'm to be beaten like a slave if I do not, I have no other choice. But do not try to bully me too far, will you, for you will mark me so it can be seen from the gallery, and that would never serve! I like a man to be—a man. But not *excessively!*"

He could hardly believe it, could not be sure even yet that it was true, and he stood very still for a moment before pulling her into his grasp again and kissing her, kissing her, kissing her, almost eating her face and throat in his delight and need.

And she responded, eagerly, and then more eagerly, and for one brief moment he thought of the couch that lay along the far wall, and remembered that time in the half-tester bed—and pushed the thought away. She was to be his wife. His own wife. Not someone who teased him, laughed at him, saw him eaten up with jealousy and laughed again, but his wife. Let others vie for her favors and consider making love to her in a greenroom and fail; he had no need of such. She was to be his wife, and there would be a house for her, a home for her, a true marriage bed for her . . .

"You must go," she said at length. "Indeed you must, dear Abel, for I am truly weary, and you too must work tomorrow."

"I shall take you home," he said, and looked about him for her wrap, but she shook her head and said softly, "No, my love. No. I must dress and prepare my table for tomorrow. The doorman will see me to a hack, never fear. Come tomorrow, my love. We shall make our plans then, but not now."

He went contentedly enough, kissing her hungrily again and holding her in a rib-cracking squeeze for a moment before shrugging into his heavy coat and leaving her framed in the light from the lamps before the mirror, her face still faintly blurred with the stain of the blow he had inflicted upon her.

As he passed the doorman, he said cheerfully, "See to it Mrs. Lucas has a hack immediately she is ready!" and shoved a coin into the man's hand before swinging insouciantly out into the still busy streets of Covent Garden.

The doorman looked after him for a moment, his long face twisted a little into a half smile, and then looked down at the coin in his hand and shrugged. They were all fools in his eyes, damned fools. He'd seen it all before, he had. Women!

That evening before he went to bed, Abel left a short note for Dorothea. He would ask her, if she would be so kind, to be sure that Jesse did not take too much brandy tomorrow. There was a matter of importance to be discussed that evening before they dined, and he wanted to be sure that Mr. Constam was feeling well enough to take his part.

Dorothea read the note, and knew at once. She folded the piece of paper carefully and put it into her reticule and went to the drawing room again to speak to Jesse.

She felt no doubt at all now. She had obtained her way so far, had she not? There was no reason that she could see why she should not continue to do so. And Abel would be much happier, she was quite sure. Much happier. She was smiling a little when she went into the drawing room.

· THIRTY-FOUR ·

STANDING at the drawing-room door and looking at Jesse properly for the first time in weeks, Abel was shocked. He sat there, unshaven, slumped in his place in the corner of the sofa and looking deflated, like a bladder of air that had been punctured long since. His flesh seemed to hang on him in folds, quite without the old elasticity and bounce that had been so much a part of him, and Abel looked from him to Dorothea, who was standing composedly beside the sofa. But she seemed quite unperturbed by Jesse's appearance, and with a sharp compunction Abel realized how very wrapped up in his own affairs he had been since Charlotte's death. He should at least have seen that the old man was so distressed and had changed so. But since he had not, there was no sense in castigating himself now. So he moved forward and came and sat down beside Jesse.

"Sir, I would speak to you on a matter of some importance," he said, more loudly than he meant to, and Jesse looked blearily at him, and raised his eyebrows with a hint of his former responsiveness, and then let his gaze wander away.

"Give me some brandy," he muttered, turning his head to look up at Dorothea, and she shook her own head very slightly and murmured, "Later, Papa. Later."

"I should prefer you would not stay, Dorothea," Abel said

irritably. "This is a matter between ourselves, in all truth, and I should have thought you would prefer not to—that you would choose to leave us alone under the circumstances."

"I think not, Abel," she said gently. "He is not very well, you know, and needs my care. And I have a—I am concerned in the matter you wish to discuss, am I not? I believe you are to talk of your forthcoming marriage?"

He reddened, and turned his attention back to Jesse. If she chose to stand there and suffer Jesse's reaction to the news of her rejection, so be it, he thought viciously; it meant naught to him. And he looked at Jesse again, and knew that the old Jesse, who would have jeered or shouted or rallied her, was no longer here, and doubted, suddenly, just what his reaction to Abel's news might be.

And then he shrugged slightly. It made no difference now. He was a man grown, a qualified professional man with membership in the College of Surgeons and in the Society of Apothecaries to his name, a man of expectations. The days when Jesse could have blighted his life by turning him out of doors, could have relegated him to the gutter again with one imperious gesture, were long since gone. Telling him now of his wish to marry Lil instead of Dorothea was no more than a courtesy; Jesse had no power over him of any sort. He had nothing at all to fear from this sodden wreck of a man.

So he told himself as he stared at him, and used the words to quell the tide of pity rising in him. For a brief moment he tried to remember the Jesse he had known, the glorious creature in the elegant clothes, swaggering with his stick under his arm through the gutters of the Dials, surrounded by eager starvelings hanging on his every gesture; tried to recall the great expansiveness that had been in the man, the huge splendor of him. He remembered the way he had looked that long-ago night at Rule's in Maiden Lane, sitting foursquare and solid at the scrubbed wooden table watching a small and scrawny child eat himself to a bursting point on the victuals he had provided; and adult Abel—successful, happy, hope-filled Abel—felt unfamiliar tears pricking his eyelids, and reached out toward the old man.

Jesse looked down at the square hand that settled on his own, lying useless on his lap, and looked up at the face before him, and now there was more than a shadow of the old Jesse in his expression. He looked pleased, filled with a cocky pride as he looked at the clean-shaven face with its long white cheeks, the full and sensuous mouth, the hair falling elegantly and handsomely over the high forehead, and gave the ghost of a chuckle. "I wrought well when I found you, eh, my boy? Made a man out of a piece of Dials rubbish, did I not?"

"Aye, sir, you did," Abel said quietly. "You wrought well, and I am very glad of it."

"As Jesse Constam says, so he does." He turned his head fretfully then, and said sharply, "You—Dorothea, you stupid creature! I told you to give me brandy! Where is it?"

"If you please, sir, I would speak to you first," Abel said hastily, and the moment of amity between them, that shred of communion, shivered and slid away. "There are some matters you must know of—though I must tell you now my mind is made up."

"Well? Well? Let's about it then! A man could die of thirst waiting for you." He was sliding back into petulant childishness again, and Abel frowned sharply.

"I am to be married, sir," he said baldly and rather loudly, not looking at all at Dorothea. "Dorothea knows that I have no wish to hold her to our betrothal, and have decided to select a wife elsewhere. She is content enough with the arrangement, I believe." Still he did not look at her, though he was very much aware of her standing there, still and contained.

Jesse looked at him, and then turned his head to look owlishly at Dorothea. "Dorothea—you spoke to me of—"

"Hear what Abel has to say first, Papa," she said softly, and puzzled, Abel shot a look at her. But she looked serenely back at him, and he returned to Jesse.

"I—you will perhaps recall the girl I—the girl that came here one night, some years ago. The friend I visited privately, and—dammit, I have no doubt you recall Lil!"

"Lil?" Jesse frowned and looked again at Dorothea, and she looked stolidly back, saying nothing, moving not a muscle of her face. "Lil," Jesse said again, and then very slowly nodded.

"Lil. A pretty child. With black hair, all curled, and green eyes. Lil." And he shot at Abel a sudden sharp look that was so totally himself, his old self, that the younger man felt a sharp thrill of anxiety shoot through him, the sort of fear Jesse had been able to arouse in him in his boyhood. "Is that the one?"

"Yes, sir," Abel said, and swallowed. "She was sent into Kent, and I found her and brought her back to London. And though you have not been much in the world since—these past weeks, to have heard of it, she has become much talked of, for she is at Covent Garden with Mr. Kemble, and is a great success. The whole town knows of her!" And he could not help the note of bitterness mingled with pride that crept into his voice.

Suddenly Jesse stood up, and a little startled, Abel stood up too, and watched the old man move heavily across the room toward the fireplace. Now he was on his feet, he looked more himself again: thinner, undoubtedly, and somewhat disheveled, but with enough of his personality there to hide the physical differences that had seemed so apparent to Abel before. He stood for a moment supporting himself against the mantelpiece, and then turned and looked at Abel, his head cocked to one side in his old characteristic pose.

"Lil. The girl that was sent away. Oh, yes, Abel. I know of the girl you mean. I have good cause to."

There was an air of chill in the room suddenly, and Abel stood staring at Jesse, and then looked back at Dorothea, who was standing with her hands clasped loosely before her and her eyes cast down, and back again. Alarm seemed to be coming at him from outside himself, from the atmosphere in the room, and it met the wave of doubt rising inside himself and made him speak even more sharply than he had spoken hitherto.

"You have good cause to? And what does that mean? You saw Lil but the once, the night she came here, and . . ."

Jesse was smiling now, a crooked knowing sort of smile, and his eyes flicked sideways at Dorothea and then back to Abel's face, and very slowly he shook his head.

"How often I saw her is no matter," he said softly, "no matter at all. After all, boy, I did not see you till you were eleven years old or thereabouts, did I?"

"What has that to do with the matter?" Abel asked, bewildered. "You do not explain yourself at all clear, sir, and I, for my part—"

"She knew, you know. My Charlotte, Mrs. Constam. She knew." Jesse was nodding now, the bald center of his head bobbing in and out of Abel's line of vision. "Oh, she knew, for why else did she behave so? She must have known, and I am glad of it, for it showed her—oh, it showed her that it was all of her and none of me. That I could have got a son upon her, more than one, had she been as a wife should be and not behaved so—"

"*Knew what?*" Abel shouted it, now thoroughly confused and full of an anxiety that he did not understand. He had nothing to fear from this man, nothing at all—he was a man made—and whatever Jesse said, nothing could come between Abel and his Lil now, and yet . . . "Knew what?" And now he was standing in front of Jesse, and his hands were clenched into fists at his side as he stared at the face so near his own.

Jesse blinked up at him, and nodded that absurdly knowing nod at him, and grinned again.

"Why, boy, that you were mine. My son, got on a whore in the Dials! She watched you and she watched me, and when I spoke—oh, she knew, she knew; did she not, Dorothea?"

"Yes, Papa."

Abel whirled at the sound of her soft voice. He had quite forgotten she was there for the moment, and looked at her now, at the smooth calmness of her face and the limpid gaze of her pale eyes, and shook his head in denial. But she, with a curious sad relish, nodded gently.

"Indeed, it is so, Abel," she said, and her voice was still soft. "Mama spoke to me of it many a time. She knew you were Papa's son, she said, and that—she knew of Lil as well."

"Knew of—knew *what* of her? That she sent her away from me *I* know, that it was she who took her out of my life—but she is dead now, and I will not— For God's sake! Knew *what* of Lil?" And his voice rose to a roar as he turned back to Jesse.

The older man was standing now with his arms raised on either side of him so that his elbows were resting on the mantelshelf behind him, and it was a posture that gave him an air of insouciance, although clearly he had chosen it to give him balance. He was staring at Abel with that same owlish expression, and nodded again, maddeningly.

"Why, she too!" he said, as though it were the most obvious thing in the world. "She too! One of my get. Like yourself! I could get a child on any that I wanted, except for her—and that was her doing, and not mine, and so I told her, many and many a time! She knew—"

"One of your— She knew— One of your— And I—" Abel knew he was babbling, could hear his own voice coming from a great distance, from depths of iciness that were everywhere around him. He could see them, looking suddenly very small and clear-cut, with light sparkling round the edges of their figures, Dorothea looking at him with an expression of vast pity and understanding upon her face, Jesse just leaning casually against the mantelshelf and blinking at him, blinking and staring.

Dorothea's voice came very loud and clear, although he knew somewhere deep within his being that she was speaking in her usual soft and unctuous voice. "It is quite true, dear Abel. She is your sister. You could never wed her, could you? Not your sister!"

He closed his eyes and saw her standing there in the darkness behind his lids as if she stood upon the stage. Small, black-haired, green-eyed—infinitely desirable—his Lil. He tried to see her as his flesh, as more a part of him than she already was, and tried to fit her face into his, seeking a denial; but he could not. Her eyes, of a color like his, her dark hair, her . . . There was no way to know, to be sure, none at all—and he snapped his eyes open and cried, "It's not true! It *cannot* be true! It is not, not, not—"

"Mama said it was so," Dorothea said in that soft, patient voice. "Mama said it was, and Papa Constam says it is so, and if once it has been said, it cannot be denied without proof, can it, Abel? You would not wed your sister! Would you?"

He was shaking his head, laughing now, shaking his head and laughing a great shrill laugh that was meant to show the world the lie of it, but that failed dismally, for it did not convince even himself.

"It is true, boy, and there's an end of it." Jesse's voice came sliding into his laughter like a hot knife through a barrel of lard. "If I say it is true, then who are you to deny it? You have no means to prove your parentage, no more than has she; Charlotte said it was so, and she knew much, did my Charlotte, and Dorothea says it is so, and she is the daughter of my Charlotte and remembers more than I do, in all truth. I say it is so, and thus it must be so, mustn't it? Charlotte says, and Dorothea says, and I say, you shall not wed her. Dorothea says you shall not wed her, and Charlotte says . . ." He was slipping back into his maudlin, drunken state again, nodding his head with imbecile wisdom, nodding and becking maddeningly; and staring at that familiar face, that fringe of graying red hair, and the collapsed old body, Abel knew that he had been defeated. It could not be true—his whole being cried out that it could not be true—but still that voice went on and on, saying it *was* true.

There came then the moment of sick horror that was to remain with him always. Rising before his eyes so vividly that it was as though it were being painted on the air before him came a picture of her lying there across his knees in the half-tester bed in Edenbridge, the light of the candle lifting the curves of her body to an agony of need; he could see himself with her, upon her, thrusting at her, being part of her, and behind it all, the face of Jesse, blank and ugly and lined, staring at the joy he had known that night and destroying it.

And he threw back his head and cried out his rage and pain and anger, his aching need for the happiness that he had almost grasped, believing it to be within his reach; and the welter of feeling amalgamated in him to a vast strength, and he launched himself across the room with all the power in him, his hands thrust out and aiming for Jesse's hateful face.

It was as though he were a child again, had come skulking soft-footed and swift through the reeking alleys in search of this man, this one man, just as he had that night long ago. But this time it was not because he would rob him that he was hurling himself through space, but because he had been robbed himself, and the huge, overwhelming anger of his loss spread through him, filled his hands with colossal power.

And quite what he did with his hands he did not know. He

heard Dorothea's cry behind him, could see his own fingers set on the old man's shoulders and shaking him, shaking him, shaking him so that his head rolled to and fro helplessly, saw the background to that head move, and knew he was hurling him about the room, and then felt his knee again describe that familiar movement, connecting with groin and then high in the belly.

And Jesse folded forward, infinitely slowly, collapsing even more upon himself like a child's house of cards, and there was a sound, a heavy, retching cough that seemed to bubble and yet reverberate through the room, and then Abel was standing very still looking down stupidly at the floor in front of him.

Jesse was lying there, staring up at him in a vast surprise, and his mouth opened, and there was again that retch and with it a gushing sound, and blood came welling up slowly at first and then with a great pulsating lift, and it seemed to be pouring everywhere, from everywere, as Jesse's face disappeared beneath its deep crimson, and it spread about his head and pooled itself upon the carpet, and Jesse's body twisted heavily, and the blood seemed to come hiccuping again, and then slowed. And then there were just the two of them, Dorothea and Abel, staring down at him.

And Abel sighed softly, like a tired child, feeling the great empty coldness inside him, and not caring at all about anything.

It seemed to Abel that it had all been happening around him for aeons of time. People had come rushing, and there had been talk and more people, and Dorothea being crisp, extraordinarily crisp, within it all, and still he sat in the middle of the sofa staring hopelessly into the depths of a future that held nothing at all. No hope of anything but misery.

She had managed just once to penetrate his inner world as he sat there on the sofa staring down at Jesse's bloody head. She had knelt beside him, not seeming to notice that her skirt was brushing in that crimson pool, and said loudly, "Abel, listen to me! He was ill these many weeks, you know that? He was ill. We must find a surgeon who will understand these matters. Whom shall I get here? Abel? Whom shall I get? Tell me—Abel—*tell* me!"

At last her nagging voice came through to him, and he stared at her blankly, and then muttered, "Bell. Get Charles Bell. From Windmill Street. He will know . . ." and lapsed back into his silent dead world, sitting there still and lumpish on the yellow plush sofa.

And all around him, activity. They bore away the shell that had been Jesse Constam, at the behest of the tall Scotsman who had come and looked and nodded, and spoken in his succinct and quiet way, and they had cleaned the blood from the carpet, though the smell of it lingered, and there had been voices, voices, voices . . .

"Lackland! Lackland—will ye try to come out o' this, man! 'Tis shock, no more, and ye need to pull your own self out of it to a degree, for there's naught that I can do for you if ye make no effort. Lackland, will ye do as I bid, damn you!"

He blinked and turned his head very slowly. Beside him Charles Bell was sitting, and he looked down in faint surprise, for he had his long and clever fingers sitting gently on the pulse at Abel's wrist, and it seemed to Abel a matter of infinite absurdity that Charles Bell should concern himself with the motion of his pulse, and he wanted to laugh. But all that came was a shrill little giggle.

"Aye, lad, I know," Bell said, and turned his head, and Abel looked up and saw Dorothea standing behind him, and she was staring at him with a look of ridiculous concern on her face, and again he found this immensely funny and again produced that shrill little giggle.

She gave Bell the brandy glass that he indicated with a jerk of his head, and then Bell was holding it to Abel's lips, and he was coughing and spluttering and pushing it away, and Bell grunted approvingly.

"That's better, lad! Now, take a deep breath—aye, like that—and again—and again. And drink again. Damn you, you great fool, will ye do as you're bid! Aye. That's it. Now, you'll be feeling a deal better soon."

And so he did. Slowly the heat came back into his hands and feet, moving stealthily from the pool of warmth the brandy had left in his belly, and with it came the memory and the knowledge of what he had done, and he closed his eyes, and heard as from a long way away a deep moan, and felt Bell's hand warm on his again; and opened his eyes to know the moan was his own.

" 'Twas a deep shock, boy," Bell said earnestly, looking at him with those dark eyes of his wide and warm and his mouth set in a half-smile of friendliness and reassurance. "A great shock, but you did your best, you did, so! There's a first time for every man to see an aneurysm go, and bad enough it is without being a man for whom you have a care."

Dorothea was beside him then, her hand, cold and rather damp, curling possessively around his. "And indeed, you wrought so well, dear Abel. You did all you could to save Papa, I know you did, and you must not feel ill about it, indeed you must not, for none but you was here, and what could you do? I saw it all, and I know, dear Abel. . . ."

He frowned and stared at her, and turned his head fretfully to stare at Bell. "What does she say? I killed him, you know, killed him with my own hands. What did she say? She's a liar, a fool, for I killed him with my own hands!"

Bell sighed sharply, a sound of mingled impatience and understanding. "Lackland, this happens to every surgeon at some time or another! That you've reached this far and escaped such an experience says more for your luck than your judgment. You could not have saved this man, not if you'd been God Almighty! That aneurysm must have been with him these thirty years or more, to have gone so spectacular as it did. I tell ye again, lad, ye could not ha' saved him had you been the devil incarnate! Ye did not kill him, nor anything like it, and you shall not get such a worm into your head if I have aught to do with the matter! You've the makings of a great surgeon, lad, but you've to learn the humility of your trade yet. You could not have saved him, and that's all aboot it!"

He stood up then and shook his head a little at Dorothea.

"He'll be a shade distraught for a few hours yet, my dear," he said softly, as Abel sat staring at him bemused with puzzlement and brandy. "See to it he's put to his bed and left to sleep. He'll be more himself in a few hours, but you can send to me if you have any doubts aboot it. I'd stay a little longer if I could, but I canna'—there's work to be done, and one death canna' become the end of a man's working day."

He was shrugging into his coat and moving toward the door, and as he reached it, he stopped and turned back to Dorothea and held out his hand.

"I forget mysel'. My dear young lady, ye must forgive me. I owe you my sympathies on the death of your father, and trust you will not find your grief too insupportable."

"He was my stepfather, sir, and had been ill these many months," Dorothea said equably, and looked back over her shoulder. "It would not be thought ill of me, I trust, to say that my dear Abel had a greater affection for him than I enjoyed, since he was his benefactor. I thank you for your concern, sir, but I shall do well enough."

"Aye, well. Yon's a fortunate man to have so—ah— Well, good day to you, ma'am. Dinna' hesitate to call me if ye're at all concerned aboot him. But he'll do well enough."

And he was gone, leaving Dorothea and Abel alone in the drawing room, and she turned and smiled at him with infinite love and pity before coming softly across the room to sit down beside him on the sofa.

· THIRTY-FIVE ·

HE tried. He tried very hard indeed, but to no avail. It was as though he were struggling in a morass of threads, all delicate, all fine and soft as spiders' filaments, but adding up to a vast and sticky web which held him fast.

When he demanded that they call the law to him, for he had killed Jesse with his own hands and with malice, Dorothea soothed him with burbles of words and offered herb cordials and sent for Mr. Bell.

When he tried to convince Charles Bell that he was not driven out of his mind by what had happened but spoke only the plain truth, the older man simply sighed and told him he had reacted so badly because he had never had any reaction to the horrors of his trade before, but would get over it in time.

He went in a state of high tension to Josiah Witney and tried to convince him, but he too refused to see his anguish as anything but a laudable expression of grief at the death of his benefactor, and offered him laudanum.

Not even Lucy could be made to believe that Abel had done what he said he had. Or if she did believe it, kept her own counsel and told Abel firmly that he was " 'alf out of 'is mind with it all, and to bite 'is tongue and get on with 'is life."

It was four weeks after Jesse's death before he could accept that this was how it was to be. He was seen by all of them as one who had tried to save Jesse's life and been temporarily unhinged by his inability to cope in the face of so overwhelming a calamity. And in a curious way, he had almost come to believe it himself. Over and over again he would try to see what had happened, try to re-create in his mind's eye those moments when he had shaken the old man's shoulders and thrust with his hard young knee at that shell of a belly, to burst the huge, fragile blister in the main artery, causing that deluge, that fountain, that vast welter of blood. But all he could see was the picture of himself and Lilith in bed in Edenbridge with Jesse's great grinning face behind, and would close his eyes in agony at the knowledge that it was all destroyed. There was no joy left for him, not anywhere.

It was curious how he felt now about Jesse's wild words just before he had died. He remembered, remembered full well, that he had not believed it when he had heard it, had seen it as yet another attempt to hold him back from his most urgent desires; had been angered not because what Jesse said was true (for how could it have been more than drunken wanderings?), but simply because he had said it. But that was all changed now. In dying with those words upon his lips, Jesse had in some subtle way created a change in them. He had invested them with a vast importance, an underlying reality that try as he might Abel could not escape. For Jesse to say with his dying breath that Lil was his sister seemed to make it so. And he carried that knowledge heavy and thick in his belly as he walked mechanically through his days and lay awake and yet dead and numb in his mind through his nights.

Dorothea was deeply happy during those four weeks. She looked after him with all the passion of which she was capable, pouring into her concoctions of flower petals and herbs all the love and sureness in her possession of him that she felt, making his bed with her own hands when he left it, refusing to let the servants do anything for him. And they grinned at each other and made lewd jokes and watched gleefully while she went serenely through her days waiting for Abel to recover himself and return to her. Her mind now was filled with plans for their wedding—with detailed dreams of how it was all to be, what she would wear, the food they would eat, the guests who would come. She was not in the least doubt, not now, that this was how it was to be.

Typically, she gave no thought at all to her status as Jesse's heiress, and was startled indeed to discover that she was. It was Hunnisett who told her of the fact, coming to the house unbidden shortly after Jesse's funeral.

"His will was there among his other business papers, Miss Dorothea . . ." the old man said, standing in the middle of the drawing room and turning his hat unhappily in his hands. His eyes were red-rimmed, and his face looked thinner than it had, but Dorothea did not notice this, and even if she had, she would not have seen these signs for what they were, expressions of real grief for Jesse. Hunnisett was perhaps the only person anywhere who mourned Jesse Constam's passing with genuine feeling.

". . . and I took the liberty of bringing it to you before I gave it to the attorney. If you would wish me to do that you have but to say, and so I'll arrange it. And I have to ask you, Miss Dorothea, what I should do in regard to the matters of the business. It's yours now, you see, you're the master now, in a manner of speaking, and I couldn't see my way clear to continuing in the old ways without your wishing it."

"Oh, dear," Dorothea had said, turning the document in her hand unhappily before giving it back to Hunnisett. "Please to do as you think best. I know nothing of these matters, nothing at all."

Hunnisett coughed, and turned his hat even more rapidly between his fingers. "Perhaps, ma'am, Mr. Abel—since he's betrothed to you, and at such time as the wedding— I know it isn't proper to speak of it now, but so it will be, and . . ." he coughed again in an agony of embarrassment. "Shall I ask him for instructions on your behalf?"

Dorothea seized on that with avidity. "Oh, indeed, Hunnisett, a splendid notion. But he is most put about, you know, quite set out of his mind with grief for Papa Constam. As soon as he is well enough, I shall ask him to come to the countinghouse to see you, and settle matters. But until then . . ."

So Hunnisett had gone away, content enough, leaving Dorothea to make further plans and spin her dreams, waiting and waiting for Abel.

He, for his part, accepted her plea for help with the business affairs that Jesse had left behind with a sense of inevitability. There was no one else to do it, just as there had been no one else to cope after Charlotte's death, and so he went to Eastcheap to spend long hours closeted with old Hunnisett and sorting out Dorothea's affairs. He found her to be a considerable heiress indeed, for all that Jesse's concern for his business had fallen off so severely before his death; Hunnisett had been an honest steward, and Abel returned to Gower Street to tell Dorothea so.

She sat in the drawing room with her hands folded neatly in her lap as he told her of her situation, walking restlessly about the room as he spoke, his hands thrust into his pockets. He looked a deal thinner and even paler than he had used to, and watching him, Dorothea felt full of love and pride; he looked as romantic a man as any woman could ever desire.

"The will is an old one, made upon his marriage to your mama. It leaves all to you; it was to be inherited by any issue of his and Charlotte's, or you and yours if there were none. So you are rich enough, Dorothea, for all purposes."

"It is all for you, Abel," she said softly. "All of it. I ask for nothing but your—"

"For me?" He spoke with a sharp violence. "For me? Such an idiotic idea! Of course it is not! Have you not heard what I said? You are his heiress, and—"

"But when we are married, dear Abel, you will be the one who— Husbands always do, do they not? And . . ."

He stopped sharply in the middle of the drawing room and stared at her, his face blank and cold.

"When we are— I told you! We are no longer betrothed," he said harshly, and she looked up at him with her eyes wide and clear of any guile.

"But Abel, you told me you wished to marry Li— You cannot do so now, so there is no longer any rub in our way! You must have a wife, must you not? Every man must have a wife! And I have my fortune now, as you have seen for yourself, so I should be a very good wife for you, should I not? Think of the practice a surgeon could found on such an income! And I know you, and understand you and care for you, and . . ."

He stared at her wonderingly, trying to see behind her blank face to the mind beyond, trying to comprehend but quite failing. "Do you not understand?" he said, and there was genuine curiosity in his voice. "Do you not *understand?* I have no love for you, not *real* love, nor ever did have. Friendship and gratitude and—and the comfort of familiarity, but no more. Does that not mean anything at all to you? That I have no passion for you?"

She smiled then, with immense sweetness. "Oh, but you will, dear Abel, when once you are recovered from the shock of Papa Constam's death, and the—when time has passed, you know, and we are wed. Papa Constam said many a time that he did not love Mama, but he did, did he not, for see how sad he was upon her loss! It was very romantic, was it not?"

He shook his head, and rubbed his forehead with one hand, and felt as though he were again wrapped in those spidery filaments, once more entangled in that web of stickiness that threatened to hold him in its strands whatever he wished to do.

"I don't understand you," he muttered, and turned to go, but she sprang to her feet and came running across the drawing room to stand beside him, her hand confidingly on one of his.

"Oh, but you will, dear Abel, truly you will! One day. When we are wed and—"

"I told you," he cried in a sort of desperation. "I told you! I have affection for you, but no more than that. Please to understand, Dorothea!"

"Of course I understand," she said. "Of course I do! You must speak first to—to her, must you not? For you must explain to her the situation so that you can clear your mind of that fatal fascination and then return to me and—"

"Oh, God!" he cried. "Oh, God, leave me *alone!*" And he flung out of the room in such a state of confusion that he hardly knew where he was going, to leave the house in door-banging haste. He walked about the streets for hours, his hands thrust deep in his pockets and his head down, staring at the cobbles beneath his feet and in constant danger of bumping into other foot passengers, for he walked so fast and furiously, and so unseeingly; but others, seeing that coatless, wild-haired figure go storming by, kept their distance and hurried well away from so obvious a madman.

But Dorothea's words had found their mark. Ever since the afternoon of Jesse's death, he had avoided it, the need to go and talk to Lil. She would have to be told, would have to understand what had happened, and why, and together they would have to cope with the situation they were in; and it was going to be hell on earth for both of them.

As the next few weeks crept by and March moved into April, and skies softened and daffodils appeared in parks and gardens, he fought with himself. There were many times when he would find himself outside Covent Garden, where still she was the greatest pull in all of London's theaterland, and would turn and flee, unable to go in through that familiar stage door and face her. And many times he would return to Gower Street in the evening, after a day spent burying himself in the affairs of Mr. Witney's shop and his own patients, aching with a mixture of fatigue and the hope that she had written to him, or called on him—had in some way sought him out.

But she never did, although she knew quite well where he was to be found, and he knew it was to be he who had to do it. He had to find the courage to tell her.

And at last, on a day in early May, when there had been a period of dreadful weather with thunderstorms every day for more than a week, and the streets had been washed clean of mud at last, to lie sparkling a little in the sunshine, he felt himself ready and able to face her. He had recovered his equilibrium in part, no longer lying awake at night for long hours in an agony of guilt when he thought of Jesse's death. But still he had to talk to her. And now the time had come.

He did not seek her out at the theater, but at her lodgings. She had taken a set of most fashionable rooms in Clarges Street, had had them done up with every elegant gewgaw she could think of, and he sat there all the morning surrounded by the frills and fripperies so reminiscent of her sitting room at Carter's End in Edenbridge, uneasy and desperately unhappy. It was eleven o'clock and she was still asleep, the maid had reported, but would come as soon as she awoke, she had no doubt; and the girl had dimpled at him in a saucy fashion and gone away, to leave him trying to find the words he would use.

He found many, planned speech after speech, but when the door swished and she was in the room with him, they all vanished, every one of them, and he sat in frozen misery staring at her.

She was wearing a robe of fine gauze trimmed with feathers, all dyed to her favorite shade of pale blue, and her hair was rumpled and her face rosy with sleep; she looked lovelier than he could ever remember seeing her, and he closed his eyes at the pain of it.

"Oh, la, sir, I am not such a fright that you cannot set eyes on me!" she cried, and he snapped his eyes open, and shook his head.

She came across the room in a drift of feathers, her arms wide. "You wretched boy! To have hid from me all these months! The last I saw of you you beat me and bade me marry you, and then disappeared! What did your Lilith do to deserve such treatment from you?"

She was about to throw her arms around his neck in her usual fashion and sit herself down upon his lap as she had done so often before, but at once he jumped to his feet and moved stiffly across the room to avoid her, and she dropped her hands and looked at him with her eyes narrowed and glittering.

"Come, Abel, what is this? You stay away from me all these months, and then when you do come to see me you treat me so! Get out and be done with it, if that is how you wish it! No man yet has behaved so to me, and none shall."

But for all her anger, she was intrigued and puzzled and made no move to go, or to force him to leave her room.

"I'm sorry," he said, and his voice was cracked and painful, and she cocked her head a little and bit the knuckle of her forefinger, childlike and wondering as she stared at him.

"What is it? Are you ill, or some such thing?" And there seemed genuine curiosity in her voice, though little true concern.

"Jesse Constam died. The day after—after I last saw you."

"Ah!" Her face cleared. "Is that all? You did not care so much for him, did you? I did not think so! But if you have had to deal with the matters of his death, well, there it is! I believe there is much to be done when people die."

She rang the bell, and the maid came in so quickly that it was clear she had been standing immediately outside the door.

"My chocolate, you bawd," Lilith said equably, and the girl grinned and giggled and flounced away, to come back almost at once with a tray of fine porcelain and a pot of steaming chocolate and a plate of very thin bread and butter.

"Will you take something with me, dear Abel? No? Well, I am very hungry." And she began to eat greedily, sitting sideways to the table and swinging one knee over the other so that her bare leg showed, and he could see she was barefooted, the soles of her feet rather grimed with dirt.

"So! The old man died! Did he leave you any of his money, Abel? He should have done, for who else is there but that stupid Dorothea of his, who—"

"Lil!" She seemed to hear the anguish in his voice, and looked up, puzzled, her mouth full of bread and butter and a streak of chocolate on her chin, for she was a greedy eater still. "What's 'a matter?" she asked, her voice muffled with the food. "Have I said aught amiss to make you sound so—"

"It is the way he died. What he told me." He swallowed hard, and then moved away to stand with his back to the wall, feeling curiously less threatened in such a position. "He— I . . ." He shook his head miserably, and she sat and stared at him, some irritation beginning to show through her surprise.

"You will have to be a little faster than this with your news, whatever it is, Abel, for I have other fish to fry, and there will be little enough time for me to dress as it is."

"He told me," Abel said flatly. "He told me that both of us—you and I—are his children. That he . . ."

She put a hand up to her mouth and stared at him above it, and said, "You and I? His— You and . . ." She moved her hand, pointed at him. "You and I, his *children*? He . . ."

And then she started to laugh, throwing her head back and

· 346 ·

laughing hugely till tears ran down her cheeks, and she had to mop at them with a corner of her robe. And he stood and stared at her, frozen-faced, until she could laugh no more and sat with her face red and her eyes glittering with it, breathless and relaxed.

"That was why I did not come to you. I could not," he said woodenly. "If we are brother and sister as he said—when he was dying—it is—we cannot . . ." He closed his eyes. "It is enough that once we did. That we . . ." He swallowed, and opened his eyes to stare at her in misery. "You see? It is all *unspeakable*."

"Oh, pooh!" she said, and grinned widely at him. "Such stuff! You foolish romantical creature, Abel! I thought better of you, indeed I did!"

"Foolish? Romant—what do you mean?"

"Why, what I say, you great gull! To believe it, for a start! How could he know? What did he know of me or mine, of where I came from, who my mother was? What could he know of yours, for that matter? It's all such a Bartholomew tale as would make a cat laugh! And you believed it! I was born in Ireland, you idiotish boy! When was your precious Jesse ever in Ireland?"

A species of hope, a curious trembling of doubt began to move in his belly, and he looked at her, and felt his face lose some of its frozen stiffness.

"What di— You do not believe it?"

She was sitting at the table again, eating, spreading a piece of bread and butter with honey and stuffing it into her mouth, quite unconcernedly. She looked up at the sound of his voice and shrugged.

"Of course I do not. Though why it should matter I cannot imagine. I do not care one way or t'other. Why should I?"

"Why should . . ." He moved then, came to the table to stand with his fists resting on it and leaning forward to stare at her. "Why should you? Damn it all, Lil, we were to be wed! You told me we would be married, and . . ."

"Married?" She leaned back in her chair then, and wiped her mouth with the back of her hand. "Oh, silly boy! I forgot all that as soon as it was said! Married? To you? *I*?"

She trilled a fluting trill of laughter. "I'd have to be clean out of my attic, and well you know it! I have all London at my fingers' ends, and you think I would settle to marry you? You're a dear boy, Abel, but you are very, very foolish, and always were! Why should I marry you?"

He was breathing faster now, his nostrils white and pinched in his face, and his lips hard against his teeth. "The night before we came to London. At Edenbridge. We— That night. I knew then that . . ."

She laughed again, that same cruel tinkle of laughter. "That night? Stupid creature! I had to make sure, did I not? You were being so particular and—and pompous, don't you remember, about bringing me to the theater? I had to be sure, that is all!"

She leaned back, stretching a little, so that her robe fell back against her arms, and she yawned, showing her sharp white teeth and pink mouth with catlike sensuousness, and then smiled at him, with real kindness in her expression.

"Dear Abel! I'm truly very attached to you, you know, and always shall be, for I have known you longer than anyone in this world, and that is very remarkable, is it not? But all this talk of marrying me or not marrying me because I am your sister—it is all such a nonsense! I care not whether we are blood kin or not, though it is clear to me we could not be! For my part you are my friend, and always will be so. No husband, but a good friend! And you shall come and visit me at any time—well, almost any time!" She laughed again. "Almost, dear heart, for I have many friends! So many!"

He was still standing there with fists clenched upon the table, his muscles knotted under his sleeves, and his face was as white as the tablecloth, though the shadows under his eyes were a violet smudge.

"You are a whore," he said, very softly and very deliberately as the anger and bitter hurt and desire rose cruelly in him. "You—are—a—whore."

And then she smiled—that long, slow smile, so practiced and so knowing—and said very softly, "Ah, perhaps, perhaps. But such a whore, dear Abel! Such a whore! For I am class, am I not? I always told you so, and so it is. If I told you who had become my—*friend*—this past month or two, why, you

· 348 ·

would be amazed and proud, indeed you would! Oh, Abel, I am having a splendid life! And I don't care whether you're my brother or the Pope of Rome, you shall share it all with me if you wish it, for you are my Abel, whom I have known so long, and . . ."

The tide reached its peak. It had been rising, filling his muscles in that same sick, familiar fashion, and now it lifted in a red foam over his head, and he moved his hands and took the edge of the table in his cold fingers and heaved it aside, turning it over in a crash of porcelain and hot chocolate, and she shrieked hugely, real fear opening her green eyes into dark slits in her face. And he reached forward and took hold of her robe at the throat and ripped it from her while she struggled with him, and then with real terror on her face stopped resisting, and he tugged and tore at the delicate fabric until it lay on the ground at her feet in tatters and she was standing quite naked before him.

She stood there, her head up, and tried to smile, as her terror ebbed, and opened her arms to him. And he stared at her for a long moment and then, very deliberately, spat hard in her face. And turned and went.

Abel Lackland and Dorothea Coombe were married at Mr. Spenser's church in Woburn Square on a very foggy Saturday in September, 1811. There were no guests in the church, apart from Josiah Witney and Richard Hunnisett, witnesses. The bride wore no special wedding gown, since the bridegroom did not wish that she should, and himself was wed wearing his ordinary working clothes. After the wedding the groom went to the shop in Piccadilly for the afternoon, to work on the plans for the new dispensary he was to open in Endell Street with Jesse's money, returning to his home in Gower Street at the usual time.

And long after they had retired to their bedroom, which had been Mrs. Constam's during her lifetime, and which Abel had forbidden Dorothea to redecorate in any way, declaring he was content enough with the room as it was and saying it needed no time or effort wasted on embellishing it, Dorothea lay awake, nursing her pain. She had not expected the experience of wifehood to be quite so sudden, so short, or so agonizing, but had borne it as best she could. And at least, she told herself, staring up into the blackness of their bed curtains, I am married to him. He is lying here beside me, my husband, and must surely one day love me. She turned her head in the darkness, trying to see him, aching to know what was in his mind, and a small sound, half gulp, half sigh escaped her. But he made no sound in return, and after a moment she turned her head back on its pillow to lie and stare into the darkness.

But he had heard her, and the sound had piled even higher his sense of self-disgust. To have used her so, simply because she was not Lil, was unforgivable. She had given him a haven during those four months of the summer through which he had lived his pain after his last meeting with Lil, had asked no questions, made no comments, offered no chiding for his neglect of her, no complaints about his long silences or the absorption in his work that had been the only sign of true life that he had displayed. She had nursed him, fed him, cared for him, had wrapped him in the balm of her total approval of him, and yet he had treated her thus.

And now they were married, and Lil was a dead thing, belonging in the past from which she should never have been allowed to emerge. For a brief moment he felt some of his old anger and resentment against Charlotte rise in him: if only she had not . . . But that was stupid, wasteful thinking, and he thrust it away, and tentatively put out his hand in the darkness and found Dorothea's. Immediately she clutched it with an urgency and need that communicated itself to him, so that he returned the pressure of her hold almost automatically.

"Dear Abel," she whispered in the darkness, the breathy sound of her voice almost lost in the muffling folds of the bed curtains. "Dear Abel. We shall live happy ever after, shall we not? For that is how it was always meant to be. I truly will be a good wife to you, truly know that I was born to be yours and you *will* be happy, I promise you. You will one day come to love me as I love you. If you will but try a little . . ."

He nodded heavily in the darkness. "Yes. We can but try." But he said it very softly.

ACKNOWLEDGMENTS

My grateful thanks to The Burroughs Wellcome Medical History Library and Museum; Macarthys Limited, Surgical Instrument Manufacturers; The Meteorological Office; Professor Philip Rhodes, Dean of St. Thomas' Hospital Medical School, London; Rules Restaurant, Maiden Lane, London; The London Library; Victoria and Albert Museum; and other sources too numerous to mention, for assistance with research.

C.R.